Dream's Sake

Jyoti Arora

V&S PUBLISHERS

Published by:

V&S PUBLISHERS

F-2/16, Ansari road, Daryaganj, New Delhi-110002
☎ 23240026, 23240027 • *Fax:* 011-23240028
Email: info@vspublishers.com • *Website:* www.vspublishers.com

Regional Office : Hyderabad
5-1-707/1, Brij Bhawan (Beside Central Bank of India Lane)
Bank Street, Koti, Hyderabad - 500 095
☎ 040-24737290
E-mail: vspublishershyd@gmail.com

Branch Office : Mumbai
Jaywant Industrial Estate, 1st Floor–108, Tardeo Road
Opposite Sobo Central Mall, Mumbai – 400 034
☎ 022-23510736
E-mail: vspublishersmum@gmail.com

Follow us on:

© Copyright: Author
ISBN 978-81-920796-9-1
Edition 2018

Printed at : Repro Knowledgecast Limited, Thane

The hope I dreamed of was a dream,
Was but a dream; and now I wake
Exceeding comfortless, and worn, and old,
For a dream's sake.

'Mirage' by - Christina Rossetti

Author's Note

'Dream' is my most favourite word in the entire English dictionary. After all, dreams are one treasure that God has bestowed on everyone without any discrimination. One may not be able to walk, talk or see. But one can always dream.

And I, if I may say so myself, dream on a wholesale basis. And now, my dream, my most cherished dream, has come true. The book upon which I spent so much of love and labour is going to be published. Finally, it is going to be read, and I hope, liked. Much liked!

I distinctly remember how this book began. I had just finished reading O. Henry's story – 'The Gift of Magi.' The sighs over it were still continuing from my heart. But with them, a wish rose up. 'How good it would be if I could write such a beautiful story,' I thought to myself.

Well, I can't dare to suggest that I have succeeded in equalling O. Henry. I can't commit such a sacrilege. But one thing I'm sure about. Dream's Sake tells a story that will remain embedded in the reader's heart for a long time.

'Dream's Sake' is the story of four friends Abhi, his sister Priyam, and their friends Aashi and Sid. Each of them is trying to recover from a past trauma which nevertheless continues to influence their present, making them insecure and hesitant to grasp what they have been longing for all along. The battle between dreams and realities and hope and despair run throughout the book. But the one thing that rises above all is the warmth of true love and affection.

Talking about love and affection, I must thank the people whose affectionate support was always there with me while I laboured at 'Dream's Sake.' I must thank my friends Anubha, Mohit and my cousin Disha who were always ready (actually more than ready at times) to point out my mistakes and help me improve my work. I must also thank Mr. Anupam Gakhar, Founder of Reading Treasure, for always giving me judicious advice, whenever I needed it.

And then, of course, there's my family without whose love and support this book would never have been possible. I wish all children had as loving a family as I have.

That's all that I can think of saying right now. I hope my readers would bless my book with their love.

Love to all,
Jyoti Arora

Chapter 1

*'In that book which is
My memory . . .
On the first page
That is the chapter when
I first met you
Appear the words . . .
Here begins a new life'*

— *La Vita Nuova By Dante Alighieri*

"*Terror does Diwali shopping in Delhi--killing 55, hurting 155,*" the old newspaper clipping proclaimed as it trembled within her fingers.

Those weren't just numbers, even if they had been correct. Those were people blown into bits. And people left behind to die in bits after them.

But Aashi had died quite enough. It was time to start living again.

She would have torn that paper and thrown it away. But her fingers didn't obey. She wanted to erase its black words entirely from her memory. But she could not, not yet, anyway. For there was her father in that paper, one among the fifty five dead.

Aashi could not let go of the dead. But it was time now for her to start living again. She had already taken her first step back into life.

Life, though, was no longer how she had once known it.

'But it won't last long. I won't let it last long. I won't...I won't!' Her head was held high as Aashi chanted these words, but her shoulders drooped. Her fingers crushed the peacock-blue fabric of her skirt. Her feet stamped at the ground, and eyes cursed the very dwelling place she had fought so hard to acquire.

'What? What you won't let last long?' Urmila asked, fixing her sleepy eyes on her daughter.

'This! This thing!' Aashi said, pointing at the house they had moved in just that day.

Renting a house for herself and her mother was to be the first happy step to her independence. But the limitedness of her finance had forced Aashi to confine herself into a structure she didn't even want to call a home.

'Oh, it just looks old but...' Urmila mumbled.

'Old! It looks ancient! They should rent it out to ghosts. Only dead people would live in such a place! And I tell you, Ma, if I live here much longer, I would surely join their group too! It's so small!'

'It's good enough for the two of us. Besides, you weren't very happy even when we were living in a bigger home. I don't know why you had to be so rude to your uncles and aunts. They were only thinking about your wellbeing. It's not good for a girl to walk out of her own home and live alone in such a dangerous city,' said Urmila.

'They were NOT thinking about my wellbeing. That house was NEVER my home and you really should stop being so afraid. The city is not going to eat me!' Aashi blazed with fury.

She knew her mother didn't agree with her decision of living alone. But then, it was the only thing Aashi could have done to escape being married to the dork of her uncles' choice. They had gobbled up all that should have been hers. There was no way she would let them gobble up her dreams and happiness too.

So, Aashi had done the only thing she could think of. She had started up quite a noisy bit of revolt and declared that she would rather kill herself than marry the guy they had chosen.

The uproar of indignant relatives perhaps cannot be compared to actual pandemonium, but there certainly was considerable sound and fury to be heard echoing within that household for the next few days. It's another matter, however, that after an appropriate display of shock and rage, and a lot more of sorrow and grief, the family's *dearest* child was given the expedient permission to leave the fold and do what she would with her life.

And so, without any hesitation or fear, and with a cheque of fifteen lakh rupees that combined in it the cost of her father's shop and house, Aashi had walked out of her grandparents' home.

She had no regrets in leaving her family. But her mother's tears did burden her heart with a bit of guilt.

'Don't worry, Ma, we'll be alright,' Aashi mumbled, regretting her fiery outburst in a second. She put her arms around Urmila's shrunken form and forced her anger to stay out of her voice. 'Everything will go just as I have planned. And I'll soon shift us to a better house too. Till then, I guess, we'll just have to make do with this stifling, miserable place.'

'Aashi, I don't mind this house, and you know that. It may be small,

8

but it's in a good locality. We are lucky that we got it so cheap,' Urmila said, patting her daughter's cheeks.

Aashi nodded at her mother's words. She knew her mother was right. But what to do if the tranquil satisfaction that came so easily to Urmila was beyond the reach of Aashi's impatient heart? After all, it was just one room attached to a tiny kitchen and tinier washroom. The rest of the area had been left vacant and converted into a garden. Aashi was sure that even that effort had been made only because the owner was too stingy to cover it up even in bricks and so, had converted his love for money into a love for foliage. A lot of time seemed to have passed however, since even this love had found an indulgence. It was now little more than a tangle of bushes where the struggle for survival had given way to total anarchy.

Curiously though, the house somehow boasted of a compact garage on the side.

'Nothing but a cowshed,' Aashi called it and looked wistfully instead at the neatly painted and properly locked garage next door.

She spent several minutes staring at this garage and then the house to which it was attached. That house was small too, according to her standards, but looked decent enough to be called liveable. It was neat at least, and properly built. But that only served to make her rented home look even more miserable.

So she turned away from it and settled down on the doorstep. Urmila had already dozed off. Aashi too leaned her head against the wall and closed her eyes. She desperately needed to call forth the dream that she had kept with her despite the loss of everything else.

She put herself on a large balcony of a palatial house and looked dreamily down at the gorgeous garden spread around. There was the steady sound of manly footsteps approaching her. She turned and looked at him, love dancing in the lustre of her eager eyes.

'If only I had blue eyes, or green perhaps! How wonderful it would have been,' she thought as she dreamed.

But then, the audacity of her black eyes was irresistible too. She had often admired it herself, feeling sure that a writer must have composed some pretty amazing lines while describing her eyes, had she been the heroine of a novel.

Of course, she was not a heroine, and life wasn't a novel either. She was just an ordinary girl, being forced to live in less than ordinary world.

But her dreams were perfect. They had perfect love, perfect romance, luxury and above all, a perfection in manly form too.

And she could almost see him, see his tall, handsome form standing beside her on that balcony. There were his arms around her slender waist, his eyes tickling her with their caresses...he opened his lips to say something, to murmur some sweet words of admiration perhaps...

PEEEP, PEEEEP, PEEEEEEP....!

The car's horn jolted Aashi back to her own little house and the mockery of a garden that was there before her eyes. Sudden dread throbbed up in Aashi's heart and beads of sweat emerged on her forehead. She hated loud noises. She dreaded them. Every loud sound reminded her of the explosion that had killed her father. It terrified her and left her trembling and feeling nervous.

But try as she might, there was no escape from such sudden loud explosions of sound. All Aashi could do was to take quick deep breaths to ease the panic and try to stop her thoughts from reverting back to that horrible day.

The horn blared again. Aashi clenched her mouth tightly, took quick deep breaths and looked out towards the road. Next moment, an old Maruti rolled to a halt near her gate.

She stared at the car and watched on as a girl stepped out of it from the passenger side and quickly went over to unlatch the gate of the house Aashi had been examining just few minutes ago. The car rolled in and came to a halt again.

'Thank God, Sid's not here yet,' the girl said as she quickly shut the gate behind her and rushed to unlock the garage while the young man in driving seat waited patiently.

'Told you we would reach in time,' the young man said, 'but you never listen to me.'

'I just didn't want us to be late, Abhi,' said the girl. 'Aren't you coming in?' she asked when the car had been driven into its garage and the garage gates secured.

'No, let's just wait here. It's past six, Sid would be here any minute.'

'That's exactly why I can't wait. You know well how hungry he would be when he comes,' said the girl as she unlocked her house and went indoors. The young man on the other hand strolled up to the little swing that stood in a corner of his garden.

'*Now at least they'd be quiet!*' Aashi thought.

She had turned her eyes away as soon as the car went inside the garage and now tried to pay no attention to the infuriating squeaks that the swing was making next door. But it really went beyond Aashi's limited power of endurance when the young man broke out into a whistling fit, quite out of tune but loud enough to startle Urmila out of sleep and make the lady look wide eyed at her new surroundings.

'Go inside, mother,' Aashi said, not bothering to lower her voice, 'there's too much noise outside.'

The whistling stopped suddenly and so did the swinging.

'Hello?' a smooth, clear voice sang out as the young man quickly walked over to the low wall that formed the boundary between their homes. 'Sorry for disturbing you. I didn't know anybody was here, or I'd have kept myself and my swing quiet. Nice sort of welcome that I've given to our new neighbours! I'm sure the squeaks of my whistle were just as terrible as the squeals of my swing!' he said, ending his long stream of words with a laugh that rang more with embarrassment than humour.

'It's okay, dear,' Aashi's mother replied, 'I wasn't sleeping.'

'Well, it sure is nice to have neighbours again. It gets very lonely otherwise. By the way, I'm Abhi, Abhinandan Mathur. You must have moved in today,' he said.

Aashi hadn't looked at him yet as she had kept her head resolutely turned away. But she had to admit that he had a nice voice. She wondered if he worked as a tele-caller.

'Yes, today. Me and my daughter and our two bags,' she heard her mother say.

'It's a pity that we weren't here to greet the four of you when you came. But now that we have met, if you, your daughter or your two bags need any assistance, I and my sister and all our bags and baggage are right next door!' he said with a chuckle.

Aashi rolled her eyes at the ridiculousness of that joke and wondered if he was habitual of trying such dull-witted retorts.

She turned her head a little and observed the neighbour that was being just a bit too friendly, as it seemed to her. She looked at him, and despite her not very benign feelings, didn't find too much to disapprove of in his person. Of course, she had to quickly move her eyes away from the stump of his left arm. But other than that, he didn't lack much in the way of her fine-tuned ideas about a good-looking man.

He was tall enough, a bit on the leaner side, but that went well with his boyish face and the curly strands of hair that steadfastly clung to his forehead, despite all his attempts to brush them away. He was fair too and had brown eyes that looked remarkably happy. And indeed, they were happy. Openly, sincerely, even eagerly happy, enlivened with the joy of a true and honest heart that loved life and desired to live it to the fullest, no matter what.

A more careful observer might perhaps have noticed some dark embers in those eyes too. But Aashi hadn't yet given so much thought to him or his eyes, nor even to his amputated left arm or his very obvious limp. There was nothing so remarkable in Abhi to arrest Aashi's attention for that long. He was handsome, but not extraordinarily so, had a charming face, but not breathtaking and his faded T-shirt showed that he clearly had no dressing sense to boast of.

And thus, it was just a wry resentment that she felt when his eyes turned towards her and forced her to get up and introduce herself.

'Hello,' she muttered in a way that threw any greeting out of the word. 'I'm Akanksha Sharma.'

'Aashi,' Urmila added helpfully.

'Akanksha, that's a nice name,' Abhi said, greeting her with a smile.

'Thanks,' she muttered.

'Sorry for disturbing you with my whistling. I didn't know somebody had moved in here,' Abhi said.

'Your whistling disturbed my mother, not me. But you did break my dream by making such a racket with your car's horn.'

'Oh, well,' he said, ruffling his hair and spreading his lips in a sheepish smile, 'you can continue your dream after I'm gone. I promise I won't break it again.'

'Yeah, as if I would get back that dream of mine as soon as I close my eyes again,' she said with a little laugh. 'It's lost forever and all because of you, Mr. Abhinandan!'

'Call me Abhi, everyone does. And I'd call you Aashi,' he declared.

Aashi shrugged her shoulders. She did not much like the way in which he had declared his decision, instead of asking her what she would like to be called. But then, she herself preferred to be called Aashi, so that was okay. Besides, she had already become habitual of finding people lacking in such polite delicacies. It didn't surprise her now. There really was too much of grossness in the real world.

'So, Aashi,' Abhi continued, entirely unmindful of the act of incivility he had just committed and preparing a question in his mind that was to shock Aashi's fine sensibilities with even a greater jolt, 'how old are you?' he asked.

Aashi looked at him with surprise. She certainly wasn't expecting *that* question and didn't know whether to laugh or be angry at his impudence.

'Oh, I beg your pardon,' he quickly said, as he read his own mistake in her shocked eyes. 'It's just that you seem exactly my sister's age.'

'Your sister?' Aashi repeated, not knowing what else to say.

'Yes, my sister Priyam. I'd call her now to meet you, but she must be busy in the kitchen with her hands deep in some batter. But why don't you join us for tea. We'll make a nice little party, all five of us.'

'Five?' Aashi's mother asked.

'Yes, you two, me and my sister and our best friend.'

'Sid?' Aashi asked, remembering the name she had overheard.

'Siddharth, actually. He comes here every day and we have tea and dinner together. Come around at six-thirty and I'll introduce you to both of them. Now I'll run off and inform my sister of the little party I've arranged. After all, she's the one to make the *real* arrangements,' said Abhi and limped inside his home.

'Seems like a nice young man,' Urmila said as she walked back to her chair.

'Too early to say,' Aashi mumbled as she settled back at her doorstep.

Chapter 2

As Aashi walked into Abhi's home, the orderliness of his little garden felt like a big relief to her eyes. Even in the dimming dusk, it looked vibrant and full of spring colours. She halted her steps and took a deep breath of the cool, fragrant air. How lovely it all felt after a day spent in the misery of her rented property.

And yet, how much more enchanting would it all have been had the place been a little bigger, with dainty white statues, gushing fountains and decorative lamps adding glamour and romance to the verdure, instead of the worn out pipe curled under the tap in a corner and a lone bulb near the main entrance throwing shadows all around.

Many minutes passed away as Aashi stood watching Abhi's garden and walking through the glorious vistas unfolding in her imagination. Many more moments might have found her lingering still, but she was suddenly disturbed by a 'hello' spoken in a manner more interrogative than welcome. The sound had come from the direction of the gate. Aashi turned and saw a young man looking at her enquiringly.

'Hello,' Aashi replied, 'you must be Sid.'

'Yes, I am, Siddharth, and you are?'

'Akanksha Sharma, I moved here today,' she said, pointing to her own home.

'Oh, okay, Akanksha,' he replied. 'Were you going in or coming out?'

'Going in.'

'Let's do that then,' Sid said as he led the way. 'So, who else is there in your family, Akanksha?' he asked after a moment.

'Just me and my mother,' she replied as Sid pushed open the door and welcomed her in.

'Oh, so you two have already met,' Abhi said as he saw them enter.

'Yes, she was admiring your garden when I came in.'

'You have a beautiful garden, Abhi,' Aashi said, 'and a nice home too,' she added as her quick eye took in the comfortable interiors.

'Well, it's okay if you complement Abhi for the garden. He works hard on it. But for the home, you must refer to Priyam. She's the housekeeper here and the head chef too,' Sid said and proceeded towards what Aashi later found out was the kitchen.

'Why have you come alone?' Abhi asked as he welcomed her to a chair.

'I tried to bring Mummy but she refused. You see, my mother's not used to being invited and would rather stay at home.'

'That won't do, I'll go and bring her,' Abhi replied, getting up at once.

'No, it's okay. She was resting when I left her.'

'Well, okay. But I don't like it. Won't she feel lonely?'

'Yeah, but...she is used to it,' Aashi said, shrugging and twitching her lips as she spoke.

'I understand, Aashi. But don't worry, we'll soon make her forget all her loneliness,' Abhi said.

Aashi nodded and gave a little smile.

'But for now, let me take you to my sister,' said Abhi, adding a more than usual cheer to his voice. 'I'm sorry but you'll have to accompany me to the kitchen because when Sid is there to help, it takes Priyam double the time to finish up her cooking. And we'll really have to hurry them up if we want to have any chance of tea before dinner time.'

When they entered the neat little kitchen, she found a girl with long black hair brewing tea over the stove.

'Hurry up, Priyam, how much time you take,' Sid was complaining.

He was leaning against the basin with his long legs crossed in front of him and a cookie jar held securely in the crook of his arm. Half a specimen of its content was in his right hand and the other half was in the process of being chewed by his strong jaw.

The picture of a man eating direct from a cookie jar contrasted sharply with Aashi's image of a dignified gentleman. But she wasn't surprised. As far as Aashi knew, gentlemen had really become a very rare breed.

'All done, Sid. Will just take a minute more. But you should really not eat so many cookies. It will make you fat,' said Priyam.

Aashi looked at Sid. There was no indication of him getting fat anytime soon. He looked strong and healthy, but not fat. Though he wasn't exceptionally handsome, he had a good and honest face and his athletic built went greatly in his favour.

15

There was an aura of placid strength about him, not merely physical but that which lies inwards. It shone out from his intense and penetrating eyes like a black fire, subdued and at peace now, but not extinct. He had a dusky complexion and a smile that brightened up on whom it shone because it was always genuine and straight from the heart. It was shining on Priyam now.

'Never, mind about me getting fat. But turn around and meet your new neighbour. You have kept her waiting for long already.'

'Oh, hi!' Priyam exclaimed, turning around quickly. 'I'm sorry, I didn't know you were standing here.'

'It's okay, you were engrossed,' said Aashi. 'Let me help you,' she added, wondering at the same time whether Abhi's judgement about their being of same age was really true.

The girl who looked at her with big brown eyes seemed much younger. Except that her eyes were so much wiser and calmer. No turbulence rocked their placid depths, and there wasn't even a hint of restlessness that flickered with such intensity in Aashi's own eyes.

Priyam had a charming face and a figure too slender to admit the possibility of curves as perfect as Aashi's. She looked a delicate and frail creature and Aashi might have been in danger of pitying her had the serene lustre of those brown eyes not told her how little Priyam was in need of that emotion.

'Oh, everything's ready. I was just making the tea…'

'Which would soon be adorning the stove if you don't pick it up now,' Sid remarked as he popped another cookie in his mouth.

'What? Oh!' Priyam exclaimed twirling around just in time to turn off the gas stove before the tea spilled over.

'See, I saved you just in time and you have no appreciation for my help,' Sid said, putting the lid back on the cookie jar and placing it on the shelf before picking up the tray of snacks. Priyam followed him with the tea tray while Abhi went to the refrigerator to take out the ketchup.

'Alright now,' Abhi said joining everyone, 'let's begin our little party.'

'Begin?' Sid questioned, popping the remaining half of a sandwich in his mouth.

'Oh, begin would be a wrong word, I see,' said Abhi, 'since you are already half-way through it! At that pace, Sid, you'd soon be a fat, bald man,' Abhi said.

'Fat I can understand,' Sid said, 'I've already been warned of that eventuality. But how bald?'

'Why, your head would swell so much with fat that all your hair will fall off,' Abhi replied.

'Maybe, but it's not my fault that your sister is becoming a better cook every day,' Sid mumbled between the bites.

Aashi smiled at the merry banter. She could see why Sid was a daily visitor to this house. Who could stay away when such love and companionship awaited him?

Abhi and Priyam's home was a perfect little haven. It had nothing to boast of luxury, yet everything to give assurance of comfort.

Unlike Aashi's home, it was fully built and had several rooms. There were two bedrooms on the first floor, and one on the ground floor as well. Aashi hadn't yet seen the first floor, but there was enough space downstairs to accommodate a comfortable drawing room cum dining space, one bedroom and a nice kitchen.

As Aashi looked around, her eyes were arrested by a photograph. It showed a couple smiling pleasantly at the camera. There was a garland of dried roses on it.

'Our parents,' Abhi said, as he saw Aashi looking at it. 'They died in a car accident.'

'Oh, I'm so sorry. It must be terrible to lose both of your parents.'

'Yes, had Sid's father not taken us in his house...'

'Then I'd have left his house too,' said Sid, with an amount of bitterness that surprised Aashi.

'You have done it, Sid. You've left him alone,' Priyam said in a low voice.

'He deserves it,' Sid replied.

'He does not,' she said, keeping her voice low, but firm.

'Well, tell us something about yourself, Aashi,' Abhi said in an obvious effort to change the direction of the conversation.

'My father's dead too.'

'Accident?' asked Abhi.

'No, work of some bloody maniacs. You perhaps remember the serial blasts that occurred around Diwali time about ten years ago.'

'Yes, many people were killed in it,' Abhi said.

'55, as the papers put it.'

'And your father was...'

'Yes, he was caught in the one that blew up in the Sarojini Nagar market. And...all because of me,' said Aashi, biting her lower lip as the sound of the bomb going off flooded her ears again.

'How can that be? Did you plant that bomb there?'

'No, Abhi. But...he would not have been in that shop had it not been for me. We had already done all our shopping. We should have left the market by then. But I noticed another dress and decided that I wouldn't leave the market before buying it too. Mummy said no, but my father never refused me anything. I was his princess. So while Mummy dragged me away from the shop, Papa went in to get it for me. Well… he never came back.'

'That's terrible!' Priyam said.

'Everything changed after he left. In an instant…everything was lost.'

'Well, you at least have your mother, Aashi, we are all orphans here,' Sid commented, trying in his own way to make her feel better.

'You are not an orphan,' said Priyam, 'Your father is alive.'

'Not for me,' Sid muttered under his breath, stuffing his mouth the next moment with another piece of sandwich.

'It must have been a big blow,' Abhi quickly added.

'It was. I did not just lose my father in that bomb blast. I lost my home too and the pampered life that I had been living. My grandparents took us to their home. My father's two brothers took up our responsibility and comfortably robbed us of our shop and house. Their wives found a free slave in my mother. Though they could never bend *me* to their wishes. My mother had no close surviving relative. She did everything to keep her in-laws happy. But…I revolted. I have left that house forever now.'

'Why now?' he asked again.

'To escape a forced marriage.'

'And what are you planning to do now?' Abhi asked, leaning a little forward in his chair.

'Start a boutique.'

'Do you have any experience?' he asked.

'And funds?' Sid added.

'I have fifteen lakhs, plus a little more that I saved so far from my salary. I've been working as a designer at a big boutique for the last two years. The clients there know me and like my work.'

'You mean they might break away from there and turn to yours?' asked Abhi.

'They might.'

'But you'll need workers, tailors etc,' Priyam said.

'I know, but till we can afford all that, I guess I'll have to depend on my mother's skill and my own hands. What I need right now is a place to open my shop in. I wish my uncles had not sold my father's shop. It would have been such a blessing now.'

'Taking up a shop on rent will add to you expenses,' said Sid. 'You don't want to spend any unnecessary penny from your limited store.'

'Hmm, you don't need your shed, do you?' asked Abhi after thinking for some time.

'No.'

'Then use it for your office. Simple.'

'Oh no, I can't!' Aashi exclaimed with horror at the thought of welcoming her rich clients in that sordid little...something! She couldn't find apt word to describe the horror she considered her garage was.

'Why not?'

'It's... it's too small.'

'So is your business. And it will just be temporary...till you can afford a real boutique.'

'But...'

'What?'

'It's so filthy!' said Aashi, making Abhi break out in a fit of laughter and causing even Sid to smile. 'What have I said that's so funny?' she retorted.

'Aashi, you seem to think of dirt and filth as a permanent evil. Don't you think that it can be cleaned?' Abhi asked. 'If we clean and get that shed painted, it will look fine. And we can easily arrange nice shelves and counters etc in it to make it look like a proper shop,' said Abhi.

'I guess...,' Aashi mumbled, her heart revolting at the picture of her covered in grime and scrubbing away at the dank interiors of the garage. Not even at her uncles' home had she lowered herself to that level. There was a servant there for such work and her mother to take care of all the rest. Besides, she was her father's princess. And princesses don't sweep!

'Well then,' said Abhi, 'we'll start the operation cleaning from day after tomorrow, that's Sunday.'

'Oh, there's no hurry,' Aashi said, 'I haven't even informed my employer yet. And she demands at least two weeks' notice from anyone who wants to leave the job. We can do the cleaning later.'

'Okay. And when did Mr. Mishra said he'd be getting the house painted?'

'He said nothing.'

'What? You took up the house without discussing it? The house desperately needs painting. You should have got it done before moving in.'

'I know it does. But...I didn't know I could ask him.'

'Hmm, I see. Well, never mind. I have his number, I'll tell him to get the job done as soon as possible. Then we must do something with that garden too. It's a horror to look at.'

'I was waiting for you to get to that, Abhi,' said Sid. 'For long you've been itching to get your hand on it!'

'Yeah,' Abhi nodded with a sheepish smile. 'But it's such a torture to see a perfectly nice garden turn into wilderness.'

'But how much money will the gardener ask?' Aashi asked.

'Gardener? Well, I don't know about that. We never had one. First my father used to manage it, and now I do.'

Aashi's mouth fell open. That was another shock for her fine sensibilities. The man of the house sullying his hands with mud and manure! Gross!

Aashi had scarcely recovered from the jolt when Abhi stuck in another blow and it appeared to her, not without some mischievous pleasure.

'Don't worry, Aashi,' he said, 'I'll teach you all about gardening. In no time you'll be managing your own little green space, without giving a single rupee to the gardener,' he said in a voice that sounded serious enough. But there was laughter twinkling in his eyes with an amount of mirth that made Aashi squirm as she looked at him.

'Okay,' she mumbled, trying to smile and keep her thoughts from bursting out on her face. She would have managed it perhaps, had her eyes been in any practice to dissemble. But they had always been too bold and frank to put on any sort of disguise. 'Well, I guess I must leave now,' she said finally. 'Thanks for everything. It's such a relief to have someone so near to turn for advice.'

'Sure,' Abhi replied, 'we are professional in giving advice. You know, we three have a super bank of brainpower among us. This Sid here is super intelligent, my little sister is super sensible and I, as you can judge yourself, am super clever. So whatever advice you need, you know where to turn to.'

'Yeah, and I guess I'm going to need a lot of it. I'm feeling so terrified right now. My mother says I've done the greatest mistake of my life by leaving my family. And I'm scared it may just be so.'

'No use worrying now, Aashi,' Sid said, 'you've done what you have done. Now bear it up.'

'Besides, now you are not alone. And even if things go wrong, we all are here for you. Are we not?' said Abhi.

Aashi's head jolted at the words and she stared at him. 'My...my father used to say that to me. How did you...I mean...'

'Maybe your father's spirit put those words in my mouth. But now that I've said them, I'll stick to them,' said Abhi, looking confidently in Aashi's eyes.

She stared at him for a long moment. And then quickly walked out of his home.

Chapter 3

'Well, that's a nice neighbour you've got yourself,' said Sid soon after Aashi walked out of the door.

'Yes, she seems nice,' Abhi said, 'but I've nothing to do in getting her here. That's her own doing.'

'Yeah, she's a big doer alright, but I'm sorry to say, a little thinker.'

'Hmm…judged that much,' Abhi replied, 'guess, we'll just have to think up for her and help her as much as we can.'

'That girl is foolish and immature and I don't think she appreciates your helping her. She clearly didn't like any of your ideas.'

'But she approved of them,' said Priyam.

'Yes, she did. But I don't know…she…reminds me of your friend Raj,' Sid said as he stretched his full length on the sofa, putting his head on the cushion that had long been moulded to his skull's shape.

'How does Aashi remind you of Raj?' Abhi asked with interest.

'You know, she's just the sort of girl Raj thrives on.'

'Oh, come on, he's no flirt,' Abhi said.

'I know he's not, but only because it's ungentlemanly to be a flirt. And Raj *considers* himself a perfect gentleman, though he's far from it if you ask me.'

'Come on, Sid, you are too unforgiving.'

'I know,' Sid mumbled. 'But I can't help it if some people get on my nerves. Raj, for example. But I must not say anything against him. After all, he appears to be an ardent lover. Right, Priyam?'

Priyam just smiled and put down the onion she was peeling to wipe her eyes. She gave a little sniff as a tear trickled down her face.

'Oh, I didn't know you miss him so much, Priyam! Just the mention of his name makes you cry!' Sid exclaimed dramatically. He propped up his head on his hand and fixed his eyes on her.

Priyam was sitting on the floor near the centre table. Her long hair were neatly plaited and slung over her left shoulder. However, some loose strands had slipped out of the confinement and made use of their liberty by touching her tranquil face every now and then.

Half a smile appeared unawares on Sid's lips as he looked at her. The sable depths of his eyes became alight with a buoyant glow, a glimmer that only Priyam's smiling face had the power to evoke.

Had Sid's colleagues or even most of his students seen him at that moment, they would hardly have believed their eyes. To them, Sid was just a surly person who rarely smiled and was always on the lookout for the opportunity of being rude and deprecatory. That he could smile too and be playful was a thing nobody could ever have imagined of him.

'Well, let's leave Raj alone now, shall we? Time for chess. We still have to finish yesterday's game,' Abhi called out to his friend.

'Oh, yeah, yesterday's game. Alright then, get ready to taste another defeat,' said Sid as he jumped out of the couch.

Sid and Abhi settled down to resume their battle of the previous day. Priyam went on peeling onions as before.

'She is so pretty, isn't she?' she asked all of a sudden as her thoughts turned back to Aashi.

'Oh yes, she's pretty. And I'd really advice Abhi to be on his guard against her prettiness. It's no good for a guy to be living so close to a girl that pretty.'

'You have no need to warn me, Sid, I won't travel on that road again.'

'But all girls are not like Neha,' Priyam protested, knowing too well what Abhi's words meant. 'I'm sure Aashi is not.'

'Maybe, but I'm still the same. Disabled, as Neha said.'

'You are not so,' Sid retorted at once. 'It was she who was lacking. She was a fool. It's good you got rid of her!'

'I think...it was more like *she* got rid of me,' said Abhi, smiling at his friend's sudden rage.

'Whatever. Now, are you going to make your move or do you intend to quit?'

'Quit? Never,' Abhi said as he quickly shifted his bishop on the board and put Sid's in danger.

Soon the two lost themselves in the game while Priyam busied herself in getting the dinner ready. The two young men could hear her humming in the kitchen, and at least one of them found it hard to concentrate on the game because of that.

Aashi was quite forgotten as the three busied themselves in their own little rituals. It was only when they were going out for a walk after dinner that Abhi thought of her, and then too because he saw her standing at her doorstep.

'Hey, Aashi, want to join us for a walk?' Abhi asked.

'Uh…okay. Let me just ask my mother,' she said, vanishing indoors.

'Great!' Sid exclaimed, 'now we can't have even our walks alone.'

'Come on, Sid, don't be so mean. She has no friend here,' Abhi said.

Sid said nothing but he still resented having to share his two friends with someone else. Their little group was nothing less than perfection to him. And it was his firm belief that perfection must not be disturbed. Certainly not by a bubble-headed girl who seemed to dance in air and never probably bothered to take a look at the ground.

But despite Sid's resentment at Aashi, and despite her being quite opposite from them in almost every inclination, she was soon to become an integral part of their group.

Aashi indeed was very different from them, different in her carefree vivacity, her lively spirit and bubbling enthusiasm that contrasted so sharply with their grim pragmatism. She lived in her dreams, and of reality, she knew little and cared even less.

But Abhi, Sid and Priyam had long ago made peace with their realities. And all their dreams, they sprouted only from the solid ground of what actually was real.

Abhi was just seventeen and Priyam fifteen when their parents died. At an age when the youth is budding with desires of success and happiness, of love and romance, they were left orphans and at mercy of their relatives.

The accident which took away their parents had also maimed Abhi for life. His left arm had to be amputated and his left leg was shattered so badly that it could never regain its natural flexibility. Only Priyam had escaped unhurt and it was considered nothing less than a miracle by those who had witnessed the accident.

Abhi had little recollections of what followed after the accident. He lay unconscious in the hospital for days and Priyam was left alone to battle the demons of grief and fear. She was old enough to know what it was to be an orphan. But the realization of being one had not yet sunk in. It remained for her relations to pound it into her heart, and relatives, it can be fairly asserted, never defer from such kindly duties, though they may ignore all the rest.

Before Priyam could realize what had happened, she found herself surrounded by roomful of relatives. Some of them wailing loudly at the loss of those they had not seen in years. Some on the other hand tried hard to squeeze out some pious drops from stubbornly arid eyes. When all their attempts failed, they merely consoled themselves by rubbing their hands to dry cheeks and drier eyes.

'What will happen to the poor children? Who will take care of them?' The questions moved around in the crowded rooms with considerable noise.

Priyam, who was sitting quietly in a corner, listened to everything without uttering a word. A steady flow of tears was the only indication that convinced everyone of the girl being sad enough. Her eyes remained fixed to the floor as she sat, watching through it, again and again, the accident that had transformed her world in an instant.

Sid, meanwhile, was sitting on a low stool right across Priyam, with eyes focused on her and ears searing with the all the kind words being spoken around. He didn't care if many a curious stares were being directed towards him. He was with Priyam, and there would he remain unless in case Abhi needed him more.

'Anil! My Brother! My Brother! My poor little Anil! What will happen to his children now? My brother is dead!' Priyam's aunt, Leela, was crying on unceasingly. 'Poor child, what will happen to you now? Your father is dead. Where will you go now? Your father is dead! How can God be so cruel? And what would happen to our Abhi now? Poor child! It would have been better had he died too, instead of becoming a cripple!'

'Shut up! How dare you!' Sid murmured under his breath, gritting his teeth and folding his fingers into fists. He had to summon all his willpower to remain still and silent, when every pore of his person was itching to silence the lady forever.

'Oh! What is to become of these children now?' Leela kept on wailing, undeterred by Sid's raging glare.

'Well, that is for you to decide,' a voice rose up from the swarm. 'They are your responsibility now, yours and Rajeev's.'

'Yes, yes, of course. And I'm not the one to shrink from my responsibilities,' said Rajeev. He was Priyam's uncle, and now the only surviving sibling of Leela.

'Yes, we will take care of them! Though God knows it is hard already to raise two daughters and two sons. But I won't shy from my responsibility. I will take Priyam and raise her as my daughter. Though it is going to be such a trial to have another daughter to raise and marry,' said Leela. 'You have it easy, Rajeev. You are taking Abhi. He will be a support to you, even though he is a cripple now.'

'Don't forget the money I will need to spend on his treatment,' said Rajeev.

'Not as much as we'll have to spend when it's time for Priyam's marriage,' Leela said. 'Nothing costs so much as a girl's marriage. Fortunately, they have this house that can be sold,' she said. 'Too bad their car is wrecked beyond repair. But we'll salvage what we can from the house. I just hope their mother's jewellery and Anil's bank balance is worth something. Otherwise it would be very difficult to take the burden of another girl.'

Sid had never thought it possible that he could hate anyone more than he hated his father. But his feelings for his father could perhaps be called benign in comparison to those that flared up against them. The man who was his father had cheated a wife, but these people were cheating two innocent children and depriving them of what little they had left in the world!

He could see that Priyam was listening to every word being spoken, and that every word felt like twisting of the knife that already had been jabbed into her young heart.

Though Priyam was two years younger than him and Abhi, she had nevertheless been an integral part of their camaraderie. She was a cheerful girl, always a pleasant company and a sincere friend. Moreover, Priyam was Abhi's sister and that itself gave her an indubitable claim on Sid's affections. She was a darling of her father and a precious companion to a doting brother. Her happy chatter never failed to bring smile on even the sulkiest of faces. Sid himself had often teased Priyam of being a chatterbox that never could remain silent.

Well, now she was silent. And her silence echoed more loudly in Sid's ears than any other sound rising from around him. He wanted her to say something, anything! He wanted Priyam to rebel against those uncles and aunts of hers, to refuse to part with her brother, to do anything, anything, except remaining silent.

'Come, Priyam, stop worrying now, child,' Leela's voice rose up again, 'your aunt would take good care of you. Come to me now, my dear child.'

Priyam's eyes shot up to meet Sid's. There was neither pleading in those eyes, nor even any resentment or feeling of rebellion that Sid would have so liked to see. Instead, Priyam's eyes filled up with terror, terror so intense that tightened every muscle in her face and drained all colour from her cheeks.

That was all that Sid could bear. 'Wait!' he shouted, 'Wait till my father comes!'

In a trice a decision had been made. A decision that went against all his promises to himself. But Sid could not let his feelings ruin his friends' life. There was a chance, and he would take it, no matter what.

'Why? What would your father do?' asked Rajeev with surprise.

'He'll adopt Abhi and Priyam and rid you of their upbringing,' Sid burst out in undisguised hatred.

His exclamation was surprising enough for everyone to gape at each other in bewilderment. Then several voices rose up at once.

'Your father?'

'Adopt both of them?'

'Why would he?'

'Both of them?' one after the other questions poured in quick succession.

'Yes, both of them. They belong together, and they will stay together. I won't let you separate them.'

'But...,' Rajeev said, 'why would he?'

'He would,' Sid replied, and without wasting any more words, took out his mobile phone and dialled his father's number. Everybody watched in silence. Rajeev and Leela looked at each other, not being able to decide whether the new development was to be considered good or otherwise. Surely, it would rid them of a lot of unnecessary trouble. But then, all the time they had just spent in calculation of their brother's wealth, well, it will have to come to nothing. Besides, what would people say?

'But...we can't let a stranger take care of our darlings,' Leela tried after a little thought, 'we don't know who your father is, what kind of man...'

Sid turned his back towards her.

'Mr. Vardhan...' he said after a moment's silence. 'Yes, it's me. No, I'm fine. Yes, I'm fine,' he repeated a bit impatiently. 'But I need you to come to Abhi's house. Your driver knows where it is.' 'I don't care how important your meeting is,' he exclaimed after a few seconds of listening to his father. 'You must come right now. No, later will be too late! It was then and it will be now...' nobody could hear what his father said, but they all saw Sid take a deep breath and disconnect the call. 'He's coming,' he whispered softly to Priyam and then turned to address others. 'My father is coming,' Sid declared, 'he'll be here in about 40 minutes. We'll wait for him.'

'Your father may be coming,' a man spoke up, 'but that doesn't mean he'll adopt them.'

'He will.'

'Why would our kids stay with strangers when we are ready to take care of them? If your father wants to help, let him give the money to us so we don't have to separate Abhi and Priyam,' Leela suggested.

'No,' was all the reply she got from the boy who stood there with folded arms, tall, firm and resolute. Sid's face looked a shade darker than it was, but his eyes were steady and heart fixed at one point.

There was only one person in the entire room who knew what it had cost Sid to do what he had just done. Sid would not have asked his father for a penny even to save his own life. But he did it for them. It was a fact that the fifteen year old girl staring at him was to stamp in her heart and repay it forever with the earnest devotion and affection so deep that perhaps even rivalled what she felt for her brother.

It was indeed not easy for Sid to turn to his father for help. It had been almost seven years since his mother had jumped to her death. And during all this time, the gulf between the father and son had become so great that they hardly ever spoke to each other now. However, by asking for help, Sid had put himself under the obligation of the very man he scorned even to call his Dad.

'But it's the only way I could...it's my only option...' Sid told himself repeatedly as he stood by the window to wait for his father.

He did not have to wait long. This time, Mr. Vardhan had evidently made sure not to give his son an opportunity of blaming him for delay. His car stood in front of the gate before the forty minutes of Sid's estimate were over.

The man who walked in the crowded room was perhaps just an inch shorter than his son, with the same athletic built and deep penetrating eyes. He was smartly dressed in a well-fitted suit and looked striking enough to make most of the younger ladies hush their babble and several men to stand up in respect.

'I've come, Sid,' Mr. Vardhan said as he walked straight to his son, 'what do you want me to do?'

Sid lost no time in explaining everything to him. It was perhaps the first time in several years that he had spoken more than a sentence at a time to the man who stood in front of him. And also the first time that it dawned on Sid how out of habit he had become in holding any sort of conversation with his own father.

'Don't worry,' Mr. Vardhan replied as soon as Sid had finished, 'I'll take care of everything. This must be Priyam, is she?' he asked looking at the young girl standing close behind his son.

'Yes...Dad,' Sid replied.

'Don't worry, child,' Mr. Vardhan said putting his hand at her head. 'I'll take care of you and your brother. I know what it is to be distanced from the one you love above everybody else,' he said looking at Sid before turning again to Priyam, 'but I won't let that happen to you.'

Priyam looked bewildered as she turned to look at Sid. She wondered if the man standing before her really was Sid's father. He didn't seem as hateful as Sid thought him to be.

But Mr. Aditya Vardhan was really Sid's father and despite the sliver of gratitude that Sid now felt compelled to admit, he still hated that man with all the passion and energy that a seventeen year old can be capable of. It was another matter, however, that despite all his bitter feelings Sid could not help but admire his father's efficiency in manipulating everyone in such a way that they agreed to everything he said and yet considered themselves as faring better than him in the dealing that ensued.

In half an hour, Mr. Vardhan had had everything settled just as Sid wanted it. He had made everyone agree that it was best for all if Abhi and Priyam stayed with him.

'I'll raise them as my own kids. You don't need to worry at all,' Mr. Vardhan declared.

'You'll of course desire to sell the house…' Rajeev ventured.

'I desire no such things. Whatever belongs to Abhi and Priyam will be made secure in their name.'

'Abhi would need a lot of medical help,' Leela said.

'He would get the best medical assistance possible. That would be my first priority. Their education will proceed unhindered and I'll do everything in my capacity to ensure their happiness and prosperous future. All I want in return is that I'll not suffer any meddling from any of you. You may come and meet Abhi and Priyam if you want, but you'll not interfere. I hope you find that fair enough.'

That was, in fact, more than what most had expected. What better excuse could Rajeev and Leela have had for forgetting the kids than that their guardian didn't want any meddling.

They held a lengthy discussion of full five minutes, and then, with bleeding hearts and tearful eyes, ceded their right of taking care of their brother's children.

***

28

For now
The anguish of the deep-fixed spear grew fierce,
And he desired to draw forth the steel,
And let the blood flow free, and so to die,
But first he would convince his stubborn foe…

'Sohrab and Rustom' by Matthew Arnold.

Priyam was moved to the Vardhan House as soon as all the funeral ceremonies were over. Abhi, however, was to remain in the hospital for a long time.

It took him eleven days just to come out of his unconsciousness. But even after that, he was kept heavily sedated. He was safe now and his life was out of danger. But a long battle lay ahead of him. The battle, that was to begin with the realization of his loss and continue till he learnt to deal with it.

When Sid and Priyam brought Abhi out of the hospital two months after the accident, a black BMW was waiting to take them to the Vardhan House. Abhi, though, would much rather have entered their white Maruti and have his father take him to their own home. But his father was dead. His mother was dead. The home that he had grown up in was lost forever. It was locked in a deep, unbroken silence now, full of memories, but empty of life.

However, while one home had died, the other stood ready to welcome them with open arms.

In the Vardhan House, Abhi and Priaym found more comfort than they had in their own home, and not any less of love and affection. Though the loss of parents could never be recompensed, yet the devotion of Sid and the generosity of his father was ardent enough to make any sorrow bearable. And Abhi and Priyam soon learned to bear theirs.

As much as Abhi and Priyam gained from Vardhan's residence, the house gained much from them too. Before their arrival, it was a place where only loneliness and resentment resided. With Priyam and Abhi, gratitude entered, soon followed by respect and love.

Abhi was too weak in the first few days of his stay there, and too much under the influence of sedatives to notice much. But Priyam's grateful heart was alert and eagerly responsive to every little kindness Mr. Vardhan showed towards them. Her heart melted at the sight of her guardian and whenever he talked to her, she could not but pity the man for his unrequited desire for reconcilement with his son.

Abhi too could not help but feel deep regard and affection for this man whom his best friend hated so much. And Mr. Vardhan too admired Abhi's courage and determination. It was however Priyam who had become especially dear to his heart.

Priyam did suspect that Sid didn't approve of her growing fondness for his father. But then, Priyam had come to disapprove his continued hatred too.

'I can't believe that Mr. Vardhan could have done such a terrible thing as to betray his wife,' she often said to Abhi. 'He's so kind and good. There must have been some mistake, some misunderstanding.'

'Well, we don't know what really happened, Priyam,' Abhi used to answer. 'It's better if we stop thinking about it.'

But Priyam could not stop thinking about it. And the more she thought, the more firm she became in her belief that it must have been Mrs. Vardhan's fault only that caused her death and turned Sid so against his father.

Of course, these thoughts were never to be revealed to anyone, especially not to Sid. Nevertheless, as dear as Sid was to her, Priyam had made up her mind never to be a cause of pain to his father. Mr. Vardhan already appeared too sad to her and Priyam wanted to do everything in her power to give him a little happiness. And if a cup of tea from her hands made Mr. Vardhan happy, not even Sid's anger would desist her from giving it to him.

Sid's own feelings were more ambivalent. He certainly did not like his friends thinking so highly of his father. However, his own deep-set honesty was forcing Sid everyday to be thankful to Mr. Vardhan. He could see clearly how well his father was playing the role of a guardian. When Sid watched them conversing and saw his father's stiffness replaced by a warm smile of affection, he could not but feel a strange pull bidding him to go and join their merry little group too. These were the moments when Sid's resentment against his father dipped to its lowest and something akin to affection made its presence felt in his heart too.

And yet, Sid hated Mr. Vardhan with every fibre of his being. At least, he believed he did.

It troubled both Abhi and Priyam, and not just because they had started loving the very man Sid detested. They really wanted to see the father and son on acquiescent terms at least.

'Why do you resent your father so much, Sid?' Priyam asked one day while they were having lunch.

'Because I hate him,' Sid replied.

'But why? He's so good. If your father hadn't agreed to help us, only God knows what would have happened to us. He's so kind and…'

'Yeah, kind,' said Sid with a scowl, 'he was kind to my mother too, Priyam, but that didn't prevent him from betraying her.'

'Don't be so hard on him, Sid. May be there was some misunderstanding?'

'No.'

'I too think, Sid,' Abhi said, 'that your father cannot be so entirely bad. If he were, he would never have bothered so much about us.'

'Y…es,' said Sid, 'I know…he's not all that bad. He… has much good in him that I might have admired and respected him for. But he's still a murderer, Abhi, my mother's murderer. How can I forgive him?'

'But how can you be so sure that he really did betray your mother and that it wasn't just her own suspicion that took her life?' Priyam blurted out before she could stop herself.

'He did!' Fire rose up in Sid's eyes as he glared down at Priyam. His fingers tightened up in fists, 'He did!' he growled again.

Priyam looked at him with terrified eyes. She could barely recognize the person who stood before her at that moment, even his voice sounded strange and unfamiliar. She shuddered visibly at his shout and choked at her own breath.

'I…I…I'm sorry, Sid!' Priyam said, her shock clearly visible in her terrified eyes. 'Sid?' she urged.

Sid closed his eyes and took a deep breath and shook his head disparagingly at himself.

'Priyam,' he said as he knelt down beside her.

'Y…y…es?' she said with an unmistaken tremor in her voice. Sid took Priyam's hands in his and held them in a firm grasp as he looked into her brimming eyes.

'I'm sorry,' he said in a barely audible whisper, 'trust me, you are the last person I…'

'I know and I'm sorry too. I hurt your feelings,' Priyam gave a quivering reply.

'Yes, you have, Priyam. But I don't blame you. I know you like him, whether it's gratitude or love, I don't know and I don't want to know. But don't expect me to love him too. I can't…even if I wanted too. We have gone too far apart. Maybe I'm wrong, but I don't care. I owe it to my mother.'

'But he helped us, Sid,' she spoke again. There was urgency in Priyam's voice now and her words came out with rapidity. 'You asked him and he never hesitated and he's been so good since then. *He* doesn't hate you, Sid, he loves you!'

'I know that! And I'm much obliged too! But, Priyam, when I look at that man, my mother appears before my eyes, as she lay there on the floor right under that balcony,' Sid pointed towards the balcony of the hall. 'She was so young, Priyam! Just about 30 years old…and…so beautiful…and there she lay…in a pool of her own blood…dead! I can never forget, I sat there, with her, until police came. And where was he? You know where? With that woman! With that woman, Priyam! And my mother dead. I know that she had told him she would do it. Did he care? No! I cannot forgive him, Priyam! I will…never forgive him! Never!' Sid almost shouted again.

Priyam nodded slightly and lowered her head. Sid continued staring at her for a moment longer, as if trying to judge whether she had understood what he had just said.

And then he began again, using a more controlled tone this time, 'I know you were only trying to help, Priyam,' he said slowly and without raising his voice. 'But please, don't talk to me about him again. You like my father, I know, and I won't stop you from talking to him. But never again, if you love me one bit, never again try to bring us closer. That would never be.'

Priyam nodded in silent affirmation.

She never did bring up the subject again. Sid's anger had shocked her too much to hazard it another time. Everything continued as it was before the incident. Sid never interfered in their relationship with his father. They never compelled him to reconcile.

It can be said however, that if the siblings failed to improve Sid's relationship with his father, they at least prevented it from getting worse. They were the only link which kept the father and son together, bound with each other with unanimity of aim.

Time passed and slowly, Abhi and Priyam became habitual of their new home. And Sid became so reconciled with the regard his friends had for his enemy that he didn't even object when Abhi joined his father's company as a trainee. His only objection, which his father felt too, was that Abhi was taking up the yoke too soon and should rather concentrate on his studies.

Abhi was pursuing an engineering degree. But he wanted to be able to support himself and his sister, as soon as possible. And he would not let even

Sid persuade him out of this resolve. And surprising though it was even to Abhi, it was Sid actually who had suggested that if Abhi was bent on breaking his back, he should as well do that in Mr. Vardhan's office.

'But won't you mind...I mean...?' Abhi asked.

'No, I won't. In fact...it relieves me,' Sid confessed. 'At least...there's someone here who can perhaps be a son to him, and, in time, take care of his business.'

'But what about his own son?' Abhi could not help but ask.

'He will never be his.'

'Why, Sid? We have been silent so far. But I must ask you again. Why don't you forgive your father? He may have done wrong to your mother. But people change, Sid, time changes them.'

'Yes, I know.'

'So?'

'I can't... I can't betray my mother. He did that, I will never. But...' Sid said after a moment's silence, 'it's good. It's good that he has you with him. You and Priyam. At least he has someone who loves him and cares for him. He needs it now.'

'Yes, we love him. And so do you.'

'No.'

'Yes, Sid, I think you do.'

'No!' Sid said with bitter firmness and turned as if to go. Yet he lingered, with his hands stuffed in pockets, eyes sometimes striking Abhi and sometimes shying away from him. It was too much to bear. He could not stand the scrutiny of his own friend.

Sid's own heart had, several times in the recent months, found him guilty of the prohibited emotion. But that it was evident to others too was a fact too painful to him. He had steadily tried to counter his growing affection for his father by hating the man with fiercer intensity. But Sid knew that he was failing, failing in the promise he had made to his mother's dead body, and he hated himself for it, perhaps even more than he had ever hated Mr. Vardhan. And it was this hate that burned in his eyes as Sid walked away from Abhi.

Priyam was standing in the doorway, a mute spectator of what had just passed in the room. For a moment her eyes arrested his advance, but just for a moment. The next instant Sid had walked past her, with downcast eyes and hands tightly closed in fists.

'Sid, stop!' Priyam called out, and ran after him when he gave no indication of having heard her.

There he was, to her right as Priyam stepped out of the big gate. He was walking on the road in a grim silence, with his eyes fixed down at some point

33

ahead of him. But before Priyam could reach him, Mr. Vardhan's car's horn announced his arrival, stopping Priyam in her tracks while at the same time adding speed to Sid's feet.

Mr. Vardhan was returning from the office and, for the first time in her entire stay, Priyam found herself resenting his early arrival. What was she to do? Her heart yearned to join her wounded friend. But his enemy's car had already stopped right beside her.

'What are you doing in the middle of the road, Priyam?' Mr. Vardhan asked.

'I...' she muttered trying to form a coherent reply. But she had no idea what to say.

'Anyway,' Mr. Vardhan said, trying to ignore her confusion, 'I'm so glad I found you here. Want to go for a ride?'

'But you must be tired,' Priyam replied.

'Tired? Not at all. Let's go,' Mr. Vardhan quickly gave directions to his driver to take them to Priyam's favourite ice cream parlour. 'Is Sid upset about something?' he asked after sometime.

Priyam nodded silently. 'He didn't see you perhaps,' she said after a moment's silence.

'He did. Why else would he have sped away into that lane?'

Priyam raised her eyes to her guardian, she wanted to say something, to tell him something that could give him a bit of comfort. But all she could do was to look at him in silence before bowing down her head and try not to cry.

'Was he angry at you?' he asked with concern.

'No,' she replied.

'Abhi?'

'Yes.'

'Because I have hired Abhi? I was afraid Sid won't like it. But don't worry, dear, I'll get Abhi a job somewhere else. It won't do to come between them. They need each other,' he said, more to himself than to Priyam.

'No, it's not that,' Priyam replied quickly. 'Sid has no objection if Abhi joins your company. He said it relieves him.'

'He said that? Then my suspicion is correct. My son doesn't hate me anymore. At least not as much as he wants to,' Mr. Vardhan said with a smile that was anything but happy. 'It gives him pain... perhaps makes him feel guilty too. I have seen it in his face often lately. That's it, isn't it, Priyam?'

Priyam said nothing.

'You know it's true, Priyam, and so do I. And that's why I'm going away.'

'Going away?' she asked with horror. 'Where?'

'U.K.'

34

'But why? You don't need to!'

'Priyam, I can bear his anger, his disgust. I have borne it all this while. But I can't bear Sid's pain. I can't see him breaking up under the load of his baseless guilt. I can't, Priyam. It's perhaps better if Sid goes on hating me, at least he is strong in that. It's too painful to see him weaken, to see him feeling lowered in his own esteem. If I go away, Sid would quickly go back to his undiluted hatred against me. That's the only way,' Mr. Vardhan said as he looked at the shops rushing past his window. A moment's silence past he turned to look at her. 'Am I right, Priyam?' he asked.

'Oh, I would rather have you here,' Priyam said as her hand quickly brushed away a tear from her wet cheek.

'Yes, I know you would. But you see the necessity, don't you? It must be painful for you too to see Sid hating himself,' Priyam gave no reply. But her silence was reply enough for Mr. Vardhan. 'You'd write to me, won't you?' he said after sometime.

Priyam nodded.

'Good. I know I can count on you. This would be my address,' he said as he took out a card from his wallet and handed it to her. 'Don't lose it.'

Priyam shook her head from side to side to indicate that she would not.

'Remember, Priyam, I rely on you to keep me abreast about what's going on with you all. Write to me as often as you can and you can always call me if you need anything. I promise I'll be with you as soon as possible.'

Priyam nodded again and looked up at him.

Mr. Vardhan's eyes were fixed on her too. 'You know, Priyam,' he began, a little hesitatingly. 'I really can't thank God enough for His mercy in handing you over to me. You've been such a blessing, child,' he said, leaning over and planting a kiss on Priyam's forehead.

Mr. Vardhan was gone the next day before Priyam opened her eyes. On the table beside her bed rested a small parcel. She opened it to find a gold chain with a radiant pearl hanging from it. 'How beautiful!' Priyam whispered to herself as she took it up in her hands and admired its simple elegance. She immediately put it around her neck and vowed never to part with it.

Abhi too found a new watch at his bedside when he woke up. Sid must have found something too, but he told them nothing and they, of course, dared not ask.

Next week, the siblings too walked out of the house that had been their safe haven for so long. The benevolent presence that had given them such loving shelter was gone, and Abhi and Priyam knew that Sid himself yearned to escape from the stifling confinement of his father's house. So, after three years, the orphans returned back to their home. It was their turn now to play a host to the friend who had sheltered them for so long.

***

Chapter 5

When Aashi moved into the neighbourhood, Abhi and Priyam had already spent four years there.

In those four years, much had changed. Abhi had risen up to a position in Mr. Vardhan's company, which, though not very grand, was at least good enough to let him manage a comfortable way of living. Priyam had completed her graduation in English Literature. Sid was teaching in a public school while continuing his studies too. He had done a couple of computer courses and was going through a third one after which he hoped to find a better paying job with some software firm. Sid had also rented a room near his school. It was another matter however that he continued spending most of his free time in Abhi's home.

The bedroom at the ground floor of Mathur's residence had been labelled as permanently his. It was used frequently too and could easily boast of having more of Sid's belonging then his rented room.

Sid's hatred against his father had resumed all its old intensity. Mr. Vardhan's exile had freed Sid of the conflict that had threatened to tear his heart in opposite directions. And now that Mr. Vardhan was no longer in front of him, Sid could rest easy in his old, undiluted revulsion.

For so many years, their world had limited itself to just three of them. Neither of them had ever felt the need to befriend any one as they had befriended each other. It was a unanimous belief among these three that any addition to their group would be unwelcome to all of them.

It's no surprise, therefore, that Sid had such a hard time in accepting the fact that their little group of three had suddenly began admitting the possibility of a fourth.

But whether he liked it or not, Aashi soon became an integral part of their group.

As months passed on, Aashi's friendship with Abhi, Priyam and Sid grew stronger. She had found all three of them to be very good and kind people, though Sid behaved a bit too rudely sometimes. Abhi and Priyam were always fun to be with. She had come to trust Abhi especially a lot in the past few months. And his amiable joviality was such a happy relief against Sid's haughty straightforwardness. Abhi was always full of fun and good cheer, and Aashi enjoyed nothing better than to go on long walks with him and Priyam.

They were now enjoying just one such walk on a surprisingly pleasant night in the month of May. The moon was shining brightly, although there were some clouds bunched together in one corner of the sky too. After an intolerably hot day, the night felt cool and comfortable.

Aashi was smiling brightly as she walked. The smile was half in response to Abhi's chatter, and half with the pleasure of seeing Sid and Priyam walk together, a couple of steps ahead of her and Abhi. The smile broadened up as she saw Sid reaching out to hold Priyam's hand when they reached a badly damaged stretch of road. He let go only when they were on a smoother track. Priyam's fingers instantly curled up in a tight fist.

Aashi was now almost grinning. She loved anything even remotely connected to love and romance. And it was clear to her how much Priyam loved Sid.

But whether Sid's feelings for Priyam were coloured with the same emotion or not, Aashi could not say.

Sid did care about Priyam a lot. But at the same time, Aashi had noticed a sort of deliberate guardedness in his behaviour towards Priyam. A certain hesitancy that restricted him and seemed to raise a warning whenever he approached too near the threshold of something more, something greater than plain friendship.

'*Maybe it's just his way to be reserved and restrained,*' Aashi concluded. '*He's certainly not the kind of man who can be openly romantic.*'

Aashi would probably have dissected Sid's character a little more, had she not been diverted by Abhi's call just then.

'Sid!' Abhi had called out.

'Yes?' Sid replied as he and Priyam halted and turned back.

'Do you think it would rain? There are clouds gathering up, see,' Abhi said, pointing towards a huge dark mass creeping on towards the moon.

'Rain? But it's no time for monsoon yet,' Sid replied without moving his eyes away from the clouds.

37

'It does seem like rain to me.'

'Yes, you are right. We should better turn back now,' Sid replied.

'Oh, it is such a pleasant evening. It would have been so good if we could have stayed out longer,' said Priyam.

'Oh, we *can* linger a little, if you want. Even if it does start raining, it won't melt us away!' Abhi laughed. 'It's been so hot lately. Getting soaked actually sounds like a great idea to me!'

'Wouldn't it be better if you ask the opinion of your *new* friend before slowing down your steps?' said Sid, twitching his lips in a mocking grin as he watched Aashi lift her skirt at the mere mention of rain.

'So what do you say, Aashi? Shall we linger?' Abhi asked.

'To get my white skirt all splashed with mud? No way! I'm going back. Besides,' she quickly added, 'Mummy would worry too.'

'Well, I certainly won't want that. Alright then, let's hurry back home,' said Abhi, quickening his steps immediately and turning his face away to hide his grin that had sprung up at Aashi's response.

The rain started just when they turned into their block. 'Run, Aashi, run before your white skirt becomes brown!' Abhi exclaimed with a show of alarm. Aashi made a face at him, but followed his advice nevertheless. She picked up her long skirt and ran away, desperate to reach her home before the rain poured any heavier.

As she arrived near her home, she spied her mother standing at the door and looking out. 'Oh, Aashi, thank God you are back!' Urmila cried out as soon as she saw Aashi. 'I was so worried about you. But where's everybody? Why are you alone?'

'We are all here, Auntie. Don't worry,' Abhi's voice rose above the pattering of rain as he unlatched his gate.

'And just in time,' Aashi exclaimed from her doorstep as the clouds roared, lightening lit up the darkening sky with all its glory and big, heavy drops started falling down with great rush.

'Ah, lovely!' Abhi murmured, closing his eyes and raising his face upwards.

'Aren't you going in?' Aashi asked.

'Go in and miss a good shower? Not until I start wearing long white skirts too!' Abhi replied.

'So what are you going to do? Stay there and get wet?' Aashi asked with disbelief.

'Exactly!' shouted Abhi, ruffling his dripping wet hair and blinking as some drops entered his eyes. Then he kicked at the little puddle that had formed in front of him and sent several muddy drops flying away.

'Oh my God, Abhi! You are acting like a little child, you know that?' Aashi laughed, feeling sure that had Abhi been a few years younger, he would have most definitely broken into a merry squeal too. She couldn't help but find it so deliciously funny, the way he stood there in the rain, his dripping hair lying flat on his forehead, eyes blinking hard against the heavy rain and his grin spreading wider and wider.

'And you are acting like your own grandmother. Just come and see how much fun it is,' he called.

It did seem like fun. Even Sid seemed to be enjoying himself. Aashi could see him smiling as he watched Priyam raise her hand. Priyam drew her hand back and smiled at the few precious drops that heaven had let fall in her grasp.

'Come, Aashi, and forget your skirt. It can be washed, can't it? Besides, no one is going to come here at this time and catch you wearing dirty clothes. So come,' Abhi called out to Aashi.

'Oh well,' Aashi murmured, looking at her mother. Urmila smiled, nodded her head and walked back inside her own house. 'Okay!' Aashi shouted and walked out into the rain. 'My hair will be quiet ruined!' she found it her duty to moan as she rushed up to them.

'Well, I suppose they can be washed too. Or do you get them dry-cleaned?' Abhi asked, leaning against the boundary wall between their houses and crossing his legs in front of him.

Aashi threw a quick punch at his shoulder and walked over to stand beside Priyam. 'What do we do now?' she asked.

'We stare at the sky and count each and every drop that falls from it. Then we go up and give the report to dear God,' replied Abhi.

'I did not come here to hear you make fun of me! My skirt is all splattered, I'll have to wash my hair again tonight and oh, I forgot to change my sandals too! They would be quiet ruined!' Aashi wailed as the sudden realization dawned on her.

'Oh, stop complaining, Aashi, and start having some fun. How about some rain dance? You like dancing, don't you?' Abhi said and before Aashi could utter any other word, he rushed indoors and switched on the CD player. 'Now, dance,' he said after coming out.

Aashi didn't need any invitation to begin dancing. She started immediately, soon pulling Priyam and forcing her to twirl too. Sid and Abhi settled themselves on the boundary wall and watched, clapping and cheering the girls and making whole lot of silly comments.

Aashi knew she had never had so much fun before. She had never danced as freely as she was dancing now, with her skirt clinging to her legs, her wet hair slapping her face with every turn she took and rain pouring down hard over her head.

'Oh, don't stop, Priyam,' she cried out when she noticed her friend stopping and walking over to the spectator's side. 'I don't want to dance alone!'

'Don't worry, Aashi, I'll come to give you company,' said Abhi, jumping down from the boundary wall.

'Yeah!' Aashi squealed as she grasped his hands and started zooming around immediately. Abhi had barely landed on his feet when he was pulled along. His stiff leg protested strongly at the speed.

And next moment, he was sprawled on the ground with one leg resting over a toppled pot and another bent crazily under him. His hand lay resting right in the middle of a small jasmine plant, robbing the poor little plant of any chance that it might have had of surviving the heavy rain.

'Oh, Abhi!' Aashi squealed, throwing herself down at the doorstep. 'Just look at yourself!' she laughed, clutching her sides, and rolling from side to side as a fit of breathless laughter overtook her.

'I *am* looking at myself and I don't find it a funny enough sight to make you laugh so!' Abhi said, pretending to scowl.

Priyam and Sid quickly knelt down to help him. Their smiles had vanished away in an instant. Sid turned his back at Aashi and focussed his angry eyes at Abhi. Abhi smiled and shrugged his shoulders.

'What a dancer you are! Amazing!' Aashi continued laughing.

'Yeah, I know. You are a good dancer too, but just try and copy *that* dance move!'

'No way! I don't even want to try!' Aashi said raising her hands up in surrender.

'Oh well, it didn't really take all that much of trying, you know. But I guess I am a natural at performing such acts! Anyway, come, let's go in. We have become wet enough, I guess,' said Abhi. 'Come, Sid,' he said, looking pointedly at his friend and forcing him to stop glowering at Aashi.

'Yeah, and dirty too,' said Aashi as she looked at her skirt.

'Never mind,' Abhi said as he led everybody in. 'It was fun, wasn't it? We've been doing this ever since we were little children,' he said to Aashi. 'But now, how about some tea? That would be great, won't it be?'

'I'll make it, and some pakoras too,' said Aashi.

That forced everybody to throw a surprised look at her. Aashi caught that look and smiled knowingly.

'Oh, come on,' she said, 'I said I won't be *forced* to work, not that I'd never do anything even if I wanted to! And I do make good tea. I'll show you all.' She kicked the floor, raised her head and marched into kitchen.

'Alright, but dry yourself first,' said Abhi. He took a towel towards her.

Aashi had, by then, entered the kitchen and was looking around for the kettle. She turned back at Abhi's voice. Her whole face was animated with the joy of the past hour. Her eyes were still glittering with merriment, and there lingered on her lips a very obvious shred of smile too. As she turned, some drops of water from her loose hair came flying towards him.

'Oh, sorry,' she said and extended her hand to take the towel from Abhi.

But Abhi gave no reply. A fragment of smile lingered on his lips too, but it suddenly started looking lost and forgotten. He looked at her and his eyes bore a look that Aashi had never seen there before.

Of course, she had seen admiration in many eyes before. But it was the first time she had seen any disturbance in *his* placid composure. It transfixed her and she could do nothing but lower her eyes in bewilderment. As she did so, a drop so far resting on her long eyelashes trickled down to make a course towards her lips. Aashi knew Abhi's eyes followed it. The warmth of his stare made her face burn as she tried to resist from smiling. But resistance is hardly the possibility when a yearning sentiment is expressed by true and honest eyes, expressed with full candour and yet perhaps with little self-knowledge.

Aashi had brushed most of her hair away from her face, but a lone strand of hair remained clinging yet.

Abhi's hand lifted on its own accord to brush it away ... the hand that still was holding the towel.

He looked at it and then at the useless stump of his left hand. His lips twitched and he seemed to hold his breath for a moment. 'Here, take the towel,' Abhi said and walked out of the kitchen.

The spell was broken. Abhi's eyes no longer held her captive.

Aashi sighed with relief and turned quickly to get the tea ready. However, it was quite some time before her mind stopped revisiting the moment and wondering what had come over her.

It had been a delicious moment. Yet, how Aashi wished that it had not been Abhi but someone else, someone with whom she could have allowed herself to fall in love with.

The only feeling with which Aashi soon began to consider the incident was of relief, relief that the charm had been broken when it did, relief at Abhi's looking down at his mutilated arm and... walking away.

41

Chapter 6

> *O stand at the window*
> *As the tears scald and start;*
> *You shall love your crooked neighbour*
> *With your crooked heart."*
>
> *'As I Wandered Out One Evening.' by W.H.Auden.*

Had it been possible for the Sun to get besotted by a girl's beauty, he might have considered himself lucky that day to see Aashi welcoming him from her window. It was after all, quite a rarity for her to be up so early. Not even her aunt's ranting admonitions had ever succeeded in getting Aashi out of bed before she herself found it absolutely necessary to do so.

But that day Aashi was up before even her mother had stirred and without having any reason to excuse this sudden aberration. Surely, the incident with Abhi was too trivial to keep her awake so.

'It must have been the rain and thunderstorm that had kept on raging all night,' she had told herself. 'It must be all that noise.'

And now, when the rain had finally stopped and a soft breeze taken its place to fan the verdure dry, Aashi felt the morning too beautiful to turn away from it.

So, she lingered on by the window, enjoying the quiet beauty and surveying the damage last night's storm had spread over Abhi's garden.

'He would shriek out in dismay when he wakes up!' Aashi thought as her eyes wandered over the disarray the garden was in. She didn't know, of course, that Abhi was already up, though his eyes were at that time fixed on a prospect more beautiful than his garden now afforded.

Abhi had left his bed as soon as the eastern sky had started to lighten up. And it was not just the worry about his beloved plants that had crowded away the sleep from his eyes. There were several happy thoughts too, recollections of the day past that had kept on revolving in Abhi's mind with too great an alacrity to let him sleep. While the face of Aashi was a constant companion through the night, what tickled him more was the happy possibility of Priyam and Sid being in love.

Before last night, it had never appeared to Abhi that the love between Priyam and Sid might be of a shade different from plain friendship. Had he not been guilty of not a purely accidental eavesdropping, he might still have not suspected it at all.

'What a pity it started raining,' he had heard Priyam moan, 'I wish we could have gone a little further, completed our whole round. The weather was so nice, wasn't it?'

'Hmm…it was. And I'd have wished the same, had there been someone to hold my hand too, over a rough patch of road, I mean,' Aashi had replied, bringing a smile on Priyam's shy face and a surprise on Abhi's.

'Don't worry, you'll surely find someone soon too. Someone just as good.'

'Just as good? Why not better?'

'Because…best can't be bettered,' Priyam had replied in a voice so low that Abhi could barely grasp the words.

Her little speech had opened up a whole new world of possibilities for him. Possibilities, that had never occurred to Abhi's mind before. And once the thought entered his mind, he lost no time in validating it by his secret observations.

They were sitting at the dining table two hours later when Abhi's covert observations received the greatest reward.

He saw Sid look up at Priyam as she quickly gathered up her long hair in a neat bun. Neither the slight smile that diffused itself on Sid's face escaped Abhi's notice nor the way his friend's face warmed up with delight as Priyam's efforts came undone in a minute and her hair came crowding back to surround her face.

Abhi's eyes shifted towards his sister. She was quietly pouring out water for them.

Her beauty couldn't have boasted of having any exquisite splendour like her next-door neighbour. But in Priyam's face, there was a grace that charmed everyone who looked on her and her amber eyes had a serenity that had a rarity of its own. The brother's heart swelled up with pride as he gazed at her.

Sure, Priyam could have won the heart of any man who looked at her. And if that heart belonged to the one he truly esteemed then…just the thought brought a wide grin on Abhi's face.

'Why are you smiling?' Sid said.

'Nothing,' Abhi replied.

'If you are planning a strategy to trap me, then it's no use. The game's mine.'

They had been playing a game of chess when Priyam urged them to the dinner table. The game, meanwhile, waited patiently for their return.

'Seems to me that you are already trapped,' Abhi said with a laugh. 'But I wasn't thinking about the game.'

'Then what?'

'Well, I was thinking about a girl who's getting prettier every day. I wonder who would marry her.'

'Aashi? Yes, I wonder so too,' Priyam said.

'He's not talking about your friend, Priyam. And Abhi, your sister never lacked in prettiness,' Sid replied.

The tone he had used would have suited the utterance of a mathematical formula better. Any other girl might have found it a strange way of complementing her beauty. More so, because lurking just behind this dry, matter-of-fact tone was an unexplained strain, almost like a regret that weighed down upon Sid's smile and made him sink his eyes into the rice on his plate. 'She has always been pretty,' he said once more, and then became silent.

Abhi's eyes remained focussed on Priyam as her face lit up with a grateful delight. She lowered her eyes and tried not to smile too much.

The joy that had brightened up Priyam's eyes at that moment was still echoing in Abhi's heart as he paced around on the rooftop. Everything felt so happy, even the sky seemed to be celebrating with a glorious spectrum of colours spread across its heights.

And to add to the moment's perfection, the wind was blowing in strong gusts too, just the way Abhi liked it. He closed his eyes, opened his arm and let the wind embrace him.

'What a morning!' he laughed and shook his head at himself a moment later. 'But time now to go to the plants.'

Abhi was just about to go downstairs, when he noticed Aashi standing near her window. That, of course, arrested his steps immediately.

He saw Aashi step closer to her window and look around. She surveyed his garden and then fixed her eyes at his window for what seemed to him a very long time.

She formed a charming picture as she stood there, half leaning, with her hand on the windowsill, looking as fresh as the morning that had just dawned. A tender smile played on her lips and she seemed totally absorbed in herself. Not that Abhi regretted it any bit. He would rather have her stand so, entirely unaware of him than to look up and find him staring at her.

But if Aashi was engrossed in her thoughts, Abhi's mind was not exactly idle too. And it was perhaps the result of his intense rumination that made him shake his head.

'Yeah, as if that would ever happen,' he spoke out with a wry smile. 'Turn back, Abhi. That road's not for you.'

He turned instantly and walked back to his room to wait there till his heart slowed down to its normal pace and it was time for him to go out and tend to his plants.

Half an hour later Aashi saw Abhi come out. She got up immediately from the chair she had dragged to the window and smiled in readiness to wish him good morning. But Abhi's head remained bent downwards, and no yearning glance flew up to meet her waiting eyes.

That was not what Aashi had expected. Surely, he couldn't have forgotten last night's incident so soon. Not that it mattered much to her, but it should have mattered to him. Searching for her should have been the first thing for Abhi to do that morning. Instead, he seemed to be thinking only of his plants.

'Fine!' Aashi muttered to herself with a mixture of anger and disappointment, 'Go and tend your stupid plants.' A moment longer Aashi waited before barging away and allowing Abhi the freedom to finally raise his head and gaze at her vacant window as much as he desired.

Abhi was still hard at work in his garden when Aashi again peeked through her window. She had never seen him in shorts and a vest before that morning. It was the first time, therefore, that Abhi's scars were so blatantly visible to her.

'*How much pain he must have suffered!*' she thought. '*And yet he's so strong and brave about it. Had it been me, I'd surely have killed myself than go through such misery!*'

Her eyes painfully brushed over the ugly, discoloured streaks running across the length of Abhi's left leg and glaring from what remained of his left arm. A quick shiver passed through her. 'Why the hell can't he hire a gardener?' she exclaimed, almost angrily.

Her smile faded away and lips curled downwards as she watched Abhi limping from plant to plant and trying to bolster them up with his one good hand. She felt like going to help him. But that would have meant putting her hands in mud. Besides, Abhi didn't like anybody helping him.

'He should get married soon and with a sensible girl. He needs somebody to put some sense into his head!' Aashi muttered. That thought, of course, led her into weaving a fantastic tale wherein a simple and sweet girl was conjured up to fall in love with Abhi's goodness and give him all the happiness that he deserved. 'He needs someone who is simple and practical, realistic and accommodating. Someone…who could manage in his limited income,' she said as she tried to determine the girl that would best suit Abhi, 'someone, in short, exactly opposite to me.'

That was okay though, because her own ideal was totally opposite Abhi too. Even though his impish grin and bright, smiling eyes had become a part of the 'perfect man' she dreamed about. The way a few of his hair always covered his broad forehead gave Abhi a sweet boyish look that Aashi could not prevent herself from admiring. But Abhi's world was too narrow and far too dull to satisfy her, restricted even more by his handicap. Besides, he lacked in other ways too. He had no style, no sense of chivalry, and not much money either.

Whereas, Aashi was waiting for a stylish, fashionable epitome of perfection. She dreamt of someone who had to be dashing, stylish, chivalrous, dignified, having good humour, good heart and abundance of money. Someone, in short, whose irresistible charm would blow her off her feet and make all her dreams come true.

Unknown to her, just such a person was already on his way towards her. She had just few more hours to wait.

Chapter 7

I do not hope to bind the wind
Or set a fetter on the sea --
It is enough to feel his love
Blow by like music over me.

—'Enough' by Sara Teasdale

'Aashi, for the third and last time I'm telling you that your mother is calling you. You better put a break on your chatter now and go to her. If you don't, I'll pick you up and throw you over the boundary,' said Abhi.

It was past eight in the evening and Aashi was still standing in Priyam's kitchen despite her mother calling her home again and again.

Aashi was very happy that day. And she had two causes to aid her happiness.

One, her rented home did not look so disgraceful now as Abhi had managed to get her landlord to paint it. Second, just that day, Aashi had also escaped the miserable necessity of having to work from her garage.

Aashi had prepared herself to go through that torture. But the old lady, who owned the boutique where Aashi worked, could not bear the thought of letting her most valuable designer leave. She knew well that she would lose half her clients if she let Aashi go.

The boutique owner was getting old too and had wanted to visit her son in Mumbai for a long time. So a deal was struck where Aashi was to handle the work of the boutique as her own with entitlement to half the earning of the business while the old lady took the much awaited vacation. She was gone for six months at least, handing Aashi full authority to run the business as she would. Aashi was happy by the arrangement and hoped to save enough money by the end of six months to be able to afford a decent office of her own. More importantly, she had heard it from the owner's maid that the lady had no intention of returning even after six months, unless her son threw her out. This, however, was hardly the possibility since he was as yet unmarried.

'Aashi!' Abhi called Aashi as paid no heed to his warning.

'Okay, okay, I'm going!' said Aashi finally. 'Was just describing to Priyam what I plan to do with *my* boutique. You know, I would...'

'Home!'

'No need to shout! Going. Bye,' Aashi retorted and ran towards the door.

A moment later, she collided with her dream and was blown off her feet, though not in the manner she had expected.

Just as Aashi had reached the door, it had slammed into her, sending the poor girl crashing down to the floor.

'Oh!' said the form that had been the cause of it all.

Aashi raised up her eyes to see who had opened the door so suddenly.

The rage that had shot up by her fall was instantly doused by one look at the handsome face and jovial eyes looking down at her. Aashi might have declared herself blessed too to have collided with him had she been able to gather back her wits with the rapidity with which her eyes had done their function.

'Who are you?' she asked.

'Aashi. Our next door neighbour,' said Abhi as he rushed to help her up. 'Are you okay?' he asked Aashi.

'Huh? Yes, yes, I'm fine,' Aashi said, trying to smile. She looked questioningly at Abhi and then at the person who had still not extended any apology to her.

'Aashi, this is my friend Raj Sinha. He lives in that big white bungalow you never fail to notice on our evening walks. So, Raj,' Abhi said turning towards him, 'when did you return from London?'

'Today,' Raj replied without taking his eyes away from Aashi, 'Hi,' he said with a bright grin, 'the stupid door came in way or I could have said that it was nice colliding with you. I hope I didn't hurt you.'

'No, I'm fine, really.' Aashi replied, trying not to appear too dazed by his dazzling persona. However, the facts that Raj had been to London and that he lived in the most beautiful house she had ever seen were not so easy to ignore.

Aashi forgot all about going back to home and could think only of how well Abhi's friend was dressed. Everything Raj wore boasted of a big brand name. He sure did not lack in good taste. And certainly not in good looks either.

Raj was almost as tall as Sid, with a fairer complexion and playful eyes that glowed with self confidence and joy of easy life. Everything about Raj spoke of richness; everything about him seemed to have a certain glow, the glow perhaps of the magic that had suddenly given a corporal form to Aashi's fantasy.

'Where's Priyam?' Raj asked.

Priyam was just coming out from the kitchen.

'Hi, Priyam!' Raj exclaimed as soon as he saw her. 'Look who's here!'

'Hello, Raj,' Priyam replied. However, her voice clearly lacked the enthusiasm that had rung so cheerfully in his greeting.

'Hey, you look fantabulous!' he exclaimed.

'I look what?' asked Priyam.

'Fantabulous!' Raj repeated.

'Where did you catch that word from?' asked Abhi.

'Geniusones don't catch words, Abhi, they create them.'

'Have a seat, Mr. Genius. When did you develop this new interest of creating words?'

'Since Priyam declared her undying love for Shakespeare. I thought I might create something too if I have to have any hopes at all. However, since I have no time to create whole dramas, I contented myself by creating new words. But, Priyam, you can't scare me with your dear Shakespeare either now. I have put enough of him in my head to keep my stand, even against you!'

'Don't worry, Raj. I have no intention of using Shakespeare against you. I don't need it,' Priyam replied. She tried not to let her amusements as well as her irritation appear in her face. All she managed however was to mitigate by her poorly repressed smile the very words she had meant to be a rebuff.

'I've heard that love makes one a poet,' said Abhi, 'this is the first time I'm witnessing that love can make you a bookworm too!'

'Yeah, but who's that worm slinking in that corner? Sid? Is that you?'

'Yes,' came the grudging reply.

'Hello, how are you?'

'Fine enough.'

'I didn't see you till now. You were sitting so quietly in that dark corner. You'd have completely escaped my notice had the curtain not moved just when I was looking towards you.'

'Well, my good luck never does last long. Anyway, didn't you promise you'd be away for two full years?'

'Did I? I don't remember,' Raj replied, 'by the way, I'm fine too. Super, as always.'

A cynical smile was all the reply he got from Sid.

'So,' Raj began again after a moment, 'what are you doing here?'

'Sitting,' Sid replied, finally leaving his window seat and coming to shake hands with Raj.

'By the way, how's Tina? Is she back too or has she stayed on in London?' Abhi asked.

'Oh, she's back. In fact, it was Tina who dragged us back here. She had some sort of break up with William, her latest ex-boyfriend. Too bad, because this time, I believe, she was really in love with him. William is a great guy and perfectly suitable for her. Don't know why he ditched her. Anyway, right now, Tina is just as busy flirting around as my mother is busy in finding a fit match for her.'

It did appear odd to Aashi to notice Sid turn back towards Raj and stop going through the newspaper that he had picked up just a minute ago. Sid's eyes turned to Raj with something more than idle curiosity.

'What kind of fit match is your mother trying to look for Tina?' Sid asked.

'You know, rich, handsome and dumb!' Raj answered with a laugh.

Sid stared at Raj for a moment, a curious spark lighting up in his dark eyes and a broad smile breaking through the sullen frown on his face, 'I sure hope she succeeds in her search,' he said and picked up the paper again.

'Thanks,' Raj muttered, sounding quite surprised.

'You're welcome,' Sid replied and once again buried his face in the newspaper.

'I know, and I'll make use of that welcome to come here as often as I can,' said Raj, countering Sid's intonations with turn of his own voice. 'You know how much I love this dear little home. And it hasn't changed at all in the fifteen months I was away.'

'Well, we like it as it is,' Abhi said, 'besides, you yourself haven't changed much too.'

'Oh, you can't improve perfection, can you?'

'*No you can't!*' Aashi wanted to shout out. But she managed to bite her words just in time. Though, try as she might, she found it impossible to keep her eyes away from Raj for even half a minute.

The evening passed away swiftly. But Raj stayed lingering in Aashi's mind.

Sitting by her window and watching her neighbour's gate soon became Aashi's sole leisure activity, and fortunately for her, the patient watches were regularly rewarded. Raj visited Priyam almost every day and sometimes stayed for more than a couple of hours. Aashi knew that to Raj, she was yet nothing more than a friend of Priyam. But to her, Raj had become a semblance of perfection.

And indeed, he was very near it, according to his out judgement too. Raj was an honest millionaire; at least as honest as a millionaire can be who wants to hold on to his millions. He never told a lie unless it was absolutely necessary to do so and he never, by himself, indulged in flirting. It was Raj's constant endeavour to be a perfect gentleman, and he tried very hard to do good because, basically he believed himself to be good. Raj was generous, never raised his voice, minded his manners perfectly and was civil to everybody, even the lowest of his servants. He liked to see himself as a perfect son, a perfect brother, a perfect friend and everybody was sure, including himself of course, that when he married, he would prove to be a perfect husband too.

It might be that Raj fell a bit short of the perfection he conceived himself to be. Yet, there was no evil in his heart and he definitely had sense enough in his proud head to know the worth of Abhi, Sid and Priyam and respect them accordingly.

Priyam especially was like a rare and precious gem to him. She was so pure and unaffected, so unlike the other girls that kept on fluttering around him. And though she tried all she could to put cold water on his warm affections, he was sure that she was the only girl who deserved the treasure of his love and devotion. And he was the only one who could give Priyam what she deserved.

Fortunately for Raj, even his mother liked Priyam and considered her a good match (though not the best) for her son.

Just a few days after her return from London, Mrs. Sinha came with Raj to pay a kind visit to the 'poor kids' as she called Abhi and Priyam.

'I really like you, Priyam,' she graciously declared to her son's choice. And then she proceeded to go over the details of the latest proposals she had received for her son. She then dismissed them all with the gesture of her own hand and said, 'But you are the best, as my Raj says. And I always say, let your kids marry where they want to unless of course they choose someone you don't approve of.'

Priyam's eyes shot towards Raj.

The effect was such that Raj immediately interrupted the flow of his mother's words. 'I told you, mother, I don't want to marry so soon,' he said. 'And when did I say anything to you about Priyam?'

'Oh, you'll marry sooner or later. And you always keep on saying that Priyam is the best and the sweetest girl. And of course, she is Mr. Vardhan's adopted daughter. And I'm sure...'

'He did not formally adopt us, ma'am,' Priyam reminded her.

'It's the same thing, child. I know Mr. Vardhan loves you like his own

51

daughter. Just as his wife, Kiran, loved my Tina. You know, Mrs. Vardhan was so fond of Tina that I dare say had she been alive, she'd surely have had her married to Sid by now. But things are so different now. That's why I don't tease Sid about the matter anymore. I used to do that you know, when Kiran was alive. But Sid is grown up now and takes his own decisions. He has given up on his father's property and made himself an orphan, but I defy anyone to call *you* an orphan when you have such a rich man as your guardian. Not that it matters at all, whether Mr. Vardhan gives you anything or not. As you know very well, we are as rich as him, if not richer. What matters is that I quite like you. You've turned out to be something like a beauty you know. Though when I first saw you, there was little indication that you will ever have anything more than a tolerable face.'

'Mother!' Raj hissed.

'What, child, I'm just praising your girl. Don't feel shy. You should have become used to by now to hear the women around you being praised for their looks,' Mrs. Sinha said, giving her head laborious nods while repositioning her hand in a way that her twelve diamond rings caught the maximum light from the lamp.

Aashi, being also present in the room, covered her mouth with her hand. She had no doubt that Mrs. Sinha considered herself a woman of great beauty. But for her son's sake, Aashi decided to forgive the lady for her ill-founded vanity.

Besides, it was true too that God had indeed endowed Mrs. Sinha with a fair complexion, pouted lips and a face that had once been in perfect proportion to her body. Now however, it seemed to have shrunk to a much smaller size thanks to the fecundity of the rest of her person. Perhaps that was the reason, as it appeared to Aashi, that the lady favoured her face with a greater share of cosmetics, in an attempt no doubt, to bring it back to prominence and also to draw the attention away from what had over time became much too prominent.

'June is always such a terrible month in India,' said Mrs. Sinha, fanning herself with her hand. 'It must be hard not to have an air conditioner. But then, not everyone can afford a comfortable life. One must be patient at all times. Patience and forbearance are great virtues. God knows, without these two qualities that are so strong in my own character, I'd have been dead and gone a long time ago. Not that I lack anything, but what with my husband's age and his many ailments, life can become a hell sometimes.'

Priyam gave no response to the lady. Aashi though tried desperately to look sympathetic as Mrs. Sinha started describing the ever cheerful patience with which she endured all the health problems that resulted from her husband's persistent longevity.

But when her efforts didn't succeed, Aashi had to resort to faking a cough and cover her grin with her hands. She hoped she had done it quickly enough to let Raj remain unaware of her humour.

'Let me warn you, Aashi,' said Mrs. Sinha, instantly turning towards her, 'if you ever happen to fall in love with an old man, make sure that his ailments are of the nature that won't trouble you for long. I wish I had someone to advice me too. It's not that I regret my choice, though I could have married better if...but then, what's done is done. But you must be careful...' said Mrs. Sinha, starting up her well used lecture that she generously bestowed on any pretty girl caught in the blessed circumstance of being in her company.

Aashi listened, nodding every now and then, but at all times keeping the path between her two ears thoroughly open. She listened to everything, but heard little. And though her eyes were turned towards Mrs. Sinha, they remained focussed only on her son.

That son, though, was busy in chatting with Priyam and trying desperately to repair any damage that his mother's effusions might have made in the road to her heart.

Priyam, on her part, watched the clock and tried to calculate the time that was still left for Sid and Abhi to come home and relieve her.

Chapter 8

Rapture's self is three parts sorrow.
Although we must die to-morrow,
Losing every thought but this;
Torn, triumphant, drowned in bliss.
Happiness: We rarely feel it.
I would buy it, beg it, steal it,
Pay in coins of dripping blood
For this one transcendent good.

— *Amy Lowell*

It was almost six p.m. when Aashi stepped out of her home next evening, fuming with a temper that threatened to become worse with the long walk she had in front of her.

'When I have money, I would never again walk in such heat!' she muttered to herself as she gave an angry push to the gate.

It had been an exceptionally hot day even for the last week of June. Heat seemed to be sweating out from everywhere as the sun slowly dragged its feet towards the west. Even the slight breeze that there was seemed oppressed by the humidity and stifling temperature

Hardly half an hour had passed since Aashi had returned from work, and before she could have taken off her weariness, her mother had handed the girl a long list of grocery.

'Tomorrow, Mummy, I'm so tired today!' Aashi moaned.

'You've been saying that for two days. There's not even a speck of salt left now and...'

'Couldn't you go to market, Mummy?' Aashi spat out with irritation.

'Okay,' said the widow, 'you're right, you work so hard at the boutique. I must not trouble you with these chores.'

'Oh, Ma! Don't say that,' said Aashi, regretting her outburst immediately. 'I'm sorry. I ...you know me, Ma! I'll go. Give me the list,' she said.

And with that, Aashi had walked out to go shopping, transferring the anger from her mother to the hot weather and the long wreck of a road that lay ahead of her.

Aashi was conscious of the worsening of her temper during last few days. Perhaps because none of her innovative schemes at her boutique had yet began to bring in a good pay off, while continuing to be a big drain on her limited resources.

She tried telling herself that matters will improve in a few days and then she would never have to worry about money any more. All she needed to do was to work hard and be patient.

Patience though, was never among Aashi's strong points. And lack of it had began to show up in her mood swings, increased irritation and more than occasional bursts of anger.

After taking over the charge of boutique, the first thing that Aashi had done was to hire a tailor that specialised in western wear. Soon the display in her boutique began to show diversity. There was not just traditional stuff as earlier, but also skirts, hipsters, capri and funky and stylish shirts and tops luring younger and variety seeking clients. With that, Aashi decided to stock up on bags, belts and other accessories to go with her dresses. And it was this pursuit that had made her roam all day in the stifling heat, straining through the markets, and scouting for the cheapest bargains and latest trends.

It had been an exhausting day, draining due to the scorching heat and depressing too because of the quibbling and bargaining Aashi had had to engage in to get what she wanted at prices she could afford. Heat, dirt, filth, rude crowd and then the cheapness of being a haggler!

It was not the life Aashi had dreamt for herself. It was not!

'Hey, what's up?' Abhi called out to her. The bag in his hand showed that he was returning from office.

'Heat,' Aashi replied.

'Is that the only reason your face looks red as a hot sun?' he said with grin.

'Don't you dare mess with me today, Abhi. I'm already very angry.'

'I can see that. But why?'

'It's so hot, and there's so much to do and nothing's working out and the boutique is losing money and I had to jostle all day through the market to get stuff for the boutique and now I have to do that again to get stuff for home and I'm SO miserable!'

'That bad, huh? Anyway, you can tell me what you need from the market. I'll get it for you. And about your huge mountain of troubles, it will wear out one day. Once your schemes pick up, you'll thank yourself for all the trouble you are going through now. So don't worry.'

'But will they ever pick up?' Aashi said, giving a furious kick to the road.

'They will, I'm sure. And soon. And once your schemes pick up, you'll quickly start earning good money. And then, very soon, you'll have your own boutique and people to do all the hard work for you. I can just see you, sitting in your air conditioned office and designing a lovely dress, while your employees run about to fulfil your orders.'

A smile finally broke through Aashi's face. 'How do you know that's what I dream of?' she asked.

'I didn't know. That's what *I* dream of for you,' he replied.

Another and bigger smile appeared on Aashi's face. 'Do you think it will ever happen, Abhi?'

'Of course, it will. And very soon. Just be patient. And now, tell me what you want from the market. I'll get it.'

'Thanks. But you must be tired too. Go home. I'll go and get it myself.'

Abhi looked towards his home. 'Well, my car's not in. That means Sid and Priyam haven't returned yet. I got stuck in the office and they had to go without me. We had to go shopping today since Priyam thinks Sid has no decent clothes left to wear.'

'I agree, hundred percent,' said Aashi with a grin.

'Don't let Sid know that. I don't think he would be as forgiving to you as he is to Priyam. Anyway, I think I'll just come along with you,' he said. He leaned over and put his bag behind the boundary wall. 'There, let's go now,' he said.

'Yeah, let's go,' she said in a tired voice as the two started walking towards the market.

'Hey, I must tell you something very interesting that happened in office today,' said Abhi. And he began regaling his companion with one amusing story after another.

Aashi listened intently, for his stories were always very interesting and full of fun. And before she knew it, she was laughing louder than what she considered decent in public places.

'Oh, my God, Abhi, I never knew working in an office could be so much fun. I wish I worked in your office as well,' she said after Abhi had recounted yet another anecdote.

'Sure, I'll tell Mr. Vardhan that his company staff desperately needs a fashion upgrade. We'll hire you as our very own in-house designer. And then you can spend your life designing dinner jackets for our computer geniuses and cocktail dresses for their secretaries.'

'Yeah, that will be fun. You do that,' she said.

'Sure, but before that, finish your shopping,' said Abhi as they reached the market.

Aashi skipped over to the grocers and then to the vegetable shop. In twenty minutes, she had bought all that her mother had put in the list and a couple of items she wanted for herself.

'Let's go,' Abhi said when she had completed all her shopping.

'No, please, I don't want to go home just yet,' she said, with her head cocked to one side in an entreating way and lips curled downwards. 'Do you mind if we take a turn in park?' she asked.

The temperature had just started to cool down and the air had become flavoured with the beautiful fragrance of rain, making her want to linger on out in the open. She just didn't feel like returning to her hot and stifling home.

Abhi's company had cooled down her anger too. But she feared all the misery of the day will pounce back on her once she was back in her house. She didn't want to go through that just yet. It was so pleasant outside.

Clouds had started gathering up in the skies, but Aashi judged them still far away to pose any urgency for them to return. Besides, the skies had been putting up a false show since several past days. The fact that the wind had risen up too only served to add to the pleasure of the moment.

'It seems like it will rain today,' Abhi said as he stepped into the park that was in front of the market complex.

'I wish it would. I could really use a wetting in the rain right now,' Aashi replied.

Abhi said nothing. But half a smile appeared on his lips as his mind went back to another rainy evening. He looked up at the sky and stared at it for a long moment, almost as if pulling the clouds forward with his gaze and urging them to let go. The clouds responded by sending a lightning stroke blazing through the sky. A gust of wind hit them and rustled away.

'How lovely!' Aashi exclaimed, taking a deep breath of the scented air. 'I wish this weather could last forever.'

Abhi's smile widened into a grin. 'Yeah,' he said.

And then his phone started ringing.

'Priyam?' Aashi asked as Abhi looked at his mobile.

'Raj,' he replied. 'Hello,' he said into the phone. 'Oh, ok, yeah we are strolling. But if you can wait, we'll be there in fifteen minutes,' he said, after listening to Raj's words.

'What's he saying? Is he waiting at your house? Oh, let's rush back!' Aashi exclaimed.

'Yeah, we are coming,' said Abhi and then disconnected the call.

'What did he say? Is he there?'

Abhi turned to face Aashi. Her face was all aglow with the sudden happiness that had burst out at the mention of Raj's name. Abhi stared at her shining eyes. He looked at her smiling lips. He turned and focussed his eyes at the park's exit.

'Yes, he is there. Let's go,' he said and started walking.

While just a few minutes ago Aashi didn't want the evening to end, all she desired now was to reach home, as quickly as possible.

'Let's hurry, we must not keep him waiting in this weather. And it might start raining any moment. My mother will worry, she doesn't know that you are with me,' she said, almost running.

Her pointed heels slid over a stone and she tripped. But Abhi's arm was there to support her.

'Be careful,' he said. 'And next time you decide to run like that, remember to wear more sensible shoes. What's the logic of breaking your legs just to look a few inch taller anyway?' asked Abhi as he cast a disparaging look at her high heels.

'I'm fine and I can manage my heels,' Aashi replied.

'Okay,' Abhi replied, 'but hold my hand. The way you are rushing, you will only trip yourself again. Here, lean on my arm…if you like.'

Her eyes travelled towards Abhi's amputated arm.

'I meant… this arm,' Abhi said. He walked to her left to bring his healthy right arm towards her.

Aashi felt ashamed at having looked so pointedly at the stump of his arm. She linked her arm into his and forced herself to walk in a more composed manner.

Before the two had covered a few metres, the clouds broke their holds and it started raining.

'We should have left sooner. Now we'll get all drenched up,' Abhi said.

'I thought you liked that,' Aashi said with a laugh.

'Oh, I do. But I'm sure you would not like to meet Raj with your hair all a mess and skirt splattered with mud,' he replied, grinning in a way that always left Aashi feeling confused. She could never know for sure if he was laughing at her or just laughing.

'Raj,' she said after a moment's silence, 'won't even look at me. So why should I worry. He comes to see Priyam, remember?'

'Yes, but it may not always be so. So you can hope on,' Abhi said, flashing yet another confounding grin and looking at Aashi with eyes full of amusement.

Aashi hated it when Abhi looked at her with that pointed stare. It felt almost as if he was seeing right through her and mocking at her stupidity. It made her squirm with irritation.

Perhaps she would have resented it less had she been capable of noticing the self-abusive mockery from which Abhi's laughter had stemmed. Abhi had learnt a lesson that day. And what amused him was that he had allowed himself to be in need of one.

'Aren't you going to take the short cut?' Aashi asked as they crossed a turning.

'I don't think so. It would be too dark and risky.'

The shortcut was a narrow lane cutting through two apartment blocks. It was notorious for never having even a single street light in working order. It was just a small stretch though and the next turn led to an illuminated track again.

'Oh come on, Abhi! It's just a small road. Will hardly take a couple of minutes to cross and in no time we'll be home. The longer route will take us another ten minutes in this pouring rain. Besides, I'm so tired!'

'No, Aashi... listen to me! I really think...'

However, by then Aashi had already turned. There was no way she was going to take the longer route while Raj waited for them. She wanted to meet him as soon as possible, and as she rushed towards him, she prayed to God to keep Priyam and Sid away for at least few more minutes.

Abhi had no other option but to accompany her as she hastened through the dark road.

They quickly covered the expanse, with their eyes fixed at the turn where they'd again come into the light. Aashi's hold tightened on Abhi's arm as he carefully guided her in the deep, unbroken darkness.

The rain was pouring hard. But over the noise of raindrops, she heard a distinct sound of footsteps. She wondered if it was Raj coming to meet them midway.

'Rain is getting heavier, Aashi, let's hurry. You are not too tired to run, are you?' Abhi asked all of a sudden.

'Huh? Wait, Abhi, we don't need to run.'

The sound of footsteps was coming closer now and they were more hurried than before. But they seemed to be coming from their back. Abhi started running, holding Aashi's hand firmly in his grasp.

59

'Stop, Abhi,' Aashi murmured, trying to make him slow his speed.

But it was to no avail, Abhi continued dragging her forward.

Someone touched her shoulder. She wrenched her arm free from Abhi's and turned back.

Lightning glinted on a metal blade in front of her eyes. A rude hand clawed at her neck. Before Aashi could realize what had happened, she saw a man running away with her gold chain in one hand and the knife in other. Abhi's arm reached quickly to support her staggering steps.

'My chain!' the cry broke out from her lips.

'Was it the one...'

'Yes, the last gift my dad gave me. The same that I told you about last week. My mother didn't want me to wear it. She was afraid I'd lose it. And I have!'

'Hey! Who was that fellow running like mad? Almost bumped me down,' Raj's breezy notes floated to them as he came strolling towards them. 'I thought I might as well stroll in the rain and catch you all midway. Didn't know you'd reach so far so soon. But where's Priyam? And why are you trembling like that, Aashi?' he asked coming towards Aashi.

'Take care of her!' Abhi shouted and ran after the chain snatcher.

'No! Come back!' Aashi screamed. 'You can't...stop him, Raj!' she cried out clasping Raj's hands in her trembling fingers.

'What happened?' he asked with bewilderment.

'My chain!' Aashi said in a hoarse whisper, 'Abhi!' she screamed again looking in the direction where he had gone after the thief, 'Oh, stop him, Raj, he had a knife! The thief had a knife!'

'What? But... I can't leave you here alone,' Raj said, 'It's not safe. Abhi should have known that before bringing you here.'

'He didn't...he didn't. I didn't listen to him!' Aashi cried out, hiding her face in her hands. 'Save him, Raj...it's...it's all my fault. He said we should take the longer route. I didn't listen to him!'

'Don't worry, he'll be fine. He would be okay,' Raj said in a soothing voice. 'You are not hurt, are you?'

'Hurt?' Aashi repeated, noticing for the first time a burning sensation on her neck. Her trembling fingers felt the wound.

'Does it hurt much?' Raj asked as he saw her wince. 'Let me take you to the hospital.'

'We have no time, Raj! We must find him.'

'But you are in pain…'

'He might be in greater. And I can deal with a little bit of pain. Let's go now,' Aashi exclaimed with rudeness that was sure to surprise her later.

'Okay, but first let me bandage your wound. It's bleeding,' he said, pulling his handkerchief out of his pocket. He stepped closer to her and wrapped the handkerchief gently around her neck.

A shiver ran through Aashi at his touch. How close he was to her! How close! She could even feel Raj's breath on her face as her eyes stalled on his.

Had it been any other time, she would have wanted the moment to continue forever. But now was not the time to linger, nor to make Raj linger with her.

'Let's go, Raj,' Aashi said and began walking immediately.

Agonizing thoughts rushed up to Aashi one after another, adding quickness to her tired feet and making her almost run towards home.

'Slow down, Aashi, you are still trembling,' Raj said as he ran besides Aashi, holding her hand in his firm grasp. Aashi looked pale and shaken and her breath was coming in gasps. Raj feared she would faint, and that would have made the matters worse.

Aashi didn't slow down. She had to find Abhi.

But Raj guided her towards her home instead. Soon they were standing in front of Abhi's home. Raj's car was parked there, and Abhi's car had just come to a stop in front of the gate. Sid was at the driver's seat and Priyam was opening the gate.

'Hi, Aashi, what are you up to?' Priyam asked as she saw her friend running towards her.

'Priyam, oh, I'm so glad you are back. Sid, Sid, Abhi…' Aashi cried out.

Urmila was standing at her window and looking out anxiously. She saw Aashi's pale face and sensed immediately that something was amiss. 'What's wrong, Aashi?' she asked as she almost ran up to her daughter.

'Abhi…Abhi…' was all that Aashi could say.

Meanwhile, Raj walked up to Sid and said, 'Sid, I need you to come with me. We must find Abhi.'

Priyam's eyes widened at the words. 'What's wrong, Raj? What do you mean? Where's he?'

Sid jumped out from Abhi's car and in two strides stood in front of Aashi.

'Aashi? What has happened?' he asked, fixing his penetrating eyes on her. 'Why's this cloth tied around your neck?'

Aashi's hand went up to her throat as her mother gasped and Priyam's eyes stared at her.

'Aashi. Are you hurt?' Urmila asked, removing the handkerchief quickly to take a look. 'What happened?' she almost screamed at the sight of her daughter's wound.

'Your chain...' Priyam murmured, 'Abhi!' fear rose in her eyes as the thought struck her, 'he has not...he has not...has he?'

Raj took Priyam's hands in his and recounted everything that had happened, taking care not to mention the knife.

Blood drained out of Priyam's face. Her terrified eyes darted towards Sid.

She looked not at Raj who stood before her, neither did she cast a glance at Aashi. Priyam's brown eyes, too shocked to shed a drop of tear, too scared even to blink, sought only one face and when they found it, lost their power to move away.

Sid nodded. 'I'm going,' he said. 'Take care of her,' he whispered to Aashi's mother. And then, without stopping to comfort Priyam or sooth away her fears, he got back into Abhi's car.

Raj too looked up at Priyam, but her eyes were still fixed at where Sid had been standing a moment ago. He cast one last, lingering look at her, and walked swiftly towards his own car.

Chapter 9

Art thou abroad on this stormy night on thy
Journey of love, my friend?
The sky groans like one in despair.
I have no sleep to-night.

— *From 'Gitanjali' By Rabindranath Tagore.*

Minute after agonizing minute passed in cruel suspense as the three women waited. No word had they yet heard from either Raj or Sid. The unrelenting hands of clock slashed away their hopes as time crawled away on its course.

Aashi would perhaps have ran away to carry out her own search. But her mother's urgings and Priyam's condition bound her feet.

Both Aashi and her mother had tried to make Priyam lie down on the couch but the girl insisted she was in no need of rest. She continued sitting on the couch, crushing the thumb of her left hand with the fingers of her right. There she remained, silent as before, giving no trouble to anybody. Only her eyes, that had not yet shed a single drop of moisture to relieve their frozen lids, refused to move away from the door.

Aashi was sitting on the floor, supporting her aching head on the couch where Priyam was sitting.

'Let him be safe...please, please...let him be safe,' the chant rang on in Aashi's heart, almost as involuntarily as her heartbeats. However, with the fear that increased with every passing moment, anger was welling up too. Anger and rage against the very soul for whose safety she was praying.

'Who had told him to run after that thief?' The rage pointed out. 'What does Abhi think of himself? He should have looked at himself before being all heroic!'

'Oh, but it is all my fault!' another little being cried out from some unminded corner of her heart.

Aashi got up to escape its voice. She started pacing around the room, looking towards the wall clock at every turn and trying desperately to sustain hope against fear and rage against self blame.

She walked up to the window and stared out. Silence echoed loudly in the air. Even the rain had stopped now. She listened attentively, often feeling certain that she had heard the sound of an approaching car. But each time, the hush of night gave lie to what Aashi believed she had heard. No car stopped at their gate, even the phone remained silent.

The clock struck one. Aashi turned and her eyes met her mother's and together they turned to look at Priyam. Priyam looked at neither of them.

Then a roar rose up to break the dreadful silence that had surrounded them for so long. The start that Priyam gave told Aashi that this time at least the sound was real.

In a moment, Aashi was at the door looking out. The roar become louder and louder till it came to a stop near the gate.

'Sid!' Aashi exclaimed, 'It's him! It's Sid!' she said looking at Priyam.

Priyam knew that already, of course.

Next moment, Sid was standing at the door, looking straight at Priyam. She bounded up from her seat and ran towards him. Her eyes stared into his and asked the question her lips could not utter.

'He's okay...' Sid said, 'hurt, but out of danger.'

'Oh, thank God!' exclaimed Aashi clasping her hands and closing her eyes to utter a silent prayer of gratitude.

'That's a relief!' her mother added.

But Priyam said nothing. 'He's okay, Priyam!' Sid said again, putting his hands on her shoulders. Priyam reached up and closed her fingers on Sid's sleeves, crushing the fabric in her tight grasp. Her eyes still peered into his. Sid nodded in reassurance and folded his arms around her as she let her face fall to his chest. Her whole body started convulsing as all the agony she had been harbouring broke loose. All Sid could do was to continue holding Priyam close to him and stroke her hair as she clung to him, finally allowing her emotions the relief of tears.

'Priyam, you want to go to him, don't you?' he asked as if trying to pacify a distraught child. She nodded, without lifting her face from where it rested on him or loosening her hold on his sleeves. 'Well, then,' he quickly wiped away the drops that had sprung forth in his own eyes too, 'let's go. Dry your tears. You don't want to go before Abhi crying like this, do you?'

'No,' Priyam replied, finally breaking her long silence. She wiped her tears and was ready to leave immediately.

'We'll go too,' said Aashi.

'It would be better if you go home and take some rest. It's no use all of us crowding in the hospital,' said Sid.

'But I want to see him!' she said.

'I think he's right, Aashi,' her mother said, 'We'll go in the morning so they can come home and rest.'

'Okay,' Aashi replied, 'but is Abhi really okay? Where did you find him? What took you so long?'

'Yes, I wish we could have found him sooner. Abhi was lying there, all bloody and in mud, stabbed and unconscious, with the rain pouring heavily over him...'

'Stabbed!' Priyam exclaimed.

'Yes, apparently the thief had a knife.'

'Stabbed?' she repeated again.

'Yes, Priyam, Abhi's been stabbed. But he's out of danger now. We took him straight to Raj's hospital and Raj has called all his best doctors to take care of Abhi. They all say that Abhi's wounds will take time to heal but pose no risk to his life. I left him only when I was sure that he'll be okay.'

'Why didn't you call us earlier?' Aashi asked.

'I didn't want Priyam to hear about all this while I was away from her. I didn't even have any reassuring word to lessen her terror. But as soon as the doctors said he'd be okay, I came.'

'But...is he really okay?' Aashi asked.

'Yes. Or, will be, soon. He's made of tough metal. He'll be here within a week. Won't he, Priyam?' said Sid.

Priyam nodded, a faint smile finally broke through her terror-stricken face.

In another two minutes, Priyam and Sid were on their way to the hospital, leaving behind Aashi and her mother to try and get what little sleep they could muster in what remained of the night.

Whether they succeeded in that or not, but next morning both were walking through the corridor of the hospital before the clock had struck seven.

It was a multi-specialty hospital owned by the Sinhas in partnership with three NRIs. Raj was more proud of this hospital than he was of any other of their business investments and was indeed thinking of repeating its success by opening another. As Aashi walked through its corridors, she could not help but marvel at the money that must have gone into such massive and well-equipped medical facility.

When Aashi and her mother stepped into Abhi's room, they found Sid standing by the window and looking at Priyam. He was guarding her repose by willing it out of his own eyes. Priyam was sleeping. Her head rested on Abhi's bed and fingers held his only hand.

As Sid saw them, he quickly put a finger on his lips and ushered Aashi and her mother out of the room. 'She's just dozed off, I didn't want to wake her up. She didn't sleep a wink last night,' he replied.

'Neither, I'm sure, did you,' said Aashi looking at his tired eyes. 'Here, have some coffee.' She sat down on the bench outside the room and poured out coffee from the thermos she had borrowed from Priyam's kitchen. Urmila opened up a box and offered sandwiches to Sid.

'I didn't realize that I was hungry. But the sight of these sandwiches does make me feel ravenous,' he said picking one up.

Aashi walked up to the door and peeped in. Even from there, she could see how badly Abhi had been injured. His face was swollen and livid bruises spotted his skin. There was a big dark patch in the middle of his right arm and his left leg was cast in a plaster. A white sheet covered him, hiding she knew the biggest wound of all, right where the brutal knife had ran through him. Aashi could not look anymore and quickly turned around.

'So many wounds!' she mumbled as her eyes met Sid's.

'Yes, but they'll heal soon, except the fracture in leg and the gash where he was stabbed. Those will take time.'

'Is it...deep?'

'Any deeper and he'd have been lost to us. All the doctors said that he is very lucky to be alive. It was lucky too that Raj was here. Things might have become difficult for us otherwise.'

'Why?'

'The doctors perhaps would have wanted to notify police first, but Raj dictated them their priorities and took care of the police too. He's quite resourceful in that way. He was here till about four and ensured that Abhi received the immediate treatment that he needed.'

Aashi nodded, not failing to note Sid's changed attitude towards Raj. Finally, he seemed to have realized that Raj was not really as bad as he thought him to be. A proud smile appeared on Aashi's face as she felt her belief in Raj vindicated.

'Priyam's awake,' she told Sid when she saw Priyam stirring.

Sid immediately got up and went inside. Aashi and her mother followed close.

'What time is it?' Priyam asked Sid.

'Half past seven,' he said looking at his watch. 'Exactly twenty minutes since you last asked.'

'How are you, Priyam?' Urmila asked as Aashi reached forward to give her friend a hug.

'I'm fine,' Priyam replied, 'Abhi's fine too.'

'Yes, of course, Sid told us,' said Urmila. She smiled reassuringly at the frightened girl.

A little after nine the doctors showed up. They gave Abhi a thorough check up and went through all his reports. Though they had nothing new to add, they managed to elicit a sigh of relief from all concerned by repeating the happy prognosis and judging Abhi completely out of danger.

'Oh, thank God!' said Aashi, 'I would never have forgiven myself...' she blurted out, realizing a moment too late what she was saying. Her eyes flew up to Sid. He too was looking at her, but as he kept his mouth shut, Aashi started feeling a strange compulsion to reveal all. 'I...' she began hesitatingly, 'he...he had told me...'

'Not to take the short cut,' Sid completed her words.

'Yes, but I...'

'Didn't listen,' he spoke again before she could finish her sentence.

'You knew?' Aashi asked shocked. 'Abhi?'

'No. he didn't tell me. What's there to tell? He never lets Priyam set foot on that road after dark, even if both of us are with her. And it's my guess that his mind lost the capacity of sensible thought after your chain was snatched, not before it.'

'Then why aren't you angry at me?'

'Because, Abhi wouldn't want me to. He would want me to forgive you.'

Aashi squirmed at the words. She rather would have had Sid scold her and pour rage at her folly. Against those, she could have defended herself. But how was one to take a stand against kindness, even if it was forced by his friend's wishes? How was one to come out clean when no one demanded any explanation or justification? It made Aashi feel guiltier than she would have felt had she been justly berated.

'Anyway,' he continued, 'would you stay here with Abhi while we go home?'

'Of course!' Finally, there was something Aashi was not hesitant to say.

'Alright, you know my number, if there's anything the matter you'll call me.'

'Sure,' she replied.

'Without delay.'

'I will.'

'Right. Let's go now, Priyam.'

Priyam was not at all willing to leave her brother's bedside. However, the combined strength of three of them finally succeeded in forcing her out of the hospital. They took Urmila with them too.

Once all were gone, Aashi settled herself near Abhi's bedside. He was still fast asleep, so Aashi had nothing else to do except listen to the usual hospital sounds coming in through the door and admire the landscape hanging on the wall right in front of her.

✳✳✳

Chapter **10**

For who is there that lives and knows
The secret powers by which he grows?
Were knowledge all, what were our need
To thrill and faint and sweetly bleed?
Then seek not, sweet, the 'If' and 'Why'
I love you now until I die.
For I must love because I live
And life in me is what you give.

— *'Because She Would Ask Me Why I Loved Her'*
by Christpoher Brennan

An hour hadn't yet passed away since Aashi had started waiting by Abhi's bedside. And she had already walked all around the room twice, adjusted and smoothed down Abhi's bed sheets three times and looked at his face several times over to find any signs of approaching consciousness. Finally, her waiting ears picked up a low moan.

Aashi turned quickly and saw Abhi's eyes flutter open. She sprang from her chair and stepped closer to him. 'Hi,' she said in a low voice, 'how are you feeling now?'

Abhi's eyes turned towards Aashi but evidently needed some time to clear the haze and focus. 'Hi,' he replied after a moment, trying to greet her with a smile, 'I'm fine, how are you?'

'I'm fine too,' she said.

'Good,' Abhi said, wincing as he tried to move his arm.

'Oh, does it hurt a lot?' Aashi asked anxiously.

'No, not at all. I'm fine. Don't worry,' he replied.

'Sure?'

'Yeah, no problem. Got your chain back from that scoundrel,' Abhi said. A grin spread out on his face, though his eyes remained dull as before.

'You did?' Aashi exclaimed, with very obvious surprise.

'Yes, it was… in my hand when Raj and Sid brought me…here.' Pain shot through Abhi and made him wince as he spoke. 'I remember the nurse gave it to Raj.' He tried to raise himself but quickly gave up the attempt as his wounds protested, making him bite his lips and throw his head back to the pillow.

'Does it hurt very much?' Aashi asked again. She adjusted his pillows and raised him a little to an inclined position. 'Is that better?' she asked, throwing back the hair that had slid over to her shoulders as she had leaned over Abhi.

'Yes, thanks,' Abhi replied. He forced his eyes away from the curls that had just a moment ago hung so close to his face. And how close she herself had been to him, tending to his comfort with such love, *'no...not love... kindness, yes, that's the word,'* he determined as feelings soared up and Abhi tried to force his still drowsy mind to push them back.

'What's the matter?' Aashi asked when she saw Abhi avert his eyes.

'Nothing,' he replied, 'you can sit down now. I'm quite comfortable.'

'Okay,' she said. She pulled her chair closer and settled down, interfering, as she did so, the sunlight pouring in from the window. Her hair, as they lay clustered on her right shoulder forced the sunrays to trap themselves in her curls, adding to their sable softness small, delicate rings of gold.

Never had Abhi found it so hard to keep his eyes in control as now when Aashi sat in front of him, her fair charms aglow with sun's radiance. Her eyes were bent downwards. She looked pensive as a little child who is subdued by the startling presence of pain and contrition in the perfect fabric of her world.

A moment later Abhi saw her long eyelashes turn up. But before he could move his eyes away, hers had caught them looking at her.

'Do you want something?' Aashi asked.

'Uh...no, nothing. Was just thinking about Priyam. How's she?'

'Priyam's fine now, I guess. She was here all night and went home only after she had heard the doctors declare you out of danger.'

'She must have been pretty scared, poor girl,' Abhi mumbled.

'Scared? Abhi, she was nearly shocked out of her senses!'

'Yeah, I was afraid of that,' he replied.

'Why did you do it, Abhi? Just for a stupid chain!' The recollection of last night's horror raised again the irritation and anger she had felt against what she considered Abhi's thoughtless bravado. 'How could you be such a fool? Going after that burly man without thinking how dangerous it could be for you! Didn't you see the knife in his hand?'

'I did, but it's no big deal. Any other guy would have done the same,' Abhi replied, shrugging his shoulder.

'But you are not like any other guy, Abhi!' Aashi exclaimed. Her voice trembled as she spoke. 'You are...'

'Handicapped?' Abhi said, flashing a grin that cut through her like a blade. She didn't want to say it, she had stopped herself from saying it, what need had he to finish up her sentence!

'Yes!' Aashi wanted to shout out, *'and you should remember that and stop*

smiling! What is there to smile about?'

But Abhi's gaze had silenced her once again. And that infuriating smile of his, if smile it really was, arrested her in perplexity.

'Do you know how worried everyone was?' she said as she tried to calm herself.

'Everyone?' Abhi asked. He was looking straight at her. Aashi's face was flushed with emotions and eyes blazed more brightly than he had ever seen them.

'Yes, and you playing superman! How could you be so foolish, Abhi?'

'Were you worried too, Aashi?'

'Now, what kind of question is that? Sure I was worried, not only worried, I felt so awfully guilty too.'

'Guilty? Why?'

'Because… it was my chain you had risked your life for. And you had told me not to take that route, and I… I hadn't listened…and it was so awful… so…oh, Abhi!' she exclaimed as her remorse clouded up her eyes, 'Don't ever do anything like that again! It was… it was…so horrible!'

'Sorry,' he mumbled, 'but don't cry, I'm okay now.'

'I'm not crying.' She forced a smile to her face. 'But I'm very angry at you.'

'Don't be,' he murmured and closed his eyes.

'Are you feeling sleepy?' she asked a little later. A nod was all the reply she received from him. 'Alright, you take a nap. I'll just go and fill the water bottle. Will be back in five minutes, okay?'

Abhi nodded again, without opening his eyes or saying anything as Aashi walked out of the room.

He heard her leaving, going out of the room and closing the door after her. He wanted to call her, but didn't, he wanted to tell her, but couldn't. So he just closed his eyes tighter and tried to squeeze her precious image out from his eyes.

But it had already been stamped on his consciousness. Even in the darkness of closed eyelids, it glowed vividly, filling his mind till there was no space left for any other thought.

Something in Abhi had changed forever. He was not the same any longer. Foolish she had called him and he agreed. He was a fool, to turn on a course which he knew would lead him nowhere. He knew well what Aashi's dreams were. He was aware too of the perfection she desired. The fact that her eyes had seen that perfection and been besotted by it was also not hidden from him. Yet, the ineffable in his heart would not quiet down.

'But it would have to…it would…have to,' he ordered himself.

The door of the room opened again. Abhi listened attentively, but kept his eyes shut. However, the footsteps that approached his bed were not the ones that he had just heard going away. Opening his eyes, Abhi saw Raj smiling at him.

'Hey, man, how are you today, Mr. Braveheart?'

'Quite fine actually. They are taking very good care of me.'

'They better do that. But why are you alone?'

'He's not,' Aashi replied from the door. 'I'm with him. I had just gone to the water cooler to fill up a bottle. And then I got lost in admiring your fine hospital.'

'It *is* a fine hospital, isn't it? I'm very proud of it myself. There is only one trouble with it. It's too close to the railway line.'

'Oh, it's not so close. You can hear the trains, but the noise is not so loud as to disturb anybody,' Aashi quickly dismissed the flaw as being too minor to subtract anything from the worth of 'Raj's fine hospital.'

'Yeah, I guess. Besides, I must not complain against what time and time again keeps on sending business here. Never a fortnight passes when somebody or the other doesn't seek the line to end his lifeline. And this being the nearest hospital, every such person is brought here. And some of them do manage to survive, for some days at least, and add to the hospital's profits.'

'Great way to turn people's misery into money, Raj,' Abhi mumbled from his bed.

'Oh well, if you put it that way,' said Raj with a cool shrug of his shoulders. 'Anyway, Aashi, guess what I have here in my pocket.'

'Umm…' she pretended to think, 'my chain?'

'How did you know? That was to be a surprise!'

'Abhi told me,' Aashi said as she placed the bottle on the bedside table.

'Oh well, in that case, here it is,' said Raj. He took the chain out from his pocket and handed it to Aashi.

'How come it is unbroken? I'm sure it snapped when he pulled,' Aashi asked.

'Oh, it was. I got it repaired. I told my mother's favourite jeweller to open the shop early. He couldn't say no to the son of his best customer.'

'Thanks, but you shouldn't have gone to so much trouble,' said Aashi as she tried to clasp it around her neck.

'Allow me,' Raj said. In a second, he was standing behind Aashi, securing the clasp as she gathered up her hair. 'There,' he waved gallantly, 'it looks good on her, doesn't it, Abhi?'

'Sure, it does,' Abhi said, in a voice that sounded tired and unwilling. Closing his eyes again, Abhi made another attempt to shut out the world, though with no greater success than the last time.

'Don't disturb him, he needs rest,' he heard Aashi whisper to Raj.

'Oh, I'm going anyway. Have a meeting to attend! Bye, dude. See you later.'

'Bye,' Abhi replied and heard Raj walk out of the room with Aashi.

There was nothing Abhi could do to alleviate the pressure weighing him down. Nothing, to blot away the happiness that had sparked up in Aashi's eyes when she saw Raj. Abhi would have loved to see her light up like that for himself. He would have loved to have Aashi look up at him as she looked at Raj. But that was just as much an impossibility as his ever being able to do what Raj had done so simply...put that chain around Aashi's neck.

'*She was right, I am a fool, a super fool!*' Abhi thought, blasting a wry grin at the epithet he considered not ill fitting.

From the tumult raging in Abhi's mind emerged a spectre that took him back to his school days. The charming form of Neha appeared before him, in all the freshness of her youth, her smiling countenance so pretty, her eyes so intriguing, even when they had turned away from him. Three years, of what Abhi had thought was love, flashed before him.

'*Love! Yeah, and how quickly it ran away at the sight of crutches!*'

Abhi had got rid of those crutches a long time ago. But the lessons that he had learnt at that time were still rooted deep in his conscience. The memories were fresh still, every sentiment still alive. And the result was that behind all his lively spirit, lurked a deep loneliness that even Sid and Priyam weren't totally aware of.

Abhi had loved, loved with all the vigour of youth, with all the sincerity of his true heart, and yet, he had lost. Now he feared even to put one foot on the path whose travails he was well aware of. He could not, he would not, never ever, fall in love again.

Abhi's guards were strong and he perhaps would have been safe had not the prohibited feeling chosen his weakest moment to make its move. He had been fighting for long already, but the battle was lost in an instant and his will surrendered. He was too weak, exhausted and in too much pain to be able to remain impervious. The nearness of Aashi as she tended him, the fragrance of her body, the touch of her hand...how could he have remained insensate to all that? The lustre of Aashi's hair, the fire of her eyes, her anger, her sympathy, all embedded themselves in the sensitive tissue of Abhi's being.

What use was it now hardening his heart again? What use wrapping the broken armour around his wound? The blow had been struck, all that Abhi could do was to keep it to himself and let no one know.

Forlorn! The very word is like a bell
To toil me back from thee to my sole self!
Adieu! The fancy cannot cheat so well
As she is famed to do, deceiving elf."

— *'Ode to the Nightingale.' By John Keats.*

Priyam looked at her brother as he sat there on the swing. It had been more than five minutes since she had come out, but Abhi was yet to become conscious of her presence. His eyes were turned up, gazing at the sky, unmoving, though perhaps looking at a lot more than the insensate piece of cloud they were pretending to observe. His face was set in the rigidity of concentration as he tried to settle something, something that refused to quiet down and in an attempt to force its way out, made breathing difficult for him.

Six whole weeks had passed since the encounter with the chain snatcher. Most of Abhi's wounds had healed. Just that day he had been to the hospital to have the plaster removed from his leg. Everything was back to normal now, on the surface at least.

But as he sat there, still and silent, Priyam knew that something there was still that hadn't healed. Something that was growing worse every day, despite all Abhi's efforts to the contrary.

Priyam had not been as blind as him while reading the working of a sibling's heart. She had seen the way his eyes sought Aashi, eagerly, almost restlessly, yet only to flit away as soon as Aashi's attention was pulled towards him.

Priyam took a deep breath and walked over to join him. The swing gave out a little groan as she settled down besides Abhi.

'Hey, what took you so long?' he asked turning instantly towards her.

'I was…washing the dishes,' she said, letting Abhi wrap his arm around her, while his eyes turned up to the sky as before. Priyam let her head rest on his shoulder as she too turned her gaze to where his was fixed.

'Nice weather,' she said.

It was a bright and cheerful evening. Many layers of clouds lay dispersed over a sparkling azure. The wind chimes hung by the door had never stopped ringing throughout the day and were still having a merry time. Right in front of them, a little bird was twittering fearlessly, pecking at the grass every now and then and looking around with small, sudden twists of its tiny head.

'Yes, perfect. Everything is perfect. Just as it should be,' Abhi replied.

Priyam nodded, though she knew very well that he was not referring to the weather at all. She snuggled closer to Abhi, her eyes studying his face as she felt him catch his breath, and stifle that unknown something that yearned for a release. Her lips parted to form a question, but she remained silent. And so did he.

It was past seven when Sid made his appearance on their door that day.

'Why are you so late?' Priyam asked Sid as soon as he stepped inside the door.

'I'm just thirty minutes late, Priyam,' Sid replied. He threw his helmet and briefcase on the couch and plonked himself down in its soft cushion too.

'Forty minutes, no, forty five. But why?'

'Oh, I had gone to Noida.'

'Noida?'

'For a job interview. Didn't I tell you about the company I had applied to?'

'Yeah, some big MNC. But why, Sid? Do you want to go abroad?'

'Not if I can find a job for your brother there too,' he replied laughing, 'All I am looking for is a nice paying job so I can afford a house where you would not mind playing a hostess. Now, can this thirsty man hope to get a chilled glass of water, or will you rather finish your chastisement first?'

'I'll get it…' said Priyam and rushed into her kitchen, perhaps to hide the sudden blush of happiness that his words had given rise to.

'*Playing a hostess…in his house…what did he mean?*' She wondered, though the excited flutter of her heart was an answer enough.

Why would he say it otherwise? Sid never said anything without intention.

He had not yet declared his love to her, nor hinted in any way his intention of getting married. But now, she knew why. Sid must be waiting until he could give her a comfortable life and a house where she would love "to play hostess." The words made Priyam's heart dance again and added a merry spring to her step as she fetched water for him.

'So how did it go?' Abhi asked Sid as she came back with a glass of water.

'Very well, I think,' Sid replied, 'there are four vacancies, I sure hope to grab one of them.'

'You will, I'm sure,' said Abhi with confidence.

'Well, we'll only find that out later, for now however, what do you say to a trip to Retreat?' Sid asked, gulping down the water Priyam handed him.

'Oh yes, let us!' she said immediately.

'Perfect. I was wishing for just such a break. Let's just get out of here for a couple of days,' affirmed Abhi.

'I would have thought that you've had enough of break,' Sid laughed, though a bit uncomfortably.

There was something in his friend's voice that had not such a happy ring as he was used to hear. Sid looked up at Priyam and found an echo of his discomfort in her face too. 'But since you are so keen on it, we'll leave tomorrow morning,' he continued nevertheless. 'It's been seven months since we went there. A visit is highly overdue. And the timing is perfect too. I just have to take a Monday off. Tuesday and Wednesday are already holidays due to Independence Day and *Janmashtmi*. So we can have a full five day vacation. There are some issues that need to be sorted out too. That tractor is acting up again.'

'Hmm...would be better if we leave early tomorrow so...'

'Leave tomorrow? Where are you going?' Abhi's sentence was cut short by Aashi's abrupt entry.

'What? You guys going somewhere?' Raj asked as he too stepped inside the house after her.

'Where are *you* two coming from?' Priyam was surprised to see Raj and Aashi together. To her knowledge, Aashi had gone to the market, and alone.

'Well, I'm coming straight from my office,' Raj replied, 'As for Aashi, I don't know where she's coming from, but by the packets in her hand, it can be guessed she's been shopping, if not shoplifting. I just picked her up from the main road, where she was trudging along with all her bag and baggage. Now you tell, where are you going?'

'To Sid's farmhouse,' Priyam replied.

'Oh, cool! Nice place. We used to have so much fun there. Remember, Sid, how we used to hold cricket and football matches in our farms? What fun those matches were!'

'You have a farmhouse too?' Aashi asked eagerly.

'Sure, and not just one. But the other one is in UK. Hey, speaking of my farm, why not go there this time? What do you say, Priyam?' Raj asked, turning expectantly towards her, 'You've never seen mine, have you? I'm sure once you see it, you'll fall in love with it. It's much nicer and bigger than Sid's. You have been to Sid's many times, let's all go to mine this time. We'll have a nice picnic there.'

'Oh yes, let us!' Aashi exclaimed with enthusiasm. 'I've not been on a picnic for such a long time.'

'But...I don't think we can...' Priyam muttered.

She hated to give a refusal to anybody, and after all that Raj had done for Abhi, saying no to him was harder than before. And she most probably would have said yes too, though only for a single day's trip.

But Priyam had caught in her brother's eyes an unwillingness to follow Raj's idea. And that was enough to make her rigid and firm against the plan. If it was to Retreat Abhi wanted to go, there they will go, no matter what.

'Oh come on, Priyam, don't be a spoil sport!' Aashi moaned.

'And may I ask why not?' Raj asked, his cheerful smile fading away into disappointment.

'Oh, it's just...I mean...Sid...'

'Sid! But I'm inviting him too, Priyam. And I think he can suffer himself to tread on my grounds for once.'

'Sid has some important business there. He can't come.' Priyam almost hated herself for being so rude to Raj. But there was nothing else she could do.

'Well then, you and Abhi come. And Sid can join us when his business is finished. Our farmhouses are just about a couple of miles from each other.'

'But, Abhi...' Priyam started but stopped short. She didn't know what to say. She never was any good at persuasion while Raj was an expert.

'Abhi won't refuse me. Would you, Abhi?'

'He would not,' Priyam spoke up before her brother could be forced to give an assent.

Raj turned towards her, surprised at the grim finality in her voice. 'Would...you?'

'We'll come some other time, Raj. But not tomorrow, please.'

'Can't you change your plans for once, Priyam? For my sake? I am a friend to you, if nothing else. Or am I not entitled to even that?'

Raj could not bear it any longer. He was not habitual of being refused. And after Abhi's stay in his hospital, Raj had hoped that he must have come at least a little closer to winning Priyam's heart. But it seemed that after all, he was still as far away from her as he ever was. He did not deserve this, an indignant protest rose up in his heart. He had become tired of being rebuffed again and again.

'Don't be angry, Raj. I didn't want to make you angry. I'm sorry if I have...' Priyam said immediately, fearful that she had hurt his feelings. 'But, Raj, Abhi's going through a rough patch...and he will feel most comfortable at Retreat. And it's been so long... we'll go to your farmhouse some other day, when Abhi would be better and Sid would be able to join us too.'

'Abhi and Sid! Can't you think of your own self for once, Priyam? You have a life too, don't you? Don't you get tired of being tied to them? Get out of their shadow for once, take a fresh breath of life and see what beautiful world awaits you!' Raj almost shouted. He tried to tone down the anger in his voice, but he was just too angry to be able to do so.

Priyam's eyes shot up at the words and stared back at him in a steady undaunted gaze.

'Oh, hell!' Raj exclaimed, 'Don't look at me like that! Go to your own damned farm house if you want to, I don't care!' he said, turning immediately to storm out of the house.

Raj knew he was defeated, and all because of a cripple and a bore. He, who had a habit of winning every challenge, had lost once again, lost to a man whom he considered inferior to himself on all counts. Of course, it was on Sid that Raj laid the greater blame of Priyam's refusal than on Abhi.

'Have a nice trip!' he said before walking out, leaving Aashi caught between anger and disappointment and rest of them looking at each other in dismay.

Neither of them wanted to hurt Raj's feelings like that, not even Sid. But then, what had happened was inevitable too. Raj, sooner or later, would have had to realize the truth. Sooner the better.

'Where are you going, Aashi?' Priyam asked as she noticed Aashi walking away too.

'Don't you think somebody should go and try to make him feel better?' Aashi shot back with an unexpected energy. 'How can you be so cruel to him, Priyam, after all he has done for your brother? Raj cares so much about you and you pay him back like this!' she exclaimed before walking out.

Raj had not yet covered a distance where Aashi's voice could not have reached his ears. He stopped when he heard Aashi coming out and turned to look at her. It was not the first time he had seen Aashi take his side, but never had he imagined that she could display such passion against her best friend, all because of him. A part of Raj felt gratified to see such concern in Aashi's eyes for what he was going through.

What Raj had yearned to see in Priyam's eyes was now looking up to him from hers, more eloquently than Priyam's shy eyes could ever have managed to reveal. And it felt good, to his bristling ego at least.

It was around seven next day when Sid carried out their bags to Abhi's car. It was the same car that had been in the tragic accident that had taken so much away from the siblings. Badly wrecked as it had been in that accident, Mr. Vardhan had had it completely revamped to suit Abhi's special needs. It looked new now and Abhi had maintained it well. However, despite all the happy journeys that it had seen since he started driving it, and despite the complete overhaul that it had been through, the memory of that fateful day remained imbibed in its deepest pores. A terrible memory, which nevertheless made it impossible for Abhi to think of parting with the car.

'Hurry up, guys, we should get going before it gets any hotter,' Sid called out after he had adjusted the bags in the backseat.

'Just five minutes!' Priyam's voice came out through the window.

Sid smiled at her words and turned to look towards the house.

As he turned, another window opened up behind him and Aashi peeked out. She was dressed up too, though it was still early for her to leave for work. She cast a quick look towards the gate before vanishing back inside her room, only to appear again as Raj's sleek red Audi came to a halt behind Abhi's old Maruti.

Sid turned immediately but before he could express any surprise, the dapper form that stepped out of the vehicle spoke up.

'Oh good, you are still here,' Raj said, 'I was afraid I might be late.'

'No, you are not,' Aashi chimed, running out from her house with a little bag slung over her shoulder.

'Hey, Abhi! Nice morning, Priyam, isn't it?' Raj called out as his quick eyes caught the two stepping out from their home.

'Raj? Hi,' Abhi called back as he locked his door.

Priyam remained silent, too surprised to say anything. After what had happened last night, she certainly hadn't expected to see Raj so soon.

'What are you doing here so early?' Abhi asked as they walked towards him.

'I knew you would leave early in the morning and I didn't want to miss you.'

'What do you mean?'

'Well, I had made up my mind to have a picnic today. And you know very well that I never disappoint myself. Aashi wanted a picnic too. So we decided that if you guys can't come to my place, that doesn't mean you will stop me from coming to yours, would you?'

'Of course not,' Abhi replied, the 'we' lingering a moment in his ears as he looked uncertainly at Sid and Priyam.

'Right, let's go now. It's getting late and your car doesn't have an A.C. even,' Raj replied.

'But...why didn't you tell me anything?' Priyam asked Aashi.

'What do you mean? Don't you want me to come?' Aashi asked. Her smile faded away a little as the cry of delight that she had expected from her friend had yet not appeared. 'I had thought you'd be glad to have someone to add some fun to your sombre little party.'

'Sure, we are glad,' Abhi said. His eyes caught Aashi's slender fingers run carelessly through her hair. 'She means we could have gone earlier, not knowing that you two planned to join us too …and your mother?'

'She's plans to visit her in-laws. She'll go there to spend a day or two, though I don't know how she can even think of her being welcome there still.'

'And had you left early then we would simply have come after you,' Raj replied. 'Let's get going now.'

'Yes, let us,' Abhi replied.

As Abhi turned, his eyes met Priyam's. The sudden turn of events had dimmed the glee that had been dancing in her eyes all morning. Abhi's eyes had brightened up with amusement though and a smile appeared on his lips, mocking perhaps the truancies of his own splendid luck.

'Come, Priyam,' Abhi said, taking a deep breath, 'let's see what more delightful surprises the day has to bring. Let's have fun!'

'I hope that means keeping away from your golden oldies, as you call the slow and boring songs you guys keep on listening to,' Aashi laughed as she took small, unwilling steps towards their car. 'Because no matter what, I never can find any fun in them. They are so boring!'

'Well in that case, Aashi, you better make a place for yourself in Raj's car because old songs are what we are going to hear all the way. May be your tastes would match better with his,' Sid replied. He did not bother to hide the irritation he felt at having all his plans spoiled.

One thing that Sid had been looking forward to was to have a quiet time away from the 'crowd'. Now, however, it seemed that the crowd was determined to follow them even inside the reserved environs of his Retreat. Nothing irked Sid more than having unwelcome people imagining themselves entitled guests and budging themselves in where he would rather have no one else.

'Yeah, come with me, Aashi. I don't want to travel alone and well…can't expect anybody else too. I've some good music too, you'd like it, I'm sure.'

'Well, okay,' she said, a bit hesitantly but not without a happy flutter of excitement. 'Bye, Ma!' she called out to her mother who had come out to see them off.

'Bye, and take care,' Aashi's mother replied bidding farewell to all of them and seeing the two cars speed off.

'Perfect start to a fine day!' Abhi chuckled. He allowed the red car to go past his, its occupants grinning and waving back at them with jubilation, a feeling that neither Abhi, nor Sid or Priyam could sympathize with just at that time.

79

Chapter 12

Somewhere there waiteth in this world of ours
For one lone soul another lonely soul
Each choosing each through all the weary hours
And meeting strangely at one sudden goal.

'Destiny' by Edwin Arnold

The farmhouse had once belonged to Sid's mother and, as the siblings had guessed over time, was the gift Mr. Vardhan had given to Sid when he went away. It was Sid's most cherished possession, not because it was a valuable piece of property, but because every leaf, every blade of grass, and even every grain of sand of that dear place was immutably linked to his mother. He would perhaps have refused any other gift from Mr. Vardhan, but he couldn't bring himself to refuse this.

Changing its name was the first thing Sid did after becoming its owner. The board of 'Aditya Farms' was quickly replaced by one bearing the inscription 'The Retreat.' That was the name Sid had given to the place which always made him go back to his childhood days.

Abhi and Priyam too had spent many a delightful days here. And as they drove towards it, a kind of delightful elation, as a child must feel when it's rushing back to his or her mother's arms, took charge of them. And in that joy, all three let their eyes ignore the red car still ahead of them and just revelled in the pleasure of returning to a favourite sanctuary.

When they reached the farmhouse, Aashi could not help but being surprised at the extreme plainness of it. The farmhouse was much too small to impress her and even plainer than what Raj's not very flattering description along the way had made her imagine. It had nothing grand or stylish to boast of. It was just a neat little three bedroom house with a couple of outhouses in the back. She looked around at the garden and was even more disappointed to notice a total lack of adornments. Sure there were beautifully designed flower beds, neatly trimmed hedges and wooden benches at every convenient place. But there were no pretty statues or gushing fountains, things Aashi considered compulsory for every garden.

'Why? Nothing at all is changed, Sid!' Raj said as he entered the house, 'I had hoped that since you are now its owner you must have brought in some freshness.'

'I'm sorry for disappointing you,' Sid replied curtly.

'No I mean, last I came here was some seven or eight years ago, right? But nothing at all is changed. Everything is as it was a decade ago, I mean, as far as I can remember.'

'Yes, everything is just as it was. We haven't changed anything,' Abhi said when Sid did not bother to answer.

'Doesn't surprise me at all. Just like you guys to keep on sticking to the past. You don't belong here, in this time zone, I mean,' Raj laughed, shaking his head.

'We are comfortable here, whatever time zone it might be,' Sid declared.

Aashi's eyes caught a lady smiling through a picture frame and she walked up to it to admire the pattern of her dress.

'That's Sid's mother,' Abhi told her when Sid did not bother to enlighten her awareness.

'She's very pretty,' Aashi said. 'But you don't look like her. You must have taken after you father, Sid.'

Priyam rushed to shelter her friend before Sid could burn Aashi with his raging glare. Aashi was quickly dragged to the bedroom she was to share with Priyam. And she was brought out of it only when Sid had gone to see a broken down tractor.

Aashi wouldn't have minded his absence quite so much had Abhi and Raj not gone along with her.

'Why did Raj and Abhi have to accompany Sid? Can't he fix his stupid tractor himself?' Aashi said with a downward curl on her lips. Priyam had brought her out in the garden and the two were sitting under a gulmohar tree.

'Why? You can't be feeling bored already?' Priyam asked.

'Yeah! There's nothing to do around here. And I'm getting tired of sitting under a tree. What do *you* do here? Don't you get bored?'

'No, I never feel bored here. I love being here. There's always something new to see or something old to admire and recollect. How can I...'

'Oh, good, Raj at least is coming,' Aashi exclaimed. 'Hi, Raj, where's the rest of your party?' she called out as soon as Raj came within hearing distance.

'Oh, still busy with an old, good-for-nothing tractor, trying to fix it up. It's a piece of junk really, much better to be sold off as scrap. I told Sid he should rather buy a new one than slog over it.'

'A new tractor costs a lot, Raj,' Priyam pointed out, 'and though the farm manages to earn its upkeep I doubt there's spare money enough to make such a purchase.'

'May be, but Sid should have calculated all this before taking it over from his father while refusing all the rest. It's a pity he's so dead-set against his own father,' Raj said, sprawling himself down besides Aashi. He looked around and smiled. 'Do you see that open ground, Aashi,' he said, 'that's where we used to play football. Me, Sid and Abhi. Abhi was Sid's best friend even at that time. Priyam was rarely the part of the team then though, right, Priyam?'

'Yes, my mother didn't like the idea of sending me too. Only once did Sid manage to persuade her to let me accompany them. That was the only time till...'

'Yes, we used to have so much fun, spending whole afternoon playing. It used to be such good fight. Both Abhi and Sid were great at football, and they seldom agreed to play cricket in which I was better than them. My mother used to cheer for me, Sid's mother for him, but you know, it was mostly Abhi who managed to steal the game. He was such good runner. He still is, if we go by the chase he gave that thief of yours!' Raj said. His words made Aashi laugh and brought a smile on Priyam's face. 'It's a pity he can't play that well now, what with his stiff leg and all that, it's too easy to beat him at any game now.'

Priyam smiled at his words and shook her head lightly. 'Why don't you try playing chess with Abhi?' she asked.

'Chess? Never, it's such a boring game!' Raj exclaimed. 'Besides, it's healthier to play outdoor games that require some exercise instead of sitting hunched on a chair playing a stupid board game.'

'Chess, a stupid game?' said Priyam.

'Okay, not stupid, but still, Priyam, it's so dull and slow. I'm never going to waste my time on it unless, heaven forbid, some accident makes me a handicap too and renders me useless for any other thing.'

That was more than what Priyam could take.

She had been avoiding his thinly veiled sarcasm for so long, trying to diffuse it with good humour. But hearing Abhi called a handicap and useless was beyond her endurance. These were the words Priyam could never hear in relation to her brother.

Raj too knew well that he should never have uttered them. But there was bitterness in his heart too and though he had decided to suppress it, the resentment continued piquing him and making him say things he would never have uttered a month ago. Not so bluntly at least.

'Don't get me wrong, Priyam,' he said quickly as she stood up in protest, 'I didn't mean it that way. I just meant...'

'My brother may lack a limb, Raj,' Priyam said, in a strictly controlled tone that nevertheless conveyed her feelings quite sufficiently, 'but he's much better and capable than many so called able-bodied men,' she declared, breathing out every word slowly and deliberately.

'There's nothing to be so angry about, Priyam!' Raj shot back at her, 'I meant no insult to your darling brother, and you know it. You, on the other hand, are the one who keeps on insulting me and my feelings. I have borne everything for your sake, but there's a limit to my endurance. This is no way to treat someone who loves you...'

'Love me? If you loved me, Raj, you'd have loved mine too, instead of mocking them at every little opportunity!' And with that, Priyam turned and walked away from him as quickly as her legs could carry her.

'There! Did you see that, Aashi? I'm always to be the one in the wrong! They don't have any fault, they are always to be the perfect ones, and I'm always to be Mr. Wrong. Even that surly fool is much better than me. He, who can't afford a tractor and yet will not part with this stupid old farmhouse, is wiser by far than I am, and kinder too, though he won't even look at his own father who raised up his friends so unconditionally. Why, Aashi? Is there something so fundamentally wrong with me? Why can't she love me?'

'Don't blame her, Raj, we have no control over whom we love,' Aashi replied.

'I don't...blame her,' Raj said, pacifying a little. 'But I'm getting so tired of being rejected and ignored and insulted. I guess I should as well have accepted Priyam's word when she had declared she would never be able to love me. But I didn't believe her, I thought... I thought I could win over her. But she hates me!'

'Nonsense! Priyam doesn't hate you. At worst, she feels irritated because you keep on trying to persuade her though she has already made her decision clear to you. You should have found yourself another girl.'

'I haven't seen any other girl who is so true and selfless. Everyone else is more interested in my money than me,' Raj said as he picked up a yellow leaf from the ground and tore it into small bits.

Half a smile appeared on Aashi's face. 'Money is a great attraction, Raj. It adds allurement to even the blackest being,' she said.

'Yeah? Then I must be worse than the blackest being in Priyam's eyes.'

'No, Raj, you are good, the best! You are so perfect...and...you *will* find love. There will surely be...or perhaps is...some girl...who loves you just for who you are...and perhaps...you just don't know it.'

Aashi barely knew what she was speaking, or why. All she was aware of was Raj's presence near her, his sadness, and a sudden, restless fire that was flaming up her cheeks and making her say things she probably shouldn't.

Raj stared at her with surprise, trying to judge what exactly lay behind Aashi's words, and the way she was looking at him.

Aashi had always been so open and free with him, always laughing and engaging him in merry conversation, especially when nobody else would talk to him. Could it be that behind all those little acts of companionship, there was something more than friendship?…could it be that Aashi…loved him?

The possibility, surprisingly, did not feel so unpleasant. There was a part in Raj that felt satisfied, almost victorious.

Aashi forced a smile to her lips and shrugged her shoulders, almost nonchalantly. 'It isn't fair, is it, Raj? Some people get all the love in the world, but don't value it, or can't recognize it. Some, like you and me, just go on hoping and dreaming about it, wondering if they would ever be loved the way they want to be loved. Why does this happen, Raj? It's so not fair!'

Raj remained silent. His eyes did not move away from Aashi.

It appeared to him that he had never really looked at her before. She was gorgeous. She formed a picture of perfect beauty as she sat there, looking up at him. Her lustrous black curls framed her face in a most enchanting way. There was childlike impetuosity in her eyes, almost an audacity that was thrilling in its very frankness. And the graceful curves of her figure were delicious and beckoning too.

Raj's disappointed heart experienced a sudden burst of excitement at the prospect of being loved by her. He could not reciprocate it, of course. But at least somebody there was who realized his worth, somebody other than those fortune seeking maidens of his acquaintance who knew nothing about love and its delicacies.

Aashi was not like them. She was sensitive and true. And despite her audacity and recklessness, had an aura of vulnerability about her that made one want to wrap a protective arm around her and put a stop to that inexplicable search that dwelt just behind the vivacity of her eyes. And besides, Aashi was Priyam's friend.

Just then, Raj caught sight of Abhi and Sid returning. 'There they are,' he said drawing Aashi's attention towards them. 'Come, we'll go and meet them.'

'You go, I'll run indoors and see what Priyam's doing,' she replied.

Aashi could not say why, but just then she did not desire to be seen by Abhi, or rather, be studied by those piercing eyes of his whose very gentleness had started troubling her. Aashi was conscious of being the focus of Abhi's gaze more often than she would have liked, but what irked her more was the sudden way Abhi looked away whenever she attempted to answer his stare. What was it that he was trying to hide from her? And why did it always make her heart feel so burdened?

She had done nothing wrong and yet she felt as if she had. And Aashi did not like that. It had begun putting a check on her free spirits and whenever Abhi appeared, she could not help but become guarded and uneasy and she did not know why. They still talked and made fun of each other in much the same way, but it all had started to feel so forced, so deliberate, so pretended. And Aashi was in no mood to pretend anything now. She needed to cool off, calm herself before she could face Abhi with any degree of confidence.

The dusk was settling leisurely over The Retreat. All that was left of the sun was a crimson fire lying recumbent in the west. And as its glow melted into the fading blue, a magnificent spectrum stretched out across the sky and reflected from the calm waters of the canal.

It was a perfect time to arrive at the canal that passed through the western boundary of the farm. Everyone settled down with a sense of relief. Although the temperature had cooled down and the evening had become quite pleasant, yet they all felt tired and hot after the long trek through the farm.

Raj climbed up to the old wooden bridge spanning across the canal. 'Are those your trees too?' he asked pointing to a small wood on the other side.

'Yes,' Sid replied.

'Really? What trees are these?' Aashi asked, much impressed.

'Mangoes.'

'How many?' Raj enquired.

'157,' Abhi and Priyam replied at once.

Priyam was sitting on a low boulder, while Abhi was standing near, gazing at the ripples that danced on the water. Soon, as Raj and Aashi asked no more questions, an unconscious silence fell over all of them. Everybody just sat enjoying the cool air and the tranquil flow of the canal.

Gently, a low, inconspicuous hum rose up over the chirping of birds as Abhi began regaling himself with a song, often breaking out in unconscious whistling.

Aashi looked at him and for once, did not taunt him for his choice of song. It had been a long time since she had heard Abhi whistle, and it felt nice to see him so relaxed. It was as if his cheerfulness was lifting a burden from her heart too.

Aashi was not the only one feeling the relief. A smile had diffused itself on Priyam's face too as she gently swayed along her brother's song.

'How much did you get it for?' Raj asked, breaking the hush and putting a halt on Abhi's humming.

'What? Oh, I don't know,' Sid replied, taking a moment to grasp what Raj had asked. 'I was quite young when Mr. Vardhan bought it. What I know is that he got it for half its price. The man who owned it was sentenced for killing his wife. So the property was disposed off cheap.'

'He killed his wife?' Priyam asked with horror.

'Yeah, brutally murdered, and cut her to pieces.'

'How horrible!' Aashi exclaimed.

'Yes, and ironical too,' Sid murmured.

'Ironical?' Aashi asked.

No one bothered to clarify Sid's words.

'Thanks for not telling me this before. I'd have been so scared of seeing that woman's ghost that I'd have simply refused to enter the farmhouse, despite all its charming beauty,' said Priyam. 'What kind of person he must have been! How frightful to have a husband like that!'

'You need not have any fear, Priyam,' Sid said, 'I may have my father's blood in my veins but I'd die sooner than cause one tear to drop from my wife's eyes,' he declared.

His eyes didn't wander away from the waning light that was trembling on the water before him. Not even to see the bright glimmer his words had raised in Priyam's surprised eyes, or joy in Abhi's face. Nor for that matter, to see the sad demise of last flicker of hope from Raj's defeated gaze. If anyone saw these reactions, it was Aashi.

She found herself inexplicably tossed between Priyam's happiness, her own happier prospects and grief of Raj's final defeat. In her bewilderment, Aashi could only look from one face to other with open lips and wide open eyes as she tried to decide whether she should rush to Priyam with delight or turn towards Raj with a word of comfort.

All she did however, was stand still and wonder at the flutter of her own heart that could not but be happy, even if the one it loved wasn't.

***

Chapter 13

Imagine something purer far,
More free from stain of clay
Than Friendship, Love, or Passion are,
Yet human still as they:
And if thy lip, for love like this,
No mortal word can frame,
Go, ask of angels what it is,
And call it by that name!

-- *Thomas Moore*

It was nearly 11 o'clock at night when Priyam entered her room in the farmhouse.

But before the door was ajar, the sound of pacing footsteps met Priyam's ears and the light from a corner lamp crept out to welcome her. Aashi evidently was wide-awake and pacing around the room with much energy.

'Oh, hi,' she said turning as Priyam entered the room, 'I thought you'd never come.'

'Well, we do stay up late when we come here. And I thought you'd have gone to sleep.'

'Sleep? How could I've slept without wishing you sweet dreams?' Aashi replied, surprising Priyam with a hug and a peck on cheek. 'I'm so happy for you!' she said, 'I feared he'd never make it clear till the last moment. But finally it dropped out of his mouth. Our Mr. Grumpy does really intend to marry you!'

'Yes,' Priyam murmured as a shy smile made her features glow with pleasure.

'You two are so perfect for each other. You know each other so well,' Aashi kept on speaking, her eyes sparkling as brightly as the smile on her face. 'It's so perfect. And it's going to stay perfect, forever, I'm sure about that. I'm so happy!'

Priyam smiled at Aashi but didn't say anything. It would have been so good had she felt that surety too. But she didn't.

87

It wasn't that Priyam felt particularly scared or terrified. Just that amid all her joy, she couldn't lose the dull feeling of apprehension that had for many years made residence in her subconscious. The accident that had taken away her parents had cursed Priyam forever to be suspicious of good fortune, for good things, her experience had shown, never last. She knew very well the undulating path that life travels, one may climb as high as the path takes, but then one has to come down. Lucky are those whose course runs smooth and unchanging, but *hers* hadn't been so blessed. Now that Priyam had in her possession the greatest bliss she had ever desired, she wondered if providence will again force her to open her grasp and make the joy fly far away.

Such thoughts remained with Priyam as she went to bed. To add to her sense of foreboding, the weather grew stormy too. The thunder clouds started announcing their presence in the sky with most deafening roars.

Priyam never was much fond of thunder, and a midnight thunder when her heart was already jostling with apprehension was perfect to pull her out of her bed and make her pace around with drapes pulled tightly over the window.

Abhi and Sid both knew how she felt in a thunder storm. And before long, she heard a soft knock followed by Abhi's voice.

'Are you okay, Priyam?' he asked.

Priyam opened the door immediately, 'Yes,' she said trying to smile. 'Don't worry.'

'Sure you're not scared?' Sid called out as he too walked out of his room. 'We can all sit together and chat if you want.'

'Oh, I am scared, a bit. Wonder when I'll stop being bothered by thunder. It's so stupid!' she said, smiling with some embarrassment.

'That's okay, everybody's scared of something or the other. Right, Abhi?'

'Sure,' Abhi affirmed. 'Let's go to the drawing room. We don't want to disturb Aashi.'

'Well, if all that booming and blasting hasn't disturbed her, there's no way our voices will. But you are right, drawing room is a much better place. We can even watch the storm from there.'

'Watch storm? No thanks! You go,' Priyam exclaimed, giving a little punch to Sid.

'Hey!' Sid retorted rubbing his shoulder, 'I thought punches and kicks come after marriage but it seems, Abhi, your sister has started practicing already!'

'Well, there's still time if you want to opt out,' Abhi laughed.

'Yeah, I came expecting a scared girl but encountered a scary one instead!' Sid quipped making both his friends laugh.

'Let's get away from here,' Abhi whispered quickly as he noticed Aashi stirring at the sound of their laughter.

'No, go back to sleep. I'm fine and feeling sleepy too,' Priyam said.

'Sure?' Abhi asked, a bit uncertainly.

'Yes, sure. I'll sleep. You go back to your rooms too.'

'Okay,' Sid replied, 'but if you feel scared, just come knocking or call. Okay?'

'Okay,' Priyam nodded.

'Well then, goodnight and take care,' said Abhi, planting a quick kiss at her forehead and walking off to his room that was just next door. 'Goodnight, Sid,' he called out.

'Goodnight,' Sid replied and turned back towards Priyam, 'You'll be okay, right?' he asked.

'Yes,' she said, focussing her eyes at his face.

Perhaps it was the urging of those eyes. Perhaps, he had waited too long already. He still halted a second, hesitating, almost deliberating a sudden urge. Then, he bent down, giving her the first token of love that was now bounding to cross the threshold of friendship and dance into the happy precincts of love.

'Goodnight,' Sid breathed, his eyes roving over Priyam's face as if it was for the first time they were seeing her. Next instant he had loosened his grip on her arms and stepped back. His eyes were still fixed on her, but now they were smiling and so was he, smiling with pleasure and surprise that reflected on Priyam's face too, as a warm glow that was forcing her to lower her eyes. In a moment Sid was gone, and she heard the soft thud of his door closing.

'Goodnight,' Priyam murmured inaudibly and slumped against the wall. She could almost hear her heart's startled response as she remained glued to the instant that had passed away so quickly and yet refused to leave her. Priyam's palms tightened into clenched fists as she closed her eyes and relived the magic again and again. Slowly her breath resumed its steadier pace and heart quieted down a little. But the touch of Sid's lips was still warm on hers, his grasp still pressed against her arms. Silently, Priyam glided into her room and laid herself on the bed. No longer did she notice the thunder reverberating in the air, no more the flash of lightning jolted her. Sid's love was with her. She was safe.

Taking early morning walks through the grounds was a routine the three friends followed religiously whenever they were in the Retreat. And even an all night long rain and storm could not deter them from this routine. And it can be safely attested too that the wet grass and muddy ground did nothing to lessen their pleasure and the freshly washed verdure and the absence of any interfering presence rather increased it to some considerable extent. And though Abhi and Priyam did not say it as openly as Sid, they too rejoiced in the fact that Raj had gone to his farmhouse on the previous evening itself, and Aashi had still been sleeping when they began their morning walk.

But a morning walk, no matter how pleasant, could not last forever. And finally, at ten a.m. they went back to the house.

As the three entered, they found Aashi waiting impatiently in the drawing room. 'Where have you guys been?' she asked immediately. 'I was just coming out to find you.'

'Well, we are back so no need to do that now,' said Abhi.

'I know,' she replied. 'Raj too is coming,' she added after a moment.

'Raj?' Abhi repeated.

'Coming here?' Sid asked, 'How do you know?'

'I…was getting so bored. You guys were taking so long. So I just called him, to ask if he was okay. He was about to leave for home.'

'So? You are not going back too, are you?' Priyam asked, with some concern.

'No, I'm not. I'm…we all can go if you guys agree.'

'Where?' Abhi asked.

'To Raj's farmhouse,' Aashi murmured and watched out anxiously for their reactions. A moment of silence followed her declaration. No one knew just how to react or reply. Priyam kept on watching her, trying to grasp exactly what Aashi was trying to tell them. Sid gave out a gruff laugh and walked away. 'What do you say, Abhi?' Aashi tried again, turning towards him.

'I say that you should have thought it out a little before forming that plan. After what happened yesterday, it would be awkward not only for Priyam and Sid, but for Raj too. I don't think going to his farm house would be a good idea, not so soon at least.'

'But Raj needs to be with someone too. You all are so happy here, and he's all alone and disappointed. *Somebody* must be with him.'

'Well, we won't stop *you* from going,' Abhi muttered.

'I knew, and I wanted to see his farmhouse so much. So he said that he would either send somebody or come himself to pick me up.'

'Have you had breakfast?'

'Yes…I didn't know how long you might take…'

'Well, you've settled everything already. I hope you'll have a nice time. If you'll excuse me now. I need to go and wash my hands,' Abhi said walking towards his room.

'But, is it okay?' Aashi called from behind.

'Sure,' he replied without turning and walked away quickly.

'Well, *that* was convincing!' Aashi muttered to herself as she walked over to the window to wait for the little red car.

However, instead of her favourite car in the whole world, a beaten old jeep drove up with a rough looking farmhand on the driver's seat.

This was not what Aashi had bargained for. Her spirits suffered another setback when she experienced the awkwardness of leaving all her friends looking out at her while she climbed alone on such a vehicle with such a companion. She looked at her fine clothes and then at the dusty seat of the vehicle Raj had sent for her. She cast a sidelong glance at the driver and found him less than pleasant or even respectful. A lump seemed to rise up in Aashi's throat, choking the voice of protest that she wanted to utter. She half made up her mind to refuse. But she could not.

She could not turn back to the faces that she knew were staring out at her with expressions too forbearing to bear. It was her own doing and she would see it through. Quickly Aashi climbed up on the jeep and focused her whole attention on gathering her skirt around her, thereby making it impossible for her to look up and wave back at her friends as the jeep drove out of the driveway and left the Retreat behind.

***

Chapter 14

It is the same! – For, be it joy or sorrow
The path of its departure still is free;
Man's yesterday may ne'er be like his morrow
Nought may endure but Mutability.

— *Mutability by P. B Shelly*

As the jeep drove Aashi to the front entrance of Raj's farmhouse, Aashi could not help but marvel at what she saw. Every inch of R.S. Farms was designed and decorated in a way to display luxury at its best. From the driveway that led to the farm, to the farmhouse itself, everything was neat, trim and luxurious. Instead of the simple cottage like in the Retreat, the farmhouse here was a grand structure, blazing white with rows of windows boasting the numbers of rooms that it had.

And right in front of it was standing the most handsome man in the world, waiting just for her.

'Hi, and welcome. Sorry I couldn't bring myself to go there. But I hope you had no trouble,' Raj said, as he helped her down the jeep and ushered her inside the farmhouse.

'No, no problem,' Aashi replied with a smile. She had forgotten all her resentment at the jeep and its driver with just one look at Raj.

'Please come in. I'm so glad you came. Now at least I can have someone to talk too.' Aashi smiled again, with pleasure now and almost thanked herself for her own perseverance.

'You have a very nice farm,' she said after Raj had ushered her to a comfortable sofa.

'Yes, but you've hardly seen it.'

'Whatever I saw while driving in is all very nice.'

'Priyam would have liked it too, don't you think?'

'I'm sure, anybody would like it. It's so beautifully managed and well groomed.'

'Yeah, but she still prefers that half-wild place of his. Anyway, when are they getting engaged?' Raj asked all of a sudden.

'I don't think they have discussed engagement yet,' Aashi replied.

'They would, soon. Once Sid has brought it up, there's nothing to stop them from rushing into it.'

'Maybe, but sooner or later, hardly matters.'

'Yes, all the same for me. But I hope they would wait at least…but as you said, it hardly matters,' Raj muttered.

A long silence ensued while Raj lost himself in his thoughts and Aashi tried to think up same way to start the conversation again. 'So how many rooms do you have here?' she asked finally.

'Six bedrooms. We also have a games room and a very nice library which I'm sure Priyam…but as you said, hardly matters now.'

'Stop thinking about her now, Raj, it's no use.'

'I know. It's no use. But it will take time to stop thinking about her.'

'I know. That's why I've come here to help you divert yourself. And one way I can do that is by forcing you to give me a round of your farmhouse.'

'That would be a pleasure,' he replied, finally breaking into a smile.

He began the tour by showing Aashi around the house. She felt strange going in and out of large, luxurious rooms. It was almost like roaming in the palace of her own dreams. But it was more wonderful, because everything was real.

'Come here, Aashi, and see this sculpture,' Raj called her towards a window when they had gone through nearly half of the house.

She quickly walked over and looked out at a dancing couple surrounded by streams of water rising up and falling around them.

'Beautiful!' she murmured.

'Yes, I love it too,' he replied, 'it looks especially gorgeous at night when the lights are on too.'

'Wish I could see it at night,' Aashi said as she continued gazing at it. 'All this must have cost a lot.'

'Not really, our residence in London cost much more.'

'My, you are really rich, aren't you? Do you ever really know how much money you have?' she asked laughing.

'Yes of course, lots,' Raj replied in the same lighter vein as they roamed around in the house.

'Is Sid's father as rich too?' Aashi asked as they stepped out and began the round of the park.

'Yes, he is. Recently Mr. Vardhan has acquired a new company that has made him even richer. But you won't judge that by his house. I guess he belongs to those who boast of their love for simpler living,' Raj said, then after a silence of few moments added, 'Mr. Vardhan once was a major partner in our hospital too. He opted out after his wife died. Had some kind of problem with my mother and decided he didn't want to have anything to do with us. Though I can tell you he respected my father a lot, and I guess, still does.'

'What kind of problem?' Aashi asked with curiosity.

'Well, my mother had something to do with busting his affair with some woman. His wife and my mother were best friends you know. My mother revealed everything to Mrs. Vardhan, and it all led to the poor lady killing herself.'

'But was Mr. Vardhan really to blame?'

'I don't know. I mean, I've met Mr. Vardhan on several occasions, concerning business of course. He seems like a very respectable man to me. But you never know. Men can go wrong sometimes, even the best of them.'

'Priyam really loves him.'

'Yeah, she loves both of them. And for her sake I hope the father and son will patch up. It won't do her much good to be stuck between the two,' said Raj.

The mention of Priyam brought a shade of sadness once again on his face. 'Anyway,' he said after a moment, 'how do you like the park?'

'Magnificent, as everything else, so neat, pretty and stylish,' Aashi said, gazing around. 'How wonderful it must be to loiter here, sitting on stylish chairs, taking small sips of tea from little and delicate teacups.'

'Yeah, you got the idea,' Raj said laughing and feeling pleased with her enthusiasm. 'You know what I always wished, whenever I came here?'

'What?'

'To walk like this, in a leisurely way, laughing and chatting and admiring the beauty of the place…with Priyam.'

'Well, everything is there, except I have taken the place of Priyam.'

Raj's head jerked at the words.

He looked at her. She was gorgeous, no doubt. And she was so much more like him in matters of taste and inclinations than he had ever found Priyam to be. But can Raj give her, or anyone else, the place in his heart he had for Priyam?

'*Never!*'

The voice of protest rose up in Raj's heart. And yet, he was aware of feeling that it would perhaps have been better had he met Aashi before he fell in love with Priyam.

But of course, that story could never be now because Raj believed that already a tale had been inscribed over his heart and there was no more blank space left to write some more. The existing marks would have to diminish first, but right now, it felt as if they had been impressed on him with an indelible ink.

The day quickly wore out into a wet evening that forced Raj and Aashi to stay indoors until it was time for them to start the journey back home. Of course, Aashi had decided to return with Raj instead of going back to 'The Retreat' to stay on with her friends.

It was around five when Raj's car sped out of the farm, thus ending what, to Aashi at least, had been quite a satisfactory visit. A day of her life had been spent in the lap of luxury, away from the mundane realities of her own world. And she had loved every moment of it. She looked back fondly at the place as Raj drove her away from it, reminiscing every moment that she had passed in it, every dialogue that she had shared with its owner, and every smile that she had managed to bring up on his handsome face. That was all she had gone there for, Aashi told herself. She had had no other expectations of course, so there was no disappointment too. Raj had been his usual affable self, a little subdued, but attentive and caring as always. He had not disappointed any of her hopes, it was another matter however that he had not raised any either.

The same cheerful music was playing in the car, yet Aashi scarcely heard it this time. Not because she had been too busy chatting with Raj, on the contrary, there had taken place little conversation between them all through the journey. All day long, it had been Aashi who had been initiating the conversation, but now she had too many thoughts of her own to listen too, too many questions to reply or parry, and far too many answers to accommodate.

Even when Raj brought the car to a halt near her house, Aashi found herself hoping her mother had not yet returned. She wanted to sit quietly and say not a word, for an hour at least. The last thing that she wanted to do was to listen to the household news of uncles and aunts from her mother.

'Well, here's your home,' Raj said, stopping his car. Aashi cast one look at her home and then at him.

'Yes, there's my house,' she murmured softly as she opened the door and got down. 'Well, thanks…for everything,' she said.

'I must thank you too. It would have been a totally lousy day had you not come,' Raj said, smiling a little.

'Next time you are in danger of having a lousy day, just remember that I'm always here for you,' she replied.

A slight smile was all the response Raj gave her as his eyes turned towards Priyam's house.

'Well then, goodbye,' Aashi said, taking a step away from the car.

'Yeah, goodbye,' he said, starting his vehicle.

'I hope I'll see you soon,' she uttered softly, more in the form of a question than a friendly wish.

'I...don't think so.'

'What? Why?' Aashi asked with shock, but by then his car had zoomed beyond the reach of her trembling voice.

The words kept on echoing in her ears as Aashi opened the gate and walked in. That possibility had never occurred to her before.

But of course, he didn't frequent these roads to visit her. It was to see Priyam that he came. Why would he come now? In all the little conversations that Aashi had had with him that day, there wasn't a one to give her even a feeble hope that he might perhaps drop by to see her. Aashi's heart sank as she realized that she might perhaps never see Raj again.

A sudden exhaustion overpowered her as she dragged her leaden steps to the door.

A week passed, a week of hectic work for Aashi, more a deliberate choice than necessity of chance. Every minute of leisure that Aashi could avoid, she did, because leisure brought thoughts and thoughts just then had no scope of having even a slight flavour of joy.

And with thoughts, she avoided company. Because when Abhi, Priyam and Sid returned, they brought all their happy cheer back with them. And it became just as difficult for Aashi to bear their happiness as it was to suffer her miserable loss.

It was just too hard at that time to laugh and chat as if nothing had happened while she felt as if her whole world had crashed into doom forever. It had been so much better when she had only a vague shadow to love and adore. At least there was no fear of losing then. Fear that was becoming more a certainty with every passing day.

A fortnight had passed and still Aashi had had not a glimpse of Raj. She didn't even know if he was still in the city or not. What irked her even more was that while she counted the days, the very girl whom Raj loved so much didn't even have a thought to spare for him.

It was getting harder now to feel so very happy when Priyam came rushing to her with a heart full of happiness and love shining coyly in her eyes.

Abhi had started forming plans about his sister's engagement and even her wedding and to Priyam's delight, she had witnessed no avoidance or a wish to delay in Sid's replies. Priyam's heart had taken up a melody of its own and Abhi had often caught her twirling to this tune that only she could hear. A faint echo of dread still ached in Priyam's heart but now it was easier for pleasure to break the barriers of her silence and reserve and murmur some soft, gentle assertions of pure bliss.

Fortunately, Priyam wasn't a girl to indulge in untamed effusions of feelings. But whatever little she shared, it only served to remind Aashi how contrary her own situation had suddenly become. Try as she might, Aashi could never forget the fact that her friend's happiness was the cause of Raj's gloom and her own hopelessness. Not that Aashi blamed Priyam for being too happy. She rather blamed herself for being a selfish and ungenerous friend who remained busy in counting her own sores when Priyam was experiencing the happiest time of her life, and that too after having suffered so much.

It was not that Aashi didn't try. But she couldn't be happy when all her joy had gone away from her, perhaps never to return. And it made her feel mean and selfish, and even more miserable.

And then there was Abhi, calmly displaying the abundance of the virtue Aashi found so impossible even to pretend at.

She had finally come to suspect that Abhi loved her. But that didn't mean that she was ready to accept his love too. Abhi should have known better. She could not love him. She did not want to love him. And she would not.

She would have liked to simply give a shake to her long curls and dismiss it all as something that was totally Abhi's problem, not hers. That had always been her way, hadn't it? But somehow, she couldn't do that now. Not to Abhi. He said nothing, and yet his very silence seemed to be controlling her every response towards him. He demanded nothing and yet made Aashi feel helpless despite all her haughty indifference. She hated it all. Abhi had no right to love her. She hated him for daring to love her.

But it was not his fault and she had no right either to think so badly of him. She despised herself for hating him.

Life had suddenly become so unbearable. And there was no way she could have escaped. Not with the loan she had buried herself under that very month.

The old woman who owned the boutique had decided that she didn't want to return. She had offered to sell the business to Aashi.

'It's a golden opportunity, Aashi,' Abhi had said when she had discussed the offer with him, 'you must not miss it.'

'Do you really think so?' she had asked.

Of course, Aashi knew that Abhi wouldn't have said it had he not been fully convinced himself. It had not been a year since she knew him, and Aashi had come to trust Abhi enough to go blindly by his word.

'Absolutely,' he had replied.

'But it'll take money, Abhi, lots of it.'

'Don't worry about that. I'll help you get a loan.'

'Oh, do you really think it's possible?' she had burst out with excitement. What just five minutes earlier had seemed so impossible to her, suddenly had started appearing easy and within her reach.

It really was a blessing to have a friend like Abhi.

'*If only… he could be content with just being a friend,*' Aashi often thought.

How efficiently Abhi had managed everything. Getting the loan, examining the deal that she had been offered, and finally getting it clinched to his own satisfaction.

And before Aashi knew it, she had become the owner of a reputed and popular boutique.

That was about a week before the trip to the farm house. How happy she was then. Everything had seemed to be going in the right direction.

The moment she had acquired the boutique, she had started dreaming of expanding it, developing it into a chain of stores, of taking it to other cities, and then, of course, to other countries.

How quickly her dreams had come crashing down. Though Aashi's business was going well, and most of her innovative schemes picked up good results, it somehow began to seem like a drag too soon. Breaking down of one dream had caused the downfall of the rest. .

There was only one hope that remained though; the hope that one day Raj would get over his heartbreak. Perhaps then he would think of Aashi and maybe pay her a visit; it wasn't important then it it were only for the sake of her friendship. He couldn't have forgotten her so entirely, could he? She just had to wait, with the hope that one day she will see him again.

Wait is a small word, easily spoken, but really hard to bear. Aashi's wait however, proved to be shorter than she had expected.

August was still looming over when Aashi returned from work only to find Raj's car parked in front of Abhi's gate.

'Raj!' she whispered to herself. How Aashi wanted to run up and confront him. But she stopped right there; in the middle of the road, her eyes staring at the car with feet suddenly rooted to the spot.

'Hi, Aashi,' the sound reached her ears. The sound she had been yearning to hear for so long. 'How are you?' Raj asked, opening the gate of Abhi's home and coming out to meet her.

'Raj? I'm so glad to see you!' Aashi murmured, finally managing to take few steps towards him.

'It's nice to see you too,' he said with a smile. 'Priyam tells me you work till very late these days and I feared I won't be able to meet you.'

'Yes…but how are you, Raj?' Aashi asked her eyes anxiously scanned his face for any sign of gloom.

'I'm having a party tomorrow, so I guess, I must be okay,' he replied, looking down on his shoes and crunching a lump of mud with them.

'Party? Oh, of course! It's your birthday tomorrow!'

'You knew?' Raj asked with surprise.

'Sure I do.'

'Well, I was just coming to your house, to invite you and your mother. I hope you'd come.'

'Oh, thanks,' she said happily, 'I would surely, but I can't say about my mother. She never goes to parties.'

'Well, you come.'

'I will,' Aashi replied with assurance. A long moment passed as both of them stood in silence. Though at least one of them was trying desperately to think of something to talk and let the moments linger on.

It was Raj however who spoke first. 'How about a walk?' he said, 'My mother is still inside, giving Priyam all the details of tomorrow's party. She won't come out so soon and…I can't go in again. Perhaps if Abhi had returned…'

'Let me just put my bag inside,' Aashi replied, rushing to unload her burden so she could fly once again and feel the surge of hope rushing back.

As Aashi came out again, she could hear the sound of Mrs. Sinha sharing her ever-expanding wisdom with Priyam.

'Poor Priyam!' Aashi muttered under her breath, 'Why does she always have to suffer her alone?'

Had it been any other time, Aashi would have rushed to relieve her friend. But now she had someone else to attend to, someone who needed her company just as much, perhaps even more sorely.

Priyam indeed was having a hard time. It had hardly been fifteen minutes since Raj and his mother had knocked on her door. But it already appeared as if her ears had been under the onslaught for over an hour.

It would have been a relief had Raj remained with them. He, at least, knew how to keep his mother in check. And then, Priyam really wanted to talk to Raj, to relieve her worry about him and try and soothe his hurt. But Raj gave her no chance. He accompanied his mother inside, stayed for two minutes and opened his mouth only to ask how everybody was and invite them all for the party. And then, without even stopping to ask if they would come or not, he excused himself and walked out, leaving his mother behind.

Mrs. Sinha, though seemed to have no intention of leaving so early. Not till she had seen what she wanted to see.

While entering the house, Mrs. Sinha had heard and seen a little something that had piqued her curiosity.

'I think we should come later, Mom,' Raj had whispered, stopping immediately.

'Why? What happened?' Mrs. Sinha had whispered back, though she could also hear the sounds that had put a stop at her son's feet. But her delicacy of manner had never included the idea of not butting in an argument. She rather thought it her sublime duty to interfere and pass a judgement. But before that, it was essential to eavesdrop a bit and know what the little argument between Sid and Priyam was all about. So she had halted near the window and took the opportunity to hear and see all that was going inside the house. Raj though had retraced a couple of steps and stood a little way away.

'But at least have a look at the letter, Sid, and see how happy he is!' Priyam was saying.

'I don't care, Priyam. And you can't force me to,' Sid replied without taking his eyes away from the book he was reading.

'I hope you won't be so rude to him when he comes,' said Priyam.

'He's coming?' Sid said, finally looking up from the book

'Of course he will. I'll send him an invitation as soon as we decide upon the engagement date.'

'My ... Mr. Vardhan? You will invite him?' Sid asked again.

'Won't you?' Priyam asked back, bewildered at such an unthinkable prospect.

'What made you think I would?' Sid threw a question back at her.

'But... we must, Sid, he's your father!'

'He's nobody to me,' Sid shouted.

'But he's still my guardian and I...I would invite him to my engagement.'

No docile gentleness trembled in her voice now. The girl knew she was right and would not let her meekness draw her back from asserting so. She had never yet interfered between Sid and his father. But there is a limit to remain quiet when you know you are not indifferent. She could not, and she would not let Sid be so cruel to his own father.

'Get engaged to somebody else then!' Sid spat out with rage and walked out of the house, nearly colliding into Mrs. Sinha. 'Oh,' he mumbled, not bothering to tone down the gruffness in his voice, 'What are you doing here?'

'I…came to invite you all, it's my birthday tomorrow,' Raj somehow managed to reply.

'She's inside,' Sid replied and walked off.

Mrs. Sinha meanwhile kept herself busy in peeking inside. She saw Priyam pick up an envelope and remove a letter from it. A peculiar mix of happiness and dread shaded the girl's face as she looked at it. Of course, this was enough to arouse Mrs. Sinha's curiosity. But what irked her more was the hurried manner in which Priyam hid the letter in a book when she noticed the lady looking in.

Now, as Mrs. Sinha talked and chatted in most unconcerned manner, without casting one glance at the book, it was the only thing that she was focused on. The lady knew that she had to have a look at the letter. It was clear that the letter was from someone she knew all too well. But curiosity demanded she should know what it contained as well.

And she got the opportunity to do so when Priyam left the lady alone to get some tea for her.

As soon as Priyam walked into her kitchen, Mrs. Sinha leaned forward and fished out the letter from the book. As she had suspected, it was from Mr. Vardhan. Not a moment did Mrs. Sinha hesitate as her eyes quickly ran over the letter and she began reading.

"Dear Priyam,

As I sit here, so far away from my only son, it's the thought of you and Abhi being with him that relieves me and assures me of his well-being. And of course, your kind letters are a blessing too.

I must confess that it has been some time since I've been expecting this particular news to snoop from letters. Every time I saw one in my mail, I always opened it expecting news of your engagement. And today, it has finally arrived."

'Oh, so that's why Raj has been trying to leave for London and has been walking around with such a long face,' Mrs. Sinha muttered to herself before quickly reading on.

Finally, what I always wished for is coming true. Didn't I always know that this day would come? It was not for nothing that I willed away all my property to Sid's wife. I knew well who she was going to be."

'Willed away all his property to Sid's wife?' Mrs. Sinha murmured to herself. Her eyes quickly scanned the rest of the letter but found nothing in it to interest her. 'to Sid's wife…' she repeated to herself again as she folded the letter and slid it back in its hiding place. 'Well,' she muttered, leaning back in the sofa, 'that changes everything.'

✳✳✳

Chapter 15

My soul is like the oar that momently
Dies in a desperate stress beneath the wave,
Then glitters out again and sweeps the sea:
Each second I'm new-born from some new grave.

—*'Struggle' by: Sidney Lanier (1842-1881)*

After an age of despair, the day had finally come when hopes started breathing again in Aashi's heart and her lost smile had found its way.

Raj was back, and she was to go to his birthday party. And that, of course, was an event momentous enough to require Aashi to spend full two hours before her mirror, and then ten minutes more to make sure the two hours had been well spent.

When Aashi was sure she had done all there was to do with her face, dress and accessories, Aashi rushed to elicit from Priyam some reassuring comments about the success of her labour.

'How do I look?' were the first words that came out of Aashi's mouth when the door opened to welcome her in. In a moment, the query had been uttered. And in that very moment too, she had realized that it was Abhi who stood before her, not Priyam.

He stood still, caught in the enchantment too potent for a mortal's heart to withstand. It was not for long, barely a few seconds at most, but those few seconds seemed long enough for Aashi to squirm between the regret of being too eager with her question and the hope that he had perhaps not heard it.

But Abhi had, because the very next moment he smiled, 'You look fabulous, as always. Though you really had no need to use so much make up,' he said.

'No need? But it's Raj's party. And I want to look my best,' Aashi declared.

'Then just let your natural beauty shine,' Abhi said. He smiled at her. His eyes seemed to caress her face.

Colour rose up Aashi's cheeks as her eyes became stilled on him.

But the smile on his face faded away as swiftly as it had appeared. 'Priyam's in her room,' he said, then turned and strode inside.

A deep breath trembled through Aashi. 'Okay,' Aashi muttered, more to herself than to him.

An unexpected knot had risen up in her throat, forcing her to take a deep breath before entering the house and running upstairs. She would have liked to ask Abhi when they would start for Raj's party, but right at that moment, she would have done anything except call him back.

Soon she reached Priyam's room. 'Priyam?' she called out.

'Come in, Aashi,' Priyam replied from her dressing table, 'I'm ready and…wow, you look…gorgeous!' she exclaimed as she turned around. 'What a lovely dress! Did you design it?'

'Yes, last month. But I had thought I would never be able to wear it.'

'What made you think that? It's a very nice dress and perfectly wearable. Just have a look at yourself and see how lovely you look in it.'

The invitation was accepted readily and Aashi walked up to the big mirror and twirled around to once again observe herself from every possible angle.

But as she did so, her eyes found themselves staring at Abhi, instead of her own reflection. Not that Aashi was wishing to see him again before her, not so soon at least. But there he was, uninvited and unwelcome maybe, but vivid to the least detail, exactly as he had stood at the door a few minutes ago. How handsome he looked and…how…totally lost…even to himself. The smile he had readied perhaps for Aashi's welcome still hanging around the corners of his mouth but, looking lost and forgotten. Those penetrating brown eyes of his groping for a way out through a chasm as he stood still, forgetful of his own very self.

She felt a strange urge to run to him and give him a hug and make him happy again.

Just then the doorbell rang.

Her gorgeous self reappeared in the mirror to sparkle in her eyes. And Abhi vanished.

As Abhi led Aashi into Raj's party, he was once again in perfect control of himself. The momentary lapse of the evening had received a thorough self-chiding and a firmer control had been pulled over his features and manners.

'There's Raj,' he told Aashi as soon as he spotted their host.

'Where?' Aashi asked. Her eyes scanned the brightly lit ground, but couldn't spot Raj. Abhi directed her gaze to Raj as he rushed to meet them.

'Hi! Good to see you all,' said Raj as soon as he reached them.

'Happy birthday!' Aashi said excitedly as he shook her hand. Abhi, Priyam and Sid echoed the greeting too.

'Thanks,' he said, taking a good look at her. 'You look lovely.'

Aashi smiled with pleasure. However, the very next moment she saw Raj look at Priyam, and could not help but feel a pinch as a shade of gloom came over his face. 'Priyam, when did you start wearing *sarees*?'

'Oh, I...I thought I might try it today,' Priyam replied.

'It looks good on you,' Raj murmured. He let his eyes linger a moment longer on her charming countenance. 'I'm so glad you all have come,' he added, not untruthfully.

He led them to a round table decked in black satin and lace. A lovely arrangement of flowers sat in the exact centre of the table adding a touch of colour to the setting.

'You'll have to excuse me now,' Raj said, almost apologetically. 'I must attend to others as well. Since Dad's not here, I have to take care of his guests too. But I'll be back as soon as possible.'

'Sure,' Abhi replied, 'get going, and don't worry about us. We'll be a merry little party.'

'I know, but I hope you won't mind me being a part of that merriment. I can hope for that much now can't I?' Raj said, looking pointedly at Priyam. 'I'll be back soon,' he added and rushed off with extended hand to greet a middle-aged gentleman dressed in a business suit and looking all stern and serious.

Meanwhile, the four friends settled down comfortably on the table.

However, two fleeting moments later Aashi started feeling restless and wished Raj would return soon.

'The music is so nice. Perfect for dancing,' she said as her foot began following the rhythm unconsciously.

'Do you want to dance?' Abhi asked, looking at anything except her.

'Can't help it,' she replied, laughing.

Finally, Abhi turned his eyes towards her. She was gazing at the couples dancing just few meters from their table. Her foot tapped the ground and fingers drummed the table. She clearly was finding it difficult to sit still. And it was getting harder for him to stay unaffected too, despite all his recently refreshed resolves.

'Aashi,' he began softly, 'would you...'

'What?' she asked turning her face towards him while still laughing at the antics of one of the dancers.

'...dance with me?' Abhi asked.

'You? You can't dance! The last time you tried me, you fell down. Have you forgotten?' she said, laughing at the very ridiculousness of the idea of Abhi dancing on stage.

'Yes, I had forgotten,' said Abhi. 'There's Raj,' he added a moment later, 'you can dance with him. He's sturdy enough on his feet, I guess.'

Aashi visibly squirmed at Abhi's words. She knew she had hurt him. She cursed herself for once again losing her tongue. But it was all his fault. He should have known better than to have made such a demand from her.

Aashi's feet stamped on the ground, though quite out of tune now. But she was determined not to let Abhi or anyone else spoil her evening. 'I wish Raj would ask me,' she said a moment later, almost with too great a display of excitement than was needed. 'I'm sure he must be an excellent dancer.'

'*So is my brother!*' Priyam wanted to cry out. But Abhi's eyes caught her and bid her to remain silent. He too had remained silent. He had already said too much, and he had only himself to curse, and this he did thoroughly well.

Raj had promised to return soon, and he did. 'Hey, guys, hope you are not getting too bored,' he said.

'Aashi was. Well, Aashi, Raj is here, why don't you go and dance?' Abhi said.

'Why don't you all come?' Raj asked.

'You know, Raj, I don't dance. But you can take Priyam and Abhi,' Sid replied.

'Well, Priyam?' Raj turned to her, but already knew her answer. As he had expected, Priyam refused with all her politeness. She couldn't imagine twirling around in front of so many people.

'Just get over your shyness once, Priyam. You can dance with Abhi, if with nobody else. Why...'

'You and Aashi go ahead, Raj,' Abhi interrupted him, 'we'll join you soon. Just let me finish my juice,' he said, showing him his half-empty glass.

'Alright then, come, Aashi,' said Raj, as he led Aashi to the dance floor. Only once did he look at Priyam, not so much with reproach as with an entreaty. 'Come soon,' he added, turning towards Abhi.

'We will,' Abhi replied, 'you go on.'

Priyam and Sid's eyes followed Raj and Aashi as they went to dance, but Abhi's stayed glued to his half filled glass which he had no intention of emptying any time soon.

'He's an excellent dancer,' Sid commented after having watched them dance for nearly five minutes.

'You dance well too,' said Priyam, smiling shyly as her eyes lit up with the remembrances of times when Sid had twirled her around to the tunes of his favourite songs, sometimes in her living room, and sometimes even in the kitchen.

'Well, I don't know about that. And I don't care, as long as I manage to please my dance partner,' said Sid, looking at Priyam in a way that forced her to lower her eyes and blush with pleasure.

Abhi could not help but smile too to see Priyam so happy. Her happiness was the only thing he asked whenever he prayed to God now. It was all he had for sustenance. He could be quiet happy as long as she was content. Being happy for Priyam was good enough. Sure, the pain of his own loneliness wouldn't leave him. It felt hurtful even now at that moment throbbing fresh and smarting in his heart. But Abhi knew all too well to be happy in misery. All he had to do was to stop feeling, to flick off the switch, to make himself apathetic to his own emotions. He had mastered that over time. He couldn't let a trifle spoil his joy in Priyam's bliss. It was a happy evening, everyone was happy, so would he . With this familiar resolution, Abhi smiled and laughed and blinked away the speck of dust that was irritating his eyes for quiet sometime.

'Where's Aashi? I can't see her anywhere on the dance floor,' Priyam said after some time.

'They are not dancing,' Abhi replied.

'They are not?' Sid asked with surprise.

'Yes, I can't see them anywhere,' said Priyam, craning her neck to search them out.

'Where have they gone?' Sid asked, looking straight at Abhi.

'I don't know,' Abhi replied and turned his face away.

Of course, he knew where Raj and Aashi were, he knew that very well. Just five minutes ago he had seen them walk into the house.

It had been nearly twenty minutes since Aashi had begun dancing through her dream. Nothing seemed real, nothing seemed possible, and yet it was happening. It was happening! The dances, the thrilling music, proximity to Raj and the jealous looks constantly being darted at her. It was all happening, it was all real, and this was just the beginning. There was magic in Aashi's steps as they moved on their own. There was enchantment in the music that reverberated the air like a racing heartbeat. And the minutes that flew away seemed to be blessed by a divine spell.

Not for a moment did it occur to Aashi that the pleasure she saw in Raj's eyes might just be momentary, a mere enjoyment of dancing with a pretty girl. Not for a fleeting moment did she care that even while dancing with her, his eyes continued to flit towards Priyam.

And when he stopped suddenly and stepped away from the dance floor, Aashi still didn't care to realize that it might have something to do with the way Priyam was chatting with Sid.

'Do you want to see my home?' Raj asked all of a sudden.

'What?' Aashi asked, trying to listen through the loud music.

'I said, would you like to see my home?' he repeated in a louder voice this time.

'Sure,' Aashi replied.

'Good, let's go then.'

'Let me just tell…'

'Don't worry, we'll be back in few minutes,' Raj said, as he saw Aashi hesitating.

As they walked towards the house, there seemed to be a purpose in Raj's gait.

'What's up with him?' Aashi wondered, as she tried to match her pace to his stride. 'Slow down, Raj,' she called out as they neared the house and Raj's gait somehow acquired greater urgency.

'Oh, sorry,' he said slowing down immediately. 'You must be tired after all that dancing.'

'Do you realize that everybody is staring at us?' Aashi asked.

A sudden dread had begun to beat in Aashi's heart. There was something wrong, she was sure about that. She could see it in the grimness of Raj's eyes. His hands were stuffed deep in his pockets and as he looked at her, there was this strange sense of fatality in his look that chilled Aashi to the very core.

'Do you care?' Raj asked without turning.

'No,' Aashi replied and continued following his steps. He led her straight to his room.

'How big this room is, and so beautifully decorated,' she burst out as soon as she entered it. 'And hey, you can see the entire lawn from this window,' she said walking quickly to the big window. 'How grand the party looks from up here!'

'Never mind the room and God damn the party!' Raj muttered as he poured out some water for himself and emptied the glass in one gulp.

'What?' Aashi asked, whirling around with shock and amazement.

'Sorry. I shouldn't have…'

'No problem. There must be something troubling you. But please don't damn the party. It's the best party I've ever been to and the most grand.'

'Well, while you are celebrating you might as well make it grand. Besides, our parties always manage to make themselves a semi-business affair, so we have to keep them good.'

'It's such a pity your father couldn't come,' Aashi said after sometime, stepping away from the window as she noticed Abhi coming towards the house too. She didn't want Abhi to see her there. He must certainly be looking for her, Aashi knew that very well, but she was in no mood to be found just yet.

'He wanted to come, but I told him not to,' Raj said, motioning Aashi to sit down. He too sat down, pulling his chair a little closer to her.

'You told him not to? Why?' Aashi asked with surprise. Things were getting too baffling and she didn't like it.

'He would have had to miss an important business meeting and besides… I'll be with him in two days. So there was no need to…'

'What do you mean?' Aashi exclaimed getting up immediately from her chair.

'I'm going, Aashi,' he said, standing up as well.

'You! You…are going?' That certainly wasn't what she had been expecting Raj to say. '*That cannot be!*' she thought. She had hardly had time…that cannot be! He cannot go away from her! '*Not like that…not so soon…*'

'Yes,' Raj replied, 'I believe it would do me good if I get away for a few months, maybe years…'

'Years? No! Please Raj, you can't go,' Aashi said as a dread filled her heart and made her rooted to the spot. She could not let him go. And it wasn't about his money. It was about him, only him and his love. That man standing before her, so handsome, so good, he was her dream, her perfect dream, how could she see him go?

'Why should I stay here? To watch them get married?' Raj smirked.

'But…'

'There's no hope now. They'll soon be engaged and then…married. I can't make a fool of myself by standing there and clapping at my own loss. I'll go to London and try and put Priyam out of my mind.'

'Oh, you must stay, Raj, it's not London that will make you forget Priyam. It will still be up to you to do that. Why should you go so far away?' Aashi cried out as the world came crashing down around her, almost choking her.

A strange fever rose up in her as she realized how near the end was of each one of her dream. The end of love, the end of romance and the end of a life that was to be sung away in his arms. The end was upon her before she had tasted the beginning. She could not let that happen!

'Maybe, but it'll be easier there. I should never have returned. It was only my hope of winning her that made me return. Now that that hope is dead too, why should I…'

'But isn't there anything else that can make you stay?' Aashi interjected. Her mind working quickly to give him a reason, or at least an excuse to linger.

'Like what?'

'Anything, or...anybody?' Aashi said as a resolution quickly took shape in her mind. She cannot let him go, that was certain and she would stop Raj at any cost.

'I don't think so,' Raj said, a little uncertainly though, as the frank admittance of her beseeching eyes trapped his.

'I can't let you go,' Aashi spoke out, plainly and with an authority that surprisingly didn't seem misplaced.

'Why? For what reason...'

'Reason?' Aashi murmured, as she took a step closer to him. She was aware of Abhi's presence just outside the door. She knew he was watching. But what did she care about his hurt when she had decided not to care even for her honour?

'This,' she whispered, touching Raj's hair with her trembling fingers, 'is your reason...' slowly Aashi rose up on her feet and pressed her lips against his. Raj took a step back and tried to resist. But she didn't let go. She couldn't let go. And how long can resistance withstand the onslaught of such delicious passion? How long can a smarting heart defy a soothing balm so generously offered, and so insistently? A surprised moment later Aashi felt Raj's arms too slide up her back and hold her tightly in their grasp. Life rushed back to her as his lips reciprocated, gingerly first but soon with a vigorous desire. It was all that Aashi had wanted, all that she was aware of.

And she wouldn't even have heard the slight creak of the door had Raj not immediately loosened his grasp. 'Who's it?' he asked, leaving her quickly.

'No one,' Aashi replied, 'except you and me. If you'll let it be so,' she said, turning and rushing out of the room just in time to see Abhi descend the stairs. She ran down them too and soon caught up with him.

'Stop, Abhi!' she called out.

Abhi stopped but didn't turn.

'Well?' Aashi said, nearly out of breath with running down the long flight of stairs.

'Well what?'

'I know you saw me.'

'Yes, sorry. I had come to call you. We must leave. It's getting late and your mother told me to...'

'I can explain,' Aashi said.

'You don't need to,' Abhi said as he resumed walking with quick steps.

'But I won't have you judging me without giving me an opportunity to explain.'

'I'm not judging you,' Abhi said without turning.

'Oh yes, you are,' she cried out, 'always, every moment of every day.'

'I'm sorry if you feel like that. But trust me, I don't think wrongly of you. I can never…'

'I know that! You are too good to think wrongly of me, aren't you? You will just make *me* feel bad about myself. But I will not have that way!'

Anger rose up in Aashi's heart. Anger, not just for today but for those many moments she had felt stifled by his benign goodness. Couldn't he be just normal for once?

'Well then, don't,' Abhi said, smiling at Aashi's petulance. What he had witnessed was still floating in the moisture of his eyes. But it was yet to sink in, it was…yet to sink in. And while Abhi sped away from it, as fast as he could, it was well in his power to laugh and smile, even though Aashi herself was walking beside him. It didn't matter, sure, it didn't. There was nothing to be troubled about. It was always to be. He knew it, didn't he? 'Even I won't have it so,' Abhi said, stopping and turning towards her.

'Yeah, as if I can help it,' Aashi said, pacifying immediately like a child under the influence of her parent's eyes. 'Abhi, maybe what I just did was wrong. Maybe *I* am wrong; and bad and selfish too. But one must be a little selfish in this world, don't you think? We don't live in heaven, Abhi. And here, there's no place for people who are too good. All they do is to make others feel worse than they are. I hate such people!'

'You hate me?' Abhi said, directly and unhesitatingly. His eyes narrowed a little at the corners but continued looking straight at her.

Aashi threw back her head in exasperation, closed her eyes tightly shut and cursed herself for once again letting her tongue go out of control. 'No, Abhi…please…you know that I don't know what I say!'

'That's not the answer to my question,' Abhi said, staring straight at her.

'No, I don't hate you,' Aashi said after a moment's silence, letting out a sigh as her shoulders drooped a little and she caught hold of Abhi's arm, 'Though I wish I did. But I can't. You are so good, so damn good! But I can't be that. I can't be so good. I don't want to be so good, Abhi. I can't. I'm mean and selfish, I know, and I…'

'Don't be so hard on yourself. You have a right to choose your love and to fight for it too.'

'I know that. And that's what I am doing. And that's what I will do,' she said, looking straight at him. 'But what do *you* know about fighting for love anyway?'

110

Abhi's head jerked at her words. He stared back at her, not turning his eyes away from her as he so often did. 'What do you want, Aashi?' he said, shrugging her hold from his arm and stepping away. 'You want me to fight for my love? For what? For the love that you can never give me? And that…I probably…no…*certainly* don't even deserve!'

'Don't say that. You do deserve, and lot more…but…oh, give me a moment to explain!' she cried out as he again started moving away.

'I don't want your explanations, Aashi,' he said. 'I understand everything perfectly well.'

'No you don't! And never will!' Aashi shouted, rushing away and leaving him just as stunned with her anger as Raj had been with her sudden love.

As for herself, she felt even more bitter at Abhi now than she ever did. He had spoiled the magic of the moment that Aashi had wanted to bottle up in her heart to colour her solitary moments for a long time. And yet, it seemed to her that despite all her resentment against Abhi, the fault was always hers. He had said nothing wrong. It was she who had shouted at him. Why had she started being so nasty with him? She wasn't such a bad girl. It was he who made her bad by being so unnecessarily good himself.

'Well then,' Aashi told herself as she ran away from Abhi, '*he can be as good as he wants to and I'll be as bad as I need to be! We'll see where it all ends up.*'

111

Chapter 16

You left me, sweet, two legacies,
A legacy of love
A Heavenly Father would content,
Had He the offer of;

You left me boundaries of pain
Capacious as the sea,
Between eternity and time,
Your consciousness and me.

— *"You Left Me, Sweet" by Emily Dickinson.*

'Where's Raj? Have you seen him, Siddharth?' Mrs. Sinha asked, as she paraded her bulk towards their table.

'No, but Abhi's gone to look for them,' Sid replied, standing up slowly and with enough display of unwillingness to compensate judiciously for the troublesome courtesy.

'Them? Don't tell me that girl is with him still. I saw them dancing together. It's so shameless, the way she's following him!

'Your son too doesn't seem to be making much effort to get away from her,' Sid pointed out. 'Maybe he likes Aashi's company.'

'Likes her company? Well,' Mrs. Sinha said, raising her hands up to emphasis her helplessness. 'I won't be surprised if that's the case. I don't know what it is with Raj! Why does he keep running after girls that are so far beneath his status?'

Sid and Priyam looked at each other. It was obvious to both of them that Priyam had somehow managed to fall from the lady's gracious opinion. It was not the only instance they had witnessed the erratic ebb and flow of this formidable force. But as a personal experience, it definitely was their very first, and thus, surprising enough to muddle them speechless. Fortunately, the one good thing about Mrs. Sinha was that she didn't usually require a response, content enough as she was with the sound of her own delightful voice.

'Anyway, let me introduce you to my friends, Mrs. Jagdeesh Thakur, and

Miss Nirupa Arya,' she said, addressing Sid and completely ignoring a very confused Priyam. This was not her usual way. Earlier, it was Priyam whom she paid such attentions while ignoring Sid. 'And this handsome boy,' Mrs. Sinha continued, beaming benevolently at Sid, 'is Siddharth Vardhan.'

Sid was forced to greet the two ladies.

'And who is this charming girl?' Mrs. Thakur asked.

'Oh she, she's only Priyam. An *orphan* whom Sid's father brought up.'

Priyam gaped at Mrs. Sinha with bewilderment. This sudden shift in the lady's perception of her relationship with Mr. Vardhan was beyond Priyam's understanding.

'It's so nice to meet you, Siddharth, after all these years,' Miss Arya gushed. 'You perhaps don't remember me but I was your mother's friend.'

'Nice to meet you too, ma'am,' Sid replied, warming up immediately to the women whom he had just a minute earlier considered beneath his notice.

'You look just like your father, don't you?' Miss. Arya continued, surveying his face with her keen eyes.

'Oh, don't talk about that man, dear. It's too hard for the poor boy, and me too. We hate him. Even my daughter Tina hates him, just as much as we do. His name always reminds me of my dear friend. She was like a sister to me, you know,' said Mrs. Sinha.

Priyam silently reached up and grasped Sid's hand, wrapping her tenderness around his fingers. More than a decade had passed since his mother's demise, but Sid had not yet recovered and to remain calm in such a situation was always painful. Perhaps the manner of her death was what made it so difficult. The misery Sid had witnessed his mother going through still buried lurid in his memory, made it really hard for him to hear or even say anything about her.

'I loved her like my own sister. And poor Kiran was so fond of me and my children too. How she adored my Raj and Tina!' Mrs. Sinha continued. 'I dare say she considered my Tina as her daughter-in-law as soon as she saw Tina as a baby. Of course, Tina was the prettiest baby anybody had ever seen,' said Mrs. Sinha. She stepped closer to Sid and put her hand on his arm. 'I'm sure that had Kiran been alive,' she said, 'she would have never waited this long, Siddharth, to get you and Tina married. Seeing Tina as your wife was the *dearest* wish of her heart, you know. Her last wish.'

Priyam's eyes flew towards Sid at the words. Her mouth suddenly felt parched. Had Sid looked down at her at that moment, he would perhaps have been shocked to see a bloodless face looking up at him. But he didn't look at Priyam. His eyes had become frozen at Mrs. Sinha.

A cloud had risen up to shade his brow at the words. A sable darkness Priyam had often seen brooding in his eyes until a few months ago. But she had thought he had lost it. She had thought her love had dispelled its gloom and replaced it with bright cheer. But here it was again, dark, threatening and seeming to overpower all the brightness that had since been shining in his life, and hers.

'Her...last wish?' he asked.

'Oh, yes, and it was the thought of Tina being your wife that made her happy even in her misery. How can you forget it? I even used to tease you about it when you were younger, don't you remember?'

'Yes...but, I...I ... don't remember *her* saying...' Sid stammered. He did remember hearing about his mother's ardent wish of seeing Tina as his wife. But it had always been through Mrs. Sinha. And hadn't Raj said that she was searching for a *fit match* for Tina?

'How could she have said this to you? You were so young. But she couldn't have been clearer to me. "Dear Maya," she said, "promise me, you'll give your daughter in marriage to Sid, to guarantee his happiness. He might be his father's son, but he's also my blood. Sid would never betray his wife, he'd never hurt Tina if he knew how much I loved her. Promise me you'll marry them, it's my last wish," she said.'

'But...you...I thought...Raj said...' Sid tried to interfere.

'Well, now that the matter has been brought up, isn't it about time you honoured your mother's wishes and give peace to her soul, Siddharth? I can't compel you, of course. You have grown up and probably don't care about your mother as much as you used to do earlier. Perhaps that's why you think nothing of going hand in hand with someone who loves your mother's killer,' said Mrs. Sinha looking pointedly at Priyam. She glared at the girl for a minute more. And then turned and walked away as if in great anger.

Her work was done. With her swift, flickering tongue, Mrs. Sinha had let loose a sting she knew well was lethal. The attack was made, all that remained was for the poison to take its course.

World swooned before Priyam's eyes as every word fell like a blow on her happy dreams. 'Abhi! Where are you, Abhi?' Priyam murmured under her breath as she looked around in desperation. Her world was slipping away from her grasp. Sid's fingers, cold and lifeless, were slipping away and Priyam had no courage to tighten her grasp. 'Abhi, come quick! Where are you?' He was the only soul in the entire world to whom she could turn for solace and help.

Little did she know how much Abhi himself was in need of just such a comfort. If her love was under threat, his was already lost. And the misery was that Abhi could not consider it as a loss too because he had never thought of it as anything else but an impossibility. He had never allowed himself to let false hope indulge his fancy, not consciously at least.

But Priyam knew none of this. All she was aware of was Sid and her empty hand from which his fingers had been drawn away.

Priyam's eyes swept the grounds to look for her brother and were relieved to find Abhi rushing towards them. 'Abhi!' Priyam whispered, and rushed to quell all her fears in her brother's unfailing love.

'What is it? What happened?' Abhi asked with concern, forgetting his own grief with one look at her terrified face.

What could Priyam say? She didn't know for sure. May be nothing had happened, maybe, everything had been lost.

'Nothing,' she murmured.

But Abhi could see that there was something that was really troubling her. 'Why are you trembling, Priyam?' he asked. 'Tell me what has happened.'

So Priyam quickly recounted everything that Mrs. Sinha had said. She could see Abhi purse up his lips and look with concern at Sid. His arm tightened protectively around Priyam's shoulders, but when Abhi spoke, his voice was toned to impart comfort and reassurance. 'Don't worry, Priyam, it doesn't matter. Sid would not let it matter. He loves you. So don't worry,' Abhi said.

Priyam nodded her head in silence, but she could not stop worrying, neither, in fact, could Abhi.

'Where's Aashi?' Priyam asked after a moment as they proceeded towards Sid, 'Didn't you find her?'

'She's coming. There,' Abhi said pointing to where Aashi was slowly approaching them.

Aashi had run away from Abhi in a fit of fury. But it soon cooled down enough to make her realize how late it really was getting. So, unwilling as she was to look at Abhi, she had forced herself to return to the table where she had left her friends.

'Okay, let's leave this place now,' Priyam murmured as the two neared the table where Sid was still standing and looking fixedly at them. Priyam watched him and trembled at the thoughts that she imagined crowding around in his mind.

But right at that moment, no thought raged in Sid's mind, no tumult hollered with passion, not even a feeble voice of protest rose as he stood there, too numb to be capable of any thought. Thoughts would come later, bitter thoughts, agonizing thoughts, thoughts that torture one to reach a decision even more torturous. For the time being though, Sid could look at his love. He could stand still and let moments pass by without disturbing him or making him go forward. He could make himself lifeless to let his life linger a little while more. Strangely, his heart kept on beating though, running through its regular motion in most placid and undisturbed manner. Well, let it beat then, very soon it would have to be divided, one part chosen while the other to be torn out. But till then, Sid was still intact, and for the time being, so was Priyam.

Fifteen minutes later, Priyam was back at her home and trying to unlock the door of her house. Somehow, the key refused to enter the lock.

'Let me do it,' said Abhi, taking the key from her. 'Come in, Sid,' he said when he had got the door to open.

'No. I'm...just leaving,'

'Leaving?' Abhi exclaimed, not hiding his surprise. Priyam too stopped in her tracks as her breath seemed to die away within her.

'Yes.'

'Why? It's Saturday. You never go home on Saturdays.'

'Yes, I know.'

'So?' Abhi asked again.

'I...have to do something. Check some papers. I have to check some papers. I must go,' Sid said. Yet he made no effort to move.

'Are you okay, Sid?' Abhi asked, taking a step back towards him, 'What's the matter?'

Of course, Abhi knew very well what the matter was. But he wanted to hear it from Sid. He wanted to see how much Mrs. Sinha's words had affected his friend. Abhi had hoped that Sid wouldn't take them seriously. It was another matter however if Abhi considered all that he knew of his friend, this little expectation of his seemed gravely ill-founded..

'Nothing's the matter. I just have some work to do. Is it so hard for you to believe?' Sid almost shouted. And then he turned and walked away. Of course, he had to return just a moment later to ask for his helmet and bike's keys. These were soon procured, the bike started, and raced away.

Abhi reached out and wrapped his arm around his sister. 'Don't worry, Priyam, nothing's going to happen. He's a bit disturbed, that's all. But he'll settle everything at night and will be his old self tomorrow. You don't need to worry at all.'

'I'm scared, Abhi,' she murmured as tears trickled down her cheeks.

'Scared? You are a silly girl! What's there to be scared about?'

Priyam removed her head from his shoulder and looked directly in his eyes. 'You know very well, Abhi, that he would do anything for his mother.'

116

'But…'

'She wanted him to marry Tina.'

'There's no proof of that,' Abhi tried to counter her fears.

'Proof? What proof is there of Mr. Vardhan being guilty? None, Abhi! And yet Sid hates him, doesn't he?'

'But, Priyam…'

'He will leave, Abhi. Sid will leave us. Sid too, will leave us.' Tears again came springing to her eyes as Priyam thought of the dreadful possibility.

'He won't. I…won't let him,' Abhi murmured as he again reached forward to shelter her in his only arm.

'You'll force him into marrying me?'

'If I have to.'

'You know he won't refuse you,' Priyam said, looking straight at him. Abhi knew what she meant.

'I won't let that stop me,' he said, after a long and painful pause. 'I can't let him leave you. I'll stop him at any cost.'

'And make Sid wretched and ashamed of himself? You'll do no such thing, Abhi. I won't let you.'

'But, Priyam…'

'Yes, Abhi,' she said, wiping her face dry, 'he can marry Tina if he wants to. I can bear that, I think. But I won't suffer him to remain tied to me with a broken conscience. He can survive a broken heart, Abhi. He won't survive broken self-esteem.'

Abhi stared at her, feeling helpless as he had never felt before. There was his little sister whose happiness he valued more than anything in the world. Now her whole world was in danger and yet he could do nothing. Priyam was right and he knew it. It was not difficult to stop Sid from reaching an untoward decision. What was impossible was to take out the sting that Mrs. Sinha's words had forever embedded in Sid's heart. All Abhi could do was pray that his friend won't take those words seriously. But Sid did take everything seriously that even slightly concerned with his mother.

Abhi and Priyam retired to their rooms to while away a sleepless night. But it only passed into a restless Sunday that brought no succour in its course. The Sunday passed into Monday, and yet Sid remained busy with his papers.

Abhi did try to explain away Sid's absence, but it was not easy as nothing had been able to prevent Sid's arrival earlier. He came whether the thunder roared its protests or the chilly winter nights tried to blind his way with dense fog. That little house was Sid's home, place where he lived, place where he laughed and place where he loved and which loved him doubly in return. How could he stay away from it? It was his refuge in illness, his sanitized alcove away from the hateful world, a place as dear to him as his Retreat was.

There could be only one thing that could have kept Sid away, only one reason, and that reason was terrible enough for the brother and sister to avoid mentioning it.

After two days, Sid appeared again at their doorstep. Though perhaps it would have been better had he still kept himself away Priyam could not even dare to ask what had kept him away for two days. It was apparent to her that could he help it, he would have maintained the distance then too. But he could not, he had to, he just had to come. Even if it meant for a few minutes, half an hour at most, he had promised himself he will come over. And as he sat there, waiting for Abhi to return, Priyam's eyes painfully observed the change that these two days had brought about in him.

It was perhaps sleeplessness that had given Sid that haggard appearance, and uneasiness of his heart that made him so restless. His knee jerked constantly as he sat waiting, casting repeated glances towards the clock and not daring to look at the one face his eyes most hungered for. 'I must go,' he said again and again, but remained sitting. He must wait for Abhi, he told himself. He could not go away without meeting Abhi.

It was a torture for Priyam to sit silent and see Sid getting defeated and wounded in a battle against himself, a battle she could not shield him, nor lull his pain away. He bore the look of a haunted man. A man haunted by the memories of his own mother who, even after her death was demanding the price of his love. Priyam knew well how Sid loved his mother, but at that moment she was on the very verge of hating the departed soul that still refused to remove its binding shadow from his sensitive heart.

Like Sid, she too wished again and again for Abhi to come. He would know how to calm Sid down. He would know what to do, what to say.

It was not that Abhi had not already tried allaying Sid's fears. On the night of the party itself Abhi had had a long talk with Sid over the phone to discuss the situation with him.

And the result of the conversation had been that Sid had gone to Mrs. Sinha the very next day to know for sure what his mother had said.

That lady loved a rambling conversation at all times. However, when it served her purpose, Mrs. Sinha was capable too of remaining focused on only one topic. And it did serve her purpose now to divert all her cunning oratory in adding cogency and absoluteness to her claim. And Sid's visit to her house gave her a very good opportunity to accentuate and make insufferable what she called Priyam's *inexcusable affection* for the man any respectable girl would hate. There was no chance of the meeting culminating in anything else but shattering of all of Sid's hopes and solidifying of Mrs. Sinha's.

There was no doubt left in Sid's mind about Tina's claim over him. The only uncertainty that still lingered was whether he should honour that claim or turn away from it to admit the call of love.

This conflict however was not an unfamiliar battle for him. It just had gained in urgency now. The fear that he was to marry Tina had always been in his mind. He had always known it. He had always wondered at it. And yet, he had allowed himself to fall in love with another and worse, to raise the same torturous feeling in her heart too. Sid knew he could never betray the last wish of his heartbroken mother. Yet, every time he tried to keep himself from loving Priyam, he invariably found himself being pulled towards her in a way that he totally failed to withstand. He loved her, he loved Priyam, and yet it seemed, he had no right to.

Sid had hoped that by freeing himself of his father's wealth, he had freed himself of that burden too. Mrs. Sinha had stopped mentioning the prospect to him and hadn't Raj said too that she was trying to find a suitable match for Tina?

If only all this had happened before he had allowed himself to put any hope in Priyam's heart. He had waited, he had kept himself in check. And just when he had started building up his heaven, the ghosts of the past had rushed out and blasted all his hopes, burying his happiness, and Priyam's under the ruins.

Sid kept himself away from Abhi's home as long as he could. For days on stretch, he denied himself the pleasure of their company, only to find himself again at the door that led to life and joy. Sometimes it was desperation that pushed Sid there, sometimes an intention to reach a final decision, which somehow, always got forgotten once he reached there. Often too there was an unconscious wish, the wish of being claimed, and thus relieved of the responsibility of choice.

But no claim was put forward by Priyam, nor by her brother. There wasn't even a shred of reproach in their eyes against the decision; both knew well Sid would finally arrive at it. They knew, they understood and they waited for the moment to arrive.

A hope sure lingered, unremittingly as is its usual torturing way. Aiding this lingering hope were numerous 'perhaps', 'maybe' and 'what ifs', most of them revolving around Tina. She was a free girl, and they had never seen her interested in Sid. She may refuse, and then Sid would have no choice but to forget about his mother's wishes. But it was all still a conjecture and one, subject to Mrs. Sinha's insurmountable tactics.

While fear and hopelessness thus crept towards Priyam and Abhi's home, a shadow of gloom already lay stretched over their neighbourhood. After the excitement of the party and the expectations that kept Aashi at home for two ensuing days, all that remained was despondency and broken dreams.

Twenty days had passed since the party; twenty whole days. And yet Aashi had not heard one word from Raj. She didn't even know if Raj had gone abroad as was his plan or refrained.

He must have gone, she often told herself. Why would he stop? She knew that Raj didn't love her and feared that she had lowered herself even more in his esteem by her stupidity. He must have left, Aashi was sure, not even bothering to say one word. He must have gone away, and with him all her dreams, all her delicious romantic fantasies...all...all her hopes! She had nothing left except to slog over her stupid boutique and crib her limited resources for every mite of good life and comfort.

Yet, despite being assured of the departure of all her fond dreams, burnt Aashi's heart was a little flame of doubt. She was sure Raj must have left the very next day, but no one had told her so. She had not heard it. And she had no intention of hearing it, even if it was true.

It was better to be uncertain. It allowed a space for hope to breathe, even if a tremulous one.

However, while Raj kept himself away from the neighbourhood, Sid came again one evening, twenty two days after Raj's party. Priyam rushed to open the door as soon as she heard his bike's roar on the road. As the sound grew louder so did the pounding of her heart. How strange it was that Sid's visit should fill her up with such dread. Earlier, she used to wait all day for the hour of his arrival. Well, she still waited for it, but with a pulsating fear of his arrival proving to be the one when the blow would be struck.

That it was inevitable, Priyam had no doubt in that. In a way, she had turned Sid's hesitating steps towards the path that could only lead him away from her.

As Priyam watched Sid drive his bike through the gates, her mind paced back. Two days ago when Sid come as unexpectedly and with same hard composure on his face, he had parked his bike outside the gate then.

Priyam knew she had managed to smile as Sid climbed the two stairs leading to the door and had tried not to look at him too pointedly as she stepped aside to let him pass in. But instead of walking straight in, Sid had halted near her, his hand reaching up, touching her hair and lingering a while by her cheek before falling down to his side again. His eyes by then had gazed long enough at Priyam's face to raise a penitent sigh.

'I can't do this, I can't!' Sid had murmured, almost inaudibly.

Priyam's eyes brimmed over again as she remembered those words. 'Wh…what?' was all she had managed to utter. The scene flashed before her eyes all too vividly. The memories were just two days old and of the nature that could never lose their sting and power to hurt and stifle her breath.

'You don't want a big engagement party, do you? Sid had said suddenly.

'What?' she had asked again, fearing she had misheard.

'We are getting engaged tomorrow evening. I'll be here at my usual time.'

Priyam had kept on looking at him as her lips formed and reformed words without giving them a coherent utterance. She should have been elated with relief. She should have jumped for joy. And yet, where was joy? Not in his eyes certainly. She had looked at Sid closely as he walked in and plonked himself on the couch.

'Sid?' she murmured, 'Are you…sure?'

'Sure?' he asked, giving out a sudden laugh, 'I'm not sure about anything, Priyam. I don't know if what I'm doing is right or not. I don't know if she'd ever be able to forgive me, her disloyal son. I don't even know if I'll ever be able to forgive myself. But I do know one thing, Priyam. I know that I can't hurt you. I can't leave you.'

Leave you… the words sounded like death knell to Priyam. There he was sitting, his long legs stretched before him and eyes looking up at the ceiling, sitting alone, though she was present in that very room.

'*You have already left me, Sid,*' she thought, '*you've already left me.*'

'You are regretting your decision already, Sid,' Priyam murmured as she sat down on the table directly in front of him.

'It will pass, Priyam. It will pass. There's a way. If you agree.'

'Agree? To what?'

'To…'

'What?' She could see him hesitate

'Priyam…I can't marry a girl who loves my mother's killer.'

'Sid!'

'I can betray her wishes, but I can't betray her trust.'

'And do you think I can betray his?' Priyam mumbled in a low voice.

'Don't make this any harder, Priyam. I beg of you.'

'You want me to lower myself to betray an old and unhappy man? Just so that you can maintain the appearance of being true to your dead mother? You cannot want that Sid. You cannot want that of me. You can't want me to be so…so…' she tried finding the word horrible enough to fit a person capable of such selfish cruelty. Her eyes glared with shocked incredulity at Sid.

'What I can't want is to make you unhappy. If you love me, Priyam…' he muttered.

'Don't, Sid! Don't lower yourself further!' Priyam almost shouted. This was not the proud and upright Sid she knew. This was not the Sid she recognized, rather a broken man, tired and trying to salvage a petty float from a sunken ship.

'Please understand, Priyam,' Sid interrupted her, 'I can't marry a girl who…'

'For God's sake!' she exclaimed, jumping up from the table, 'You have always known how much I love him. It is just an excuse that you want, isn't it? Just an excuse to justify yourself, either before me or your mother? Well then, you shall have it. I love your father and think of him as the best and kindest man I've ever met. I love him and shall always respect him to my utmost. There, you have your excuse now. Go and fulfil your mother's wishes with a clear conscious. Go and marry the girl you think she chose for you. Go!'

Priyam didn't know whether what she had done that day was right. She didn't know the effect her words had had on Sid, except that he had walked away soon after and just as suddenly as he had appeared.

She didn't know what it was that Sid had come to tell her now. All she was aware of was that he was there, standing before her, and that his eyes were just as lambent with love for her as they had been before Mrs. Sinha had said a word to mar their perfect joy.

'How long before Abhi comes?' Sid asked before entering in.

'He might come any time now.'

'Good,' he said and walked in, putting his helmet and keys at their usual place. 'I wish he won't be late today. We must finish up that game we started last week. You haven't disturbed it, have you?' he said, walking over to his favourite couch.

'No,' Priyam replied and walked away to fetch him a glass of water.

'Thanks,' Sid said, emptying the glass quickly. 'Why's the water not cold?' he asked.

'There was no power supply all day.'

'As usual!' Sid smirked and began setting up cushions to one side of the couch.

Priyam watched him arrange the cushions and tried to remember how many days had passed since he had enjoyed a nap on that couch. Then after a moment's hesitation asked, 'Would you stay for dinner?' The question sounded strange when directed towards Sid. But so much had changed since the days when his presence at the dining table used to be as unquestionable as Abhi's or her own.

'Yes,' Sid said as he kicked off his shoes and sprawled across the sofa. Priyam looked at him for a moment, bit her lip and quickly walked over to the kitchen.

When Abhi came back from office, he couldn't help but stand and stare at the recumbent form on the sofa and try to decipher its meaning. A quick look at Priyam too didn't reveal much.

'Hey, Sid,' he said.

'Hi, what took you so long?' Sid asked, without getting up or even opening his eyes.

'Yeah,' Abhi said, wanting to ask the same question in return but instead just said, 'but this is my usual time.'

'I guess I was waiting for you too impatiently,' Sid murmured.

'What's up?'

'Just that we need to finish that game we started last week. And I intend to beat you hands down today.'

'Chess? But a week has passed, Sid. I've even forgotten who moved last,' Abhi replied, not at all fooled by the cheerful words. He was too familiar with all the modulations his friend's vocal chords were capable of. Mere words could do little to deceive him.

'You did. Now it's my move. Freshen up quickly,' Sid replied and got up finally as Abhi walked off to his room. He rearranged the cushions, putting them back to their rightful places. A moment he lingered near the couch that had for so long been his favourite resting place, almost caressing it with his eyes. 'Now the game,' he murmured, almost as if ticking off an item in a mental to-do list.

Priyam watched him from the corner of her kitchen. Sid was following the old routine, trying as if to live a day from the old and happier times. And yet, where was the nonchalance of unconscious habit? Where was the spontaneity? All that Priyam could see in his moves was deliberateness, a slow and painful unfolding of a plan, and she dreaded to imagine what lay at its end.

Sid talked much that evening, allowing no space for thought to creep up to his mind. He looked at everything, devouring every little inconsequential bit of the house as if to fill up a huge empty space in his own being. Neither did his eyes avoid Abhi's nor Priyam's, often lingering at the latter in fact, unconsciously perhaps, but unhesitatingly.

After dinner, Sid proposed a walk too and insisted on walking a little further than their usual course to relish the cool and calm night. The cheerful vivacity he had adopted for the evening accompanied them all the way.

It was only when the three were about few metres away from their home that the siblings sensed Sid slowing down and become sombre with each step. All his merriment seemed to creep away and soon all that remained to interest him was to watch his boots trample the mud.

'I...want to tell you something,' he began after sometime.

Priyam's fingers curled up tightly, her nails digging into her palms. Her eyes remained bent down. Of course, she knew he had to tell them something. She had been expecting it all evening. She knew too what that something was. The words, as yet unspoken, had already burnt through her heart many times. Sid had decided to marry Tina. He had reached the decision. But hadn't Priyam herself forced Sid to it? He had agreed to marry her, if only she could have agreed to his conditions. Now all was lost, all, except his friendship. That would never be lost. That was hers still, to cherish, to treasure. It wasn't what Priyam had come to wish for, yet it still was a lot and one can manage to live with such a blessing in one's grasp.

Priyam was ready, she was prepared to take the blow, yet, there rose in her heart a cry to tarry a little longer, to delay a little bit more.

'*Not now, not now Sid, please, not now!*' the words started beating hard in her heart.

But Sid had already delayed till the last moment.

'I've got a new job...' he said.

'*A new job? Is that it? Is that all?*'

Hope flared up for a moment. Spontaneous congratulations would have followed immediately, and yet, Sid didn't seem to be expecting them. There was something else, something of greater weight to be revealed and Abhi and Priyam waited in silence for Sid to complete his sentence.

'...in Bangalore,' he said.

'Bangalore?' Priyam gasped. '*Why? Why Bangalore? Why so far?*' It was not what she had expected. It was not what she had feared. It was worse, much, much worse. And where was the need for it? Why was he going away? Hadn't she herself given him up?

'You are going away?' Priyam heard Abhi ask.

'Yes, but it's an excellent opportunity for me.'

'But Bangalore is so far away...' Priyam couldn't resist from saying.

'Not as far as...I mean...posting in Bangalore is just temporary. After that, I hope to get some offshore posting.'

Priyam stared at Sid. She couldn't judge whether what burnt all over her was pain or rage. She felt Abhi's fingers envelop her hand. She looked at him and then back at Sid. There was nothing to be said. There was no protest to be made. But she had not bargained for this. She felt betrayed. And it was yet too sudden a shock to allow for the comforting outlet of grief. If anything, it was not grief or sorrow that bit into Priyam as she dragged her steps towards her home. There was more of rage, a sudden infuriation against her utter defeat, a defiant denial against her absolute loss.

'When?' Abhi muttered.

'Tomorrow,' Sid said.

Up shot Priyam's eyes again, only to find that Sid's were already turned towards her. Dark gloomy eyes from which every spark of life seemed to have been quenched out and replaced by spent ashes of all his dreams…and hers.

He was going tomorrow, *going*. Away from her, forever. It was one thing to see Sid with another, but not to be able to see him at all! '*How could he be so cruel!*'

'That's…abrupt,' she heard Abhi say.

'No, it's not,' she thought. '*It's planned, deliberately planned.*'

'I must leave now,' Sid was saying. 'I still have some packing to do.'

'Okay,' Abhi murmured, his head bent low and eyes fixed to the ground just a step ahead of him. 'Tomorrow, what time?' he asked.

'6:30.'

'Evening?'

'No…morning.'

'Okay,' Abhi said looking up at him, 'I'll drop you.'

'No.'

'No?'

'No,' Sid said, gently but firmly. By then they had reached their home. Abhi stepped forward to unlock the door. Sid made no move to enter. 'My keys and helmet,' he murmured to Abhi.

'Okay,' Abhi replied and went in. Priyam remained standing outside, leaning against the boundary wall facing the door.

'Priyam…' Sid called out softly and after a moment's hesitation. Her eyes were already fixed on him, and they remained there. She neither said a word nor moved. 'I…' Sid said, walking slowly over to her, 'brought something for you.' he held out his hand. Priyam looked at it and saw a gold bracelet nestling in his palm.

'It's yours!' she gasped, recognizing in an instant the Buddha engraving in its solid gold centre. It was the same bracelet Sid used to wear till it became

125

too small for him. His mother had had it made for him on his ninth birthday. He couldn't wear it now, but he kept it close nevertheless, cherishing it like a dear memory.

'Yes,' he said, looking fondly at it, 'I want you to have it.'

'But...' Priyam tried to protest, however, by then Sid had lifted her arm and clasped it around her slender wrist. It was a perfect fit.

'There,' he murmured, 'something to remember me by.'

'As if I could ever forget you!' Priyam could not resist herself from crying out. 'Why must you leave, Sid? Why can't we be friends still? What harm could come of that?'

'I must...'

'Why? Don't you trust me?'

'Do you think that?' Sid asked in return.

'Then what are you afraid of?' Priyam cried out, 'That I'll make you do what your father did?' She didn't want to say that and regretted her words the second they escaped her mouth. But he deserved it! And he deserved much more. She was prepared to kill her every dream to let him fulfil his mother's. What reason had he to take away from her his friendship too? Did his mother forbid him even that?

'Don't...say that, Priyam.'

'What does it matter now, Sid?' Priyam said, faking a little laugh, 'You are going. Now I'm free to say and think whatever I want. And I will say this. Your father never betrayed your mother. He never loved another woman. But you do! You do, Sid. You've betrayed Tina even before you married her. And every moment of every day you spend with her would be a betrayal too. You are no better than your father, Sid. You are worse, much worse!' There, she had inflicted on Sid a wound more severe than he was leaving on her. It hurt Priyam just as much, and yet she did it. Why, she didn't know and just then, she had not the sense enough to care, or even to try and quell her fury a bit.

It was not Sid she was angry at. Yet Priyam was conscious of rage and resentment bubbling up in her mind. She wanted to revolt, to shout out and make herself heard just as she used to do when a child. Grief had trapped her into silence and calm endurance. Grief again was bringing her out of it. There's after all a limit to what one can endure. More than that and the being reverts to its inherent nature. The tyrant fate had once forced Priyam into subjugation. But now she wanted to revolt, now she wanted to raise her voice in resentment. She had lost everything. She had a right to be angry and to show it too.

'What else can I do, Priyam?' Sid asked, his hand still holding hers, his fingers clutching her tightly enough to leave behind another mark besides the gold bracelet on her wrist. But neither Priyam was conscious of Sid's hold, nor he of the pressure he was exerting.

'You always knew what you had to do, Sid,' Priyam said, 'but you love me, and you can't deny that.'

'It doesn't matter now.'

'It still does to me.'

Just then they heard Abhi coming out. It was time... for Sid to leave. Yet, his fingers wanted to linger a little longer on Priyam's arm, his eyes thirsted yet to look on her, but they had to let go, *he* had to let go. And he did.

'Take care of yourself,' Sid murmured and turned quickly to walk towards Abhi who was just then coming out.

'When shall we hear from you?' Abhi asked as he handed Sid his keys and helmet.

'I'll call you as soon as I can and give you my new number.'

'Okay, and all the best for your new life.'

'Yeah, my new life. Thanks. Take care of yourself and Priyam,' he said, giving Abhi a quick hug before strapping on his helmet and climbing on his bike.

In a minute, the roar of Sid's bike faded away into the silence of the night.

He was gone.

Sid was gone.

And Abhi and Priyam were left alone once again. Left alone to peer into the dark that had engulfed him and listen to each other's silence. That was all that was left with them, a deep, impenetrable silence.

Chapter 17

Sail fast, sail fast,
Ark of my hopes, Ark of my dreams;
Sweep lordly o'er the drowned Past,
Fly glittering through the sun's strange beams;
Sail fast, sail fast.
Breaths of new buds from off some drying lea
With news about the Future scent the sea:
My brain is beating like the heart of Haste:
I'll loose me a bird upon this Present waste;
Go, trembling song,
And stay not long; oh, stay not long:
Thou'rt only a gray and sober dove,
But thine eye is faith and thy wing is love.

— *A Song Of The Future by Sidney Lanier (1842-1881)*

The sun unfolded its glory in its proper hour, not a minute late, not a minute early. The birds too trilled their apathetic melodies and the whole world revived itself with its usual bustle.

But there was no waking up from the nightmare that still dazed Priyam's eyes. The darkness of the road had given way to light. Did it matter though? The gloom of last night was forever now entrenched in her being, never to lighten, never to admit even a ray of light, never even to hope for one. But it didn't matter. Neither to her, nor to the rest of the world.

The routines of life continue, and they must. What did it matter if life had flitted away? The existence still remained, and existence must be maintained. Sure, Sid was gone, but the milkman had come. The milk had to be taken and boiled. Sure, Sid would never come back to her. But the water supply had arrived in its due time, and water had to be stored for the day. Sure, Sid would perhaps never again tread on the lawn, or revel in the warm comfort of the house. But the plants had to be watered nevertheless, and the house required just as much cleaning as before.

Everything was done. All the dictates of the clock followed. A new day had begun, and it yet had to run its entire course before it could hope to rest its weariness in the dark secrecy of night. But it would end, sooner or later, to give way to another dreary day. But an evening must pass before that… an evening without Sid. Sid wouldn't come. He wouldn't. Nevertheless, the evening would come still, and pass away too, somehow. But now it was yet a day.

The clock had already passed the hour of nine but Abhi was still at home.

'Aren't you getting late?' Priyam asked Abhi.

'I'm not going today.'

'Why?'

'Just…don't feel like going,' he said.

'Don't worry about me, Abhi. I'll be okay,' Priyam said.

'I can take a day off if I want, can't I?' he almost shouted.

'Sure,' Priyam replied, breaking a little morsel from her sandwich and stuffing it into her mouth, 'but there's no need. Besides, he's not going to fade away in a day. But life… must go on. We still have each other, there's reason enough, I guess.'

'Yes, guess so too,' Abhi murmured, forcing himself to control his rage. He felt helpless and bitter, but that could in no way excuse his venting his rage at the one who had after all suffered the greatest loss.

'Priyam,' Abhi said after a quiet moment, 'would you do me a favour?'

'What?'

'Next time you pray, ask God if He used a black ink to write our fate with. There hardly seems to be any other colour in life.'

'I would,' Priyam replied with a wry smile, 'but, would He listen?'

'Yeah, doesn't seem like it. Perhaps, His ears have been stuffed by Mrs Sinha's voice too.'

The more Abhi thought about Sid's departure, the more bitter he felt. It wasn't Priyam's gloom alone that made him miserable. Abhi himself felt hurt too by the way his best friend had gone away, to battle his demons alone and let them deal with theirs, whatever way they could.

Abhi could have dealt with his. They were his old familiars. But he already felt weighed down by defeat when Priyam was forced in the field too. How sure he had felt of Priyam's happiness. How sure he had been about Sid's firmness. Now that very firmness had led to the fall of all her joy.

How Abhi wished he could do something, anything. If only he could give a good shake to Sid and bring him back to his senses. Sid had surrendered his will to a dead woman, but had he given up his brains too? How could he do it? How could Sid do this to Priyam? If only he could bring Sid back for once and show him Priyam's ashen face as she went about the house, too shocked to sort out her feelings, too numb to grieve, and still standing frozen in the moment that like a black hole had sucked in everything and had left behind nothing but a dull bewilderment.

The delicious softness of Priyam's brown eyes had vanished into a steely frigidity that stared out in disbelieve. They grieved not. No amount of tears could have done justice to the bitter betrayal that Sid had left behind, the betrayal that scraped at her heart like the scar that, though it does not bleed, presses on a vital vessel till life is squeezed out.

The day had crawled its tedious way towards evening. Television had laboriously flickered through several long hours without managing to regale even a moment. Abhi's impatient fingers were fuming through odds and ends of at least six movies, in addition to a dozen of news programs and countless commercial breaks. Priyam was sitting quiet and patient, letting her eyes follow the tread of the minute hand as it sliced away what, not very long ago, had been the most awaited hour of the day.

Just then the doorbell rang, followed soon by Aashi's voice. Abhi's finger jerked to a stop. He looked towards the door.

'Coming, just a minute,' Priyam replied to Aashi's call and got up to open the door. Abhi too stood up, quickly switching the television set off and preparing to leave the room as soon as possible.

'Hey, what's up? I saw your car in the garage. How come you are home so early? Aashi asked even before she had stepped in.

'I didn't feel like going to office today,' Abhi replied.

'No? Why, that's a surprise. Are you sick or something?'

'No, I'm fine,' he replied and turned to leave. Aashi shrugged her shoulders with annoyance as she watched Abhi make his rapid exit. 'Good riddance!' she muttered under her breath, 'I didn't come to see you anyway.'

'Sit down, Aashi, you look tired,' Priyam said.

'Oh, yes, I am. But what's up with Abhi? Is he really sick?' she asked as she sank down on the sofa.

'No,' said Priyam. She settled down on the carpet, her arms encircling her folded legs and chin resting on her knees.

'Then why... hey, where did you get that? It looks expensive,' Aashi exclaimed as her eyes fell on the bracelet around Priyam's wrist.

'It's Sid's.'

'When did he give it to you?'

'Yesterday.'

'Yesterday? He came yesterday? Why didn't you call me? I told you to call me if he comes. I would have given him a piece of my mind. Because he certainly seems to have lost *his* brains, you know!'

'And a lot more besides,' Priyam muttered, as a wistful smile made its brief appearance on her face.

'Why? What happened? Did Siddharth...? What has he said now?'

'He's gone,' Priyam replied.

'Gone?' Aashi repeated, shocked by the chilly finality of Priyam's tone.

'Yes,' Priyam replied. 'Gone.'

'When? What happened? Are you okay?' Aashi's anxiety poured forth. She quickly left the sofa and sat down beside Priyam, wrapping her arms around the stricken girl. 'What happened?' she whispered.

Few moments sufficed to tell Aashi everything and fewer to let her understand what had befallen on Priyam the night before. 'Oh, Priyam!' she burst out, 'How could he do this to you? How could he!'

'Don't blame him, Aashi, he couldn't help it,' Priyam tried a feeble but urgent defence.

'He couldn't? It seems to me he very well could, Priyam! Principles and conscience and all such shit are all very well, but a promise can never be more important than a true heart! And it isn't even certain if all that Mrs. Sinha is saying is true or not. And he broke your heart just to keep his dead mother's dreams alive? How could he?'

'If Sid broke my heart, his own is broken too,' Priyam pleaded.

'The bigger fool that he is!' Aashi spat out with infuriation.

'Don't blame him...'

'Whom should I blame then, you?'

'Yes, me. I had built up dreams of perfect bliss. They had to break. And I knew it all along. I knew it all along, Aashi. And yet I built up my foolish hopes, demanding a fortune from a beggar that my fate is.'

'Oh please, don't start cursing your fate now. We make our own destiny and with our own deeds spoil it too. And that's exactly what you have done

131

too, Priyam. All you had to do was tighten your clutch and your perfect bliss would have been here with you still and forever. You should at least have tried like I...I mean...you should have done something! And Sid, he's the greatest fool of all!' Aashi burst out. She could not believe what Sid had done, and try as she might, she could never bring herself to look at things from his viewpoint, or even Priyam's. 'What's the matter with all of you; such perfect specimens of goodness!' she continued, 'I tell you, if you were only a little less good, you'll all be a lot happier!'

'Oh, I hope he'll be happy,' Priyam murmured, bending her head down to bury her face in her arms.

'Will you stop thinking about Sid for once and start thinking about yourself?' Aashi cried out with exasperation. 'It's all very well and good to care for others, Priyam, but not at the cost of your own happiness! That is simply foolish,' Aashi exclaimed with fury.

'That's right, I totally agree with you there, Aashi,' a voice called from the doorway.

'Raj!' A rush of feelings coloured her face, and a sudden thrill started banging hard against her ribs.

Raj was still in India! He hadn't left! He was still there, close by! But why? Was it because of her? Was it? Oh, let it be because of her!

But then, Raj hadn't come to see her. He had come to see Priyam. He must have heard of Sid's going away. Had he come to try his luck once more? Had Sid's betrayal revived his hopes again! Well, that would be the end of all her hopes then.

'Hi, Priyam,' Raj said softly as he stepped in through the open door.

'Hi,' Priyam replied, getting up.

'Are you okay?'

'Yes.'

'Siddharth came to our house yesterday, late at night... why didn't you tell me anything, Priyam? No one told me anything! It was just yesterday that I came to know through Sid what my mother has done.'

'Do you know if it's the truth?' Aashi asked.

'No, I have no idea. But something might have been done! If only I knew...I could have persuaded my mother, I...but don't you worry, Priyam. It's not too late even now. I can't let this happen to you.'

'You can't do anything, Raj,' Priyam murmured.

'We'll see about that,' he muttered, 'Where's Abhi? Why didn't he do anything? Couldn't he put some sense in his own best friend?'

'I tried, Raj,' Abhi replied as he came down the stairs. 'I tried.'

'But why didn't you tell me anything? Why didn't you…'

'I didn't know you've changed your plans.'

'Well…I was…had some important business to finish,' Raj mumbled, trying not to look at Aashi. But he did look and there was a strange self-consciousness in his eyes that escaped neither Aashi nor Abhi.

'Sure, that's a reason enough,' Abhi replied.

'I…must leave now,' Aashi murmured as she quickly gathered up her stuff. 'Mummy would be wondering why I'm being so late,' she explained as she hastily walked towards the door.

'Okay, see you later,' Raj said, quite casually, but with a lingering look that followed her form as she escaped.

Raj did see her again, not that evening but the very next. It was seven p.m. and Aashi was enjoying a cup of tea with Priyam in the little open space that Abhi had somehow transformed into a garden. She got up to look out when his car stopped at her gate.

'It's Raj,' she told Priyam who was sitting beside her. 'He's coming here,' she added when Priyam gave no response.

Priyam had been with her since morning, more on her own insistence however, than Priyam's desire. Aashi knew that left to herself, Priyam would have stayed indoors all day, filling all her leisure with uninterrupted indulgence of grief. But Aashi would not have it so. And it wasn't just because Abhi had demanded it as a particular favour before leaving for office.

It felt nice to be trusted by Abhi, and Aashi knew she needed to justify that trust, to nobody else though but her own self.

So soon after Abhi left, Aashi stepped inside her neighbour's house.

'What are you doing here at this time?' Priyam asked.

'I'm here to make sure that…'

'Has Abhi sent you here?' Priyam interrupted her.

'Yes. He thought you needed a dose of vitamin A.'

'Huh?'

'Vitamin Aashi, silly! Get ready now. I'm going to take you shopping.'

'I don't need to buy anything,' Priyam replied.

'Well, but I do. So let's get going. We'll have a girls' day out.'

'Really, Aashi, I don't feel like…'

'Don't worry,' Aashi interrupted her, 'I promise you I won't drag you along all through the market. Just two or three shops where I have placed some orders, that's all. And then, we'll go somewhere for lunch. Come along now,' she said, forcing Priyam to go and dress up for the outing.

133

All day long Aashi forced her company on Priyam. All day long her attempts continued to keep her friend engaged, to keep Priyam's mind too busy to have any leisure to fall back in gloom.

Aashi took Priyam for shopping and then, after having lunch at a Chinese restaurant, to her boutique. There, she had kept Priyam busy and at the end of the day determined that her friend had proved to be such a help that she absolutely must agree to come there every day. Aashi knew that the wound Priyam had suffered could not be healed in a short time. But she was determined to do all she could to palliate it a little.

Again and again Aashi's jokes and sallies attempted to raise a smile on her friend's face and were often blessed with success too. The day had passed quickly that otherwise would have proved too long for Priyam. Now the two friends sat quietly in the garden, sipping tea and waiting for Abhi to return. It was then that Raj made his entrance.

'Hi Aashi,' his cheerful voice sang out as Raj opened the gate. 'Oh, Priyam, hi,' he quickly added as soon as he saw her. 'Good to find you two together.'

'I was just leaving,' Priyam replied.

'Oh, but you must stay now. Where's Abhi?'

'He hasn't come from the office yet. Had some meeting,' Priyam replied, sitting down again, but quite unwillingly.

'How are you?' Raj asked.

'Okay,' Priyam replied.

'Any news from Siddharth?'

'No.'

'He didn't call?'

'No.'

A couple of incoherent rumblings escaped Raj's mouth as he quickly turned his face away from Priyam.

'What happened?' he heard Aashi ask and turned back to see Priyam standing. 'Where are you going?'

'Home,' Priyam replied.

'But why? Abhi's not back yet.'

'I must start getting the dinner ready. He would be hungry when he gets home.'

'But...' Aashi mumbled with surprise. 'It's only seven,' she pointed out.

'Are you still angry at me, Priyam?' Raj asked, getting up too and taking a step closer to her.

'Angry at you? Why would she be angry at you?' Aashi asked, trying to figure out Priyam's strange behaviour. There was something she was missing out, something that Priyam had not revealed despite being with her all day long.

'Guess I became a bit too frank yesterday,' Raj replied with a shrug of his shoulders, burying his hands in his pockets.

'You had no right to blame Sid, least of all my brother,' Priyam muttered in a tone almost too dry to be possible for her.

'Yeah, right. One gentleman breaks your heart and the other stands and watches and does nothing. Yet they are not to blame. The blame is all on me, because I can't bear to see you like this.'

'Well then, perhaps it would be better if you don't see me at all,' Priyam shot back.

'Did you see that, Aashi?' Raj exclaimed as Priyam walked away from them and entered her own home. 'And I had thought that at least now Priyam would come to respect the value of my love!'

'Don't blame her, Raj, she's not herself.'

'I don't blame her. You don't need to defend Priyam from me. But why does she always misunderstand me? It was just my concern for her that made me say those angry words. She doesn't understand me at all!'

'Understanding? Few can boast of excelling in that art, Raj,' Aashi said with a wry smile.

'What do you mean?'

'Just that understanding a person isn't so easy. Had I known that you were still hoping for her love…'

'No I'm not. You know I gave up that hope long ago.'

'But you just said…'

'I don't know what I just said. But I know that I no longer wait for her. I did hope to gain her friendship and good opinion, but not her love. That would never be mine, Sid, or no Sid. I've finally understood that.'

'Then,' Aashi began with a quivering lip, 'why did you not go?'

'To London? I wondered when you would ask me that,' Raj said, sitting down again and looking straight at her, 'and also that having stayed, why didn't I meet you.'

'Well?'

'Well,' he began, trying to arrange his few well thought out words in their proper order, 'do you remember you gave me a reason for not going away?'

'I am sure I don't have such weak memory to make you doubt that!'

Aashi could not help but laugh at the silliness of his query. Can a girl forget her first kiss? And that too, a kiss given under such circumstances?

'I hope so too,' he smiled back.

'And?' she had to ask.

'And, all these days I was trying to find a reason against that reason.'

Those were not the words Aashi had been expecting and their unfamiliarity surprised her into silence. 'Did you...' she began finally, 'find that reason?'

'No, not yet,' Raj replied. 'And...when I saw you yesterday... and...after what happened...it suddenly dawned on me that...I don't need to. I mean, it would have been foolishness. Love in itself is a precious gift, and such ardent love as you must have for me that made you take such a step, it would have been an utter stupidity to deprive myself of its pleasures. Besides, I've always admired you, and liked you...'

There, a new start was made, a hesitant start for sure, but a determined one nevertheless. And once Raj had told Aashi of his decision, it might be imagined that several lengthy speeches must have followed from both sides, trying to out-excel each other in their profusion of love. Let it suffice that almost an entire hour was spent in saying what needed to be said. At the end of this hour too it needed a phone call to remind Raj of the necessity of departure. However, by the time Raj left, he already felt himself to be sufficiently in love again. As for Aashi's happiness, well, several hours needed to be passed before she could calm the pleasurable little tremors of her heart and feel firm on her feet again.

If this sudden shift of affection seems surprising, it was just that for Raj too. He was more bewildered by this turn of his own feelings than anyone else could ever be. When Raj lost Priyam, he had considered it a loss of all his future happiness. He had believed himself quite incapable of feeling any joy ever again, having lost the greatest joy of his life.

But here he was, sitting in Aashi's garden, not a month after his defeat and yet not sad enough, not rending his hair out, feeling quite comfortable in fact and actually looking forward to a happy future which certainly was in his grasp now.

Raj still felt a bite of resentment for sure, but found his heart strangely intact and already warming up to the charms of another. And there was nothing wrong in that. What use would it be to mourn after a girl who was never his and give the same pain he had suffered to someone who loved him just as much. One should always move ahead, Raj reminded himself, trying to put logic behind the baffling breach in his code of conduct. One must leave past grief to the past. That would be for everybody's benefit. And didn't Aashi deserve his love just as much as Priyam? She surely was in no way inferior to Priyam. And didn't he deserve a chance of happiness too? Didn't he deserve to be loved too?

Raj's attraction towards Aashi was definitely more spontaneous than his love for Priyam had been. While his desire for Priyam had resulted from an elaborate appraisal of her worth against those of other girls of his acquaintance, his inclination towards Aashi was against all his conscious wishes.

'When will I see you again?' Aashi asked him as Raj got up to leave.

'Soon,' Raj could not help but reply.

'Tomorrow?' Aashi asked again.

'Sure.'

'I'll wait for you,' she murmured.

'I won't make you wait long,' he whispered back.

Aashi watched Raj walk up to his car. If only he could have stayed a little longer. How her eyes had yearned to admire his perfections. She waved to him as he started the engine and sped away. In a moment Raj had vanished, but Aashi had the promise of his return. She had him, her most wonderful dream, her dearest wish, her wildest and most impossible fantasy. She had him. Raj was hers, hers only. Her face burned with joy, her palms sweated and feet seemed to be unsure of the ground under them. She wanted to shout out her joy, she wanted to squeal with delight and run off to Priyam.

'*Priyam! Oh!*' she had entirely forgotten her! How could she? Aashi looked towards the house next door. Abhi's car was in the garage. '*When did he return?*' Aashi thought with a surprise. They had been sitting outside all the time. She should have heard Abhi's car. But she didn't. And well, she was glad of it. And it was good too that he had come back. Now she won't need to sit with Priyam. It would have been so impossible to contain her joy. And it would never do to be jumping the couch when she knew how contrary the situation of her friend was.

But Abhi was back and Aashi was free, free to run indoors and hug her surprised mother. To tell her all her joy and laugh at her reaction and advice of restraint and decorum that must follow. Free too to run to the mirror and wonder what it was in her that Raj most admired. And she had to relieve her grim pillow of the fortnight's sad burden too and weigh it down with ecstasy that was pressing so to break all barriers and overflow.

137

> *Your hands once touched this table and this silver,*
> *And I have seen your fingers hold this glass.*
> *These things do not remember you, belovèd,*
> *And yet your touch upon them will not pass.*
>
> — *'Bread and Music' by Conrad Aiken,*

A week had passed since Sid's departure. A week that, for Priyam, was nothing but a trudging sequence of numb days and wrenching evenings. She slogged through the day like an automaton and looked forward to the evening to be alone with her memories. Nights saw her lying like a dead log on her bed, going over the same memories and bathing them afresh with her tears.

Priyam's condition could not but affect Aashi too and cast a gloomy shade over her rising sun. Living just next door and having taken it upon herself to be Priyam's constant companion in her distress, Aashi felt compelled to pass her days in careful reserve. It was only when evening fell and they separated, that the girl allowed her wings the liberty to fly and her feet to dance to the rhythm of her heart.

Ever since the declarations had been made, scarcely one evening had passed when Raj had not showed himself at her door.

That day too, when Aashi, her mother and Priyam reached home, they saw Raj's car parked right before Aashi's house.

'Oh, he's already here!' Aashi exclaimed, quickening her step just as Raj stepped out from his car.

'There you are,' Raj said, welcoming them with a broad grin. 'Hi Priyam,' he added in his gentlest tones, 'how are you?'

'Fine,' Priyam replied and excused herself from the company. Raj and Aashi watched her enter her home before turning to each other again.

'Have you been waiting for long?' Aashi asked as Raj.

'Yeah, for over an hour,' Raj replied.

'Really? Then why's your car still so warm?' Aashi asked with an arched smile after examining his claim by laying her hand on the car's bonnet.

'Well, it did feel like an hour,' he shrugged.

'Honest, when did you come?' Aashi asked again, responding to his dramatics with a merry laugh that was exactly what he had calculated to evoke.

Raj knew perfectly well how to make Aashi laugh and fall in love with him all over again. There never was a dull moment when he was there with her.

And Aashi could not help but marvel at her own good fortune. Admiration sparkled in her eyes and love rode a roller-coaster in her nerves just at the sight of Raj. But then, he was her perfect dream come true!

'Five minutes ago,' Raj replied, putting his arm around her shoulders, 'you are just in time. And now that you are back, let's go for a long drive.'

'Now?'

'Why not? It's a beautiful evening,' he remarked, staring up at the sky.

The month of September was already half-way through. And though the days were still too warm, evenings had started to be pleasant and cool. Some stray post-monsoon showers were still left in the air to sprinkle the ground or sometimes even drenching it, and if nothing else, to add a spectrum of clouds to the evening's romance.

'But...' Aashi still hesitated. She knew her mother did not approve of such *going-outs* with Raj. That evening too, while on their way home, she had been trying to persuade Aashi to be a little reserved, a little less frank with her ardour. In short, to be a little more in control of her emotions and actions.

'I'll ask your mother if you are worried about that,' Raj said, taking her hand in his.

'No, that won't be necessary,' Aashi replied. She after all, knew what she was doing. And besides, she trusted Raj, and trust doesn't allow hesitation. 'Just give me a moment and I'll go tell her,' Aashi said and rushed indoors.

Raj was left alone outside. He started gazing at Priyam's house. His lips twitched and some unintelligible words garbled out from his mouth against Sid.

To a less frequent visitor, the house may perhaps have looked exactly as it was before. But Raj's familiar eyes could not help but feel the vast difference that had taken place. It was no longer a happy house, no longer ringing with laughter and joy of companionship as it used to do earlier. The laughter was quiet now, lost, as it were, in a deep and impermeable silence. Even the garden looked unkempt and withering away into despondency.

Yet, there was little he could do. He had tried talking to his mother, but could get nothing out of her mouth. Communicating with Sid was out of question. For one, his relations with Sid had never been too genial, and also,

Priyam would not approve of it. And Raj was determined not to do anything to make Priyam turn even more against him. But it wasn't easy, it wasn't easy to be standing there and looking at the walls of her home and imagining her sorrow without being able to do anything about it.

While Raj thus stayed worrying about Priyam, she was sitting in her room quite oblivious of his gaze turned towards that very place. But then, when was she ever aware of it even before? And how could she now, surrounded as she was by thousand different recollections. That was all Priyam cared for now, to be alone with her memories.

Priyam was all alone in the house, but the silence that engulfed her seemed strangely soothing too, perhaps because silence echoed Sid's words, Sid's voice, that was stamped on her heart for ever. It had been exhausting to focus her attention on anything else but Sid, tiresome to laugh and smile at Aashi's jokes. And now Priyam longed to rest. To put her aching head on the cold window sill and just gaze into the silent sky, letting her mind roam where it would, letting her eyes water if they would and letting Sid's unseen presence fill every pore of her body until the awareness of all else dissolved away into nothingness.

Days crawled away, months changed calendar pages too. It was mid-October now. More than a month had passed since Sid's departure, time enough for Aashi to feel comfortable with her happiness and for Priyam to start adapting to life lived in telephonic conversations.

That comfort, at least, had still been left unto her. Sid had given Abhi his new phone number as soon as he had got a new phone. At least he had not broken that link. However, the frequency of his calls was just as erratic as his visits had been just before his going away. He called and accepted Abhi's calls too. As for herself; Priyam never tried his number nor phoned him. And she didn't unless asked for. More often than not, she simply contented herself by hearing his voice that floated out from the speaker-phone Abhi had recently installed.

It was during just one such overhearing that Priyam caught the question that seemed strangely out of place.

'Did you...check your email today?' Sid was asking.

'No,' Abhi replied.

'I...sent you a mail. Go through it when you get the time. Okay?'

'*Mail! Sid's mail! Oh, how wonderful!*' Priyam rushed out of the kitchen at the words.

Priyam's hands were covered in flour as she stood listening to Sid. But the conversation soon ended. No hint came through regarding the contents of the e-mail. Nothing to tell her what it was about. But her face had lit up nevertheless. Finally there was something better than two minutes of succour coming through long distance calls.

Abhi, though, didn't feel quite well about this e-mail. Somehow, he felt it in his heart that it would only lead to more harm than good. And he wished Priyam had not learnt about it.

Priyam though, was quite oblivious of Abhi's concern. Besides, there was nothing left to scare her now. The worst had already taken place. What else would there be for Sid to say or write that could hurt her more? There wasn't anything left to dread any further losses . There was still a glimmer of hope though! Hope that lingered despite everything!

Perhaps it had occurred to Sid that all his mother could have wanted was to see him happy. Perhaps Sid was regretting his decision and thinking of coming back. But of course, that was too much to expect. He would never go back on his decision, never betray his mother's wishes. Then, what could Sid have written in that e-mail that he couldn't have said on phone?

Abhi went up to his room where his computer was. Priyam followed a few moments later. When she reached Abhi's room, he had already switched on his computer and was waiting impatiently for the system to boot up. His fingers drummed on the mouse as he stared into the screen.

'What has he written?' Priyam asked, even though she knew that he could not have logged onto the net so soon.

'I don't know,' Abhi replied. 'but...' he said turning towards her, 'why don't you get us some more tea while the system gets started.

'But you've already had tea,' she complained. How could Abhi make such a request at this time? He knew how impatient she was to read that mail.

'Yeah,' he grinned, 'but I'd really like another cup. Don't worry, you know how slow this system is. Your tea would come here quicker than his mail.'

Priyam said nothing. She stared at Abhi for a moment and then walked out of the room.

Hardly five minutes had passed when Priyam walked back in with tea and biscuits. 'Oh, why have you started reading it alone? Couldn't you wait for me?' she broke out with some anger at Abhi's strange thoughtlessness. But he neither looked up nor gave any reply. 'Tea,' she said, placing the cup near him, 'What has he written?' she asked.

'Nothing,' Abhi replied.

'Nothing?' Then why did Abhi look so disturbed? There must be something in the mail that Abhi did not like. What could it be? Why was he shaking his head so and looking so grim and displeased.

'What is it, Abhi? Is Sid okay?' Priyam asked, fear beating at her heart.

Abhi looked up at her but said nothing.

'What has he written?' she asked again.

'He's concerned about you,' Abhi muttered.

'Is that all?' Priyam asked, but already knew it could not be. There was something else, something that Abhi feared would hurt her more. Why else would there be such anger in his movements? Why such desire to keep her from reading the mail?

'Yes,' Abhi replied, moving the mouse pointer to close the mail.

'I want to read it,' Priyam said. Abhi's hand halted and he stared at the computer screen as if trying to reach a difficult decision.

'Please!' she insisted.

'Okay,' he sighed and got up from the chair. Priyam looked at Abhi for an uncertain moment but soon took the seat he had vacated. Her eyes greedily scanned the screen, hoping to see a special note addressed just to her. There wasn't any. But she could live with that. Next, she proceeded to read the mail.

'Hello Abhi,

How are you? And, Priyam?

Everything here is fine. Life has again settled down to a set routine. Though it's just for a short time. By March next year I'll get an off-shore posting. Tina hopes that I'll be posted to London. She has many friends there. As for me, I no longer care where I am. I've already left my friends far away.

Mrs. Sinha, Mom, as I'm now supposed to call her, is trying to fix an early date for engagement and marriage. I'll inform you when anything gets finalized.

Abhi, I don't know if what I'm doing is right or wrong. I've already erred once by letting Priyam build up dreams that I had no right to inspire. All that was a mistake. Maybe, by crushing these very dreams I'm just doing a graver wrong.

And yet I dare to ask a favour of you. I know you'd understand. I don't ask for forgiveness, Abhi. Neither from you nor from Priyam. I don't deserve any. But it would make my life a little easier if I could be sure of her recovery from the feelings my selfishness has given rise to. I wish I could undo the mistakes I committed. Wish I could take away the pain I've given her. But I can't.

You can, Abhi. Help her leave the past behind and walk ahead. Only a new life can help one forget the old miseries. Give Priyam that new life. Give her a new love. I'm sure you'd be able to find for your sister a person who would give her back all the happiness and joy she has lost.

Just do this one last favour for me, and I'd stay forever indebted to you.

Take care of her…

Sid.'

Abhi watched Priyam carefully as she read the e-mail again and again.

Her lips were trembling and eyes seemed to be staring with disbelief at Sid's words. There were no tears in her eyes. She had wiped them away, perhaps to make space for the seething rage that rose in her at every reading of the words that seemed to mock her from the computer screen.

'Priyam?' Abhi murmured.

'The day after tomorrow is Sunday,' she said.

'So?' Abhi asked.

'So, you can look in the Sunday matrimonial.'

'There's no hurry, Priyam, you are only....'

'I'm old enough to get married. He has asked a favour of you. You must not disappoint him.'

'We can wait.'

'For what?'

'Till you are ready...'

'I'm ready now, Abhi,' she said, 'more than this, I'll never be. And you know that, don't you?' she asked.

Abhi nodded his head and breathed a deep sigh but said nothing.

'Just get me married,' Priyam continued, 'as soon as possible. So at least *he* can breathe easy.'

And before Abhi could say anything, Priyam got up from the chair and ran out of his room. Not to cry. She had done with crying. Sid did not deserve her tears. Mistake! All those moments she so cherished were mistakes! How could he call their relationship a mistake? And wasn't it enough for Sid to separate himself from her? He wanted to remove himself from her heart too, to force someone else's thoughts to cloud away his memories? As if that was even possible! How could he even think of her belonging to someone else?

Priyam stood in front of Sid's photograph. But instead of love, it was rage that glowered in her eyes now as she looked at him. 'You want to see me married? To see me happily settled? Alright then,' she said, 'I'll yet grant you your wish, Sid! I'll give you what you want. I'll get married, and before you!'

Chapter 19

'If this is as it ought to be,
My God, I leave it unto Thee'

— *'Dora' by T.E. Brown*

The month of November dawned with a promise of settlements, grim and unwanted maybe, but decisive and final. New relationships were forged, putting a firm seal on the breakdown of the earlier ones.

Priyam was engaged, a few days later Sid too went through the ceremony. Another engagement was solemnized a few days later, though only informally and in the privacy of Raj's car. It was to be kept secret from everyone else. Diamonds, however, have a way of announcing their presence on a girl's finger. Unsurprisingly therefore, scarcely a day had passed since Raj had slipped the ring on her finger and its glitter had already proclaimed Aashi's happiness to everyone.

Priyam's engagement took place in the first week of November. There, after all, couldn't be any dearth of interest in a girl so pretty and so well connected as she was. That Mr. Vardhan had a special interest in Abhi and his sister, was an open secret in Abhi's office, confirmed repeatedly by Abhi's rapid rise in the company. And that Abhi doted on Priyam and could do anything for her was also not hidden from anyone. So as soon as he let drop a word about getting his sister married, the buzzing of grapevine was diligent enough to bring before him, even before the week had passed, a long list of suitable candidates.

Perhaps, Abhi may have taken some time to sift through the heap, had it not been for the desperate endeavours of an exceptionally eager young man. His name was Manish, and he was blessed to be an only son of what he humbly acknowledged as a very well-to-do family.

Manish had joined Mr. Vardhan's company about six months ago and had soon established himself as the computer wizard of Abhi's team and everybody's good friend. He had good looks and a very innocent looking smile. And Manish was already so in love with Priyam that he utilized every opportunity of visiting Abhi's cabin just to look at her photo.

A couple of felicitous remarks dropped by him had got Abhi to discuss with him his sister's future and allowed Manish to dutifully reply that any man would consider himself fortunate to be wedded to her. 'At least I would,' Manish had coyly declared.

Abhi discussed the matter with his seniors and colleagues, and they all had only good things to say about Manish. There didn't seem any reason to doubt Manish's deserving.

Abhi didn't like rushing Priyam into a new relationship. She was not ready, he knew that well. But there was no reason to wait either. Sid was not going to return. And maybe, Manish, with all his charm and goodness, was the perfect person to make Priyam happy again. At least, Abhi hoped he was.

And so, before many days had passed, Abhi invited Manish and his family to his home. The Damle family came over to see Priyam and was abundantly delighted with her. It didn't bother them that she was parentless because they did not harbour any expectation of dowry.

'It's not the money that the bride brings that makes a happy family, but her own personal virtues and adaptability,' Manish's mother declared with substantial good sense. 'A girl must be of adjusting disposition; one who could keep the family united and always put the family's good above her personal desires.'

'Yes, that's what is of real value. And I'm sure our Priyam has everything that we want in a daughter-in-law. She will fill our home with happiness,' Mr. Damle declared before he stepped out of the house. 'By the way, when are we going to have the pleasure to meet your guardian? I'm quite looking forward to meet that gentleman and embrace him as a close relation that he is soon going to become.'

The possibility of quick fulfilment of this desire however was sacrificed by the eagerness of his son to enter into the bond and reluctance of Abhi and Priyam to inform Mr. Vardhan about the same. Manish insisted, till acquiesced, on holding the engagement as soon as possible. And both Priyam and Abhi procrastinated the duty of informing their guardian till just two days before the ceremony. And by then, it was too late for Mr. Vardhan to be able to change his plans and fly to India.

Had it been left to Priyam alone, she would never have got the courage to pass on the information to her guardian. It had been more than three months since she had sent a letter to him. Three months, during which time had taken place the downfall of all her life's hopes. Yet Mr. Vardhan knew nothing about the matter. And Priyam had no courage to tell. He had gone away from India secure in the knowledge that his only child was with his friends. What would he say to know that his son had alienated himself from the only two persons on whom he relied for comfort and happiness; that both sid and Priyam were doomed; that the union the old gentleman dreamt of and had blessed not very long ago would never materialize. Priyam couldn't tell him. She just could not.

Abhi understood her hesitation, and took upon himself to share the *happy* news that he knew could bring no happiness to the listener. That evening he took up the phone and carefully dialled Mr. Vardhan's number.

'Hello…sir, this is Abhi,' he began.

'Abhi? What a pleasant surprise?' Mr. Vardhan's voice echoed out from the speaker. Priyam's hand instinctively reached up to the chain around her neck. Her fingers grasped the pearl pendant that had stayed close to her bosom from the day Mr. Vardhan had gifted it to her. How many years ago had that been? 4? 5? Oh, but how far away it seemed!

'How are you, sir?' Abhi asked.

'I'm okay, son. Quite okay. But you tell me, is everything alright there? Why did you call?'

'To inform you about Priyam's engagement.'

'Ah, finally! That blessed day has come. So? When's the happy day? I hope Sid would have no objection to my presence at his engagement ceremony.'

'I don't know about that, sir. But he could have no objection to your attending Priyam's engagement.'

'What do you mean, Abhi? They couldn't be getting engaged separately, could they?' said Mr. Vardhan with an uncertain laugh.

'They are, sir. Priyam's engagement is after two days, and Sid's, about a week later.'

'What do you mean, Abhi? How can that be? Speak clearly!' Mr. Vardhan's shock burst out from the phone. Priyam could hear the tremor in his voice, but could do nothing except spend the next ten minutes watching Abhi relate everything to him.

The siblings could not see their guardian's face but could very well feel the shock and anger that he must have been hit with.

Priyam kept on expecting his call in the following days, but it never came. Not that day, nor on the next two. Even the day of her engagement passed away without hearing a word from Mr. Vardhan.

Two days passed away in a flurry of preparation. And before the sun downed on the sixth day of November, a bright band of gold encircled Priyam's finger and proclaimed possession in the glitter of the tiny diamond that adorned it.

It was this ring that engaged her eyes after all the bustle of the evening was over. Everybody had left. It was almost 11 p.m., time enough for even

Aashi and her mother to retire to their home. The mother and daughter had been their only guests apart from the people accompanying Manish and his family. The clamour had passed away and only silence remained behind. Silence that surrounded Abhi and Priyam as they sat alone in the living room that was still bearing the marks of the ceremony held.

Priyam sat staring at her hand, at the glint of the metal that had sealed the bond. She turned her head a little and noticed Abhi watching her.

'Look at this diamond, Abhi, how shiny it is,' she said, without bothering to intone the excitement that should have followed the words.

'I'm looking at your eyes, Priyam, and there's not a single spark of joy in them,' Abhi replied.

'I'm tired, Abhi.'

'So am I, Priyam, of all this. I thought I was doing the right thing. But now, I don't think so anymore. This is not right. It should not happen like this. Let's put a stop to this.'

'Stop to what?'

'This…this engagement, this wedding…we can still back out. This is not right. Neither to you, nor to Manish. We should put an end to all this.'

'Now? After everything has been arranged?'

'I don't care about the arrangements. I don't care about anything. I care about you, and your happiness. Look at yourself. You have got engaged today and there's not even a spark of interest in your eyes. Not a flicker of excitement. You don't at all care for any of this shit.'

'You are right. I don't,' she muttered in a tired voice.

'Then why?'

'You know why.'

'He wanted you to move on, Priyam. But you are not moving on, nor even trying to. You are not leaving anything behind, but carrying it all buried deep inside you. It will kill you, Priyam, it will stifle you.'

'Let it then. At least *he* would breathe easy,' she murmured, still staring at the ring.

'And me? How do you think would it make me feel?'

'Abhi, you always say that whatever happens, happens for the best.'

'Yes, but…'

'Well, then let it be.'

'What if I don't? I have done a mistake in starting all this. But I'll put a stop at all this now. I can't allow you to…'

'Don't forget, Abhi, if Sid can run away, so can I. I'll elope. You can't stop me from marrying,' Priyam muttered, fully conscious of the bitter cruelty of her words, yet past caring.

'You won't do that to me.'

'Don't try me, Abhi, you don't know what I might or might not do. Just don't try me. I beg of you,' she said and got up from the sofa.

'Where are you going?'

'To my room. Good night,' she said, turning to go out of the room.

'So, you are determined to ruin yourself?' Abhi called out to her.

'I'm determined to get married,' she said without stopping.

'Are you happy with…?

'That isn't necessary.'

'For me, it is!' Abhi said, walking upto her. 'You are all I have to look for happiness. And if you are sad, how can I bear it?' His hand clutched her shoulder and shook her angrily as he spoke. She stumbled backwards, but her eyes remained fixed on him.

'Don't think about me, Abhi, you have sorrow enough of your own,' she said, looking up at him. For a moment the icy rigidity melted away from the brown depths of Priyam's eyes, but only to be replaced the very next moment by a sterner attempt at apathy and immutability.

'No, I'm content,' he said, 'all I want is for you to be happy.'

'So am I,' she said as she turned and walked out of the room, 'and for the same reason,' she said, and then ran up the stairs before Abhi could utter another word.

Abhi watched her climbing the stairs and a shuddering sigh escaped his lips.

It should have been the happiest day of his life. It should have been a day full of excitement. But all he could feel at that moment was a heavy crushing ache in his heart and a sense of having done something gravely wrong.

There was this unremitting foreboding of approaching disaster that Abhi could not take out from his heart. The day sped by past his eyes once again. Every time he tried to remember the one moment in the entire day, that one moment on which he could build up his hopes for Priyam's wellbeing. He did not doubt Manish, or his family. They all appeared very nice people. Nor was it that Abhi didn't want her to move on. Sure, he no longer had any hopes from Sid.

But what pricked Abhi was the reason behind Priyam's insistence to rush into this union. She was not ready, and yet she was forcing herself into a relationship that held no meaning to her.

'I hope you are happy too, Sid,' Abhi muttered after Priyam left him alone.

He walked up to the side table and picked up a photograph. There they all were, still together, still happy. It was taken just last year and yet, how far ago those days seemed now. Abhi stared at the picture. The faces peeking out of it were still the same, yet, how the persons had changed. 'I wish you could see her now, Sid,' he muttered, 'I wish you could come here and see with your own eyes the *happiness* you have given her,' he said, not entirely without bitterness.

Sid did come to their house again, and in the same month, but six days after Priyam's engagement and two hours since his own.

'Sid? How come...' Abhi exclaimed to see him at the doorstep so soon after his engagement.

'Didn't you expect me?' Sid asked, cutting his question midway.

'We did hope that you'd come. But...is the party over already?'

'No, but I managed my escape.'

'But why? It was quite a nice party,' Abhi said, welcoming him in.

'You didn't stay long either,' Sid replied.

'We stayed long enough, I think.'

'Yes. Thanks for coming,' Sid answered.

He had by then walked up to the middle of the living room. Here, he halted and looked around, throwing a loving glance at every corner of that dear room. 'Where's...Priyam?' he asked a moment later.

'She was here just a moment ago. Priyam?' Abhi called out to her. 'There she is,' he said as Priyam came out of the kitchen with a glass of water for Sid. She walked up to them and silently handed the glass to Sid.

'Thanks,' Sid said, surveying her face anxiously, 'how are you?' he asked.

'Fine,' she replied with a suitable smile. 'Congratulations for your engagement. It was a very nice party.'

'Yeah, I guess.'

A short silence ensued after his words.

'So,' Abhi spoke up finally, 'how long are you here?'

'All night. My train leaves at 6:30 in the morning. And till then I hope to find a refuge here.'

'It's a humble refuge compared to the place you could have stayed in.'

'Suits me better though. Priyam, don't go back into your kitchen. You can delay your hospitality a little, can't you?' Sid said as he caught Priyam on

149

her way out of the room. She stopped, looked at him for a moment and then walked up to a chair. 'Thanks,' he said.

'No problem,' Priyam replied and sat down, trying to appear as unaffected by his presence as possible.

'Where's the chess-board?' Sid asked as he glanced around the room once more.

'Folded up and stowed away,' Abhi replied.

'That photograph…is that Priyam's…?'

'Yes. He's my fiance' Priyam completed the sentence he could not.

'Manish Damle, that's his name, isn't it?'

'Yes, it is,' Priyam was again the first one to reply.

'What kind of a guy is he?'

'He's much liked in the office for his good humour, intelligence and helpful nature,' said Abhi.

'He's very good-looking too. You like him, Priyam, don't you?'

'*What does it matter if I do or not. He satisfies your purpose, doesn't he?*' Priyam wanted to shout out. 'I have no reason not to,' she replied instead.

'Good.'

'Thank you,' she muttered and got up from the chair, walking out of the room before Sid could stop her again. He watched her but made no attempt to call her back.

Time flew away swiftly that evening. And even before Priyam could have her fill of Sid's face, it was time to turn away and go to bed. Too soon had come the time to bid him goodnight. Although Priyam had talked but little all evening, she had still had the pleasure of listening to his voice. And now as she walked up to her room, she could not help but wonder when, if ever, would she have that opportunity again.

There he was, standing near the door of what was still called Sid's room. He was looking at her, Priyam knew. She dared not turn, yet his gaze was upon her and her every pore tingled with wrenching pain. With leaden steps Priyam climbed upstairs and closed her door.

It was a little after eleven, sleep was still a distant wanderer. So Priyam walked up to her window and stared out through closed panes. The night air had already acquired a biting chill that warned them of a bitter winter. Yet the night sky was just as beautiful as before. The moon was just as bright and serene, but then, when was its serenity ever disturbed by the turmoil of the lowly earth. It might listen, it might hear, it might stand witness to many a secret pain and masquerade as a sympathetic companion of the dark. But it could not feel the pain it witnessed, it could not experience the grief it shared. All it could do was to shine and follow the dictates of time.

That night as Priyam stood at her window, she felt just as apathetic to everything as that impervious sphere of light, just as insensate, just as lifeless.

Priyam didn't know how long she remained standing there, nor what time it was when she finally decided to lie down on her bed. But she couldn't have slept for half an hour when she got up again. What it was that had awakened her, she had no idea. There had been no sound, no sudden clap of lightning, no threatening roar of thunder. Yet there she sat, breathing hard under a sudden oppressiveness that had overwhelmed the sleep out of her eyes. Her eyes stared at the door, as if waiting for someone to announce his presence. Surely there was someone outside her room. Someone standing motionless and still, and yet being tossed in the raging sea of desire and indecisiveness. Priyam could almost feel his hand on the door, aching to make a knock, and yet resisting. She too waited, staring at the lifeless face of the wooden door. Minutes crept away, time remained standing, caught as if in the perplexity of the moment.

And then, it was over.

In a moment Priyam was at the door, pressing her ear to its cold surface. But that was not enough. She opened the door and ran towards the staircase. There he was, halfway down the stairs. Sid halted, perhaps turned too. But it was too dark and Priyam's eyes were bleary. A long moment passed away in tortured silence. Then he moved again, not towards her but away. A few soft footsteps receding down the stairs… a gentle creaking of the downstairs bedroom door…

That was all.

He was gone.

Priyam dragged her feet back to her bed and strained her ears to hear him move again. But no sound whispered in the night, no unwilling steps surrendered to the pull of heart's desires again, no beating heart sought to find solace in a sympathetic breast. All that had been won over, and everything else that could have been life, given over to loss by a determined will. Sid had won the final battle, broken whatever still fettered him to Priyam, and set himself free to sail away.

Priyam kept on watching the door for a long time. But Sid never retraced his steps. He was gone and all Priyam could do was to hug her knees close to her and refresh, with her tears, the remembrance of the night when he had not so turned away from her but had lingered on to leave on her lips the imprint of his love.

But that was in a different life.

And that life was no more.

✳✳✳

Chapter 20

For each ecstatic instant
We must an anguish pay
In keen and quivering ratio
To the ecstasy

For each beloved hour
Sharp Pittance of years
Bitter contested farthings
And coffers heaped with tears.

— *Emily Dickinson*

It was only 8:32 by her watch, early enough for Aashi to grudge the very workload that was speeding up such a pleasing bulk to her bank account.

'Hi! Hurrying off so soon? What's the rush?' Abhi asked when he saw Aashi coming out of her home. He was sitting on his swing and going through the day's newspaper. Seeing Aashi however, he left it on the swing and walked up to the boundary wall separating their houses.

'Yes, there's so much to do and so few days. If I don't hurry now, I'll have to sit there till Diwali is come and gone.'

'As if you'd be allowed to do that,' Abhi laughed, ignoring her brusque tones.

'I know, Raj doesn't even allow me there after evening. Evening time is his time he says,' Aashi said, giving Abhi's statement the turn that suited her better.

'He should be glad that your boutique is prospering so well.'

'All boutiques do well in the festive season,' she shrugged.

'No wonder, festivals and weddings are such excellent excuses for you girls to horde up on clothes. Whether you need them or not,' Abhi laughed.

'You cannot have any such complaint, Abhi,' Aashi shot back. 'Priyam is hardly the girl to do anything like that. She doesn't eve care what colour or cut she would like in her own wedding *lehenga*.'

'And aren't you glad about that? You at least have one customer who trusts you with such total faith. I've heard designers like that,' Abhi said, trying to make light of the matter that had already evoked a familiar fear in his heart. Aashi's words didn't surprise him though. Priyam showed the same indifference to everything concerning her marriage. Everything, except the date. That she wanted to be as early as possible. The rest Priyam accepted without even a word.

'Yeah, but I would like *her* to start complaining once in a while,' said Aashi. 'Will she ever be able to forget Sid?'

'Their bond is just too strong. They... neither of them would be able to forget,' Abhi replied in a low voice.

Aashi looked up at him, at his worried face. Her hand half lifted itself to reach out to him with a reassuring touch.

'But don't worry,' he said, looking straight at her, 'they've seen enough of life to know that it rarely, if ever, is perfect. Not everyone is so blessed with the fulfilment of all their dreams you know. Most are just left with a handful of broken shards. The tighter you grasp them, the more they hurt.'

Aashi's hand dropped to her side and she took a step back.

'*A handful of broken shards,*' the words echoed in her mind as she stared at Abhi.

But it was not her fault. It was not! And she had the right to choose her happiness. No matter what the cost!

Fire blazed from her eyes. But she remained still and silent.

'You must leave now,' Abhi said, taking his eyes away from her and turning to stare at a nearby plant instead. 'I'm sorry I delayed you so much.'

She turned away, only to retrace her steps in a moment. 'By the way,' she began, 'I'd be late today too.'

'Okay.' Abhi replied.

'I'm going with Raj to watch a romantic movie, and then he'd take me to a very nice and expensive restaurant,' she added, taking care to stress the words she knew carried maximum strike.

'Okay,' Abhi repeated, not caring to notice her various intonations.

'Why? Aren't you going to lecture me again?'

'I only told you to return early because I don't like people here talking crap about you. But since you don't mind...'

'Yes, I don't mind,' Aashi replied, 'my mother doesn't mind. Why should you? If there's anyone in the world who could put restrictions on me, it's Raj. He's there to protect my honour and me. You need not bother.'

'You made that abundantly clear yesterday itself,' Abhi replied with a twisted grin that could surely have rivalled the ambiguity of a world famous smile. But of course, Aashi was in no mood to dwell beneath its various layers. Neither did Abhi give her a chance to. He turned his face and let her stomp away, throwing all her fury at the rusty gate. It easily produced the loud screech of protest that she herself felt too dignified to indulge in.

It had became too much of a routine those days to have their meeting ended in a walkout. Every time they spent some moments alone, it invariably ended in either Abhi slinking away from Aashi's biting fury or she fuming away from his haughty complacency.

Never once did Aashi turn while rushing away from Abhi. Nor did she even once stop by to see if he was still standing and looking at her. She could feel his eyes on her very well and knew that he was. And so she rushed away, trying to get, as quickly as possible, out of his visual range.

But then, she knew that it was useless. There was no escape from Abhi. Even when she reached the end of the road and climbed into the bus, she felt those eyes still upon her, staring at her with that all knowing gaze of his and mocking her with their disapproval. Why won't they ever leave her alone? Why would they keep on following her, keeping a constant guard, even when she was alone with Raj? Aashi hated that stare, she hated those eyes and, she hated him. Yet, try as she might, she couldn't despise Abhi the way she wanted to. He was just too good…too damn good.

Exactly fifteen minutes after Aashi left, a visitor arrived at Abhi's gate, and exactly fifteen seconds later, he walked into the house with firm stately pace.

'Priyam, come quick! Mr. Vardhan is here,' Abhi called to his sister as he ushered the gentleman in.

The door of Priyam's room opened immediately. 'Uncle!' Priyam's voice rang out, soon followed by several thuds as she almost tumbled down the stairs.

'Easy, Priyam!' Mr. Vardhan laughed, 'You'd break your neck one day if that's the way you come down the stairs.'

'Oh, it's so good to see you, Uncle!' she sang out, her smiles barely managing to mirror the pleasure she felt.

'Yes, it's good to see you too, both of you,' Mr. Vardhan replied, stroking her head and smiling at Abhi.

'This really is quite an unexpected surprise, Sir,' Abhi said smiling.

'No, it isn't. I've been expecting him since…' but Priyam let her sentence remain unfinished. The mention of her engagement would hardly have given any pleasure to her guest, or to herself.

'Oh, I know it's very early. But then, this is the only place where I could expect such a warm welcome. So I told my driver to bring me here. And I do hope that I'm early enough to join you in breakfast. Am I?' Mr. Vardhan said, smiling at Priyam.

'You are just in time, Uncle. Give me five minutes,' Priyam smiled back, trying hard not to let her eyes get clouded by the memory of another one so like him who too so often had claimed her hospitality with equal candour and confidence. She soon skipped away to her kitchen, but not before satisfying herself about Mr. Vardhan's health and extracting from him every little detail about the duration and schedule of his visit.

Abhi looked at Priyam with a glad mix of relief and pleasure as she chatted away. It had been many days since he had seen her so animated, and with genuine happiness too.

Mr. Vardhan soon settled down uncannily on the sofa his son always preferred. His eyes lazily swept over the room, halting a moment at Sid's photo before travelling on to Manish's picture standing much nearer on a small side table. It was placed directly under the lamp-light but far away from all the other frames.

'What's his name?' he asked.

'Manish Damle,' Abhi replied.

'He works with us, doesn't he?'

'Yes, Sir.'

'You like him?'

'Yes, sir, everyone likes him.'

'I'd like to meet him. Have you invited him to the party?'

'No, Sir, his name was not among the list of invitees.'

'Oh, forget the list. Invite him, his entire family. Send them a special invitation,' Mr. Vardhan said, waiting for Abhi to give an affirmative nod. When that was done, Mr. Vardhan fixed his elbows on his knees and linked his fingers in the exact way Sid used to do when preparing to settle something of great importance. 'I hope all the arrangements have been made,' he said.

'Yes, Sir,' Abhi replied, 'everything has been finalised. It would be a grand party, true to our company's tradition.'

'Oh, I wasn't talking about the party,' Mr. Vardhan interrupted, 'What about Priyam's wedding?' he asked, making Abhi go over every little detail.

By the time Priyam brought in the breakfast, Mr. Vardhan had gone through and approved everything with just two essential recommendations. One, he could not let his child get married in the banquet hall Abhi had booked, and two, he would not allow anyone except his long trusted caterer to serve at the wedding.

Abhi knew that caterer and had even talked to him, finding even his simplest of menus too far above his own budget. But that didn't stop Mr. Vardhan from picking up his phone and shooting all the necessary orders to his secretary. 'There, that's done,' he soon said, 'now about the venue.'

But deciding upon a venue took a little more time. Abhi refused to entertain the idea of holding the wedding at any five-star hotel. Priyam shook her head at Mr. Vardhan's plan of using either his bungalow or the Retreat. And Mr. Vardhan, of course, would not bear to have his daughter marry in a place less worthy.

'Well then, the only other option I give you is our guesthouse. It's spacious and its rooms can house all your guests with ease too. It would be the perfect place for your marriage,' Mr. Vardhan concluded. Neither Abhi nor Priyam could think up of any objection to the plan. 'Good, it's settled then. I hope you don't mind my being so interfering,' he added, with a little smile.

It saddened him just to think Priyam getting married to someone other than his son. But he had determined not to let his feelings interfere with his duty. Priyam was his daughter, and she will get married as his daughter. He would not spare any expense in her wedding ceremony.

'No, of course not. But...' Abhi tried, but before he could utter another word Mr. Vardhan interrupted again.

'Those are the only two changes I require,' he said. 'For the rest of the stuff I declare myself quite content with your good choice and judgement.'

'Thank you, Sir,' Abhi breathed with obvious relief. He knew well what pleasure it would give to his guardian to splurge on Priyam's wedding. Still Abhi wanted to keep all the expenses to himself. Mr. Vardhan had already done so much for them. Now that he was independent and earning well, Abhi didn't want to still be leaning on to Mr. Vardhan to meet their wants. He didn't want to take an undue advantage of his guardian's benevolence and be seen like appropriating the money that rightfully belonged to Sid and Tina.

The Diwali party, for which Mr. Vardhan had arrived back in India, was an annual affair that gave the company chance to host all its present as well as future benefactors and carry out a great relation building exercise. It was always held two days before Diwali, and was an eagerly anticipated event by those who had hopes of getting the coveted invitation.

There was one person however, who needed to be lovingly cajoled every year just to be present there. Priyam never liked being part of such a high-brow event even though her own brother, ever since he joined the company, was an active member of the organising committee. She felt lost among the fancy throng and didn't like to enjoy a party when Sid sat alone in his room.

But this year there was no Sid to think of and since her future family was invited, Priyam's presence was imperative too. She was glad therefore to know that Aashi would be coming to the party too, as Raj's girlfriend of course.

But Priyam's gladness couldn't have equalled Aashi's thrill at the prospect. For one, it was the first party she was to attend as Raj's declared girlfriend and an undeclared fiancée. But what felt even better was that she wouldn't need to solicit a lift in Abhi's old Maruti. She didn't yet know which of his several fancy cars Raj would choose to bring that day. But that didn't stop her from picturing herself getting down from a sleek beauty that sometimes was sexy black and sometimes elegant silver. Aashi could even see the face of the uniformed guard that respectfully opened the door for her while Raj waited with eagerness to take her hand in his. Together they would walk to the party hall, Raj in his sartorial best and she looking stunning in her newly designed dress. She even practiced the smile she would give to all those staring at them, the admiration in everybody's eyes proclaiming the two of them the most handsome couple in the entire gathering.

What a pity it was therefore that never, in all her mental rehearsals, had Aashi prepared for the presence of a third. A third that demanded her continuous attention by petulant complaining and walked, not just besides Raj but actually between them, maintaining an impervious barrier between Aashi and her love. What made it worse was that it had been Raj actually, as Tina declared over and over, who had forced her to attend the party.

'His mother must have ordered him to do it,' Aashi told herself.

That however, could help but little as a way of consolation for the shattered dreams and lost hopes, especially when Aashi could very well see every eye drawn towards Tina, or rather towards her tiny designer extravagance.

'I hate such stuffy parties!' Tina declared as the three of them walked in, 'What does it matter if it's Mr. Vardhan's party? Even his son's not here. If Sid didn't think it necessary to come, I'm sure I could have been excused too.'

'Take it easy, sis,' Raj tried to pacify her, 'you never know whom you might meet in such parties. May be it won't be so boring after all,' he said laughing.

It needed just fifteen minutes to show Aashi how well Raj knew his sister. Very soon she experienced the great relief of seeing Tina engaged in a very animated conversation with a tall, blonde English gentleman. And fortunately for Aashi, the gentleman continued to engage Tina's interest all evening and even succeeded in being her chosen partner in all the little events that required the participation of couples.

Tina didn't seem to remember that it was her father-in-law's party she was flirting around in. Nor did Mr. Vardhan seem to mind her a bit. In fact, the two were so unmindful of each other's presence that neither of them bothered to seek or greet the other.

There was one particular group of guests, however, that received the host's almost undivided attention. Mr, Vardhan welcomed them himself and gave special instruction to the serving staff to take extra care of them.

'Oh, don't worry about us, Mr. Vardhan,' Mr. Damle responded with much humility. 'We'll be fine. Besides, it is enough for us that you have accepted my son as your daughter's husband. I just want to assure you that we will do everything to keep Priyam happy. She will be as much a daughter to us as she is to you.'

'Thank you, I hope so too. She deserves all the happiness in the world. You would never have found a better girl for your son than Priyam. She is a gem, and I do not just say this because she is my daughter,' said Mr. Vardhan.

Mr. Damle nodded and then he and Manish walked off with Mr. Vardhan as he went to greet his other guests. Mr. Vardhan duly introduced them to all of his important guests. They greeted everyone most humbly and made every effort on their part to play the role of good hosts, they being now family of Mr. Vardhan.

Mr. Damle received another very pleasant surprise when he recognised one of his distant relatives among the guests. So he and his son left Mr. Vardhan to spend some moments with their much esteemed relative. This gentleman was a minister of state now. Naturally, he had some difficulty in recognizing Mr. Damle and his family. But Mr. Damle soon managed to raise the minister's brain cells out of their slumber and sustain their wakefulness long enough to let him follow the trail of relations that bound them together.

'But didn't you live in Pune?' the minister asked, adjusting his bulk on his ever-shifting legs.

'Yes, yes,' Mr. Damle said, 'you remember us right. We used to live in Pune. But we shifted here a little while ago. . We live here now. My son, Manish, works with Mr. Vardhan and is soon going to be his son-in-law.'

'Oh, very well. Nice to know that. It's real pleasure to see young people progressing so well. How's your other son? Is he still working in Pune?'

'Other son? What other son? I have no other son,' Mr. Damle replied.

'No? Was it Manish then whose wife died? If I remember you correctly...I did hear something concerning the sudden death of your son's wife and her relatives dragging you to court. What was it?'

'Wife? Sudden death? What are you saying?' Mr. Damle exclaimed. This certainly was not what he had expected to hear from his relative. 'There must be some mistake. You don't recollect us clearly,' he added with a laugh.

'Maybe, I meet so many people, I can't recollect them all,' the minister droned in nonchalant voice. His eyes by then had fished out someone of greater importance at the far corner of the hall. 'If you'll excuse me now,' he said quickly, 'I must go and meet someone.' He had wasted enough time with the Damles and it was time to see some more profitable company. So before Mr. Damle could utter another word, his long distance relative had put in a long distance between them.

Priyam, however, wasn't so blessed with the choice of company. With her brother running from one corner of the hall to the other in an attempt to manage everything all at once, she had no other option but to remain in company of her future mother-in-law.

Aashi did try to give her company some times, but the allurement of being with Raj soon won over the compulsions of camaraderie and she could do little but flash understanding smiles to her poor trapped friend while she herself glided dreamily across the hall with her handsome prince on her side.

It was truly a magnificent party with grandeur flashing in every corner. Aashi felt as if she had stepped into an entirely different world. Certainly, the doors had been finally opened, welcoming her into a world she had only dreamt of. And yet, she felt at home here, as if she was finally where she belonged, where she deserved to be. It was a mistake of providence to raise her up in a middle class household and that too as a dependent relative. It was good that destiny had realized her mistake so timely and rectified it so marvellously.

Aashi now had everything she had ever desired, and it was just the beginning of life that she could already see gleaming before her, so lovely with youth and beauty, so enchanting with love and romance and so glittering with luxury and grandeur. What else could she want more? Aashi had found the perfection she had desired. Nothing else mattered.

The two days after the party flew away in a flurry of activity as Aashi raced against time to finish orders before Diwali. She even had to hire some extra workers to meet the festive rush. The festival day soon enough and she was happy that she could managed to satisfy most of her clients.

Aashi too was perfectly satisfied with her dress and her carefully applied make up. She was ready and looking forward for her most eagerly awaited guest to arrive.

159

Well, Raj didn't make her wait too long. The clock had barely stuck eight when Raj entered her gate.

'Hi gorgeous! Super Diwali!' he sang out from the gate. 'What were you doing?'

'Waiting,' she replied.

Since last half hour Aashi had done nothing but stand just inside her door, waiting for Raj and keeping her fingers firmly in her ears to block away the sound of crackers.

That was the only thing she hated about Diwali. The air was just too full of booms and bangs. And every cracker that burst left her shaken and feeling edgy.

It had not always been like that. She had loved crackers just as much as everybody else. But one single, cursed bomb had changed everything.

'What took you so long?' she said, rushing up to him, still keeping her fingers in her ears.

'Oh, the usual stuff. But now I'm absolutely at your service till midnight, or even later if you choose,' he replied, wrapping his arm around her.

'That can be decided later. But first, come in,' Aashi said as she hurried Raj inside.

Her eyes glittered with happiness, as they always did when Raj was close. But it was with dread that her heartbeat was racing right at that moment. And even Raj's presence was not sufficient guard against the terrifying sounds echoing through the air outside.

'And now,' she said when they were inside the house and she had wiped the sweat away from her forehead, 'where's my present? You didn't forget to get me one, did you?

'Dare I do such a thing? I love my life, dear, and I wish to see it continue for long!' Raj laughed, fishing out of his pocket a carefully wrapped box.

'What's in it?

'See for yourself,' he said, smiling fondly at her excitement.

'A mobile phone! Oh, just what I wanted! I love it! Thanks!' Aashi exclaimed as she lifted it from the case and let her fingers admire its sleek smoothness. 'It's so beautiful!'

'I'm glad that you like it. Anyway, what's keeping Abhi and Priyam indoors? Some special guest? Manish and his family maybe...' said Raj, answering his own question.

'Nah, neither Manish, nor his family have come. Nor have any plan of doing so, as far as I know. It's so sad, don't you think? This is Abhi and Priyam's first Diwali without Sid, and...at least Mr. Vardhan should have come. But he isn't even in the city today! Priyam said he had to go away for some urgent meeting. I'm sure Mr. Vardhan's business could have waited till another day. He should have known how much Priyam would need him today, don't you think so too, Raj?'

'Well, I can't say anything about Mr. Vardhan. If he is away today, then it must really be something important. As for Manish and his family, I'd rather they stay away.' Raj muttered, settling himself down on one of the four folding chairs that formed the principle furniture of the room. 'She's much better with us. But if Manish comes, we'd have no option but to leave Priyam to him. And I don't think he has any idea of what she needs.'

'He seems quite in love with Priyam though,' Aashi commented.

'Yeah, I suppose he does,' said Raj.

Just then there was a knock at the door and Abhi walked in. Priyam followed him close, holding a box of sweets in her hand.

Raj got up eagerly to exchange Diwali wishes with them.

That was soon done. Then they all sat down to enjoy the sweets and snacks that Urmila and Priyam brought out from the kitchen.

'Well, guys, we have chatted quite enough and eaten more sweets that we should have,' Raj said after fifteen minutes. 'Let's go out now and have some good blasts.'

'You mean crackers?' Aashi asked with evident unease.

'What else? Don't tell me you are scared of crackers!' Raj laughed.

'She is,' Abhi was the one to reply.

'But that's ridiculous!' Raj exclaimed, shaking his head in disbelief.

'No, just an after effect of the bomb blast that took away her father,' Abhi explained.

Abhi knew well how terrified Aashi was of crackers. Just last evening he had seen her all trembling and drenched in sweat when she returned from office, having encountered several fiery celebrations over the way.

Abhi himself was not a stranger to fears that lurk behind after a trauma. He had battled with several such fears and was still fighting against some. He yet had to see a month when he did not wake up in the middle of night, having re-lived the terrible accident again in his dream. The only difference that time had produced in Abhi's nightmare was the replacing of his father's face in the driver's seat with his own. Just a dream, Abhi had always told himself. Still, not once had he touched the steering wheel of his car without silently praying for safety. Yes, he knew well what fear was.

But there had been no such experience to aid Raj's understanding. He had been in a couple of small accidents, but had suffered nothing worse than a few dents on his car.

'But one can't celebrate Diwali while sitting indoors,' Raj said.

'No way, I'm happy in here with my friends. If you want crackers, you go out alone,' Aashi replied.

'Oh, come on. We must learn to grow out of our childish fears. We'd never manage to do anything if we keep on hugging our fears like that.'

'But she's really scared, Raj, I've seen...' Abhi tried again.

'Oh, please, Abhi, she'll never know how much fun there is in a cracker if she never tries her hand at one.'

'No really, Raj. I can't,' Aashi pleaded, shaking her head vigorously. 'I haven't bought any either.'

'Neither have we,' Abhi added.

'I have some in my car. I'll bring them. Let's all get out first,' Raj said and quickly walked out. By the time the rest of them came out, he had already brought a big packet full of all sorts of crackers and was busy rummaging through it. 'Here it is,' said Raj after fishing out a rocket from his store. 'Come, Aashi,' he called her, 'we'll send this off together and it will go up brightening the sky with our love.'

'Not a chance!' Aashi gave a nervous laugh. 'I'm not going to be tricked by your sweet talk. I told you, I'm not touching any of those.'

'Oh, come on, Aashi! Don't be such a coward!' Raj said, pulling her by her hand. 'Don't you trust me?'

'Don't! Don't force her!' Abhi cried out, 'She really is terrified of crackers.'

'Butt out, Abhi. I know what I am doing. I don't want my wife to be scared of anything. Besides, it'll only take a few seconds. Once it's over, Aashi would want to do it again and again. I know her, she's a bold girl, not scared of anything, right Aashi?'

But Aashi had stopped listening. Only one word kept on ringing in her ears. *'Wife! My wife!'* How sweet those words had sounded and with what delicious authority had Raj uttered it. Oh! She would do anything for him! And all he wanted was to light a cracker. She did not love him enough if she could not fulfil even his such a little wish.

'But, really, Raj...' Abhi made another attempt.

'Alright!' Aashi cut him short, 'I'll do it,' she declared, silencing Abhi with a slant look of her eyes. He had no need to defend her, nor any right either. 'You are right,' she continued, turning towards Raj, 'I must not be coward. Let's do it.' Sure her voice trembled as she said that, but then Raj slipped his arm around her and Aashi was ready to die at his command.

'Good girl, I knew you'd agree,' Raj said, smiling with all his charm. 'There's nothing to be scared about,' he continued in his gentlest of tones, 'Just light it with this candle and step back. Simple. See, I can let it go from my hand even. No need of any holder. I'll just hold it like this, you light it, step back and see how it flies off from my hand.'

'No, Aashi, that's too dangerous!' Abhi called out.

'For God's sake, Abhi, stop scaring her like that!' Raj called back. 'Don't listen to him, Aashi.'

Aashi didn't, but she could see Abhi clearly enough and she could see the terror on his face. He stood near his gate with his hand tightly clutched at its rusty body. As she looked at him, his lips moved in a silent plea to refuse. But refusal to Raj was out of question, and Aashi had become quite habitual to ignoring Abhi's words anyway. She didn't quite approve of the tone with which Raj had shouted at him. But it was easy enough to forgive Raj and follow him and do what he bid.

All that Abhi could do was watch as Aashi's trembling hand lit the match. She brought it closer to the fuse. 'God!' his hoarse whisper echoed in the chilly air. Love, pain, fear and a fervent prayer for her safety, all reverberated at the same time in that one word. And that word was the last that Aashi heard that night.

The small flame touched the fuse. The fuse hissed and sputtered as smoke bellowed out. Sparks blazed past her and the rocket zoomed up. It went up just as Raj had promised. Its burning stars bloomed over the sky, dissolving away the darkness just as Raj had predicted. But Aashi saw nothing of that. She fell face down on the ground, unaware of even the utter darkness that had come crowding to her eyes.

Chapter 21

Oh, could we weep,
And weeping bring relief!
But life asks more than tears
And falling leaf.

—'Nurse No Long Grief' by Christina Rosetti.

Yes, Aashi was blind. Blind, without any hope of reprieve. She just didn't know it yet, lost in a dense slumber that she still was.

But Abhi wasn't asleep. He hadn't been able to taste that palliative since her accident.

Aashi lay unconscious on the hospital bed and he could do nothing but sit quietly and watch, letting his fingers have the liberty to hold hers tight in their grasp. Sometimes a tear escaped the bonds of his tired eyes, but that was alright too. She could not see and there was no one else in the room.

He gently lifted up Aashi's hand and touched it to his lips, letting its smoothness rest against his cheek. Several moments crept away in this stillness, several more would have followed had Abhi not felt her fingers twitch. He tightened his grasp and waited awareness to finally dawn on Aashi. Her head moved slightly and fingers reciprocated by lightly pressing against his. A low moan escaped her lips.

'Aashi?' Abhi breathed in a whisper and waited. Some moments passed though before she moved again. 'Aashi?' he tried again, rubbing his thumb over her fingers.

'Humm?' Aashi mumbled, slightly shifting her head towards him.

'How are you feeling?' he asked, leaning closer to her.

'Abhi?' she asked in a voice barely above a whisper.

'Yes, how do you feel now?'

'What...what are you doing in my room? Switch on the light,' she mumbled.

'You are not at home, Aashi. You are in the hospital. And it's light enough. Your mother and Priyam were here too, but I sent them back home.'

'Hospital?'

'Yes.'

'Hospital? Why?'

Abhi wished Aashi could go back to sleep. He didn't want to tell her. He didn't want her to know.

'Abhi?'

'Yes, I'm here,' he said. He took a deep breath before going on. 'Remember the rocket you were trying to...'

'Rocket? I was...Oh! Rocket! I was...Raj? Where's he? What has happened, Abhi? Is Raj okay? He was holding the rocket. Is he okay?' she was fully awake now.

'Raj is okay. His hand is a little blistered though. But then, he should have known better than to do something so foolish. Fire crackers are not something you can mess with so childishly.'

'He knew what he was doing. It must have been my fault,' Aashi cut Abhi short. 'I remember...I lit the fuse and...it shot up, and...what happened then, Abhi? I don't remember!' she said, getting more and more terrified as she spoke. 'Am I burnt? Is my face scarred? Abhi? Tell me!'

'Doctors say the scars will heal in a few days. They are not very serious.'

'Thank God! I hate scars! They look so ugly.'

His lips widened in something that might have been mistaken for a smile. 'I know,' he said.

'But why's everything so dark? I can't see a thing.'

'There's a bandage on your eyes. Some...sparks...fell into your eyes. But don't worry,' he quickly added. 'Raj has sent your reports to a specialist in London. I'm sure there's still something that can be done. You don't worry at all.'

'Still something that can be done? What do you mean, Abhi? Why do you sound so grim and serious? It's not that I'm turned blind or something!' Aashi laughed.

'That...is what the doctors fear.'

He didn't want to do it. He didn't want to be the one to tell her. But there was no one else, and it would have been cruel to keep her waiting.

'What? That I'm blind? Don't be stupid!' she laughed again, though not with her previous nonchalance. 'Abhi? I'm not blind!' she exclaimed when no reassuring reply sounded from him.

'I sure hope...'

'I'm blind! I'm not! And Raj would tell you so. Where's he? Where's Raj?' Aashi shouted, more with terror than fury.

Just then the door opened and Raj came striding in.

'Call Raj. I want Raj,' Aashi ordered Abhi.

'No need for that. I'm right here, my love. At your service as always,' Raj said. 'Good to see you finally awake and missing me. How are you feeling now?' he asked, leaning over her to peck at her lips.

'Fine now,' she smiled, 'but Abhi had me so scared a moment ago!'

'He did, did he? Well, Mr. Abhinandan Mathur? What have you to say to that?'

'Nothing,' Abhi replied.

'He told me that I'm blind. That's a lie, isn't it, Raj? I'm not blind, am I? What do your doctors say? Abhi is lying, isn't he?' Aashi's fears revived themselves on her face as her hands helplessly groped around to reach up to him. Raj took her fingers in his and pressed them gently.

'Don't worry about anything, Aashi. I've sent your reports to specialists in London. I'll not spare any expense to make you see again.'

'I...I'm...really? Blind?' Aashi mumbled, feeling too dazed to speak coherently. Just then, a thought even more terrifying than her blindness stuck her. 'Oh, Raj, does your...does your mother know?' she exclaimed.

'Yeah, I'm afraid she does. And it has given her a fine reason to...she was against you even before, I mean... and now...' Raj twitched his lips and looked at Aashi, his eyes bearing a shade of sadness and anxiety, perhaps for the first time in his life. He saw Aashi lower her face, her lips trembling with wretchedness. 'But you don't worry about that,' he added quickly. 'Just get well soon.'

'You won't leave me, Raj, would you?' she asked in a little voice. That was the thought that terrified her more than her blindness.

'No, Aashi, never. No matter what,' Raj murmured, wrapping her in his reassuring hug.

Abhi watched them for half a second and quietly walked out of the room. 'I would never leave you,' he heard Raj assert as he stepped out through the door.

But Raj did leave her, and not before many days had passed.

Raj however, wasn't the only one to go away. Even before his exit, Priyam's fiancī had to rush off to Pune.

'It's to settle some unfinished business...a dispute... related to our ancestral property,' he told Priyam on the evening before his departure. He had come to see her before going away, just so she would not worry.

166

'Must be very important,' Priyam uttered, without actually caring what she said. But she was determined to be polite and patient with her fiancī. Manish loved her. He was going to be her husband. And it was not his fault.

'Of course. It's important or I would never go away at such a time. But you don't worry at all. I know our wedding date is very near. It's already 27th November today. But I assure you I'd be here in perfect time. No need to worry about that.'

Priyam nodded.

'It's just a matter of few days. Though I admit,' he said, lowering his voice and smiling a little, 'every day away from you would seem like a decade.'

Priyam lowered her head at the words.

'You would miss me too, won't you? What would you do to pass the time?'

'Work.'

'At what? Building up dreams of our happy future?' he asked, smiling again.

'At Aashi's boutique. Aashi is in hospital so it's up to me to take care of everything. And then, there's some shopping left too.'

'Oh, that reminds me. My mother sent this list. Though I feel ashamed even to give it to you. But these are the names of our close relatives. Mother says, though even she doesn't like it, but it is customary for groom's close relatives to get gifts from bride's family. Clothes and such things, you know.'

Priyam nodded and took the list from his hand. Her glance stilled at it for a moment as she noticed that the list had over thirty.

'I really hate asking you this,' Manish continued. 'But what to do? Customs must be followed. Otherwise we would never have asked you for anything. You know how much we are against dowry.'

Priyam folded the list and leaned forward to put it on the table. As she did so, her chain slipped out from her shirt. She immediately put it back inside again.

'Doesn't it feel wonderful, Priyam, to see our wedding day so near!' Manish said, as he stared dreamily at her. 'I can't believe I'm really marrying the girl I love,' he continued. 'Yes, it's true, Priyam. I love you, I have loved you ever since I saw your picture in Abhi's office. Loved you with all my heart. Do you love me too, Priyam? Say that you love me too, with all your heart,' he said, moving closer to Priyam and taking her hand in his, 'Well?' he asked again.

'Yes,' she replied, pulling her fingers out of his grasp, 'I love with all my heart too.'

'Oh, Priyam!' he exclaimed. His hand started inching closer to her again.

Priyam got up immediately and walked up to the window.

'I'm so happy,' said Manish, getting up too and following her. 'But now, I must take your leave.'

'Okay,' she said, 'have a safe journey.'

'I'll miss you so much! I wish I can have something to remember you by,' Manish whispered in Priyam's ear, trapping her so she could have no opportunity to inch away.

'What do you want? A photograph?' she asked, forcing away the urge to give him a rude push.

'No, a photograph will only make me miss you even more.'

Priyam tightened her fists as his breath touched her cheeks. But she would not push him away. She would bear it, and much more that she knew would follow in few days. If this was what Sid wanted, then let it be.

'Then what do you want?' she asked.

'Something that always remains close to your heart. This chain, for example.'

'You want my chain?' Priyam burst out in disbelief.

'You always wear it. If I have it, it would be like having you around.'

'I can't give it to you! It's a gift from my guardian.'

'And as a gift I demand it too. A gift of love.'

'Anything else, Manish, I'll give you anything else. But it's Mr. Vardhan's gift,' she pleaded.

'Come on, I know you love it a lot, and it's as a proof of your love that this chain will lie around my neck. Proof of your love for me,' he said, unclasping it quickly and putting it around his own thick neck. Priyam recoiled at the touch of his cold fingers and did finally give him that push. But he had taken what he wanted. 'There, doesn't it look good on me?' he grinned.

Priyam didn't answer, just stared at Manish without blinking.

She did not love him. But she had respected him all this long, and considered him a good human being. But what had just happened froze her with shock.

Manish didn't bother to notice her stare though, engrossed as he was in his newly acquired possession. In another two minutes he walked out of her door, not once turning to see if Priyam had waved to him or had banged the door shut behind him.

But Priyam did neither. She just slipped down on the floor where he had left her standing and let its cold surface receive her burning tears of wrath.

Her fingers clawed at the skin where his hand had touched her to rob her of Mr. Vardhan's parting gift.

Parting gift! The words evoked another and more terrifying thought in her mind. 'My bracelet! Thank God he did not want my bracelet!' Priyam spoke out aloud. Her eyes stared through tears at the golden metal encircling her wrist. Maybe next time he would. But she can't let him have it! She won't. There was no way she would let Manish's fingers touch one particle of Sid's bracelet. She must hide it! She must hide it! The resolution made Priyam spring up on her feet and look around desperately to find a secure place for the precious emblem of love. In a week, everything she had would be Manish's. But not the bracelet. He would never be able to touch it. Never!

It was the first day of the last month of that year. Afternoon was just inching away to let the evening spread its spectrum. The sunlight that had kept Abhi, Priyam and Aashi outdoor all that afternoon was now just a pale shadow of its previous glory. And yet they lingered outside, despite the rising chill in the air.

'It's time you use that shawl, Aashi,' Abhi said as he caught Aashi rubbing her arms.

'No, I'm not cold yet. What time is it?' she asked. She was sitting on the swing, her legs folded up and hands idly fiddling with the corner of her skirt.

'Nearly five,' Priyam replied, handing her the orange she had been peeling.

'Thanks,' Aashi said.

It was her first day out of the hospital, reason enough for her friends to ignore all their work for the day and spend all their time with her.

However, there was one person that had remained absent, not just that day, but on the previous one too. Raj wasn't there. He was not with her when Abhi and her mother brought Aashi back from the hospital. Neither was he at home, waiting to welcome her back with Priyam. He just wasn't there.

Had Raj's mother cast a spell on him too? Surely, if she could break the bond between Sid and Priyam, their relation was on too incipient a stage to withstand her pressure. And she was pressuring Raj. Aashi knew that very well.

Aashi wanted to trust Raj, to trust his love, but no matter how hard she tried, Mrs. Sinha's hatred always ended up seeming more powerful than Raj's love.

'Hey, don't squeeze the orange, Aashi, eat it,' she heard Priyam calling and realized that her hands were indeed wet with juice. She immediately put the piece of orange in her mouth.

169

'Here, wipe your hands with this,' Priyam's voice fell to her ears again as a towel was put into her hands. Aashi took it silently and rubbed her hands dry.

Just then, a car stopped in front of their gate.

Was it Raj? Aashi waited to hear his cheery voice. But the sound of the car wasn't familiar, neither was the thud of the closing door.

'Hi, kids!' the voice that rang out in the evening air belonged to Mr. Vardhan. 'Enjoying the sun?'

Disappointment flooded Aashi's heart again. Just like in the morning when she was alone in the garden and had felt sure she heard Raj's red Audi stop in front of her home. She had even run to where she thought the gate was and had landed face down on the rose bush instead. And no Raj had rushed to lift her up. The car had just started up again and left. It couldn't be Raj, surely. He would never run away from her like that.

Would he?

'Yes sir, but it's nearly down now,' Abhi replied to Mr. Vardhan, giving him a welcome hug.

'Guess I should have come earlier then. But I thought you guys would be running around too, gathering all the little odds and ends before the big day.'

'Well, we decided to take a break for the day,' Priyam replied. 'There's hardly anything left to do and besides, we still have two days.'

She had not told anyone about what Manish had done. Abhi had noticed the chain missing from her neck and the bracelet from her wrist, but he didn't like asking. And she didn't tell. She had no intention of backing out from the marriage. Besides, it little mattered what kind of person her groom was.

'Two? Oh, I don't think so,' Mr. Vardhan replied. 'You'll have to wait some more days, Priyam, before you get married.'

All eyes turned to stare at Mr. Vardhan as he walked over and settled down on a chair. Aashi couldn't see, yet even she could very well judge the merriment in his voice.

'What?' Abhi exclaimed.

'Mr. Damle called me today morning. They want to postpone the wedding till 18th December.'

'18th December? But how can they do that? Everything's been fixed and… why this sudden change?' Abhi asked, wondering at the same time why Mr. Damle contacted Mr. Vardhan instead of him. Had they any problem with the date, they could have easily discussed it with him. In fact, Manish had visited them just yesterday. He hadn't said a word about any change in plans. He had actually rambled on about how the approaching day had made him rush back from Pune even though he had not found the people he had gone to meet.

'What can I say?' Mr. Vardhan shrugged. 'Must have been something unavoidable. But don't look so worried, Abhi. I've already talked to the caterer and re-arranged everything.'

'I'm not worried, sir, but it did come as a shock. Why did they...?'

'Talking of shock, here it arrives...the whole big bundle of it,' Mr. Vardhan interrupted Abhi's words.

Abhi turned to see what Mr. Vardhan was talking about. He did try to suppress his humour then, but only managed so far as to tone down his free laugh into a low snicker. But before Aashi could ask the explanation for this sudden burst of humour, another car stopped near the gate and the voice that followed answered her unasked query.

'Oh, how good it is to see you all here sitting so idly,' Mrs. Sinha's voice boomed out, 'I wish I could be so calm and happy too. But I never get a moment's peace! I just heard the sad news...'

'I would have thought the news would make you happy,' said Mr. Vardhan, interrupting her flow of words. 'I, personally, am quite happy to know that Priyam and Sid are going to get married on the same day.'

'What?'

'Wasn't postponement of Priyam's wedding the news you were talking about? I thought you were. But then, how could you have known, both your children being away and you being so busy. But what were you talking about?'

All eyes stared at him. Even Aashi turned towards the direction of his voice. Their faces bore the same expression of surprise and shock. The reason however was different.

'Postponed? Why?' Mrs. Sinha exclaimed.

'Raj?' Aashi gasped.

'Where's he gone?' Abhi asked.

'And Tina?' Priyam enquired.

Questions poured out from every mouth. But it was to Mrs. Sinha that Mr. Vardhan decided to offer the satisfaction of reply. 'Yes, Priyam's wedding has been postponed till 18.'

'Really? But why?'

'Oh, what's there to say? World is getting just too whimsical these days. Plans change without warning, people run away, or throw away their decisions at the whim of a moment. Am I not right, Mrs. Sinha?' he asked as Abhi and Priyam watched on with bewilderment.

They had never seen him talking so graciously with her. But now, Mr. Vardhan actually seemed to be enjoying himself. The same of course could not have been said about Mrs. Sinha. She suddenly seemed more alert and as if it were...more guarded. The news didn't amuse her much after all.

'Oh, I'm just glad that my kids aren't so whimsical. They are very obedient kids. They never do anything against my wishes,' she replied.

'Oh, don't take me wrong, ma'am. I was talking about people in general. I'm sure disobedience of kids wasn't the tragedy you were mourning about.'

'Of course not. It's Mrs. Thakur, she's grossly sick. I was just going to her when I saw you here. It's such a bother, you know. I had to meet the dress designer today to order some design changes in some of Tina's dresses. Designers are such nuisance. You have to make everything clear to them. Otherwise you will just end up wasting money and getting nothing good in return. Meeting with designers is such a bother too. You are lucky, Priyam, you can't afford dress designers. But the regular stuff available in the market should be good enough for you. I know the designs there aren't much good, but then, you need to start living within your means now and make compromises.'

'And just what do you mean by that, ma'am?' Mr. Vardhan stopped her, without bothering to feign politeness any longer.

'Oh, nothing. Nothing really. Just that… I know Manish is a very nice young man. But he only belongs to middle class you know. And one must learn to live in one's means, and not keep on looking towards others. I mean… please don't take me wrong…but now that your son is getting married …and will have a wife very soon…I mean…family, it will be better for people not to expect anything from your property anymore. Your property belongs to Tina and Sid and...'

'You forget, ma'am, my son has already renounced my property. He does not wish to have even a cent from my property. And let me inform you that in the recent revision of my will, I have taken all his wishes into consideration,' Mr. Vardhan said, enjoying no doubt the sudden bleaching of Mrs. Sinha's face.

'But Aditya, he's your son. I'm sure children make mistakes but it's a parent's duty to take care of them and not let them commit a blunder.'

'I'm afraid I've lost the right to command my child by committing so many sins myself, didn't you yourself say that once?'

'No, I mean, but...he's your son and...'

'He doesn't think so, you made sure of that long time ago,' said Mr. Vardhan.

'I did nothing wrong. But he's still your son. You should not deprive him of his property. How can you...' Mrs. Sinha flared up with anger and indignation.

'You know very well that I always do what I want to do. And right now, I want you to leave,' said Mr. Vardhan.

'I was leaving any way. I don't have time to sit idle,' she said. Then she turned towards Aashi and said, 'I have to prepare for my daughter's wedding and also to buy some designer dresses for Tanya, my soon to be daughter-in-law. Even though she's still in London with Raj. But I must buy something for her, she's sure to come with him to attend Tina's wedding. I have no time to lose.' And Mrs. Sinha got up from her chair, smiled at Mr. Vardhan, looked askance at Aashi, and then paraded herself back to her waiting car.

'Don't listen to her, child,' Mr. Vardhan said to Aashi, as soon as Mrs. Sinha had walked out of the gate, 'there's seldom any conformity between her words and the truth.'

'But her words do have a way of turning into truth, Uncle,' Priyam said, just as shocked by what she had heard as Aashi was. She couldn't believe that Raj could betray her friend so blatantly. And yet, his mother possessed powers as potent as black magic. There was no telling what she would do.

'Sir, you mentioned earlier that both her children were away,' Abhi asked, 'do you know where?'

'Well, I don't know where Tina is, and you'll be surprised to know, neither does her mother.'

'What do you mean?' Abhi asked.

'Oh, Tina is a free spirited girl you know. But as for Raj, he couldn't be in London so soon. He just left this afternoon.'

'Today afternoon? But how can you be so sure?' Abhi asked again. He had never seen Mr. Vardhan to be so aware about the whereabouts of Raj or his family.

'Oh, we are...doing a joint project. But that's all I know,' Mr. Vardhan concluded hurriedly

'So Mrs. Sinha was right,' Aashi mumbled in a shaken voice, 'she was right, Raj's gone. And he gave me no chance to stop him this time. No chance to...' she couldn't continue further.

'He'll come back, very soon,' Mr. Vardhan tried to comfort Aashi again. 'Raj is not a bad kid. He's the best of the lot. He has his faults I know, but deceit is not one of them. And if it gives you any comfort I'll tell you this, he's the only one of the family I'd trust, even with a secret. He won't betray anyone, Aashi.'

But Aashi by then had got up from the swing and was fumbling furiously towards the gate. Abhi rushed after her and quickly took hold of her hand.

'Go away!' she shrieked and gave him a push, 'Go away!' she repeated as she crashed into first his gate and then her own. She quickly unlatched it and stumbled inside. Abhi grabbed her arm, tightly this time. She tried to fight

173

him off as before. But he didn't let go, not till he had handed Aashi safe into her mother's arms.

And then he turned his feet back towards his own home where Mr. Vardhan and Priyam were still sitting in the garden. He settled himself beside his sister and Mr. Vardhan and lost himself in the same silence that enveloped his two companions.

'Uncle,' he heard Priyam's voice after a while, 'why did Kiran auntie like Tina so much?'

'Kiran liked all children. And Tina was a pretty baby, and her best friend's daughter. But there's nothing more to that. The rest is all that devil woman's fabrication. You have no idea what she's capable of. She ruined my life and separated me from not just my wife, but my only son too, two persons that were more precious to me than my own life.'

'She seems to take a particular delight in engineering separation, doesn't she?' Abhi grumbled.

'I don't know what she delights in or not,' Mr. Vardhan replied, 'all I know is that she broke the heart of an angel and drove her to an untimely death. She destroyed my home, my love. And I did love my wife, whether you believe it or not.'

'We do. We know you can never betray anyone. And we also know how much you loved Kiran Auntie. And no matter what the world says, I know you could never have done anything to hurt her.'

'Thank you,' Mr. Vardhan said, his smile fully expressing the pleasant surprise Priyam's words had given him. He perhaps had lost the hope of such absolute vindication long ago. If only Sid could feel that way too. He would not care then what the world said or thought. 'Yes, I did love her. I still do,' he said. 'She was just like you, Priyam, simple and innocent with a heart full of love and trust. My world revolved around her. And to Kiran, I was the whole world. She clung to me like body to soul. But when body and soul separate – death comes,' he recounted, looking neither at Abhi nor Priyam but staring at the darkening depths of the skies above. Priyam and Abhi though looked only at him. This was the first time they had heard their guardian refer to his past, the first time that he was unravelling the wounds of his heart and letting them have a glimpse of what lay beneath the layers of cheerful self-assurance and proud dignity.

'What had happened?' Priyam asked softly when he fell silent.

'What happened? I really don't know, Priyam. I must not put all blame on that devil woman. I was to blame too. Had I given Kiran a little more time... I should have seen how lonely she felt when I busied myself in my work and let Kiran manage the long lonely hours anyway she could. I should have been aware, but I wasn't. And Kiran didn't tell. And then, she rediscovered her old friend. Rather, her old friend rediscovered her. And I was glad. Though I didn't quite like Maya even at the first time I met her in our college...we all studied in the same college. But I was glad. My wife had a friend now and that had relieved me of what little compulsion I felt about sparing time for Kiran. I devoted myself in building up a business empire, and Maya Sinha devoted herself to bringing down my empyrean world.' he said, looking towards them and yet beyond them as it seemed, perhaps, at the time long gone by.

He didn't know why he was telling Abhi and Priyam all this. He had never bothered to explain himself to anyone before. But then, Abhi and Priyam were not anyone else.

'I should have never admitted that woman in my house,' he began again after a silence of several moments. 'I knew that Maya was angry. I knew she thought that we had betrayed her. But the way she behaved, the love and affection she showered on Kiran, I just couldn't see what lay beneath all that. I just couldn't...'

'But, why was Mrs. Sinha angry with you?' Abhi asked.

'Because I did not marry her. I married her friend instead.'

'She wanted to marry you?' Priyam exclaimed. That possibility had never occurred to her before.

'Yes,' Mr. Vardhan affirmed, 'evidently she did. And she had made herself believe that I loved her too. Although it was clear to everyone else that it was her friend instead whom I adored. And when I finally married my love, Maya's love for me turned into hate'

'What did she say?' Priyam asked.

'She said several things, and in a voice loud enough for a lot many people to hear. But in few days, she found herself another wealthy man and became the talk of the town by marrying a 45 year old widower. They left India and settled abroad. That was a huge relief. I thought I had got rid of her forever. But eleven years later Maya reappeared again. I remember, Sid was about ten at that time, a happy budding boy who adored her mother and tried in every way to be like his father. He was proud of me at that time you know. I was still his Super Daddy, although one that remained absent for long durations though. That was his only complaint. Until *she* came back, that is.'

'But why did you allow her to befriend Auntie again? You should have...'

175

'I know, I should have. But I didn't want to spoil my wife's joy at seeing her old friend again. And Maya did seem so repentant, seeking forgiveness and reconciliation with such vigour. So I let them be alone, busy as I was in expanding my business. I let them alone. Let my little lamb *enjoy* the company of a fox. She ate my love away. I don't know how she did it, but in two months she made my wife believe that I was betraying her. She told Kiran I was having an affair with my own secretary. My poor Kiran, she couldn't bear it. She went into depression. She stopped talking to me, hated the sight of my face.'

'You should have kicked Mrs. Sinha right out!' Abhi exclaimed.

'I tried that too. But she declared it was her duty to guard her friend from my evil ways. I even threatened her. But nothing worked. So I decided to move out of India. I had even bought a house in Manchester. I don't know how, but Maya found it out and informed Kiran of the new house I was buying for my new family. That was all that Kiran could bear. She went into frenzy, as my servants later told me. My scared boy tried to call me. But Maya told Sid that she had already informed me but doubted I would bother to come. Of course, she hadn't. And when I returned to India with the key of my new house, my home was already dead. There was a crowd gathered at my gate. And inside lay my love's corpse, and my child sitting beside his mother's dead body, as much lost to me as the departed soul.

'Why didn't you tell Sid? Why didn't you explain?' Priyam burst out.

'What do you think, Priyam? I did all I could, but Sid was just a child. And he had seen too much agony and heard too much evil. There was no remedy for the wounds his mother's condition had left on his tender heart. The more I tried, the bitter he became. He hated everybody, raged at every little thing and shrouded himself into an impermeable shell. The sun that had once brightened our home with his cheer was now hid behind dark cloud of gloom and bitterness. Doctors warned that Sid might slip into depression too. So I took him to the new house I had purchased. But he missed his home, yearned for the place where his mother had lived and died. I was forced to bring him back. But I changed his school. I didn't want Sid to study where Raj was studying too. And that was the best thing to have happened to Sid ever since Kiran's death. For in that school, my son met you two and started living again. You gave Sid a new life, kids, or I fear he'd have ended his existence long ago.'

176

'Don't…say that, Uncle,' Priyam pleaded, it was horrible enough already to think of Sid being all alone and so far away from them.

'It's true, child, you two are the only ones binding Sid to life. You two *are* his life. And if that woman thinks she can take Sid's life away from him again, then she should better think again. Because I won't let her. Not this time! Never!'

Abhi looked back at Mr. Vardhan. 'What would you do?' he asked.

He didn't know what Mr. Vardhan was up to. Whatever it was, he just didn't want anything to happen to add to his sister's woes. Abhi had no hope left of Sid's return. And besides, Priyam was getting married too. Things had gone too far now to allow any alteration. Too far, even for Mr. Vardhan to turn them around.

'Oh, nothing much,' Mr. Vardhan replied, 'except of reviving some old relationships and putting everyone in its rightful place.'

Chapter 22

To catch some fragment from her hands
That else would fall into the sands
And lie lost and disintegrate:
For this I wait: for this I wait.

— *Beauty - Kenneth Slade Alling*

'I'm sure Raj would return soon,' Abhi tried once more to reassure Aashi.

Those days, the sentence had become more like a refrain for Abhi. Whenever he was with Aashi, he had to say it again and again, and at every time face her stark refusal to either believe or entertain any hope.

Yet Aashi needed to hear those words. She would admit no hope, but it was a relief still to see Abhi so steadfast in his. Even though she declared the words mere lip-service, blatant lie even, yet she hungered for them at all times. She hungered to hear Abhi say it. Somehow, it sounded so true and comforting when brought out aloud in his voice.

'He would not,' Aashi said dryly, giving her usual reply to his assurance.

A whole week had passed since Aashi's discharge from the hospital. A whole week, and yet all she had heard from Raj was a quick phone call that had served only to confirm that he indeed was in London. 'I can't tell you anything now...things are too uncertain...' that's all that Aashi had got from him. No intimation of his plans, no promise of return either. Raj had said that he was missing her. He had replied in affirmative when Aashi had asked if he still loved her. And then he had added that he must rush off because there was someone waiting for him. The call had been disconnected even before Aashi could ask whether that somebody was a girl called Tanya. But she asked the question nevertheless, from the silence around her. And the reply she got was the reply she didn't want to hear and yet, couldn't help but suffer from every apprehensive beat of her heart.

'He would come back, I tell you. You are just being stupid suspecting Raj like that. He would never betray you,' Abhi repeated. His hand reached out to take hold of Aashi's arm as they approached a damaged portion of the road.

Abhi really hoped and prayed for the speedy fulfilment of the assurances he kept on pouring in Aashi ears. Raj's sudden disappearance was disturbing him too, giving him an uncanny sense of *deja-vu*. What happened to him he didn't want Aashi to suffer too. Abhi prayed again and again that she wouldn't have to, that the separation was but temporary and that Raj would overcome soon whatever was keeping him away from Aashi.

'Don't try to give me false hopes, Abhi. Even you know very well that Raj's mother would never let him come back to a blind girl whom she never approved any way. I've lost him forever. I've lost everything, my eyes, my future…everything and you know it just as well as I do,' said Aashi.

'You must not lose hope, Aashi. You haven't lost anything. Your sight will come back. Doctor said that after operation…' Priyam tried, gently pressing her fingers around Aashi's. She knew well how volatile her friend's emotions were at that moment, ever ready to flare up in rage or to burst out in agonized tears. She and Abhi tried their best to keep Aashi calm and hopeful, but with the passing of each day with Raj being still away, managing her temper and even predicting her responses was becoming quite tricky.

But Abhi and Priyam knew Aashi needed them, and both were there for her, whether Aashi wanted them or not. More often, she did not. She preferred staying confined in her house, surrounded by nothing but her memories and the pain they evoked. But Abhi would not let her do that. Even on that evening, Abhi had literally dragged Aashi out of her house and forced her to take a walk around with them.

No longer did Abhi seek to avoid Aashi now, no longer keep up the pretence of indifference. Indifference could only be applied to his own suffering, not hers. She was in need and he was ready to do whatever was required of him, no matter what resulted from the proximity that he had so steadfastly tried to shun before.

'You know the truth of operation as well as I do, Priyam!' Aashi shouted in reply to Priyam's words. 'Didn't you hear what the doctor said? There's a national backlog of over one million eyes. It'll take years for my turn to come to get donated eyes. And by then my career would be over and love lost forever. Don't try to fool me! Go away, and leave me alone. At least I'll be rid of your lies!' Aashi shouted, jerking Priyam's hold on her hand and rushing away from her and Abhi.

'Where are you going?' Abhi called out.

'Home! And you need not follow me!'

'Okay, but…that's not the way towards home,' he said, walking up to her.

'I don't care!' Aashi shouted back, just as her foot tripped on a little bump. But Abhi was already there to catch her before she hurt herself. 'Leave me!' she cried out, hitting him with her fists.

179

'I will, let me first drop you home,' Abhi replied, still maintaining his grasp on her.

'I don't want you to!' Aashi cried, breaking down in tears, 'I don't want you…I want Raj! Why's Raj not here, Abhi? Why has he left me? Why has he left me alone?' she mumbled through her tears as he pressed her to his heart and held her close.

'Shhh…don't cry, Aashi…' he murmured gently as Priyam walked up to them too. 'Don't cry, he'll come back, I tell you, he'll come back,' Abhi whispered in comforting tones, slowly guiding Aashi's steps back towards her home. By the time they reached her door, Abhi had calmed her down into silence and made her wipe her cheeks dry. 'Okay now,' he said as he led Aashi to her door, 'promise me you'll go straight to bed and not shed even one more tear.'

'As if I can help it,' she replied, sniffing and rubbing her eyes dry.

'But you must, Aashi. You must be strong. Priyam's wedding is coming so close and I do need you to be strong. Be a good girl and…'

'I'm not a good girl,' Aashi mumbled, jerking her head and giving a toss to her loose mane.

'Well, try being one for a change then,' Abhi said, giving a short laugh, 'But now go and have some rest. Tomorrow I'll take you to your boutique.'

'My boutique…I don't know how much longer will it remain so. There's still so much of loan that remains to be repaid. How will I…'

'Now, don't start worrying your head again. As I said, let all you worries rest till after Priyam's wedding. Besides, you already have able workers to follow all your suggestions and a very capable designer too. It's lucky you hired her before…Diwali. Sunita is really diligent and sincere. She's keeping your boutique right on track. And your mother has proved herself quite a capable manager too. You don't need to worry at all about it,' he added cheerfully. 'Now go and have a good sleep,' Abhi said, raising his arm to ring the door bell. 'Be ready by nine tomorrow morning. I'll take you back to where you belong.'

Abhi was just easing his car in the parking of Mr. Vardhan's guest house when his mobile started ringing. He looked at it and saw Aashi's number flash on the screen. 'Hey! What happened? Are you okay?' he asked anxiously as he received her phone. Hardly half an hour had passed since he had dropped Aashi at her boutique. What could have happened in so little a time, he wondered.

'Where are you?' Aashi asked.

'At the guesthouse to see if the decoration work is going on schedule. But why?'

'I want to go home.'

'What? But why, Aashi? I've just dropped you at the boutique. What has happened?'

'Nothing. I just want to go home,' she replied. Abhi could judge from her voice that she either was crying or on the verge of it.

'Now? But Aashi…'

'Okay, sorry. You are busy, I know.'

'Stay there a little longer. I'll come and pick you up as soon as I'm done from here.'

'No, don't bother,' she said, clearly stifling a sob, 'I'll catch an auto. I can't stay here a moment longer,' she declared, and disconnected the phone.

Something must have happened to hurt her, Abhi felt sure. And just as sure was he that there was no way he could stay put in the guest house, decorator or no decorator. He dialled Aashi's number, 'I'm coming, wait for me,' he told her, and quickly reversed his car.

Abhi didn't want to waste even a second, knowing full well that Aashi can very easily fulfil her threat of attempting her journey back home alone. There was no telling these days what she might or might not do. Once, Abhi had even caught her raging across the road alone after having fought with her mother. He didn't want to give her another opportunity to put herself in danger again. So he raced through the rush hour traffic, guilty even of driving a little recklessly, a thing he had always considered nothing less than a sin.

'What happened?' he asked even before he had brought his car to a full stop in front of her boutique.

'What took you so long?' Aashi snapped instead of replying.

'I came as soon as I could, Aashi,' he replied, getting down from his car and walking up to her, 'the roads are still crowded with office-goers. But what happened to you? You sounded disturbed.'

'Let's go,' she said.

'Okay, but let me first tell your mother.'

'No need. She knows you are coming to fetch me.'

'But… it'll just take a minute.'

'I said let's go!' Aashi shouted, stepping down the stairs that led up to her shop and on which she had been waiting since receiving his call. She walked straight out on the road. Abhi had no choice but to follow her. Fortunately he caught sight of Aashi's mother looking at them from inside the boutique. He made a quick gesture and received an affirmative nod from her before taking hold of Aashi's arm and guiding her towards the car.

'Do you mind if I take you to the guest house instead?' he asked.

'No, take me wherever you want. As long as you don't ask me to feel a texture or guess out a colour combination. And don't expect me to approve a design by following your descriptions. My ears are not my eyes and neither can my fingers show me if the embroidery patch has come out as I designed it or not. But I can tell where my designs have been altered. No one can fool me in that! She thinks she can run my boutique as she wants and even fiddle with my designs just because I can't see, then she must think again.'

'Who?'

'Sunita, who else? I'll tell her who the boss is, I'll…I'll… fire her.'

'But she's a good designer, Aashi. And she's trustworthy too. If you fire Sunita you'll have to find a new one,' Abhi replied, guiding his car out of the lane at a pace much slower than the one he had used to zoom into it.

'I will, I don't need her. I'll find a better one,' Aashi muttered, tears streaking down her face.

'You do need her, Aashi, whether you like it or not. You have to admit that she's the one who's managing your boutique right now. Neither Priyam nor your mother can do it without her. They are not designers. Besides, didn't you yourself change your own designs almost till the last moment? Why should you mind if she does that too? It's a part of creative process.'

'You don't need to lecture me like that. My mother has done that enough already. Alright then, let her rule over my boutique. I won't say a word. It's no use anyway. Nobody cares what I say or feel. Nobody understands!' Aashi sobbed, turning her face away from Abhi. 'And don't you dare smile like that at me!' she cried out after a moment. Aashi obviously didn't need her eyes to feel the sting of his gaze upon her and that hateful smile playing on his lips.

'I'm not smiling at you,' he replied, instantly curbing his lop-sided grin that she hated so much.

'Yes you are! You are always mocking me with that twisted smile of yours. And I hate it!'

'Well, but don't worry. We won't let anyone rule over your boutique. It's yours and will remain yours. And very soon you'll learn to sketch out beautiful designs again. But you'll have to practice hard for that. And once you get used to…'

'I don't want to get used to, Abhi!' Aashi cried out, 'I don't want to get used to being blind! I want to get out of this darkness! You don't know how it stifles me! You don't know anything! Nobody knows! And yet you go on preaching.'

'You are right, Aashi, I don't know what it feels to be surrounded by darkness. But I do know what it is to be lonely and hopeless. I know very well the pain you are going through right now. But by not trying to rise out of it, you are only making it worse. You must remember, Aashi, pain is not a medal that you must wear on your sleeve. It's a force you must fight against and never, never let it win.'

'I said I don't want to hear any preaching.'

'I'm just trying to…'

'Don't!' she cut him short again, 'don't try anything. Don't try to force me back in life that doesn't belong to me anymore. Don't try to make me hold on to hopes that are long dead and buried. And don't drag me out every evening to make me learn my blind way about. I don't want to learn the way. I don't want to!'

'What do you want to do then? Stay in your room and fret?'

'Yes, I want to fret. And I'll fret. I can do that still.'

'Alright then,' Abhi said, trying to keep his smile out of his voice, 'fret all you want but after Priyam's wedding. Till then I forbid you to fret and sulk,' he said, bringing his car to a stop in the guesthouse parking.

'You can't forbid me anything!'

'I can and I will. I forbid you to get down from this car and follow me. You must stay here and wait while I go talk to the decorator.'

'I have no interest in following you!' Aashi countered, wiping away her tears.

'Good then, stay here.'

'I won't,' she said. She got down from the car and banged the door shut.

'Easy!' he exclaimed, 'my car is too old to withstand your fury. Divert it all on me instead,' he laughed and wrapped his fingers around her extended hand.

'Shut up and walk,' she hissed, conscious of an unwilling smile creeping to the corners of her mouth. 'No, stop!' she exclaimed suddenly.

'Why? What happened?'

'My phone. It's in the car.'

'I'll get it,' Abhi said and unlocked his car again. He knew how important her phone was to Aashi. It was the last gift she had had from Raj. It was not just a mobile phone for her, but a companion she didn't like staying away from. Its cold body perhaps filled up a void that Raj had left behind, replacing the warmth her palm yearned to feel. It was an emblem of what had been and what perhaps would never now be. Sometimes Aashi held it close to her heart, bathing it with her tears and showering it with kisses when she was sure of being all alone. At other times she felt like throwing it away and filling her ears with the sound of its breaking into bits.

'Is this guest house very big?' Aashi asked after they had walked a few paces.

'Yes, and beautiful too,' Abhi replied.

'I wish we had come here earlier, before Diwali. Now I'd never know how it looks.'

'Sure you would. I would show you everything. But first let us see what these guys are up to now.'

The meeting with the decorator didn't last too long. Since everything had been settled already, there were only some minor matters that needed to be sorted out. That was quickly done and within half an hour, Abhi was free to entertain Aashi.

'Aren't you glad I came along? You'd have quite ruined the setting otherwise by choosing yellow flowers! And why were you so against the water fountain in the centre? It would look gorgeous, I tell you. I'm glad I was here to salvage Priyam's wedding from the certain ruin you'd have brought upon it.'

'Sure, her wedding is salvaged. It doesn't matter of course if I'm ruined in the process. Your ingenious suggestions will raise our budget by ten times at least.'

'Oh, don't worry! Mr. Vardhan would pay.'

'That's exactly what I don't want to happen. He's already doing too much.'

'By being away all the time? Nice sort of help and support that he's being for you!'

'It must be something very important or he wouldn't have gone,' Abhi replied, even though Mr. Vardhan strange unexplained trips were troubling him too. He had flown away on second December and as yet, there was no news from him, nor even any information as to where he had gone.

'Anyway,' he shrugged, 'Let me take you around the place now.'

Abhi gave Aashi a leisurely round of the place, describing to her every little thing, mentioning every least bit of detail that he considered necessary to help Aashi see the place with her mind's eye.

After Aashi had *seen* everything that there was to see in the guest house and was fully satisfied that Priyam's wedding was being held in a deserving venue, the two returned back to Abhi's home. And here Aashi remained, under the watchful eyes of Abhi.

It was four in the evening. Boredom had pushed Abhi and Aashi out of their home, and the pleasant winter sun had pulled their feet to the road. They were now enjoying a leisurely walk in the winter sunshine. And Aashi, at that time at least, was feeling cheerful enough to smile readily at Abhi's silly jokes.

'Where are we going?' she asked when she sensed being turned onto a different road than the one in front of their home.

'On the main road,' Abhi replied.

'Main road? No! We must turn back!' Aashi exclaimed. She stopped immediately and turned around. 'There's...there's too much traffic here. I'm scared,' she added and refused to budge an inch forward.

The reason for her refusal wasn't really what she had given to Abhi. She was not scared of the traffic. She was scared of coming across Mrs. Sinha. She didn't want to go waddling like that on the road just opposite Raj's house. No way was she going to take a step further and be mocked by his mother who might be returning to her home or stepping out of it just at that moment. 'Let's turn back,' she pleaded.

'Don't worry, Aashi,' Abhi said, taking her hand in his. He knew well what her fear was. 'Mrs. Sinha isn't here,' he told her.

'Are you sure?' Aashi asked in a little quivering voice.

'Hundred percent. Most probably she has shifted to the hotel where they plan to hold the wedding. That would mean she is in Jaipur right now.'

'Two days ago?'

'Yeah, but it's today only that I found out.'

'Oh,' Aashi breathed with relief, 'okay.' she mumbled and allowed her feet to finally take her further. 'Do you think...' she began again after a moment.

'Yeah, Raj must be there too. There's not even a week left now. He must have come back,' said Abhi. 'And...Sid?' he added, pronouncing the name of his friend in quite a different tone of voice.

'No, I don't think he would go there so soon,' said Aashi.

'No! Sid...there...in that taxi!' Abhi said, his eyes fixed at a taxi standing at the intersection and waiting for the traffic light to turn green.

'What? Sid? Is he here? Did he see you?' Aashi asked excitedly.

'Yes, it is him. I mean,' Abhi hesitated a little. 'It does look like him. But what's he doing here?'

'Did he see you? Is he coming?'

'No,' Abhi replied with disappointment ringing clear in his voice. 'The light's turned green. He's gone.'

'But was it really Siddharth? Are you sure?' Aashi asked again as she tugged furiously at his arm.

'Yes, I think so. But then, it is getting a bit dark. It might have been someone else too.'

'Well, if it was really Sid, we'll sure hear from him soon. Maybe he'd come visiting you guys.'

'He was going in opposite direction right now.'

185

'But he'd come back, I'm sure,' Aashi insisted, 'or at least call.'

And that was what Abhi too expected Sid to do. There was no other reason for Sid to be in Delhi, except that he wanted to see them before flying off to Jaipur and get married.

But the evening passed away without any other indication of Sid being in the city. Abhi kept on expecting to see his friend walking through his gate, or at least calling him on the phone. But neither the phone got fortunate enough to receive Sid's call nor the gate had any opportunity to welcome the eagerly awaited visitor.

'Are you sure it was him?' Aashi asked him next day.

It was evening and the two were strolling after dinner, waiting for Priyam to finish her chores and come out to join them too.

'It did look like Sid,' Abhi muttered.

'But he would have called at least had it really been him.'

'If he had wanted to call,' said Abhi.

'Well, Sid is moody, I must admit,' Aashi said, 'and there's no telling what his so called principles might force him to do.'

'Well, maybe it wasn't Sid after all. I could easily have been mistaken. It was getting dark and…'

'That's what I think too,' Aashi declared, 'It couldn't have been him. What would he be doing here at such a time? Sid would either be in Bangalore or in Jaipur where the wedding is to be held. Nowhere else.'

Little did they know that the person they were talking about was in neither of those two places. Sid was at that very moment roaming around in a city he had never visited before and searching for a face he had never ever seen in his entire life. And all this, on the behest of the very same man whom he once hated to be recognised as his father.

Chapter 23

At last, when all the summer shine
That warmed life's early hours is past,
Your loving fingers seek for mine
And hold them close—at last—at last!

—'*At Last*' -*Elizabeth Akers Allen*

'What are you doing, Abhi?' Priyam called from the stairs. She had heard him fumbling in the kitchen and had rushed down to find out why.

'Nothing. Just preparing breakfast,' he replied, taking out a couple of eggs from the refrigerator and putting them gently down on the platform.

'But why? I was just coming. Do you have to go anywhere early?'

'No, I just thought…anyways, I'll have to do it all after two days. So I thought…' The slight catch in his voice did not escape Priyam even though Abhi had kept his face turned away from her. 'Don't worry,' he said, almost succeeding in steadying his voice, 'I won't torture you with any of my experiments today. Just my standard omelette and bread and tea…just the way you like it. You can go back to your room and get ready.'

Priyam moved, though not towards the stairs. Instead, she rushed straight to her brother. Her fingers tightened around Abhi's shirt as she buried her face against his back. 'Wha…Priyam?' he quickly turned around to witness her tear soaked face. Her arms tightened around her brother. He could not help but reciprocate too.

'I wish I could stay here forever,' Priyam sobbed, pressing her face harder against him.

'This day had to come some day, Priyam,' Abhi sighed, 'but I admit, it has come sooner than I had foreseen…and…not exactly as I…' a trembling breath overtook the rest of his words as a couple of tears trickled down his eyes too. 'But we'll be okay,' he said, as soon as he could speak again, 'we'd be okay, won't we, Priyam?'

She nodded, still clinging tightly to him.

'Both of us?'

Another nod was all the reply Abhi could get from her.

'Promise me.'

Finally, her face turned up towards Abhi. He looked so tired and his eyes betrayed more than he would have allowed them to at any other occasion. Priyam felt like hugging him again and crushing herself into him, never to be separated ever. Abhi was all she had in the name of family. And she was all he had for comfort and love.

Priyam had never felt as helpless as she felt now, never so wretched too. When Sid had still been with them, marriage had always been a word that was to result in closer bonding, never, as it was now, in such a painful separation.

'Promise me,' Abhi murmured again.

'Yes Abhi,' she replied, stemming the flow of her tears, 'we'll both be okay. We owe this to each other.'

'Thank you,' he whispered as his arm encircled Priyam again and his lips pressed against her hair.

A stream of music rose up in the next room, detaching Priyam from her brother. 'Your phone is ringing,' she said, taking a step away from Abhi. Abhi rushed away to pick up his phone.

He returned to the kitchen just two minutes later. 'It was Mr. Vardhan. He's back. He was calling from his home, in fact.'

'Did he tell you where he had been to?'

'No, and I didn't ask either. He wants us to shift to the guesthouse today, before our guests start arriving.'

It was nearly noon when Abhi led Priyam and Aashi to their rooms in the guest house.

'This would be my room,' he said as soon as he reached the first room, 'and this...' he led Aashi to the next room, 'count the steps and keep your hand on the wall,' he instructed, 'yes, this is Priyam's room. And right in front of it is your room, here.'

'Okay, okay, I got it,' Aashi replied, 'your room, ten steps, Priyam's room and in front of it, our room.'

'Good. Now you two just have a look at your bags and see which one must go to which room. And, Aashi, if you have forgotten anything, let me know. I'll bring it when I go back in the evening to bring your mother, and the rest of our bags.'

'Aren't you going to help us?' Aashi asked.

'In a minute. Let me just call Mr. Vardhan and tell him of our arrival,' Abhi said and walked away from two girls. However, even before Priyam had ordered all the bags to their proper destinations, he walked back to join them again.

'What happened?' Priyam asked.

'He's on his way here.'

'So? Why are you worried?' she asked.

'I'm not worried.'

'Then?'

'I don't know... I mean... Mr. Vardhan has brought some guests from wherever he had been too. And he's keeping them at home.'

'What? What else did he say?' Priyam asked, just as surprised at the news as her brother had been.

'I didn't talk to him,' Abhi replied, 'his mobile was busy so I called home instead. His servant, Mohan, picked up the phone. He told me that Mr. Vardhan had left for the guesthouse half an hour ago, soon after he had had an early lunch with his guests. Mohan didn't know who these guests were, just that they were quite old and the gentleman looked quite sick too.'

'Must be the Uncle who lives in Agra. I mean, he's the only one I've ever heard Mr. Vardhan mention. So it must be him. He's old too and infirm.'

'Yeah, must be them,' Abhi shrugged, hardly sounding convinced though.

Neither in fact was Priyam by her own surmise. She knew very well that Mr. Vardhan's parents were long dead and he didn't have any sibling either. Neither had they ever heard him mention any other relative in a tone of any great fondness. Who was it then that had been given the privilege of enjoying the hospitality of the Vardhan House? As long as Abhi and Priyam had known Mr. Aditya Vardhan, they themselves had been the only lucky ones to be allowed that privilege.

Ever since the death of its hostess, the house had turned hostile to all and any of its visitors. The precincts that once had resounded by the jovial cheer of frequent parties, now guarded in solemn silence the memories and moments that still hung spectre-like in its very air. Mr. Vardhan did receive guests whenever he was in India, but never in the Vardhan House. Nor did he ever see an occasion to hold a party within its walls ever again.

Abhi and Priyam, therefore, were highly curious to know who these special people were. But of course, they had no other option but to wait for Mr. Vardhan's arrival at the guest house to know for certain.

It took almost half an hour for Mr. Vardhan to make his appearance. Abhi, Priyam and Aashi had already familiarised themselves with their rooms and stowed away most of their luggage in the cupboards and were, in fact, just settling down for a quick lunch when Abhi saw him enter the dining room.

'Enjoying your meal, kids?' Mr. Vardhan smiled as he strode towards them, 'The manager told me that you were here so I came straight in.'

189

'You look tired, Sir,' Abhi said, getting up from his chair. Priyam did the same.

'Oh, I am, exhausted,' Mr. Vardhan replied, settling down heavily on the chair Abhi had pulled out for him. 'Age catches up with everyone you know. And I didn't get to sleep much for the last few days either. But I'll rest now. I'll take a long nap. But I needed to see first if everything was going okay here,' he said, ordering a cup of black coffee for himself.

'Won't you have something to eat too?' Abhi offered.

'No, I've had lunch back at home.'

'With your guests?' Priyam could not help but bring it up.

'I called and Mohan told us that you have some visitors,' Abhi explained quickly. He could see that Mr. Vardhan had not expected to be met with such a question. And something in his eyes gave Abhi a queer feeling of having stumbled upon something that had been intended to be kept a secret.

'Oh, well…since you know…'

'We know nothing, Sir,' Abhi remarked.

'You won't stop calling me Sir, would you, Abhi?' Mr. Vardhan smiled.

'It has become a habit now, Sir, I mean…'

'Never mind, call me whatever you want. I'll still be who I am, won't I?'

Abhi cast a look at Priyam. It was too obvious to them how Mr. Vardhan had deliberately changed the direction of the conversation. What they couldn't figure out was why.

'So,' Mr. Vardhan asked a little later as he took small sips from his steaming cup of coffee, 'everything okay here? I hope there's no problem.'

'No, Sir, everything is going as per schedule. No problem.'

'Good, everything should be top class, perfect and extra special. After all, it's going to be a very special wedding you know, one that people would remember for a long time. Especially the Damle family,' he added. 'Oh yes, it's going to be a memorable day for them, that I guarantee. But for now, if you don't need me, then I think I better go to my room and catch up on my sleep. See you later, kids,' he said, and then quickly walked away.

The next morning saw the inevitable onslaught of relatives. Abhi had invited only ten families from both of his parents' sides. Out of these, he duly hoped that only four would find it impossible to ignore the invite or excuse themselves from honouring it. As it turned out however, as many as seven families managed to arrive for the big event. Uncle Rajeev and his family arrived even before breakfast was laid on the table. Other guests too, with their several children and some grandchildren kept on trickling all through the day. Aunt Leela however could make her appearance only after the lunch time, a great misfortune for her as she and her family had to make do with a hastily put together meal that could not match up the lavish spread served for the lunch.

With the arrival of guests arrived their various suggestions, advices, demands and even complaints, all vying against each other to be heard and met with prompt action. All day long Abhi found himself rushing from one corner of the property to the other, giving directions and approving or disapproving changes. His office colleagues did all they could to lighten Abhi's burden. Some of them had arrived there in the morning and all worked almost as hard as Abhi did.

It was another matter however that the help and support of his entire team could not take away the empty space that had been created by the absence of Sid. At every decision Abhi had to make he felt like turning around and asking 'What do you think, Sid?' At every little thing done or bought, Abhi hungered for the approval of the one whose opinion he had always valued above his own.

It was seven thirty in the evening. Aashi was dressed and waiting to be taken to first of the many ceremonies of Priyam's wedding. Priyam had wanted to take Aashi to the beauty parlour with her. But her aunts had conveniently pushed Aashi aside and let her remain standing while they drove away in the cars. Abhi had found Aashi trying to grope her way back to her room. He had helped Aashi to her room. But he was too busy to linger with her for long. No one had bothered about Aashi after that. No one had come to assist her. Even her mother seemed to have forgotten her.

Aashi could imagine her scurrying around, fulfilling everybody's demands and trying to be of service to each and every one. Aashi hated her mother slaving like that for anybody. She hated the way her mother let everybody take advantage of her. But right now, it seemed like a blessing that kept her away. All Urmila did was cry when she was with Aashi and rend her heart out at the great misfortune of her daughter.

Aashi knew Urmila considered her blindness a punishment for hurting the sentiments of her elders. Aashi's accident had given her mother another opportunity to assert how wrong the girl was in walking out upon her family. And to this she was steadily adding low voiced but insistent pleading of reconsidering the decision and going back to where they belonged.

'Go back? Never!' Aashi muttered under her breath as she ran her comb through her hair. 'I'd rather kill myself!' she said, putting the comb down and gingerly touching her curls to judge if they had been smoothed neatly enough.

If Aashi still had her sight, she'd have spent at least half an hour in designing an elaborate hairdo to go with her lovely dress. But now, all she could manage was to tie them up in a ponytail or let them hang loose on her shoulders. She preferred the latter, of course.

Having smoothed her hair, Aashi had nothing else to do but wonder what she should do next. Should she try and apply some makeup too or just take consolation in Abhi's words that she needed it not?

She decided it was better to trust Abhi.

As Aashi sat there, waiting and thinking, she could not help but remember all the merry plans she had made for Priyam's wedding. She was supposed to be the best dressed and best looking girl in the whole celebration. And Priyam had even given her the permission to tease her groom as much as she wanted. Of course, at the time when the plans were made, it was still Sid who was supposed to be Priyam's groom.

The two girls had made a pact that they would dance for the whole night on each other's wedding. Actually, Aashi had made that pact and Priyam had agreed. And Abhi had added to it by saying he'd dance more than them on both weddings.

But of course, all that was a thing of the past. None of that was going to happen now. Never!

Just then a gentle knock sounded at her door. 'Who's it?' Aashi called out.

'Preeti. Abhi has sent me to help you.'

'Preeti? Oh, come in, the door's open!' Aashi replied, feeling more than glad to hear the sound of a girl she had met only once before. Abhi had introduced them at his birthday party. She was his friend Ajay's fiancé and was a trained beautician 'Hi, Preeti, how are you? And how's Ajay?' Aashi asked as soon as the door opened.

'Both of us are fine, thank you. Ajay's downstairs with Abhi,' Preeti replied as she entered the room. 'They sent me up to help you get ready,' she added, walking up to the dressing table. 'Let me start with your hair first,' she said as her nimble fingers started working with Aashi's luxuriant curls, moulding them and pinning them up in a way that assured Aashi of the girl's skilfulness and good taste. In about fifteen minutes Preeti gave Aashi's head a final touch up and shifted her attention to her face. Just then another knock was heard and the door opened up to let Priyam enter.

'Hey, Priyam. You took a long time getting ready today, didn't you?' Aashi laughed as her friend walked up to her and put her hand on Aashi's shoulder.

'And I hated every moment of it,' Priyam replied, 'with Leela Bua being there by my side. How dare she pull your hand out of mine and push you back?'

'Never mind, Priyam, your brother ensured that I did not miss out on anything. See, I even have my own personal beautician. And by the way, I've been dying to ask you, does your dress fit okay? How does it look?'

'Perfect in every way and so does your own,' Priyam replied. 'You look gorgeous.' she added just as Preeti finished her work and made Aashi turn towards her friend.

'Well, that's good then. Thank God I had finished all our outfits before Diwali, otherwise…but…I don't look too made up, do I?' she asked, bringing about a sudden forced change in her voice. 'Abhi would laugh at me if I…'

'Not at all. You look fabulous. But talking about Abhi, here he is. You can ask him too if you don't believe me,' Priyam replied, getting up to answer the knock at the door.

Aashi didn't need to ask Priyam how she knew it was Abhi at the door. She knew his style of knocking just as well as Priyam. Ever since her accident, Abhi had often come seeking her in her home. But never once had he yet taken the liberty to enter without knocking, even if the door was open.

A sudden thrill rose up within Aashi. She knew Abhi must be looking straight at her at that moment, looking at her with that irresistible, magnetic stare that only his eyes were capable of. Nothing and nobody had ever complemented her with an intensity as his silent gaze did. And Aashi waited to feel that complement again. She had never done that before. But then, so much had already changed. She had enough admiration flowing towards her before. And Abhi's hadn't been particularly welcome either. But now Aashi found herself hushing up her own breaths as she focussed her attention at his footsteps.

He entered the room. She heard the door close behind him.

'*Now he would say something stupid and irritating to mask his feelings,*' Aashi thought.

But she was prepared to face Abhi's attack. She was ready.

But…why was everybody so silent? Had he left? It was him, Aashi knew, and he *had* walked in, she was sure about that too. What was he doing then? Why didn't he say anything? Was he looking at her? 'Abhi?' the sound escaped her before Aashi could stop herself.

'Yes?' the reply promptly came.

So he was there after all. He had not left. Well then, he must be standing there staring at her all the time, just as she had expected.

'Well?' Aashi asked, getting up from her seat.

'Well what?' Abhi asked. His eyes, which so far had been arrested by her face, were now forced to wander downwards and follow the movements of her hands as Aashi touched and twirled the graceful folds of her *lehenga*.

193

'How do I look?'

'It seems to me that you know that already,' Abhi replied, and Aashi could hear the same old battle between desire and control in his voice. His face however remained as grim as before and his eyes kept on roving over her form, unmindful even of Preeti's presence.

'Now, that's a pretty satisfying answer. Thank you very much,' Aashi grinned, turning away from him as Preeti carefully arranged Aashi's *dupatta* around her shoulders. .

'You are welcome,' Abhi replied, finally moving his feet and eyes away from Aashi.

'Stay a while,' Priyam spoke up, 'you look tired.'

'Nah, I'm okay. I just came to see if you two were ready. Guests have already started arriving. Manish and his friends have also arrived. Any moment you'd be called down too. So I thought I'd let you know and…'

'And?' Priyam asked.

'Have a quite word with you while I can,' he replied, accompanying his words with a shallow laugh. 'You are okay, aren't you? Do you need anything?' he asked, as Priyam snuggled close to him and his arm reached up to envelop her in his reassuring hug.

'No, I'm okay,' Priyam murmured, shrinking herself closer to Abhi as the finality of the moment settled over her heart.

Several sounds rose up in the corridor, giving them a clear indication of her various aunts approaching to take her away.

'Well then, it's time,' Abhi said, freeing himself from her, and planting a quick kiss on Priyam's forehead.

Within moments a veritable swarm of over-excited ladies stormed in. Abhi quickly walked up to Aashi and removed her to a quieter corner. 'Will you do me one more favour?' he asked as Preeti joined them in the corner too.

'Sure, Abhi, what do you want me to do?' the girl asked.

'Just stay with my sister. Don't leave her alone. She needs the company of friends today, not strangers, so stay close to her.'

'I will, don't worry,' Preeti replied

'Yeah, me too,' Aashi added, 'and if anyone tries to push me away this time, I know how to use my elbows and knees too. I'll shove *them* away!' Aashi declared.

'That's the spirit,' Abhi laughed, 'but I've claimed you for myself today. You'll come with me.'

'But why?' Aashi asked defiantly, as her mind tried to disentangle itself from his words. *Claimed you for myself...*what was it ringing behind those words that had felt so heavy and leaden as it entered her heart. Aashi had to take a deep breath and swallow hard to relieve herself of the sudden weight. It wasn't so easy however, especially as she felt Abhi step closer to her.

'Why?' he said, 'because that's my only chance of getting a lovely girl to walk by my side. And you are looking quite good today actually.'

'Thanks, but if you think that complement is going to make me stay behind, then you are wrong,' Aashi replied, trying hard to suppress her smile but failing miserably.

Abhi's attention though had suddenly been drawn towards his aunts who had so far busied themselves in surveying their getup in front of the mirror or comparing the room to the ones allotted to them.

'I dare say,' Leela's voice rose up above the cackle of the rest. She had lost some weight over the years and her skin had also begun to show signs of not a very pleasant or comfortable aging. That however had had no diminishing effect on the shrillness of her voice, nor her temper either. In fact, both had gained a good deal, if one took into account her daughters and their steadfast adherence to their mother's good example. 'It's going to be a very lavish party. A bit too lavish, I think,' she kept on pouring out her judgements, 'for it's just a ladies *sangeet*, but then, it's his money. He can throw it away as he wishes. And really, Priyam, you should be thankful to your aunts and uncles. It wasn't an easy decision for us to give up the children of our dear dead brother and let them go with a stranger. But we made that sacrifice, for your good, you know. We knew that we'd never be able to give you the wealth that Mr. Vardhan would. All we could have given you was love, and a growing up child needs a lot more than that. So you should be thankful that we let you go with him.'

'Oh, we are thankful, *Bua*,' Abhi replied even before Priyam could open her mouth. 'It was the best thing you could have done for us. And let me assure you, Mr. Vardhan has given us a lot more than just shelter. And the love we have received from him far exceeds the money you see him spending here.'

'I know...I know...that's why I say you should be thankful we didn't keep you from going with him. It'd have been so selfish of us. But now, let us not waste any more time. It's already past eight. Let's go now, Priyam,' she said, taking a firm hold of her hand, fearful perhaps that the poor girl will fall if not held tightly enough.

Abhi sent Preeti after them as they took Priyam out of the room. Priyam looked back at her brother and saw him holding Aashi's hand. A smile flickered across her face, a smile of hope. Abhi saw that smile and knew what it meant. A slight twitch of his own lips was the only reply he could give, but it was sufficient to wipe out Priyam's pleasure in an instant and replace it with a sigh instead.

Indeed, as Abhi stood there, with his love's hand held firmly in his own, his imagination was allowed the liberty only to wander to the limit of just that evening. He had planned out a special surprise for Aashi. It was to be an evening she would never forget, and a one that would build up his own load of happy memories, of moments that would forever be cherished in his lonely heart. That was all Abhi had decided to hope for. That was all he had allowed himself to look forward too.

'Ready, Aashi?' he asked as soon as he had heard the noise of all his aunts fade away behind the closed door of the elevator.

'Yeah,' she replied in not too cheerful a tone, 'let's go.'

'Why? What happened?' Abhi asked. He saw an unmistakable shadow of despondency pass over Aashi's face. Her lips trembled as she tried to convert her grief into smile.

'N…nothing. Let's go,' she managed to say.

'No, tell me or I'm not moving one step from here,' he declared.

'It's nothing, Abhi. Just a stupid habit…'

'What habit?'

'You know, when I could see, I never left for a party without throwing a final glance at the mirror to make sure everything's okay.'

'Everything is okay, Aashi. You look lovely and you know it too.'

'Yes, but…it isn't the same. Not half as satisfying. If only I could know…'

'How you are looking?'

'Yes, but…' Aashi let her sentence remain unfinished.

'Okay, let me see.' Abhi said, making Aashi turn towards himself.

'Well?' Aashi asked, waiting to hear just how Abhi would describe her looks while maintaining his show of utter indifference.

Aashi knew his words would satisfy her. Ever since her accident, Abhi had served as her eyes, describing to her everything that she wished to see and in such details that her keen imagination had no difficulty in raising up the picture in all its vividity even through the impenetrable darkness of her eyes

'Well, if Raj had been here he would have said,'… Abhi began.

'Raj isn't here!' Aashi retorted. Raj had left her, alone and at a time when she needed him most. He had gone away and Aashi didn't want to even hear his name. Not when she was already struggling hard to be happy in Priyam's happiness. Not when it was already too hard to keep up her promise of being happy and cheerful. And how dare Abhi even try to pretend he could imagine what Raj would have said or not? How dare he use the crutches of Raj's name! 'Raj…isn't here!' she repeated, taking a step away from Abhi.

But in a moment his hand had stopped her. 'I'm sorry,' he breathed, making Aashi turn towards him once more, 'I'm sorry, I shouldn't have…' he said again in a deeply distressed tone as his fingers gently picked away the protesting drops that had rushed out from her eyes.

Aashi nodded and forced herself to take a deep breath to calm herself. 'Bet I look horrible now,' she said a moment later, drying her cheeks further and trying to diffuse the moment with some touch of humour. The smile though, that Aashi stretched on her lips was too awkward to be convincing. And her attempts at cheerfulness didn't fare any better either.

'You are looking gorgeous, Aashi. You have designed this dress yourself so it cannot but suit you to perfection,' Abhi said, in a carefully weighed tone.

'I know that,' Aashi mumbled, trying to move away again.

But there was Abhi's hand on her arm, and she had not the liberty to step even an inch away.

'Your hair,' she felt him run a finger through her long curls, 'are perfectly set. Preeti has done a good job. Your hairstyle looks elegant, without being too showy and over-the-top kind of thing.' His deep voice still hovered in the realm of dry, matter-of-factness.

There was something in that voice however, coming as it did from an utter darkness, it seemed to surround Aashi with an inscrutable force and made her listen attentively as he let out each of his carefully selected words. Words that were plain enough, and yet…

'Your eyes,' Abhi continued, picking up a trembling drop from her curled eyelashes, 'though they cannot now see, will still force many to look only towards you.'

'They will?' Aashi heard herself murmur.

'Yes,' he replied, 'and these ornaments that you are wearing, artificial maybe,' she felt a light touch on her dangling earrings, 'seem more alluring to me than the brightest diamonds.'

Aashi could not help but notice the way his voice dwindled till it was just a whisper. But what longing echoed in that whisper. Longing… potent enough to tremble through every pore of her being, entering into her like burning, igniting pain.

'Your face,' his fingers stopped tinkering with her earring and caressed her face instead, 'as fresh and enchanting…as…'

197

'As?' she whispered, barely able to draw in her breath. What was happening to her? Why did her face burn so and why was there such loud thumping within her ribs. She realized that her face was turned up...towards him...and she was conscious too of his fingers creeping down towards her trembling lips and his breath approaching a little too close to her face. Her toes twitched, tightening, fingernails dug into her palm. She waited...

'As...' he whispered.

She heard him suck in his breath and hold it, letting it out a long moment later, slowly, regretfully.

'As...it always is,' he said, with an abrupt change of tone and a quick retraction of himself and his roving hand, 'that I think is sufficient description for any young girl to feel satisfied with. Shall we go down now?'

'Ye...yes...sure,' Aashi managed to utter. A strange trembling had overtaken her, a trembling that she had not felt for the first time but which had always left her confused and bewildered. That was perhaps what Aashi hated about him. The way Abhi could make her feel. The way, she didn't want to feel with him. How could he evoke in her the emotions she had reserved only for her love? How could he make her feel so powerless...so utterly incapable of moving away from him? First it was his eyes, and now it seemed even his voice knew that cunning. How Aashi had hated him for everything he had forced her to feel, including a strange unfathomable sense of guilt. Yet, as she now walked out of the room and stepped into the elevator, her fingers entwined with Abhi's, his low smooth voice humming away his calculated nonsense, and the scent of his cologne intoxicating her senses, did she still want to push him away and throw sarcastic comments on him?

No, because now she needed him and besides, there was nobody else to turn too. Selfish? Aashi knew she was that and had in fact prided at her being so. It was the most practical way to survive in this world, she had always believed. Somehow though, it didn't feel quite so good now, as it had done before.

The elevator soon brought them to the ground floor and as the doors opened up, pandemonium rushed in.

'Why's everyone shouting?' Aashi asked, putting her hands to her ears as a great onslaught of noise knocked against her.

'No one's shouting,' Abhi laughed, 'they are just trying to make themselves heard over others. And very soon, you'd have to join the battle too.'

'Never! I'm not so vulgar as to shout out like that.'

'Yes, I know. You only shout out at me,' he chuckled and guided her steps towards the garden. 'Anyway, here we are, two steps going down, remember? Careful now.'

She nodded and carefully stepped out into the garden.

'Is everything looking as we planned it?' she asked Abhi.

'Yes, everything is as you planned it. I did not forget any of your suggestions or plans. I hope your memory is as good too,' said Abhi.

'What do you mean?'

'Just that I hope you remember all your plans and promises?'

'Which plan or promise are you talking about?'

'That you would dance all night on Priyam's wedding. Let's see you fulfil your promise. And I will fulfil mine too and dance along with you.'

Aashi halted her steps at once. 'You...remembered?' she said.

'Didn't I tell you? I have super memory.'

'No use, I'm not going to dance,' Aashi declared.

'May I ask why not?'

'I'm not going to make a fool of myself before so many people. If I go on the dance floor, I'll only end bumping against others and making a fool of myself. And I won't have that!'

'We'll see,' Abhi replied, 'now quiet down, my dear aunts are coming this way. Don't let them see your fury. It gives bad impression, you know,' he laughed, reclaiming the hold of Aashi's fingers.

Aashi didn't utter another word, but that didn't stop her from repeating in her heart the resolution she had just declared to Abhi. He can make a fool of himself if he wanted to. There was no way she would let him make a fool of her. How ridiculous it would look...a blind girl dancing with a lame man!

'*No way! Never!*' Aashi was resolved.

So what if the DJ was playing all her favourite songs? So what if the pulsating music wafting on air had already given rise to an eager tingle in Aashi's feet. She was already finding it too hard to stop her hand from beating the rhythm against the folds of her *lehenga*. But that didn't mean that she was ready to dance! She would not! Never!

199

Chapter 24

I thought that my voyage had come to its end
at the last limit of my power,--
that the path before me was closed,
that provisions were exhausted and
the time come to take shelter in a silent obscurity.
But I find that thy will knows no end in me.
And when old words die out on the tongue,
new melodies break forth from the heart'

— *'Gitanjali –37' by Rabindranath Tagore.*

'*That* was sudden!' Abhi remarked, watching Mr. Vardhan walk away with Priyam and Manish.

'And unexpected!' Aashi added. 'What would Manish be thinking?'

More than two hours had passed since Abhi and Aashi had stepped out into the party lawn. Fifteen minutes since the *sagan* ceremony had been over, and just two minutes since Manish had taken hold of Priyam's hand and made an ardent request.

'Let's go and dance, Priyam,' Manish had said, 'I can't wait any more to take you on the dance floor.'

'No!' Priyam had refused of course, with a suitable show of coyness, 'I can't dance!' she had urged.

'Oh come on, I've been waiting for this moment since morning,' Manish had countered her frantic protestations, almost pulling Priyam out of Abhi's shadow where she had sought refuge against his proposal. 'Abhi promised me that you'll have at least one dance with me. You can't refuse me now.'

She didn't. But even before Manish could take her a step away, a hand had reached out and pulled Priyam back.

'I'm afraid, son,' Mr. Vardhan spoke up, sheltering Priyam under his arm, 'you'll have to wait a bit longer.'

'What? Why? I mean…' Manish sputtered, carefully parrying the feeling of getting insulted by the abrupt removal of his bride from his side.

'Oh, don't feel bad, son. It's not your fault. But really, Abhi,' Mr. Vardhan said, turning to glare down on him, 'you should have known better than to raise such hopes in this young man. Don't you know how inauspicious it is for the groom to dance with the bride before marriage?' he almost scolded.

Abhi stared at his guardian with shock as well as bafflement.

'That's…' *ridiculous*, Manish had wanted to say, but bit his tongue at the last moment. It would never have done to risk offending Mr. Vardhan. He had not got the full impunity to do so yet. And Manish was too wise to risk anything that might affect his future prosperity.

'And Priyam,' Mr. Vardhan had then turned to her, 'you have done enough walking for the day. You should now go and sit with your aunts,' he said with all the sternness he could muster against her. But his voice soon softened again and a smile broke through his exaggerated frown as he added, 'you can dance all you want after your marriage. I won't stop you then.'

With those words Mr. Vardhan had led both Priyam and Manish away from the dance floor. And as Abhi watched on, his sister was deposited to the safe custody of her aunts while her fiancé was being taken further away.

'But why did he do it, Abhi? Is it really so inauspicious for a bride to dance?' Aashi asked.

'What I would like to know is, since when did Mr. Vardhan start believing in such things?' he said, scratching his head. His guardian's behaviour was becoming much too baffling for him. But of course, there was little that Abhi could do except to trust in Mr. Vardhan's wisdom and try not to worry too much. 'Well,' he said taking a deep breath, 'what do you want to do now?'

'Whatever,' Aashi shrugged.

'Well, then let's go on the stage and join the dancers. You have a promise to fulfil.'

'I've already told you at least ten times that I don't want to dance. I would not,' she declared and took a step back.

'Oh, okay,' Abhi relented, 'if that's what you wish. I won't force you. But we can at least go and cheer the other dancers, can't we? I can see Ajay and Preeti dancing, we can go and applaud them. You can have no objection in *that*.'

'Okay,' Aashi replied in a little voice, 'but I won't dance!' she reminded Abhi again.

'Alright,' he replied and led her up on the dance floor.

Aashi felt the floor vibrate under her feet as several young people pounded upon it in tune with the music. Instantly a thrill rose up in her. How she wished to join her own energy to the beats and twirl away in ecstasy.

And it was her most favourite song too that had started reverberating the air around her.

But all she allowed herself to do was to stand in a corner with Abhi and clap.

'Hey, Abhi, why are you standing so still like a stick?' Ajay's voice rose up over the music. 'Move yourself a bit, *yaar*. You are on a dance floor and the music is so good too.'

'I would, but my friend here doesn't want to dance. We just came up to cheer you two on, Right, Aashi?' said Abhi.

'Ye...s,' Aashi agreed, not however so emphatically this time. The music was just too beckoning and the pulsation under her feet was already making it impossible for her to stand still.

'And she won't change her decision, no matter what. Right, Aashi?'

'Is it...very crowded?' Aashi heard herself mumble and bit her tongue immediately. The words though had already escaped her mouth.

'Not where we are,' Abhi replied, and Aashi could have sworn he was already grinning.

'But...what if I trip? What if I fall over somebody?' Aashi still hesitated, even though her feet had already begun to move as Abhi's arm slid around her and made her sway to the rhythm.

'You won't. I won't let you fall, and there's no question of you tripping over anybody. Trust me.'

And indeed, there already had formed a secure circle around them as five of his friends, including Ajay, surrounded them. There were enough people to crowd up the dance floor, but none was allowed to break that circle. Abhi's friends had formed a ring of safety for him as they danced along with their own partners.

'I do, but...' Aashi's sentence remained unfinished as Abhi surprised her by making her twirl to the music. 'Oooh!' Aashi laughed out with nervous excitement, 'Don't do that!'

'That was fun, wasn't it? Just keep on holding me. We'll be fine, really,' he said as he tightened his grasp on Aashi's hand and smiled to see her move to the tune despite her many protestations.

Aashi couldn't help it either. The music throbbed loud and fast, just as she liked and she could easily notice that all her favourite songs were being played. She was slow and awkward at first but soon the magic of the music took away all her inhibitions. The floor was even and smooth under her feet and there was no jostling and shoving around her to scare her off. But more than all this, there was Abhi's reassuring presence, his firm hold on her hand. She had nothing to fear.

'See, how easy it is?' Abhi said, smiling to see her joy.

'Yeah, it isn't as hard as I had imagined it to be,' Aashi said.

If only she could stop thinking about Raj. She didn't want to remember the one who had forgotten her so easily. She didn't want to remember her various dances with him. But try as she might, Raj's face rose up again and again before her and often when Abhi's arm encircled her, Aashi caught herself imagining being held by Raj instead.

'Abhi, is this the same suit you wore on Mr. Vardhan's party?' she asked, as her fingers caressed the smoothness of the fabric.

'No, it's a new one.'

'It feels so smooth,' Aashi said, 'what colour is it?' she asked as the music started again after a momentary break.

'Brown,' he replied. He took hold of Aashi's hand and started moving in step with the rising beats.

'Brown! I hate brown!' she frowned.

'Well, it's good then that you can't see it,' he laughed.

'And what colour is your shirt? And tie?' she quickly added.

'Oh, shirt is a lovely bright yellow and with bold red checks. I'm not wearing any tie though.'

'Awful! Leave my hand right now, mister! I'm not dancing with a clown! You should better have worn your faded jeans and tee-shirt than this horror!' Aashi cried out and tried to loosen her hand from his hold.

'Hey! I'm actually looking quite good, you know. So don't you dare call me a clown,' Abhi said, He drew her closer by wrapping his arm around her slender waist.

A sudden tremor raced through Aashi as his breath caressed her neck. There was his cheek rubbing ever so gently against hers as they moved along the music. Aashi's fingers tightened slightly at his shoulders, her back stiffened.

'Yeah, looking good and colourful!' she said. 'Couldn't you wear something nice for a change, Abhi? It's your own sister's wedding you know?'

'Nice? What do you mean by *nice*?' he asked, pretending to be deeply confused and highly displeased.

But there was pleasure dancing on his face and a deep, deep longing swimming in the moisture of his eyes. And his eyes at that moment had fixed themselves on her smiling lips.

'Like…an all black suit or…'

'An all black suit? Hmm…' he muttered, without moving his eyes away, 'can it have lines over it?' he asked.

'You mean stripes?'

'Maybe, and can the shirt be not black but like…steel grey?'

'You are wearing that?'

'But I'm not wearing any tie. You know I hate wearing ties.'

'You are wearing a pinstriped suit?' Aashi asked. Her fingers quickly checked out the style of the collar and ran down his front to count the buttons.

He looked down at her roving hand, his fingers tightened on hers. 'Maybe,' he said. 'So you lied to me?' she exclaimed, giving Abhi a hard punch on the shoulder. 'I really do hate you, Abhi!'

'That's not the first time you are telling me that,' he laughed back, 'and I willingly give you the permission to hate me as much as you want.'

'I don't want your permission for anything. And I *will* hate you as much as I want,' Aashi shot back.

But she knew that never again would she be able to hide herself behind that emotion. She may never love Abhi the way he deserved to be loved. But neither would she be able to reciprocate his kindness by cruelty as she had done so far. That comfort was lost to her forever.

'So we both agree on something at least,' he laughed, 'concentrate on the dance now, you are missing the beats.'

'Pinstriped suit, black and grey…you must be looking good. Black always looks good on you,' she mumbled as she tried to form a mental picture of them dancing together.

'Of course, I'm looking utmost handsome today; in fact, quite dashing really!'

'Oooh! Stop it, Abhi. You need not be so vain!' she squealed and hit him again.

'Excellent! I praise you and you listen with open mouth and don't even think the need to thank me for the complements I showered on you. I praise myself a little bit and I'm declared vain? Ha!'

'Ha to you too! I'll say what I want to. You can't stop me.'

'Well then, all I'll say is that with so many eyes staring enviously towards me and my companion, I've every right to be vain, for today at least.'

'What? Are people looking at us?' Aashi asked horrified. She had almost forgotten that she probably was surrounded by a lot many dancers. They had been dancing so uninterruptedly that it had actually felt to her that they were the only ones there. But now Abhi's words brought consciousness rushing back to her and she immediately began to worry if she was making a spectacle of herself.

'Sure they're looking and I can assure you many young men would rush to grab your hand if I let them. But I warn you, I'm not going to do that. I'm not going to let anyone take you away from me...today. Not even if you order me to.'

'I won't,' Aashi replied. She stepped back towards him and reciprocated the tightening of his clutch by putting her free hand over his shoulder too.

It was the shoulder from which protruded the stump of his amputated arm. And even though her eyes had always shied from looking at it directly, her fingers didn't hesitate now to rest over it. 'It's been so long since I last danced,' she continued after some moments, 'and...I love dancing, Abhi,' she could not help but add as her curls flapped in the air while Abhi floated her around the little circle his friends had formed.

'I know.'

'You do? How?' Aashi asked, gasping as she moved to the fast beats.

'Well,' he replied, 'you do sometime forget to draw your curtains close.'

'You watched me?'

'Didn't you want me to?' he asked.

'No! I mean...I didn't deliberately keep the curtains open...not always... I...I mean...' sometimes it had been just plain forgetfulness too. But she knew Abhi was not talking about those instances. He was talking about that one day when she had actually wanted him to see, yes, to see...and suffer.

Aashi herself didn't know just what it was that had prompted her to do such a shameless thing. She had done it only once, and that too under the intoxicating influence of Raj. He had brought a new CD and his portable CD player and the two of them had spent almost an entire hour moving along to its music in the limited space that her room afforded. She *had* noticed the window open, she *had* seen Abhi moving inside his room. And yet, she didn't draw the curtains. She was too furious at Abhi to try and shield him from any pain. And it had felt too good a way to make it apparent to him how much she loved Raj, and how far above him her darling prince was.

The message, evidently, had been taken.

'Oh! You shouldn't have!' words fell over each other as she stumbled between past and present.

How much had changed since then, how much! She had changed, if not him. Abhi was still the same, just not hateful now. Aashi's feet stopped moving as a throbbing dread burnt up in her heart, echoing perhaps the very pain that must have passed through Abhi by what she had made him see. And he *had* seen, seen it all. There was no doubt in that. He had seen them dance, dance in the most intimate way and culminate their bliss in a passionate kiss.

205

He had seen it all!

Horror dawned on Aashi as she remembered that evening. There was no way she would ever be able to compensate for all the pain she had given Abhi. No way she'd ever be able to hope for an apology, not that she considered herself deserving one either. 'You…shouldn't …have,' she muttered again, her head bending low and fingers crushing the delicate fabric of her dress.

'I know,' Abhi replied. There was not a bit of anger or resentment in his voice. He had accepted her act just as uncomplainingly as he had accepted everything else. 'But why have you stopped dancing?' he asked a moment later. His voice had resumed its normal carefree tone, 'I hope you are not tired already?'

'No, of course not,' Aashi said, trying to complement her words with a suitable smile.

'Well then, keep moving. And stop only when you are tired and want rest.'

'That won't be for a long time,' she managed to laugh as she started moving again.

'I hope not,' he murmured, letting his voice get drowned in the louder sound of the blaring music.

Abhi knew he should rather be attending to his guests instead of dancing. He was the host after all. And he most definitely should already have sought Manish out and soothed away any ill feeling that might have risen out of Mr. Vardhan's strange behaviour. 'Well, I will, later,' he told himself. It wouldn't matter if he played a truant for some time. Just for some more time.

Soon, Aashi's feet began to play with the music again. All unpleasant memories were relegated away as the joy of the moment repossessed her in its enthralling grasp.

It didn't matter if it was Abhi she was dancing with. It didn't matter now how awkward he looked while dancing. She couldn't see and by what she could sense, he was dancing smartly enough. She was smiling now, and she had not smiled with such pleasure in many days. Her face was flushed with delight. And she knew Abhi was happy too.

And it felt good to be finally giving him some reason to smile. After all, he loved her more than anyone else ever would. And it was an honour to be so loved. Why had she been so bent upon fighting against such a love earlier? Abhi had never made any demand from her. He never would. So what if she would never be able to reciprocate his feelings. So what if she would never be able to love Abhi the way he loved her. It was delicious nevertheless to be so cherished. And she would repay by giving him utmost respect. She cannot be his lover, but she would be his best friend. Now that Sid was no longer with him, Abhi did need a 'best friend.' And so did she; with Priyam getting married.

The music kept on spinning Aashi on her feet as several resolutions took shape in her heart. And for the time being at least, Raj's face faded out of her mind. Aashi closed her eyes and watched herself twirling away in gay abundance with another young man, a dear friend, looking most handsome in a pinstriped suit and grey shirt.

It was the day of Priyam's wedding. The time was past eight thirty, and Priyam had just been informed that the *baraat* had arrived and was being welcomed. All her dutiful companions, except Aashi, had rushed out to witness the welcome ceremony. Soon she would be called too. It was time.

It was the end of time.

Priyam looked down at her henna painted hands. A desire flared up to scrape her smouldering palms clean of the decorative stain, to banish Manish's name from her hands. But she would not. She would bear his name like a proud token, token of disgust…and of revenge.

'Please! Can someone tell the band not to murder such nice songs!' Aashi's voice startled her. Priyam had almost forgotten her presence in the same room.

'What?' Priyam asked, having missed out on half of what Aashi had said.

'They are torturing me! Tell them to stop or at least sing in tune!' Aashi moaned, putting her hands to her ears.

The singer accompanying the band though kept on wailing away in happy unconcern the notes and often the lyrics of the songs he was supposed to be singing.

Outside, Abhi was busy in welcoming the *baraat*.

The welcome ceremony took a long time to get over, but finally after almost an hour, Abhi accompanied Manish into the *pandaal*. The Damle family followed close and behind them swarmed in the rest of the *baraatees*.

With the welcome over, Abhi went to stand in attention near the stage as Manish settled down on his seat and his nears and dears surrounded him for the first round of photography.

A tap on shoulder made Abhi turn around.

Mr. Damle's face beamed at him as he turned, 'All the arrangements look good, Abhinandan. Nothing seems to be lacking. But where's Mr. Vardhan? I've looked all around but he's nowhere. Hasn't he arrived yet?'

'He must be here somewhere,' Abhi replied. He looked around him and tried not to let his own unease appear in his voice. But the fact was that Abhi was deeply troubled. He trusted his guardian more than anybody else in the world. Yet, Mr. Vardhan's behaviour had only become more bizarre over the day.

Abhi had seen Mr. Vardhan enter the dining room in the morning with such merriment in his step that would have surely been converted into a little jig had he been a bit younger. '*This* is going to be the happiest day of my life!' he had declared while sitting down with them for breakfast.

This happiness had however declined with the decline of the day. As the sunset and dusk crowded over, Mr. Vardhan steadily grew more and more agitated. Abhi himself had witnessed several workers scurrying away after getting razed by Mr. Vardhan's fury. Soon after the sunset, his car was seen zooming out of the guesthouse, only to return an hour later and be driven to the small back entrance of the building. But all this was nothing in comparison to what Abhi had witnessed while coming out of his room after getting dressed for the evening.

Abhi had just opened his door when he noticed a waiter carrying a tea tray, with *two* cups, into Mr. Vardhan's room. And then, before he could conjure up any explanation, Mr. Vardhan and the waiter both stepped out of the room. The waiter carefully locked up the room, turned on the 'do not disturb sign' and left after handing over the key to Mr. Vardhan.

'Be ready,' Mr. Vardhan ordered as he dismissed his man. 'Are you ready, Abhi?' he quickly added as he caught the young men peeking out from his room.

'Uh...yes, yes, Sir,' Abhi stuttered as he stepped out into the corridor to join his guardian.

'Good, let's go then,' Mr. Vardhan responded. He put his keys securely in his pocket.

From under his door however, light kept on pouring out and a couple of hushed voices met Abhi's ears even where he was standing. Who those people were, he had no idea, nor why they had been locked like that in the best and most luxurious room in the entire guesthouse. The only thing that was clear to Abhi was that the person who was striding along with him was guarding a secret. And that no matter what, he would never know what it is till Mr. Vardhan himself thought it proper to divulge.

Abhi had tried to find out the waiter however, but the man seemed to have vanished away too. And as time progressed, Abhi was left with no choice but to give up his search and concentrate on other pressing needs instead.

'Oh, there's Mr. Vardhan ! I wonder how I missed him? He's standing right at the entrance!' Mr. Damle exclaimed. 'I'll go and meet him,' with that Mr. Damle left Abhi to walk up to the one more worthy of his attentions. Abhi watched Mr. Damle for a moment but soon his gaze shifted to his guardian instead.

Mr. Vardhan was pacing near the entrance in the most impatient manner, looking again and again at his wristwatch. 'He already has two people locked up in his room,' Abhi muttered under his breath, 'who else is he waiting for?'

Soon however Abhi's eyes were pulled away to gaze instead at Priyam, being escorted in by Leela and party.

Dressed in a stunning pink and blue *lehenga* and dolled up in her bridal finery, Priyam slowly walked up to the stage. Aashi too was walking behind her, being escorted this time by her mother. But Abhi saw only his sister, his pretty little sister, his angel...walking out to take up the yoke of humanity.

Abhi stared at Priyam, at the delicate smile that she maintained, at the resolute steady stare with which she met his eyes. Where was his sister in all this? Where was Priyam? The girl who was moving towards her waiting groom had nothing left of the girl she had been. Abhi forced himself to take a deep breath and blink away the tears that had risen up. He took a step away from the stage and turned his eyes towards his guardian once again.

Mr. Vardhan was still near the main entrance of the *pandaal*. He had stopped pacing and was busy talking into his cell phone instead. The call soon ended and Abhi saw him click off his cell phone, flip it over in the air and catch it triumphantly. Immediately he left his position at the entrance and walked in towards the stage. His steps once again treaded the carpet with cheerful energy and his face beamed at whoever met his gaze.

'So, Abhi,' Mr. Vardhan said as he stepped close to him, 'guess it's time for the show to begin.'

'Sir?'

'Oh, never mind, just wait and watch!' he replied, as he too focused his eyes on Priyam. 'I knew Priyam would make a pretty bride,' he told Abhi. 'Her groom would really have to make some hectic efforts to match up to her.'

'Oh, Manish is looking handsome enough,' Abhi replied, turning to gaze a moment at the *sherwani* clad and inexorably grinning groom.

'Oh yes, Manish is. He's all dressed and decked up. Almost looking like a prince right now, waiting to possess his catch, isn't he?'

Abhi nodded, without realizing what he was nodding his approval to. His eyes were staring at another approaching form. The waiter he had been searching for all around the guesthouse had suddenly materialized and was, at that moment, actually walking towards them. However, before Abhi could ask a word about him, Mr. Vardhan had already excused himself and rushed on to interrupt the waiter's path.

No word passed between the two men, but as Abhi watched on, Mr. Vardhan took out his room's key and put it into the waiter's hand. The waiter instantly closed his fingers on it and walked away. And then Mr. Vardhan came back to Abhi.

Priyam by that time was just a couple of steps away from the stage. Abhi saw her glance up at Manish and immediately lower her eyes. She did not look up again. She could not. Just one look at her handsome groom had filled her heart with repulsion. She kept on advancing her steps unceasingly, and yet, with every step she took forward, her heart recoiled further away from the man she was going to marry.

She wanted to stop. She wanted to run away. She looked up at her brother. He had done all he could to make her relent. She looked at her guardian. How well he was bearing it all. She knew he had looked at her as the only means of securing happiness for his son and himself. And with every step she was taking, she was trampling away on each of his hopes.

'*Stop me!*' she wanted to whisper in his ears. '*Don't let me do this!*' she wanted to cry out. But all she did was take another step and climb up on the stage. It was too late now to stop...too late...and...for whom? Sid himself was getting married at that moment, wasn't he? He no longer belonged to her and...she no longer belonged to anybody.

She turned towards Manish and raised her head. No longer did her eyes shrink from his gaze. She looked up at him and stretched a smile in response to his indefatigable smirk. A big garland of roses was put in her hands. Her arms lifted up.

'Stop, Priyam!' the cry resonated in the *pandaal*.

'Sid!' Abhi's voice followed close.

'Yes!' Mr. Vardhan's jubilation didn't lag far behind.

World swooned around Priyam as she turned and saw Sid coming in.

Chapter 25

My hungry Soul he fill'd with Good;
He in his Bottle put my tears,
My smarting wounds washt in his blood,
And banisht thence my Doubts and fears.

What to my Saviour shall I give
Who freely hath done this for me?
I'll serve him here whilst I shall live
And Loue him to Eternity

—*'By Night when Others Soundly Slept' by Anne Bradstreet*

'Stop, Priyam!' Sid called out again, 'You can't marry that man! You must not!'

Priyam looked at Sid. And then she looked at the crowd around her that had started talking in not too hushed whispers. There she was standing on the stage, her hands holding the wedding garland and her groom just a step away. And there was Sid, asking her to stop. And the crowd deciphering all kinds of meanings from his call.

Priyam's heart had fluttered up with joy to see Sid standing there. Her steps had moved forward on their own to rush up to him and hide herself in his arms. Sid had come back! He had come back to her! Her heart's desire had come true and there was nothing more to wish for.

But it was too late. Too late.

A moment more Priyam gazed at Sid, just a moment, and then, she turned away to look up again at the one whom only *he* had made her destiny.

Sid wanted her to get married to someone else. Well then, she would get married. She *must* get married. She must.

Priyam's arms lifted up again, to finally put the garland around Manish's neck.

But, where was that garland? Why were her hands empty?

Priyam felt herself move. She felt herself being slowly turned away from Manish. Two sturdy hands held her in a firm grasp, supporting her and gently leading her away.

'No!' she protested, trying to loosen herself and turn back. Perhaps she had been in danger of falling. She didn't know. She didn't care. 'No!' Priyam cried out again as she was forced to climb down the stage, 'Where are you taking me?'

'To your rightful groom,' Mr. Vardhan's voice echoed in her ears, 'the man you were standing with is just an impostor.'

Priyam's feet stopped moving. She looked up at her guardian. 'Sid is not my groom!' she spoke through clenched teeth, stressing every syllable of her miserable words.

Priyam loved Sid, loved him with every fibre of her being. But he had no right to play with her like that! What did Sid think that he would come back and start living life from where he had severed it? As if what he did didn't matter at all? As if… she was a plaything that Sid could throw away at will and then pick up again as and when he felt like it. She would not even look at him again.

But Sid was already there before Priyam, looking at her with eyes that still shined with the same honesty and love that Priyam had always adored. His hands reached out to her and grasped her fingers in their warm and gentle hold. Fire blazed from Priyam's eyes as Sid lifted them up and pressed them to his lips. She snatched her hands away and scorched him with her burning stare.

He could yet read the eloquence of those eyes. He could yet hear the voice of her unspoken words.

'I know…' Sid replied, bowing his head and taking a step back, 'I…had no right to come back…I…the way that I…I had no right to come back,' he repeated, looking up again and meeting her eyes, 'but I couldn't let you marry that man!'

'And why not?' Manish shouted out from the stage.

'What is this, Abhinandan? Who is this man? And how dare he say that? Mr. Damle raised up his voice.

Abhi didn't know how to pull himself out of the tumult between relief and alarm that Sid's entry had given rise to. On one hand, it was just what he had been wishing for all along. On the other hand, he could already hear derisive words rising up to sully his sister's character. A part of Abhi wanted to welcome his friend back with a joyous hug, while the rest of him burnt to throw Sid out and forbid him even to touch the air around Priyam!

'Who *is* he?' Mr. Damle asked again.

'He is…' Abhi began, turning to look at the one who once was his best friend.

'My son,' Mr. Vardhan gave the answer before Abhi could utter any other word. 'And he dares to interrupt your son's wedding because your son is already married.'

Abhi staggered back at the declaration.

Priyam's eyes flew up to her guardian.

'Married? Manish is married?' Aashi's was the only voice that managed to echo the thunderbolt.

'Lie!'

'That's a lie!' Manish and his father spoke up at once. 'And an insult!' Mr. Damle quickly added. 'Who told you such bullshit?' Mr. Damle shouted.

'Well, my dear Mr. Damle, here's a bit of news for you,' said Mr. Vardhan. 'Do you remember the conversation that you had with a relative you discovered among the guests at my party? Perhaps you thought that nobody heard it. But guess what? Somebody did. And what he couldn't hear, I found out from your very same relative and my good friend.'

'I don't know what you are talking about. As far as I remember, my son was never married,' it was Mrs. Damle this time to counter the accusation.

'Then of course you wouldn't even remember your grand-daughter who was just four months old when you murdered Swati, her mother,' Mr. Vardhan said. 'But whether you remember it or not, I have proof and witness that you harassed your daughter-in-law for dowry and then killed her when she refused to satisfy your greed further.'

This was more than what Abhi could take. Horror swept over his face as he listened to each flaming word being spoken. For the first time it dawned on him with what blind haste he had finalised the match. How easily he had allowed himself to believe in the goodness so blatantly self-professed by Manish and his family. He, who prided himself in being capable of reading a person inside out. How he had been blinded when he should have been the most careful!

Abhi's eyes darted towards Priyam. She was standing with her eyes glued to the floor. There was not a shred of surprise on *her* face.

'What is this, Abhi?' he heard his Uncle's voice. 'Were you getting Priyam married to a murderer?'

'Don't listen to them, Abhi,' Aashi whispered. She had forced her mother to move closer to him. Soon, her fingers too found Abhi's hand and entwined themselves tightly into his, as she tried to impart whatever comfort she could. 'You didn't know, Abhi. It's not your fault,' Aashi urged.

'It is. I should have known. I should have been more careful. What kind of brother marries off his only sister with such blindness?'

213

'But it's okay now, Abhi. Everything has come back to just as it should be. Even Sid is back, isn't he?' Aashi tried again.

Abhi was not so sure though. Sure Sid was standing there, right beside him. But, was he back? Was he back for Priyam, or just to save her and then to go back again to his own distant world?

'All baseless lies!' Mr. Damle added. 'You can't prove even one word you have so brazenly spoken.'

'Oh, yes, I can. Even though Manish did try to stop me from finding out the truth. You went to Pune too, didn't you, Manish, on 27th November?' Mr. Vardhan asked. 'Let me guess, you must have learnt that someone was trying to enquire about your past and so you rushed to Pune to give fresh warning to the neighbours and Swati's parents against divulging anything. Too bad your trip didn't fetch you any benefits.'

'You can say whatever you want. Nobody believes you anyway. Come Abhi, let's not waste any more time. We must get on with the wedding,' said Mr. Damle.

But Abhi didn't budge from his place. His eyes were fixed on Sid and he needed no proof to verify the truth of his friend's claims, nor of Mr. Vardhan's.

'No,' Abhi said, 'Priyam will not marry Manish. Not with my permission at least,' he declared, looking straight at his sister and silencing with one look any objection that she might raise.

Priyam's eyes had shot up at the pronouncement, but she lowered them again. Rage still seethed in her heart, and the desire was still strong to take her revenge to its culmination. But Abhi's eyes forbid her to take even one little step further on the road to self-destruction that Priyam had felt so fortunate to have chanced upon. She was not to marry Manish, and that was that.

'This is an insult! We won't bear this!' Mr. Damle thundered as several voices rose up to back him up. 'We'll call the police! We'll sue you,' he declared.

'Don't bother,' Sid replied, 'the police are already here.' And sure enough, there stood just near the entrance a small team of uniformed men, guarding, as it seemed, an elderly couple and a small girl. Near her stood a middle-aged lady, her hand over child's head and eyes staring with undisguised disgust at Manish. And near them stood the waiter whom Mr. Vardhan had given the key to his room.

'But before you meet the police, won't you kindly meet these - my special guests? They have all come here just in the hope of meeting you,' Mr. Vardhan added.

'We have no need to meet anybody,' Mrs. Damle shouted.

'I know why you are doing this,' said Manish. 'I always did feel that Priyam didn't love me quite as well as she should. Now I know why. She already was having an affair with your son. I did hear about it in the office. I did not believe it then, but now it's clear to everyone,' he sneered.

'Is that why you are trying to break this relation by raising all these false accusations against us? But you can't prove anything,' shouted Mr. Damle. 'There never was any Swati in my son's life. And there arises no question of these being her parents and sister, nor is that girl my son's child.'

A hush fell over the crowd as the words escaped his mouth. Manish winced and the mouth of Mrs. Damle fell open.

'It does say a great deal when a person denies something that hasn't yet been revealed,' Mr. Vardhan replied, smiling smugly as Mr. Damle unravelled his own deceit. 'I guess I won't need now to display all the proofs that I've gathered. Take them away,' he ordered the waiting policemen.

In less than two minutes, the groom and his family was whisked away. Their relatives took the path of the exit on their own.

'There, one good thing accomplished!' Mr. Vardhan said with a satisfied grin. 'What did I tell you, Abhi? They'd never forget this day!'

'Neither would any of us, Sir, but…why didn't you tell all this before? I'd have immediately called the marriage off,' Abhi asked.

'And they would have as immediately put the blame of the break up on Priyam and you. Many people would have believed them too. You couldn't have gone around telling the world the truth. And even if I had prohibited you from doing anything drastic, do you think you'd have succeeded in acting natural? There was too much at stake, you know. And there was no way I was going to allow anything that might make them suspicious. They would have easily denied everything. We had no proof. We couldn't have done much against any of them. So you see, I kept silent. The only person who knew about it is Raj.'

'Raj?' Aashi murmured.

'Raj was the one actually who heard the conversation that started everything,' Mr. Vardhan continued. 'He would have told it all to you, Abhi, but fortunately I met him first and he revealed everything to me. I told him to keep it a secret and to help me in further investigations. To gain some time, I persuaded Mr. Damle and his delightful son to postpone the wedding. They, of course, obeyed and gave me sufficient time to investigate their past,' said Mr. Vardhan with a grin. 'However, Raj soon became too trapped in his sister's escapades and his mother's histrionics,' he continued. 'So I told him to pass on the information to Sid without letting my name in, and of course, bind him up with a promise of secrecy too. I needed help. I had found out the truth, but I still had to find Swati's family.'

'Wait a minute!' Abhi exclaimed. 'We thought we saw you on the crossing near Raj's home, about a week ago. Was it really you?'

215

'Yes, it was him,' Mr. Vardhan replied. 'Sid had come to make up with me and to inform me about Manish's deceit. But as you know, I wasn't here that day. But he called me up, revealed everything that Raj had told him. Of course, I already knew it all. In fact, by that time I had also discovered where Swati's parents lived. But they were too scared for the life of their young son, a boy of fifteen now. They said that Manish and Mr. Damle had threatened to kill the boy if they tell anyone that they had a daughter who was married to anybody called Manish Damle. So I sent Sid to find Swati's sister. I had heard that she lived with her husband in Nagpur. She had all the proofs and also Swati's child. I was sure that even if Swati's parents get scared at the last moment, her sister would stand firm. I had heard that it was she and her husband who had filed the case against Manish and his father. So while I was trying to persuade the parents, I told Sid to rush to Nagpur.'

'Yes, and so I went to Nagpur,' Sid said. 'But the address Dad had given me was old. Swati's sister had moved out of that house a year ago. I had to follow a long chain of acquaintance to discover them. It was only yesterday morning that I finally managed to meet them. Swati's sister immediately agreed to accompany me. So I booked our tickets and informed Dad.'

'Yes, and what a relief I got when I received Sid's call. It was like finally everything was going as it should. Till Sid called me again with the news of flight delays. That turned everything upside down once more.'

'Oh, so *that's* why you were so agitated during the day,' Abhi asked with a smile. Everything was getting clearer now.

'Did it show? But of course, I am no actor, you know. And it was really frustrating too. Fortunately, Sid did manage to bring the lady and the child here on time, didn't he? Of course, I had my contingency plan ready too. But I really didn't want to do anything that drastic!'

'And I'm so glad he did,' Aashi exclaimed, echoing everybody's sentiments in her words. 'But...what about Tina? You were supposed to get married today, weren't you Sid?'

'Yes, that's correct. Sid was supposed to get married to Tina today. But you see, he can't because Tina too is already married.'

'What?' Abhi and Aashi shouted at once.

'Yes, and Mrs. Sinha has put the blame of it on my head as well,' Sid informed. 'She phoned me from London when I was busy trying to follow Raj's leads. She called to give me a long speech that, in fewer words, meant that her daughter was married and that it was all my fault because I had not given Tina the love she deserved. 'You are after all your father's son,' she said. 'Your father ignored my love and you ignored my daughter's love. Well, he paid the price, and so would you. Priyam, I dare say, is as much lost to you as Kiran is to your father.'

Mr. Vardhan put his hand on Sid's shoulder. 'Well,' he said, 'I guess I should be grateful to her for saying that.' That finally made Sid realize who really was behind Kiran's death.'

Sid nodded and lowered his head. Mr. Vardhan patted him on the back. But when that didn't satisfy him, he stepped up and gave Sid a tight hug. Sid did not resist him this time.

'This is super!' Abhi exclaimed. He looked at Priyam. She had tears in her eyes.

'But what made Tina change her mind?' he asked a moment later. Priyam too looked up with curiosity but kept her mouth sternly shut.

'Raj at play again,' Mr. Vardhan said, 'he knew that neither Sid nor Tina had any love for each other, nor ever would. Both had agreed under the influence of Mrs. Sinha's black magic. Tina, Raj knew, was still in love with William, her ex-boyfriend. So Raj decided to re-unite Tina with her love so Priyam could be re-united with hers. It was actually quite easy. All we needed to do was bring William and Tina together and Raj was sure things between them would mend on their own. And that's just what happened. I invited the young man to the Diwali party and Raj made sure that Tina came too.'

'So *that's* why she was dragged in between us that day! Oh, I so hated Raj for bringing her along. I never knew that it was…but he could have told me!' Aashi said.

'Well, one thing that we had decided upon was secrecy. We didn't want to raise false hopes in any of you. We might have failed too, you know. There was no surety.'

Aashi nodded her head. Abhi let out a small smile too. They had no intention to argue against Mr. Vardhan's wisdom.

'Fortunately though,' Mr. Vardhan continued, 'all Raj's predictions came true. Before the party was over, Tina had forgotten all about Sid. And William had realized his mistake in jilting her. Result? Before you were out of the hospital, Aashi, Tina had already eloped to London with William.'

'She ran away!' Aashi exclaimed.

'Yes. Unfortunately, that compelled Raj's departure as well. He was sent away to look for his sister.' Mr. Vardhan added.

'So *that's* why he left?' Abhi asked, stressing every word as he spoke. 'That's why he couldn't tell anyone where he was going or why?'

'Yes, I had forbidden him.'

'Where…is he now?' Aashi heard Abhi ask. Her own throat felt dry all of a sudden but she dared not ask for a sip of water. She didn't want to choke on it and make a spectacle of herself.

'Raj is in London,' Sid replied, 'trying to make his mother come back to India.'

'Enough about other people!' Leela's voice rose up to interrupt him. She had had enough of conversation she could scarcely understand and had no part to play in. 'Has anyone thought what will happen to our Priyam now? Her life is spoilt. Who will marry her now? First it was just postponement. We had to cancel our tickets and change all our plans. Now the wedding has got cancelled altogether!'

'Oh, we might yet have a wedding here,' Mr. Vardhan declared, answering at once all the hushed and not so hushed lamentations rising up around them. He walked up to Priyam and ushered her to a nearby sofa. Pulling another chair, he too sat down beside her.

'Priyam,' he began, taking her hands in his and fixing his eyes on her trembling little form, 'I know what Sid did to you is beyond forgiveness. But you will forgive him, won't you?'

Priyam looked up and stared at her guardian. Her eyes flew up to Sid. He was standing just a step away, waiting, she knew, for the absolution. Did he too think it was so easy to forgive what he had done?

'No,' was all that she had to say.

'But Sid loves you, Priyam, and you...'

'I...know Sid loves me,' Priyam interrupted him, speaking slowly and deliberately, 'he loves me so much that...he...he told me to get married...to someone else. And I would never forgive him for that.'

'But Priyam...' Mr. Vardhan tried again, turning towards Abhi for assistance.

But Abhi remained silent as he watched the battle his sister was going through. He could have made it easy for her. He could have told Priyam to give up her resentment and accept the love of Sid. She did love Sid, there was no doubt in that. But would it be okay to force her so? Sid had hurt her, and Priyam did have a right to choose for herself. Abhi just hoped she would finally let her love win over everything else.

However, while Abhi remained silent, there was one person who could not.

'Why are *you* silent, Siddharth?' Aashi spoke out before Mr. Vardhan could urge Priyam again. She had inched up to Priyam and now stood behind her sofa, both her hands resting on her friend's shoulder. 'It was not your father who caused Priyam so much pain. It was you. Don't *you* have anything to say to her now? How can you stand so quiet and make your father to win the forgiveness for you?'

'What can I say, Aashi?' Sid replied, without lifting his eyes. 'There's nothing that can lessen my guilt. I...I don't deserve to be forgiven.'

'To that I agree hundred percent,' Aashi declared. 'You don't deserve Priyam's forgiveness, and you don't deserve her love either.'

'I know that. I threw away my heaven with my own hands. I must not hope to repossess it again,' Sid said, drawing in a long trembling breath and staring at the one who still had her face turned away from him.

'Oh, for God's sake, Sid!' Aashi cried out in sudden exasperation. 'What's wrong with the three of you? I never saw anyone more ready to throw away your love as readily as you guys do. Would it kill you to assert your love for once and try to save it? You still love her, don't you?'

'I do, I do with all my heart,' said Sid.

'And yet you threw her into living hell! You have no idea what she went through, Sid. Now, at least say that you are sorry! And you better be sorry!' Aashi shouted.

'I am sorry!' Sid exclaimed. He took a step forward and fell down on his knees in front of Priyam. 'I'm sorry, Priyam. I...I was a fool. But I love you. Please forgive me, and let me come back, I promise I'll never leave you. I'll never go away again, not into a living world at least,' Sid urged, finally tripping over all his reservations to let his feelings burst out.

Aashi felt Priyam turn towards Sid and could not help but break into a broad grin. It felt good to have shouted at Sid. She had wanted to do that since a long time. But it felt even better to push him towards making Priyam relent. If only Priyam too would give up her resentment now and accept her own love. There were already too many people yearning for their love. The world could do without two more voices joining in the mourning for the deceased joy. Sid and Priyam must get back together. '*Sooner, the better,*' thought Aashi.

Priyam could feel herself relenting too. All her anger, all her bitterness was already seeping away through her eyes. But what could she have done? Perhaps it would have been better had she kept looking away. She could withstand Sid's pleading voice, she could yet stay firm against the touch of him on her hands. But how was Priyam to remain adamant against his eyes, his eyes that were turned up to her, too intent at the face they were fixed upon to be even aware of the moisture that dripped from their edges.

'I don't deserve your love,' Sid said as a sob trembled through Priyam, 'I don't deserve even your forgiveness, and yet...would you please...let me come back? I want to live again. But my life is here, with you. Save me again, Priyam, as you did so many years ago. Look at me, Priyam,' he urged as she closed her eyes, 'don't shut me away. Priyam, I died the day I severed myself from you. Can you bring me back to life once again? Please!'

'Oh Sid!' the cry escaped her lips. In a moment Priyam was in his arms, fervently nodding a yes as he pressed her close, feeling the rush of life coming back after, as it seemed, ages spent in purgatory.

'I love you, Priyam. I love you so much!' he mumbled as she clung to him.

'Don't ever leave me again. Don't ever go away,' she urged.

'He won't,' Mr. Vardhan answered for his son, 'neither from you nor me. Right, son? You are finally done with walking away, aren't you?'

'Yes, Dad,' Sid replied, 'I'm done with all my walking aways, and I'm not going anywhere now,' he smiled. He picked away Priyam's tears and wiped his own face dry too.

'Well then, welcome back! But you took a long time in coming back, didn't you?' Abhi beamed as he rushed forward to hug his sister, and of course, the soon to be brother-in-law.

'Good, all's settled then, just as it should be. The only thing that remains to be done is to get these two married. Right, Aashi?' Mr. Vardhan asked. He walked over to Aashi and put his hand over her shoulder.

'Yes, of course,' Aashi replied. 'Let's get them married, finally. I'm so happy! This is just as it should be. And all thanks to you!'

'No, not just to me. Don't forget that there were three persons involved in it – me, my son and Raj. Me and my son are here, but Raj, I'm sure would be dying to know how it all ended. What do you say, should we call him?' Mr. Vardhan asked.

'I...no...he...you call him,' Aashi stuttered, not quite sure of what Mr. Vardhan meant by asking her that question.

However, Mr. Vardhan had already stuffed his phone in her hand, 'Come on, talk to him. Give Raj the good news. Raj has been missing you just as much as you missed him. Talk to him now and give him his reward,' he said and walked some distance away with Abhi to give her some privacy. 'I just wish he were here today. This celebration is incomplete without the man who played such a crucial role in bringing this happiness about.'

'Don't worry, Sir,' Abhi replied, keeping close to his guardian and making sure to look at him and not let his eyes divert elsewhere, 'Raj would come soon,' he assured.

How could he not? The ardent request had already been whispered into the phone. What was there now to keep Raj from honouring it? He would come. He would come soon.

***

220

Chapter 26

*Unto a broken heart
No other one may go
Without the high prerogative
Itself hath suffered too.*

— *'Unto a Broken Heart' by Emily Dickinson*

It was a lazy Sunday evening. Abhi and Aashi had spent the last two hours enjoying the sun from the roof of Abhi's house. It was still only four in the evening. But the sun already looked tired and spent out as it rushed to its night quarters, pulling its drowsy light up from the earth and encouraging the shadows to stretch themselves into a comfortable ease.

'Here's your tea,' Abhi said as he put a cup in Aashi's hand. 'You are feeling sleepy, this will wake you up.'

'Me? No, I'm not at all sleepy,' she claimed, breaking out into a big yawn the very next moment. 'It's a lovely weather today, isn't it?' she added soon and lifted her eyes up towards the sky. 'The sky must be beautiful, bright blue. Are there any clouds too?'

'No, it's a clear sky,' Abhi murmured absent-mindedly. Not for once did his eyes turn up to gaze at the sky above. He looked at her instead. At the delicate wisp of smile that rested on her lips. An exact replica of it soon emerged on his mouth too.

How like a little child Aashi looked as she sat there, her feet huddled close to her and hidden away in her shawl, hair held together in a tight braid and face looking up, as calm as the sun subdued by the bitter winter chill.

How close she was to him…just a couple of steps and he would be beside her…

In a moment imagination warmed up with a tremulous desire. Would it be so wrong if he just stole one little peck off those enchanting lips? *'Just… one little kiss…'*

But before the vision could be translated into reality, Mr. Vardhan's words rose up like dark phantoms, their shadows looming menacingly over the handful of infantile hopes that had somehow taken shape in the past few days.

'*Me, my son and Raj.*'

How could Abhi forget those words! How could he forget?

He closed his eyes, tightly, only to open them again a moment later and fix them once again on Aashi's face.

Aashi's eyes however remained wide open, blind to the entire world but roving busily, Abhi was sure, in the many-coloured world of her dreams. How Abhi wished to have one little peek into her dreams and find out if he formed any part of them. To have just one little look and see what it was Aashi was thinking about at that moment.

'*Must be about Raj,*' he thought as his own smile drooped down from the corner of his lips.

'*Me, my son and Raj,*' the words echoed again through the rising chill.

Why did it have to be Raj to play such a vital role in bringing Sid and Priyam together? Why couldn't it have been anyone else?

The heel of Abhi's boot kicked the dead stone under his feet. He was now indebted forever to Raj for saving his sister and her happiness. It was too great a debt to be ignored or forgotten. Yet, there was no denying the fact that it was certainly not gratitude that Abhi felt beating in his heart as he stood so close to Aashi, while she remained far away from him.

So what if she had stopped hating him as she used to do. So what if she waited every evening to have tea with him.

'Why are you so late? I've been waiting for you for so long!' had become Aashi's routine complaint that greeted Abhi every evening as soon as he stepped out of his car.

But then, in the absence of Priyam, Sid and of course Raj, Aashi had only Abhi to fill the void and pass away the long lonely moments.

It had become their routine to have the evening tea together and then to escape the confines of home and go for a long leisurely walk. Conversation between them was no longer restrained. There, however, did pass many long stretches of silence as Aashi brooded over her fate and Abhi could find nothing but to stay close and be ready to say "here" when she called his name.

Their conversation often hovered around Sid and Priyam. There was one name however, that was getting steadily relegated to only occasional references. Talking about Raj was just too painful for Aashi, and it might be said of course, not too pleasurable for Abhi either.

Sure, Aashi understood why Raj went. But what she could not comprehend was what was still keeping him away. Raj did say that he would return soon. And of course, he had started calling her too. He did still seem in love with her. But why wasn't he returning? Why was he letting his mother fetter his steps? Didn't he know how much Aashi needed him? He had done his duty as a friend. He had done his duty as a brother. When would he start thinking about her?

Many questions hovered in Aashi's heart, many doubts clouded up her thoughts. And she had the perfect misfortune to be free to dwell in them too. She had not yet started going to her boutique again. And all day long she had nothing to do except ponder over her gloom and make herself depressed. Abhi's return in the evening did dispel some of the gloom, but the lonely nights never failed to strip her of every positive thought that Abhi had so laboured at in the evening.

Just some such miserable thoughts had probably risen up again in her heart as Abhi lost himself in silence.

'Abhi, do you believe in God?' she asked all of a sudden, breaking the chain of his thoughts by giving voice to her own troubled ones.

'Don't you?'

'I...don't know. It's getting really difficult to. I mean, sometimes I do, and then it gives me hope. I feel that everything will turn out alright in the end. God will take care of everything. But mostly, it seems as if...I'm only deluding myself. There really doesn't seem to be anyone up there, Abhi.'

'I know. Sometimes it does get hard to maintain our faith. But what we witnessed on Priyam's wedding night...'

'Was the result of effort of three men. Had it been left to God alone, Priyam most probably would be within the bloody fangs of the Damles and Sid would have become a Sinha by now.'

'*That* I admit is not a very pretty picture,' Abhi replied, laughing.

'No really, Abhi, what if there's no God? What if...'

'That is a terrible thought, Aashi.'

'But what if it is true? What if there's no one listening to us? And even if there's such a thing as God and He is, as you say, looking down at me, what makes you so sure He would do something for me? He doesn't seem to be doing much of a good these days, you know.'

'I know. But what can we do? We have no other option but to hold on to our hopes and wait...'

'Are you...holding on too, Abhi? To your hopes?' she asked.

A long silence passed, as Abhi tried to utter a convincing no. Yet, no was not the answer. But saying yes was out of question too.

'Abhi?' she called again.

'I...I'll be back in a moment. I hear my phone ringing downstairs,' saying this, Abhi quickly escaped.

A shade of sadness came over Aashi's face. 'And yet, you keep on wishing for my hopes to come true,' she said, ending her words in a sigh.

'I'm back,' Aashi heard Abhi's cheerful voice after about five minutes.

'Who was it?' she asked.

'God.'

'Huh?'

'He called to tell you that your loneliness is about to end soon.'

'What do you mean?' she asked.

'Priyam called to let us know that they'd be back in India in two days.'

'Two days! That means day after tomorrow. That's great news,' Aashi exclaimed, 'but two days is such a long time too. How would I wait so long?'

'You really must learn a little patience, Aashi,' Abhi laughed, 'you really must learn how to wait.'

'Oh, I hate waiting, you know that,' she declared.

'Well, try to imagine all the happier moments that would arrive when the wait is over. It won't seem so long then.'

It was just this advice that Aashi wanted to try out next evening. There was still an hour for Abhi to return and she had already positioned herself in her garden, ready to catch the first sound of his car driving up on the road.

She was happy. Priyam was coming back after a fortnight long honeymoon trip. Not next door for sure, but it wouldn't matter so much. Mr. Vardhan wouldn't grudge Priyam visiting her best friend or inviting her over. But there were still so many hours to while away alone. If only Raj had been there, he wouldn't even have let her notice Priyam's absence.

But then, Raj himself was the one who was more gravely absent than Priyam. Aashi knew why Priyam was away and when she would return, but there was no knowing as to what still was keeping Raj away from her.

'Come back soon, Raj,' she spoke aloud as she waited for Abhi. 'Or at least tell me for sure when you'd be back. I can't bear this suspense any longer. How can you do this to me? It's not fair!'

'Certainly not, and I'm ready to bear any punishment you want to give me,' Raj's voice breathed down her neck and two sturdy arms clasped Aashi from behind.

Lightning blazed through the girl as her eyes closed shut and fingers clawed at her chair. It couldn't be! It couldn't be! 'Raj!' she breathed out the dear darling name.

'At your service,' Raj answered. He came out from behind and knelt in front of her.

'What are you doing here? How did...when...how?' words skipped over each other as Aashi caught hold of his hands and pressed them to her heart. Raj was back...he was finally back and she had forgotten all her complaints. He was back. Nothing else mattered, not at that moment at least.

'I returned this afternoon,' Raj said, 'I didn't tell you before because I wanted to surprise you and see your charming face light up with delight. I didn't want to make you wait.'

'Thanks a lot for that!' Aashi replied, 'I'm already half-dead having to wait for Sid and Priyam. Waiting for you would have surely finished me off,' she admitted with a laugh.

'And I couldn't have risked that,' Raj declared, smiling to see Aashi's face warming up with pleasure. 'But you must have become so bored of sitting all alone here. Come, I'll take you for a walk. It's a lovely evening. Let's go,' he said, tugging at her hands to make her stand up.

'Now? No, I can't. Abhi would return soon. He hates having tea alone. We must wait for him.'

'Oh, come on, you'll soon be far away from him. So it's better if Abhi gets used to being alone now. Besides, there's no need for you to spoil your evenings for him.'

'What do you mean?' Aashi asked, trying to focus her attention on his first sentence and not to battle with his last. It was not Raj's fault of course. He didn't know just how many evenings Abhi himself had spoiled for her. She would tell Raj, but later. First, she must find out what he meant by her being soon far away.

'We are moving to London,' Raj told her. He quickly explained how Mrs. Sinha had simply refused to part with her daughter and had managed to persuade her husband to break all his ties with India and settle down in London instead.

Raj had been sent to make the necessary preparations. His parents were to arrive a month later and stay only for as long as it would take to sell off their various properties in the country.

'You're going away?' horror clouded her face as Aashi pronounced the words.

'Not alone, silly!' Raj laughed, 'We'll all go.'

'But Raj, your mother? Has she agreed?'

'I'll make her agree. She'll have to agree. Mom knows how much I love you. She has seen how I missed you when I was there, so far away from you,' he declared.

The confidence in his voice brought back Aashi's smile. If Raj was so

225

sure that he would succeed in turning his mother around, then of course, she had no reason to doubt him. Raj was capable of doing anything. If he said he would make his mother agree, then he would.

'You may have missed me, but you have no idea what I went through,' she said, 'I didn't even know if you were ever coming back. Why did you go away so silently, Raj? I was so sure that it was my blindness that had driven you away. It was so awful when you went away without even saying a word to me. You could have spared five minutes for me, couldn't you?'

It was not a complaint. There didn't seem like any reason to complain, now that Raj was back. But Aashi wanted to tell him how bad she had felt without him. She wanted Raj to know so he could seek to recompense by his sweet words and well, sweeter gestures. An expectant smile beamed on Aashi's face as she waited. But what followed was certainly not what she was waiting for.

'I...could have spared many more, Aashi,' he said, 'and the truth is that I...did come to see you. But...'

'You came?' she gasped, 'When? But I never...'

'It was on the day I left for London, in the morning. But I couldn't come in.'

'So it *was* you!' Aashi burst out, 'I thought I heard your car! But why didn't you come in, Raj? Why didn't you talk to me?'

'I...I felt if I did that, I would end up revealing everything, or worse, not being able to go at all. I knew you needed me by your side. And I should have been here, with you. But I had to leave, I had to go to make sure everything ended up fine with Tina and William. I couldn't have left India without seeing you. And when I saw you, you looked so helpless...I couldn't bear it. I mean seeing you sitting on a hospital bed was hard. But seeing you groping around helplessly...it was unbearable, Aashi. So I drove away, as fast as I could. Had I lingered, I probably never would have been able to leave you. But I had to. It was necessary.'

'So you ran away!' Aashi couldn't believe what she was hearing. She pulled her hands from his grasp and stood up with disbelief.

This was not what she had expected. This wasn't what she had expected of *him*! And yet, he was not lying. And it wasn't a jest either. Aashi's smile quickly faded away as realization dawned and surprise gave way to shock.

'I shouldn't have. I know what I should have done, Aashi. But I...you were in such misery...and I had to go away...'

'So you decided to walk away without saying a word to me. And I, like a fool, rushed towards the sound of your car and fell face down in rose bushes.

226

But what do you care about that? You had to make sure your sister was okay and your ex-girlfriend was okay and your mother was okay. It didn't matter to you if I was okay or not.'

'That's not true, Aashi. It's only because I...'

'couldn't bear to see me blind and helpless, right?' Aashi completed his sentence. 'Then why have you come back now? Don't you know I'm still as blind as before? Not as helpless maybe, thanks to Abhi's training, but just as blind, Raj.'

'It doesn't matter. I love you. It doesn't matter!' The rapidity of his words gave ample evidence of his desperation. 'Why don't you understand? You know how much I love you!' Raj urged, taking hold of her hand again. But Aashi pulled it back once more.

'You know, Raj, now, I'm not so sure,' she said and entered her home, closing the door firmly on his face.

Chapter 27

To feel my hand so kindly prest,
To know myself beloved at last,
To think my heart has found a rest,
My life of solitude is past!

But then to wake and find it flown,
The dream of happiness destroyed,
To find myself unloved, alone,
What tongue can speak the dreary void?

— *Dreams by Anne Bronte*

'Aashi? You've been crying? What happened?' Abhi asked as soon as she opened the door for him. His briefcase was quickly put down on the floor as he freed his hand to wipe away her tears.

'I hate Raj!'

'What happened?' Abhi asked, 'Did Raj call? What did he say? Why are you crying? He'll be back, I'll make him come back!'

'Raj *is* back! But it'd have been better had he never returned!' she cried out.

'He's back? Oh, I mean, that's great. Why are you crying then?' Abhi asked, wiping away Aashi's tears again and cajoling her to a chair.

Soon Abhi managed to pacify her enough to have her tell him everything. And Aashi did tell him, each and every word that had passed between her and Raj, like a little child recounting her misery to a sympathetic parent and knowing that he would make it alright. He would take care. He would understand. And he did.

'Yes,' Abhi said, 'that was wrong of Raj. But you should have tried to understand him, Aashi, instead of flying at him like you did.'

'Understand? Yes sure, I should have…just how a person can run away from me when I needed him most and still claim to love me!'

'Raj really does love you, Aashi, his going away has proved it like nothing else could. It was his love that made it so hard for him to see you in misery.

He must have felt guilty at bringing this on you. And also because he had to leave you when you needed him. You must try and understand what Raj must have felt at that time. The terrible guilt that…'

'Guilt? You think it was guilt?' asked Aashi. Her anger cooled instantly at that word.

She well knew how hard it was to deal with guilt. She could yet remember what horrible things her own guilt had made her do. Raj had only run away. That was not as bad as resorting to pouring poison over someone whose only fault was that he was just too good and loved her too much.

'Yes, Aashi, I really think it was guilt that drove him away,' Abhi replied, closing his eyes and trying to shut out the protest against being Raj's advocate. It wasn't easy to try and patch up the very road that he knew would lead Aashi away from him. But, what else could he have done?

'And he really loves me?' she asked, wiping her tears.

'Of course.'

'But what if my blindness disturbs him again? What if his mother strictly refuses to accept me? What if…'

'Stop thinking such negative thoughts, Aashi.'

'I think it would be better if I stop thinking altogether! That's what makes it so hard, Abhi, thoughts! It would have been easier perhaps if…if I could throw all my thoughts out, don't you think?'

'On the contrary, I think that you really should have stopped and thought a little bit before turning on Raj like that.'

'I have a heart, Abhi, and the blessed heart reacts. I am not a sponge like you that absorbs everything and nets out nothing .'

'Well, but a sponge is a very useful thing, you know,' he commented with an easy smile, 'it mops up well and lets things remain clean and clear.'

'Yeah, clean and clear. But…how do I mop up this mess that I've created? I closed my door at Raj's face, Abhi, how do I welcome him back?'

It, however, didn't take very long for Aashi to clear up the matters. Even before her maid brought in the tea for the two of them, she had already dialled Raj's number on her cell phone. It didn't take long either in forgiving and being forgiven and before Abhi had finished his tea, Raj had already been invited back.

That was the first evening when Abhi found himself going for a walk alone. But of course, he knew there were many more to come, too many in fact.

Thankfully, Sid and Priyam were returning next day. He would have them at least. Not all his evening would be so alone then. But some would still have to be. It was… inevitable.

229

'I'm so glad you are not angry at me anymore,' Raj said as soon as he entered Aashi's house, fifteen minutes after she had called him. Abhi, by then, had already made his escape. 'I'm so glad you've forgiven me,' Raj continued.

'Well, I've been favoured by the company of some very forgiving people, you know. I must have learnt something, I think,' Aashi replied, smiling as Raj wrapped his arm around her shoulders and made her sit right next to him. 'Besides, Abhi told me that it was your g...your love that made you...'

'Well, I must thank Abhi then for taking my side.'

'And also for taking such good care of when you were away,' she replied. Now was her chance to make Raj aware of all that Abhi had done for her. 'Had he not been there, I...I don't know if I would have been here either. I felt so depressed, so...but Abhi never let me lose hope. You know, never a day passed when he did not assure me that you would return, that you loved me and would surely return. And he was right, as always.'

'Oh, I had to return. I would not have survived long with my heart left behind here, so far away from where I was.'

'Yes, but I did not believe that you would. It was Abhi who kept on telling me not to despair. He's so good, he never...'

'He's a good man, I know. But you tell me, who's taking care of your boutique now?'

'You remember the designer I had hired a month before Diwali? She takes care of everything. I'm so glad I didn't fire her in my madness. I had absolutely decided to get rid of her. But Abhi told me not to. He made me see sense and realise how much the boutique needed Sunita. Mummy also goes there to keep an eye on things. Abhi keeps on telling me to go too. I haven't agreed yet, but maybe I will, soon. Now that I don't feel quite so helpless. I can even walk unaided you know, all the way to the market and back home.'

'Nonsense! You don't need to go to your boutique and you don't need to walk unaided to market or anywhere else. Don't you give yourself any such silly trouble. Once I marry you and take you to London, I'd hire a full-time attendant for you, and a chauffeur too and whoever else you need. You'll have your own car and won't need to walk anywhere.'

'That will make me even more of a handicap than I am already!' Aashi laughed, delighting in Raj's concern and already beginning to imagine how it would be to have that sort of luxury. 'Abhi says I am not to think of myself lacking in any way. He says it doesn't matter if I'm blind. I'm still as capable as I was before and I don't need to depend on anyone.'

'Absolutely. But a little pampering did no one any harm. And I want to pamper you like a princess, my princess. And I will do it whether Abhi approves of it or not.'

'He will most certainly not! He says I'm already too much of a princess and what I need is to become more *normal*,' she laughed. How different Raj and Abhi were, she thought, and yet, both loved her and she loved both of them.

She loved both of them? '*No, absolutely not! Maybe…but not in the same way,*' she concluded.

'I don't care,' said Raj, and his voice told Aashi that he wasn't too pleased about something.

'What happened, Raj?' she asked.

'Nothing, I hope. Except that…I seem to have lost the only fan that I had.'

'Huh? What do you mean?' she didn't quite get what it was that had made Raj talk like that.

'You know, Priyam thinks that Sid and Abhi are the best. Sid thinks so about Priyam and Abhi and Abhi believes that there's no one better than Sid and Priyam. You were the only one who thought that I was the best. Please don't change your mind now. I want to remain best for at least someone in the world!'

'What? What are you saying, Raj? Are you jealous of Abhi? But why?' she laughed at what seemed to her an absolute absurdity.

'Why? It's been half an hour since we've been together and all you have to say is what *he* says. Can't you forget Abhi for some time? I'm back now, Aashi, and I want to talk about us.'

'Yes of course, me too,' Aashi quickly replied, 'I…oh, I didn't realise. But you are the best, Raj, and would forever remain so. You are my perfect prince and no one else can be that.'

But why was she saying that? Where was the need to explain? That was understood, wasn't it?

They continued sitting together for half an hour more. And for all that time, Aashi did manage to remember not to mention Abhi again. Of course, she had to bite her tongue a couple of times and halt mid-sentence as well, but she managed to carry out a pleasant discourse without mentioning Abhi's name. It was just a habit she had acquired because she had been living in only his company for so many days. But now that Raj was back and Priyam and Sid were coming too, she would soon recover of it. Very soon, Aashi knew, people would start teasing her about never having anything to say except what Raj had said.

But before that, there still was a huge hurdle to overcome.

'What are we going to do now, Raj?' Aashi asked after some time.

'Whatever you want to do,' he said.

'No, I mean, your mother...she would not...I mean...'

'She would agree. She will have to. I'll take you to my home tomorrow. My father will be there too. He's a good man, Aashi. And when I tell him how much I love you, he will not say no. And together, we'll make my mother say yes too. Tomorrow.'

***

I am alone, as though I stood
On the highest peak of the tired gray world,
About me only swirling snow,
Above me, endless space unfurled;

With earth hidden and heaven hidden,
And only my own spirit's pride
To keep me from the peace of those
Who are not lonely, having died.

— *'Alone' by Sara Teasdale*

'You want to get yourself killed, girl?' the driver of the car shouted as he brought his vehicle to a skidding halt.

'Yes,' she shouted back.

'Watch it!' Raj cried out as he pulled Aashi back. 'What are you doing, Aashi?'

'Going back to where I belong,' she said, her voice still shaking, thanks to her recent encounter, not with the oncoming vehicle, but a lady whom she had hoped to call mother.

'Okay, wait, I'll drop you,' Raj entreated, taking hold of her hand.

'You...should, and right here. I'll find my way back on my own.' She removed her hand from his grasp. 'Bye,' she mumbled and began walking.

'Wait, Aashi!' Raj called running after her, 'hear me!'

But she had heard quite enough for the day. Now, all that she wanted was to escape to the loneliness of her home and hide there till all the world, Raj included, forgot about her very existence.

Things had gone too grossly wrong in Raj's attempt to let her mother see Aashi as her daughter-in-law.

Aashi had stepped inside Raj's home with a heart beating with happy hopes and dreams that seemed too near coming true. But nothing had happened as they had predicted.

Mrs. Sinha had agreed readily enough to meet Aashi. She had, in fact, made quite a loud ado in preparing to welcome her future daughter-in-law to her home. But the first thing that she had done was to send her husband, the person on whom Raj's plans really rested, away from home. And she provided Mr. Sinha with such good reason that it didn't really seem like an excuse at all.

Mrs. Sinha had personally welcomed Aashi indoors, detaching her from Raj's care and guiding Aashi's blind steps inside with timely instructions about each and every obstruction in her way. Only once did the kind lady forget to inform Aashi about a costly vase. It shattered into tiny pieces as Aashi collided with it. But Mrs. Sinha was quick to admit that it was not Aashi's fault but her own and that she should have been more attentive to Aashi's needs instead of turning and talking to her maid for *just* a minute.

This small accident notwithstanding, the gracious hostess remained at all times quite eloquent about her approval of her son's philanthropy and his decision to marry such a gravely disadvantaged girl, despite having a whole retinue of princesses falling over each other to get related to him.

Mrs. Sinha declared herself quite ready to bow to her son's choice. But then, she had always been an indulgent mother. And she was confident too that Raj would stand by his decision, even if the decision gave him nothing but regrets. She was sure that Raj would remain present and attentive to the needs of his helpless wife, even at the cost of his own life and happiness.

Mrs. Sinha, in short, had declared herself quite ready and eager to welcome in her family the girl Raj *thought* he loved, and had already framed up apt replies to be used in case her various high status friends commented upon the unsuitability of the match. How did it matter after all if the girl Raj was marrying had no mentionable past nor present. It was the future that mattered and the girl, of course, was wise enough to secure her future by attaching herself to them.

It must, therefore, be because of her own tempestuousness if Aashi had to stumble out of the house just when Mrs. Sinha was in the middle of one of her kindest speeches.

'Don't you let her words disturb you,' Raj insisted, following Aashi as she rushed away from his home, 'I love you and that's all that matters.'

Her feet halted at the words and she turned towards his voice. 'No, Raj, love...doesn't matter at all,' Aashi tried to stifle her breath that was threatening too urgently to come out as a sob. 'I am blind, Raj, but it's time you open your eyes and see into what gloomy darkness you are throwing your bright future. And thank your mother for me. She made me see sense and saved me from a life of repentance and regret,' Aashi said, turning back again and resuming her long walk into loneliness. But in a moment she stopped, 'and Raj,' she began again without turning, 'I would wish and pray that the girl you'd chose from the *retinue of princesses* would be better deserving of you than I can ever hope to be. Good bye,' she said, and then walked quickly.

'Wait, Aashi. I cannot let you go alone. At least wait till I call my driver. He'll drive you home. If you say no to that, I'll come walking after you all the way.'

That finally forced Aashi to halt her steps and accept the ride back to her home in Raj's car, accompanied only by his driver.

'I'll see you soon,' Raj said as he helped her into the car.

'No, you won't,' she replied, turning her face away.

It was past seven-thirty when Abhi heard a car stop in front of Aashi's home. He knew well where she was coming from. And since past hour he had been waiting to hear the news and forcing himself to hope for the success of her trip.

Abhi walked up to the window of his room and stood staring at her window. It was closed now and the curtains were drawn too, giving him no indication whether joy rested behind them or grief was rending its heart out.

But he kept on waiting, hoping to catch a glimpse of Aashi. Abhi didn't have to wait very long. He heard a noise and saw Aashi coming out of her home with her arms full of cards and gifts that Abhi knew Raj had given her. His eyes followed her as she entered the garage. She dumped her load in the centre and started groping around, looking for something. Her search stopped at a glass bottle. She took it back to the pile of cards and gifts, bent down on her knees and started emptying the bottle over it.

It took Abhi just a minute to run into her garage.

'Aashi! What are you doing?' he shouted as he sprang towards her.

'What now? Have you become blind too?' she muttered, putting a match to the kerosene soaked pile.

'Why did you...why...what are you doing, Aashi? Where's your mother?' he asked again as he pulled her away from the fire.

'She's inside. And you don't need to raise such an alarm. I'm only... burning my dreams away.' She shrugged herself free from his hold and stepped closer to the burning pile again.

'Come back now,' he finally said, 'you've burnt everything.'

'No, not everything.' She pulled out her mobile from the pocket of her jeans. 'One thing still remains.'

'Don't! Don't do it!'

'I must.'

'It's a very good phone, Aashi, and you love it.'

'No, I don't.'

235

'You are being too rash, you'll regret it later. You have become so used to having a mobile.'

'You can buy me a new one, can't you?'

'Not such an expensive one.'

'This is too good for me anyway.'

'You don't want to do this, Aashi, think again.'

'Didn't I tell you? I want to get rid of thoughts. Thoughts are what make everything so hard.'

'But…'

There…' she said, throwing the phone into the flames, 'that's done.'

His hand flashed out and caught the phone as it fell. 'You really shouldn't have,' he said.

'Is it burnt?'

'It's burning.' Abhi switched the phone off and bestowed it to the safety of his own pocket.

'Good.' She turned away quickly enough to give Abhi no opportunity to read her face. 'Let's…go now.'

'Let me douse this fire first. Do you have any idea how dangerous it could have been? You could have hurt yourself even.'

'While you are just next door? Not a chance!' she tried to laugh, but ended up trying to stifle a sob however.

Abhi didn't want Urmila to see Aashi in that condition. So he led Aashi to his home, his arm wrapped securely around her shoulders. Aashi did not cry, she did not let even a tear a trickle down her eyes. But his arm could very well sense the little tremors welling up within her.

Together they entered the living room.

'Here, sit down now,' he said as he gently pushed Aashi down on a chair. 'Do you need anything?' he asked as he knelt down beside her and pressed his fingers on hers.

'Y…yes,' the words, as they came out of her mouth, could not remain untroubled by the tears that soon followed.

'What?' he asked, standing up in readiness to do her bidding.

Aashi too stood up slowly and extended her hand to find him. Abhi immediately grasped her fingers.

'Can you…give me a hug?' she pleaded.

Her heart was breaking and she had nobody else to turn to for comfort. She had just burnt all her life away. She had just put to fire all her dreams. Her love was dead. DEAD. She herself had burnt its pyre. Even her father wasn't

236

there to hold her tight in his arms and squeeze away all her pain from her.

'No,' she heard him say.

'Okay,' she nodded, the burden of utter defeat weighing down on her.

There was no strength left in Aashi to utter any other word. An inexorable sense of loss pressed hard on her and seemed to be pulling her down, crushing every fibre of her trembling self into one tortured mass of nothingness.

But before she could fall to the ground, Abhi's hand was there to support her.

'I meant…' he said, 'I can…only give you half a hug.'

She threw her arms around him and let him cradle her weary head near his heart. 'Don't be so sad,' Abhi kept on whispering, holding Aashi tight as her misery convulsed through her eyes and poured down on his heart. He waited for her to calm down enough to be able to talk coherently. 'Stop crying now,' he said. 'It's Mrs. Sinha, isn't it? What did she say? But you must not mind whatever she said. You know Mrs. Sinha, she's like that to everybody. You must not mind her. Since when have you started caring about what people say, anyway?' he asked.

'I don't care about what she said,' Aashi managed to utter through her sobs. 'I care about the truth in what she said. I don't care about her, Abhi, I care about Raj. She was right. I'll only make Raj's life miserable. He deserves a much better girl than me.'

'No Aashi, you cannot give up like that. You must not. Mrs. Sinha wasn't very fond of you even before the accident, was she? Nothing's changed, Aashi. She's just as bad as she always was and you are just as good. Nothing's changed. Raj's still with you, isn't he?'

'I'm changed, Abhi! I'm no more the bright eyed, independent girl Raj fell in love with. If he could not bear to see me floundering for one evening, how'd he bear it all his life? He cannot long be happy with me, and I would not make him miserable. What if it's just guilt that's keeping him with me? What if even Raj has started regretting that he ever fell in love with me? He never does any wrong. He would never leave me. But it's best…it's best that…I let him go. It didn't take him long to forget Priyam, it wouldn't take him long to forget me too. He would soon find someone else to lavish his love upon.' Those were not easy words to speak. But Aashi pushed them out with just as much rapidity as she had used to pull the pall over all her brighter hopes.

'And you?'

'I? I already have you, don't I?' she said wearily, resting her head back against him and letting the rhythm of his heartbeats lull her to peace.

'But you don't love me, Aashi, I'm…I'm not your dream,' Abhi said. Half a smile rose up on his face to contradict her words. He really must teach her

237

to control her tongue while in temper. Abhi was sure Aashi would regret her words as soon as she cooled down. He must not let her little speech beguile him into hope. He must not.

'I'm done with dreaming, Abhi.' A sigh shuddered through her as she detached himself from him and groped her way back to a chair. 'It's time I start accepting realities.' She wiped her eyes dry and forced herself to take a deep breath. 'And…the reality is that whenever I am in need, I find you standing beside me, not my dream. My dreams have given me nothing but pain. But you always tried to take all my suffering upon yourself and give me all the love and support I needed, whenever I needed it. I'm not sure that my dream still loves me. I know that you do.'

'What…are you trying to say, Aashi?' he asked, peering at her face with eyes that were more troubled than elated at her words.

It was not so easy however to keep on turning away from the delicious possibility. Yet, it could not be true. She was saying all this only because she was angry and hurt. She didn't really mean any of it.

'I mean that I…I want to accept that love, your love…that has often shielded me from the hurts of the world. I want to hide in it forever now, Abhi, I want to hide…from Raj, from his mother…from the entire world. I am being selfish, I know, now perhaps more than ever. And it is true too that I am turning towards you because I want to turn away from *him*. I know I don't deserve to seek the very salve that I so often have abused myself. But…I need you, Abhi. And I'm not ashamed to say it. I need you to marry me so Raj can marry someone else. I need you to hide me within yourself so he can no more be troubled by me. I lay my claim on your love, Abhi, because I know it is mine, has always been mine. It's been a long time since I recognised its worth, now I lay my claim on it. And I promise to honour it with every little bit of my own worthless being.'

'Do you have any idea what you are saying?' he almost shouted.

'Yes, Abhi, I do realize what I am saying. And it is not being said in a fit of temper. I'm calm now. See, I'm not even crying. If I marry him, none of us would be happy. But if I let him go and trust myself to your love instead, there's a fair chance of happiness for all of us.'

'Tell me this, can you really imagine yourself being happy with me?' Abhi had never spoken to her with such rage. But then, he had every right to be angry. And she was ready to bear his anger. He would understand. Aashi knew he would. He loved her.

'Imagine? I don't have to imagine, Abhi. When I look back at the days since the accident, each and every moment of cheer and happiness that I've enjoyed is because of you and Priyam. And that is proof enough to validate my decision. But of course, you are not bound to accept it. I just wanted to say…'

'You've said quite enough for a day, Aashi. Better become quiet now and think it over.'

'I will. But I'm not going to change my decision. I won't have my love turned into a regret. I would rather let it go than hold it close, like a dead burden that weighs down on you till you can no more breathe. I'm not going to be the reason for his misery. Never!'

'Of course, you'd rather make me miserable!' he muttered, walking up to a chair near her and throwing himself into it.

'Well, you must have become quite used to it by now. So it doesn't matter,' she said, with a little laugh accompanying her words. Her hand reached out to him.

She had lost her love. It was time now…to let his win.

You stars, who these entangled fortunes give,
O tell me why
It is so hard to die,
Yet such a task to live!

—'Song' by Katherine Philips

The week ended. The week that, for Abhi at least, meant nothing but uncertain bliss and certain disquietude. Aashi, as she had promised, remained firm on her decision. Nothing that Abhi said could make her change her mind. Abhi could see the paradise that he had considered only a vain hope coming on its own towards him. Yet, he was not sure it still belonged to him.

Sure, Aashi had burnt away every token of Raj's love. But his memories still resounded in every beat of her heart. She had even returned the engagement ring to Raj, and turned a deaf ear to all Raj's entreaties. Yet, hadn't Abhi often spied her caressing her unadorned finger and letting tears run down her face when she imagined herself alone? When Aashi talked, there was no more any mention of her dear dreams and hopes. She had killed them all. And the demise of her dreams weighed down hard at the fulfilment of Abhi's.

Abhi's good fortune had resulted from Aashi's ill luck. And this didn't taste much like victory. If only his bliss had not risen up from the ashes of hers. If only there was some way to rebuild Aashi's lost castle and let it glow with the light of his own love.

If only...if only...if only...thoughts kept on battling in Abhi's heart, and deprived him of all his peace.

But while Abhi remained fighting with his own happiness, Priyam welcomed it with open arms and declared her world perfect because of it.

'Oh, I just can't stop being amazed at how well the things have come up to be!' Priyam exclaimed yet again.

It was also a Sunday evening, and Abhi and Aashi were sitting just as leisurely in Mr. Vardhan's garden as they had sat in Abhi's house just a week ago. But this time, Priyam and Sid were there too.

'Everything is just as it ought to be, isn't it?' Priyam added.

'Yes,' Aashi smiled, 'just…as it ought to be.'

Of course, it had been Aashi who had passed on the news to Priyam. It didn't matter if Abhi still didn't feel quite so certain about her resolution and hadn't bothered to inform anyone about it. Aashi saw no reason to keep quiet. For one, she knew that the news would make her friend very happy. And indeed, it had. Priyam had laughed, she had cried, and hugged Aashi again and again and declared her world complete. Sid, on his part, had also confirmed that Aashi would never regret her choice. Aashi, of course, knew that already.

Besides, telling it to someone had also added a sort of solidarity to her own resolve. Aashi knew she could not back out now.

'Well? So when are you two going to get engaged, Abhi?' she heard Priyam ask.

'When are you two going to London?' Abhi's voice countered Priyam with a question of his own.

'Dad will go back in a week. But we won't, not any time soon,' Sid replied, 'I've just joined the company. It's going to take me a lot of time just to understand our business here. Till then, Dad would have to manage it out alone in London.'

'I wonder if we'd ever need to go there at all,' Priyam added. 'You know, since Mrs. Sinha wants to settle there, Dad might just as well decide to settle here. At least, I hope he does.'

'Better if he does,' Aashi commented. 'It would never do for you two to be so near them and so far from us. Right, Abhi?'

Abhi chose not to answer. His eyes travelled from her to Priyam and Sid. Behind them, he could see Mr. Vardhan approaching with an old album in his hand. It had finally become possible for the old gentleman to bring it out even when Sid was there. Abhi could discern a new energy in his guardian's pace. Mr. Vardhan almost seemed younger now as he strode on, his grin broadening with every step he took towards them.

'Abhi?' Aashi tried again.

'What?'

'You don't want them to go away, right?'

'Doesn't matter what I want, Aashi, life doesn't follow the dictates of our wants.'

Sid stopped rocking his chair and stared at Abhi.

'Well, I'm sure Priyam doesn't want to go away. I'm sure she cannot bear even the thought of being separated from you.'

Sid's frown deepened as he saw Abhi's eyes fix themselves on Priyam. Mr.

241

Vardhan had handed her the old album and Priyam was quickly going through it to find one particular photograph that she wanted to show to Abhi. She was smiling as she went through the album, often pointing something out to Mr. Vardhan who had settled close to her and was peering into the album as well.

'Give some credit to Sid and Mr. Vardhan at least, as long as they are with Priyam, she'll bear anything,' said Abhi.

'It would be much better though if all she has to bear is an excess of happiness,' Sid interrupted him. 'So get engaged to Aashi as soon as possible. There's no sense in wasting time in useless thoughts.'

Abhi looked at his friend, responded with a smile, and said, 'Let's go in now, it's getting cold.'

So the group moved indoors, to continue their leisurely party. Hours passed on and it was only at dinner time that the party broke up as Priyam excused herself to the kitchen to see if her help was needed there. Aashi waited with the others for some time, but soon was forced to move away as well.

'Be careful!' Abhi exclaimed, as she tripped over a step leading out of the room. 'Where are you going?'

'Only to the kitchen. At least Priyam would have some topic of conversation other than your office and your work.'

It was true. Ever since Sid had joined his father's business, there scarcely passed an hour between them when the two friends did not lose themselves into a lengthy discussion of company's affairs. And while it was a source of delight for Mr. Vardhan, who had done nothing since the last half hour except watch Abhi and Sid and smile, the conversation had not been of the nature to raise any interest in a girl like Aashi.

'Alright, but be careful,' Abhi replied.

'Oh, it's okay. I better get used to it,' she said, removing her sandal and rubbing her toe, 'it's going to be a part of my life for a long, long time…if not for ever.'

There was just a hint of sadness in Aashi's voice. Abhi's ears though were quite tuned to catch even that little hint.

'No, certainly not. You'll recover your sight soon,' he said. He got up and walked up to Aashi to escort her safely to Priyam.

'Yeah? When?' she said, smiling to see Abhi still clinging to his hope when she had long given up hers.

'Soon,' he repeated.

'Oh, stop it now, Abhi. You don't have to remain repeating this lie. It stifles me more than this darkness. Stop giving me this false hope. It's useless.'

She did try to maintain her smile and keep her frustration out of her

242

voice. But her attempt really wasn't very successful.

'No, Aashi, it's not useless,' Abhi replied, stopping midway. 'Hope is what guides us, Aashi. Hope is what keeps the heart going. A hope is like bright, life giving sun. We must never...'

'Yeah, sun!' Aashi cut him short. 'And we remain leaning against this sun till we get blinded by its light and can see the truth no more. But I'm not going to do that anymore. And *you* need not preach, Abhi. You are not a very hopeful person either. You had no hopes of ever winning my love, and that's a truth that you can't deny.'

'But I have got you now, haven't I? So you see, even miracles can take place,' he said. 'Besides, it's not true that I never hoped for your love. I did, every moment of every day, I just...didn't like admitting them, to my own self even. But I hoped nevertheless, and wished and prayed...'

'Well, it's good that God favoured your prayers over mine then. You *are* a better person than me, Abhi, and far more deserving...'

'Don't say that, Aashi, please!'

It was true that his prayers had been answered, but now Abhi felt almost guilty of ever having uttered the words that had sought this very happiness for him. He felt guilty of having prayed for the fulfilment of his love even though he knew that it could only occasion from the failure of hers. While he was so blindly wishing for his happiness, wasn't he in reality asking misfortune for Aashi? It almost seemed like what had happened to her was somehow all his fault. And he must now make amends. He must do something to rectify the wrong done. He must. No matter what it might cost him.

'The decision has been made, Abhi,' Aashi continued. 'God himself has decided in your favour. So you see, I have no scope for hope left. Besides, I have decided to stop deluding myself with false hopes. They only blind us, Abhi, till we can no more see the reality. But I've seen reality now. And I'm not going to let false hope blind me again.'

'But it's no use giving up to despair, Aashi...'

Aashi could not help but smile, a sad little smile, at his concern. 'Don't worry, Abhi, I'm not giving up to despair. I'm only giving up false delusions to put in their place clear and solid realities. Despair would have been a too easy choice, I know. It would have ended the story long ago. But you never let me seek its shelter,' she said, adding a little laugh to her words that she knew sounded too grim to please him. 'You live too near me to let me have the liberty of that escape.'

'Don't you dare say such things.'

'But it's the truth. I didn't just lose my eyes in that accident, Abhi, I lost

243

away all my life, as I had viewed it once. Had it not been for you, I'd have done it long ago…'

'You'll get your eyes back very soon, I promise you that.'

'Yeah, right. What are you going to do? Kill someone and gouge out his eyes and stick them up on me?' she almost laughed at the absurdity of his claim.

'Probably. Why not?'

'Okay, so what are you waiting for, Mister? Do it quickly,' Aashi said, freeing her hand from him and walking in the direction that she thought led to the kitchen.

'I will,' he said, stepping up to her and redirecting her feet in the correct direction. 'But promise me you'll never again talk of dying.'

'I won't, Abhi. I don't like it either. But, sometimes it does get very hard, doesn't it? And I'm just learning the skills of your trade,' Aashi said, giving him a mock salute. 'But don't you worry, Abhi,' she added, 'I have grown up now. I will no more cry over broken dreams. I have accepted that I'll never get back what I have lost. But I'll try to be happy in what I still have, instead of mourning the loss of the world that could have been. And I know I'm not alone in this struggle. You are with me, and you'll get me out of it too, won't you?'

'Yes,' he murmured.

'*Mourning the loss of the world that could have been…*' the words remained ringing in his ears.

'Of course,' he added.

'*Mourning the loss of the world that could have been…*'

'I will,' he declared.

✳✳✳

Remember me when I am gone away,
Gone far away into the silent land;
When you can no more hold me by the hand,
Nor I half turn to go yet turning stay.

—'Remember' by Christina Rosetti.

Abhi's eyes opened up, though his mind remained entangled with the dream that had just ended. It was good that he had not lost it in his sleep. He could go back to it again, and pull every dear emotion from its magical fibres and re-live all those sensations. He had scarcely known before how sweet, how blessed a dream can be!

A smile lit up on his face as he saw that dream again, this time with wakeful eyes. And a couple of drops trickled down his cheeks.

He looked around. He could see all his plants waving gently with the untiring wind. Their colours though were still shrouded in dull greyness.

He looked up. There, the morning star was already preparing to retire. It was tired too, just like him.

It had been a long night, a very long night. A night that had seen him roam ceaselessly in his small garden while wandering in the lanes of past and peeking into the paths that beckoned from behind the mist of future. When he had sat down on the old swing and closed his eyes, he didn't know. But he was awake now. Although, he would have liked to go back to sleep and continue that dream.

His dream.

Not hers.

But he had stayed up all night to plan out the continuation of *her* dream.

The night was over now. Light was finally creeping out.

A smile broke out on his face. The tumult that had stayed with Abhi all night was resolved. The restive flight of the storm had passed, leaving behind everything washed and appearing clean and clear. A decision had been taken. And why not? All his hopes had been fulfilled. All his dreams had come true. Now, it was time to make true his love. He loved her, didn't he?

Abhi could relax now and let himself enjoy the calm. There was still time enough. It was not yet day. Aashi would not wake up for several more hours.

He leaned back at the swing again and started giving it small pushes with his feet. He liked the way wind ruffled through his hair. He wondered how it would feel to fly away on its wings, free and unburdened.

His eyes turned to gaze at the tiny buds that were getting more eager by each day to welcome the fast approaching spring. Wherever Abhi looked, the February wind seemed to be rousing the verdure to shake up their wintry drowsiness and get dressed up in their vernal finery. His tiny garden was already bursting with marigold and big, beautiful *dahlias*. And yet, there was space for more and the more stood ready in promise.

The Retreat too would soon burst out with beauty. Priyam and Sid were planning to go there next week. Priyam and Sid, two names that really belonged together. Priyam...his little sister, not little anymore. Soon she would have young ones of her own. What would she name them? Would any of them resemble him? He wished they would, even if in some tiny way.

He wished...

'Hi Aashi! You are up early today,' Abhi called out from the swing as soon as he spied her coming out of her house. He himself was dressed and ready. On his side fluttered the day's newspaper, still unread.

'Abhi? Hi! What are you doing at home? It must be past ten, isn't it?'

'No, it isn't. It's just about 9:30. That's why I said you were early.'

'Oh, if you do think 9:30 is early for a girl to wake up,' she said, 'do tell that to my mother too. It would save her a lot of useless urging.'

'Have you had breakfast?'

'No, have you had yours?' Aashi asked.

'Long enough ago to require a second helping,' Abhi replied. 'So count me in too. I'll be there in a minute.' He got up from the swing, picked up the paper as well and took it back inside.

When Abhi emerged from his house, he carried in his pocket two small packages. He locked his own home, closed his gate shut behind him and quickly walked past his car that had been waiting outside since an hour at least.

'Good that you are here today,' Aashi told him as he helped her prepare some sandwiches. 'It's never much fun to sit alone and eat. I always wish for someone to sit with me and talk while I stuff myself full.'

'Not impossible, if you could bring yourself to leave your bed early and join your mother when she has her breakfast. Neither of you would be alone then.'

'Or,' Aashi interrupted, 'you can stay late every day and give me company.'

'That must surely mean that I'm not such a bad company after all. Thank you very much.'

By then, the sandwiches were ready. He handed the plate to Aashi, picked up the tea tray and together they walked back into the drawing room.

'Well, even if you are,' Aashi said, 'I can't complain. I scarcely have the luxury of choice, you know,' she said with a little smile. There was no need to hide her emotions from Abhi. He knew her too well. She put down the plate of sandwiches carefully down on the table and then settled down herself.

'I know,' Abhi said, sitting down beside her, 'but today at least I have something to recompense.'

'Yeah? What?' she asked.

'Let me finish my sandwich first.'

'No, tell me now.'

'I said let me eat first. Won't you even let a hungry man finish his meal in peace?'

'No, I won't, tell me first,' she said, groping around for Abhi's plate.

'Don't dare touch my plate!' he said as he lifted his plate high in air. 'I think I better go out and eat in the garden. My food is in danger here!' he said.

'My garden. Yeah, now I really do have a garden. And it smells wonderful these days,' said Aashi. She pulled her hand back and turned her face towards the open window. 'Are there many flowers blooming, Abhi?' she asked.

'Yes, it looks magnificent,' said Abhi, looking out through the window too.

It was a clear, bright day. Aashi's garden looked just as splendid as his own, and was just as ready to unfold the greater splendour that was to come. All thanks to his own labour. But, it hardly seemed worthwhile. She could see none of it.

Aashi did try to feel content with the wind that remained active all day long and didn't even show much sign of fatigue even after night fall. She kept reminding herself how she had never really bothered about how beautiful a flower was or how clear was the sky. And it was indeed enough of pleasure, if one knew how to satisfy oneself, to breathe in the warm fragrances and feel the balmy crispiness of the brightening sun. And then, she could always ask Abhi, as she often did, to describe just how everything looked.

Still, it really wasn't the same. Nothing was the same.

Life, though, was still going on. Just as it always does.

'So, am I going to get my gift now or are you going to make me wait even more?' Aashi asked when Abhi had finished his sandwich and cleared the table.

'No, your wait is over, Aashi,' Abhi answered, sinking back in his chair. 'It's time now for you to get what you want.'

'Well?' She extended her hand to receive what she was sure must be a

247

ring. At least, that was what she hoped it was. Abhi had already taken a long enough time. She hoped he finally had reached a decision.

Abhi placed in her hand the small velvet box. 'Oh, it's a ring, isn't it?' she said, rubbing her fingers against its softness, 'It better be nice, I've given up a very expensive one to make way for it.' It did take Aashi some effort to maintain the easy smile she had brought up on her face. But she managed it.

Abhi, on the other hand, didn't make any such effort. 'You never should have given it up,' he replied.

'Don't start that again, Abhi. I have decided, and I'm not going to change my decision,' Aashi cut him short.

'Why are you doing this, Aashi? Don't throw your love away with your own hand!' he said as he leaned back in his chair and fixed his eyes on her.

'He is not my love any more. You are.'

'No, I'm not.'

'Well, if that is your decision, then I have no love. I don't love anybody and nobody loves me. But… it is not the truth, you know it, Abhi, and I know it too. You love me. You still love me, don't you? Why then can't you accept my love?'

'Because it is not mine.'

'It will be, I'll make it yours. I promise,' said Aashi, reaching out to touch his hand. 'I won't betray you, Abhi. I would be true to you, to your love.'

'You mean you'll force yourself to love me? Would that make you happy? Would that make *me* happy?' Abhi asked while his fingers crushed hers in desperation.

'Yes, we'll all be happy. Why don't you understand, Abhi? I can't force my blindness on Raj! I can't ruin his life. You said yourself that he isn't used to seeing pain in his world. His world is bright and glittering, Abhi. There's no place in it for the darkness of my blind eyes. I won't let my gloom stain the bright sunshine of his life! And if you can't help me out here, I would be left with no choice but to seek some other means.'

A trembling drop broke down from Abhi's eye as he listened to Aashi's feverish speech. 'Don't be so cruel to me, Aashi. Have some mercy!' he begged.

'I can't force you to marry me, Abhi. You can say no, if you want to.'

'Do you think…'

'I don't think,' Aashi cut him short.

'Then you won't change your mind?'

'No.'

'That leaves me with no option.'

'Yes, you have no option. You better marry me. And I hope that's what you have decided. And I hope that this little box contains my new engagement ring,' she said. She flicked her hair behind her shoulder and focussed her attention again on the little box in her hand.

'No,' said Abhi, reaching out to open it for her, 'it's a ...'

'Pendant?' she asked as her fingers quickly discerned its smooth polished surface, cut in a heart shape. What was the meaning of that now?

'For your chain.'

'Oh, but...' she was still confused. The pendant was heavy and she could judge that it was expensive. It felt like solid gold with a little something sticking out of it from the middle.

'Put it in your chain and let me see how it looks,' he urged. Aashi complied, her mind still trying to decipher the meaning of this unwarranted gift.

She quietly removed the chain from her neck, threaded the pendant in it and reached behind her neck to clasp it back again.

Past flashed before Abhi's eyes. Had Raj been there, he'd have immediately reached out to do it for her. But Abhi could only watch and wait.

'There,' Aashi finally said after struggling for a whole minute, 'how does it look?' she asked, touching it lightly.

'Lovely,' he replied. 'Would you promise me one thing?' he asked, quickly clearing his throat to banish the sudden hoarseness from his voice.

'Sure, you've promised me so many things. I can promise you one.'

'Then promise me that you'd always keep it close...close to your heart just as it is now.'

'I would, Abhi, I promise.'

'Don't ever lose it.'

'I won't.'

'I mean,' he quickly added, finally managing to take control over his voice, 'since it's a bit expensive. That's diamond, you know, the little thing that's there in the middle.'

'It is? But why did you spend so much, Abhi? We are not even engaged yet,' Aashi said. She lifted the pendant up in her fingers and felt what Abhi had said was a diamond.

'You like it, don't you?'

'Oh, it's diamond. I love it,' said Aashi, 'thanks so much. But do tell me how to calm down my mother when she sees it. I'm sure she'd scream and fall in a fit for my accepting such an expensive gift.'

'Don't worry, she'd understand,' he said, smiling at the success of his gift. If Aashi could see, he was sure, there would have risen up in her eyes a sparkle brighter than that diamond.

Well, her eyes would sparkle again, very soon. Abhi had promised her that. And then, all her dreams would come rushing back to her. And she would have no reason then to hold back her hand. She would reach out, she would grasp them in her fingers, give them a place once more in her heart. And then, she would be happy again.

'Alright, I must leave now,' he said as he got up from his seat.

'Okay, see you in the evening,' she said.

She was smiling. Her fingers still were toying with her new pendant. A corner of Abhi's mouth moved a little to attempt a smile. But he had quickly to purse up his lips and mute his own breath into silence. In his pocket waited the second gift that he had brought for her. But before he gave it, there was something else that Abhi wanted to do.

'Do you...love me, Aashi?' he finally asked the question.

He saw Aashi's head jerk. *That* certainly wasn't what she was expecting.

'Do you love me, Aashi, even if a little bit?' he asked again.

Aashi's face turned towards him. Her lips parted without making a sound. They were waiting perhaps for her to recover. But then, it was okay after all. He was the man she was going to marry. He, of course, needed to know if she loved him, or could love him.

'Y..yes...' she finally uttered.

'Well then, say it.'

'Say what?'

'I love you.'

'Huh?'

'I love you.'

'Oh, I do, I...love you.' It wasn't a lie after all. She did love him. Just not in the same way as she loved Raj.

'Feels dry without a hug,' he said.

Aashi felt him come closer to her. She took a determined step forward as well. Why not? She had said she wanted to marry him. Why should she keep him away still?

'I love you,' she repeated, letting her arms wrap themselves around him, and her head to nestle close to him. Somehow, it didn't seem quite so forced after all. But then, he was her friend and she had already experienced the reassuring comfort of being sheltered in his arm.

But he would not have it so. He lifted her face up. She felt his fingers brush her hair away from her face. It was not what Abhi had planned, yet...

He asked no permission. He begged no favour. His lips found hers, slowly...gently...pouring his soul into her. It was not a kiss of pleasure. It was not a kiss of passion. But of an emotion sadder far, and more, lot more intense.

Her fingers dug at his back, trying perhaps to steady the sudden tremor radiating through her pores. The irresistible warmth of his love chipped away at the cold resistance that was her only guard. A thirst blazed up in her as well, and an echo of many long past moments. Moments...that had knocked against her heart every time and sneaked inside despite her resolute denials. Aashi felt his lips pressing harder. She felt hers respond, hungrily, hastily, to suck out all his pain from his heart and let it melt through her body. His lips stilled against hers. Hers waited.

He stepped away. She staggered and clutched at him for support.

'I love you too,' a low whisper carried his words to her ears. He pulled out the second parcel from his pocket and put it in her hand. 'Your world,' he said, 'I'm giving you your world back.'

'W...what?' her own voice sounded strange to Aashi. 'Abhi?' she called.

But by that time Abhi had already walked out of her home.

He banged the car door shut. Habit prompted him to close his eyes and utter his usual prayer. A smile rose up to interrupt it. He didn't need to pray for his safety that day. So he prayed for his success.

Aashi heard his car start up. She heard it roll away. Where was he going? She gasped for air, stumbling towards the door. Her hand pressed at her bosom. It would take some time for her heart to calm down to its steady pace. Her cheeks were wet. But...she had not cried. Those were not her tears! She felt her legs shaking under her weight. In a moment she was sitting down on the floor, slumped against the cold wall.

What was it that had suddenly started banging against her ribs? What was it that had risen up to choke her breath away and let it escape only as a sigh?

The chimes from next door gave a beckoning ring. An old ache rose up from somewhere deep within. She wanted to cry out. She wanted to cry out loud and hard till there were no more tears left in her. 'ABHI!' she shouted out his name. But she knew he wasn't there. He had gone away.

'Oh!' the word that escaped Aashi's lips sounded more like a cry than a mere exclamation. A strange force seemed to envelop her.

Strange? No, not at all strange. It was in fact, too familiar. Much too familiar.

Memories raised their phantoms and began dancing before her eyes. Fragments of the past started rising up from the dust of time. They rose up, they swirled around her, they came together and went apart again, mixing and mingling with each other. They all bore only one face...Abhi!

There was Abhi...arresting the motions of her heart with his eyes as she stood rain drenched and waiting for him to hand her the towel. There was Abhi again...running after the thief for her chain. There...he was on the

251

hospital bed, turning his eyes away to hide his love. Oh, there again, watching her kiss Raj! In the guest house … there was his hand on her hair, her ear-ring, her face…his breath approaching closer to her…closer still…Oh why hadn't he kissed her then!

She felt his arm around her, the sound of his heartbeats rose up in her ears. She wanted him to hold her again, close to his heart. Forever!

And she still had no idea what it meant.

Her hands were trembling. Her heart was pounding. She longed to call out his name. And in her heart rose a yearning to call Abhi back and tell him she loved him? She loved *him!*

She loved him? She *loved* him? What, then, had she been doing with Raj? Was it just a girlish fascination that she felt for him?

'*No! How can that be?*' she still fought with her feelings.

But the battle had already been lost.

'I don't know! I don't know anything!' she cried out. 'How can I love Abhi? I love Raj! Oh, Abhi, what have you done to me? Why do I love you?'

She had never wanted to fall in love with Abhi. And yet…it seemed to her now that she already *was* in love with him! All the shields she had so far erected against him had proven to be very weak. Far too weak.

That was it. That was why she had hated Abhi so much. That was why, it had always hurt her so much to hurt him.

But now there was no hurt. She felt lighter at heart than she had felt in many past months.

'I…I must tell him. His love has won.' The thought revived her. 'I must tell him.' She jumped back on her feet. 'I love him.'

But how? She had already burnt the only phone she had. 'Why am I always such an idiot!' she wailed, hitting the wall behind her with her hand. Something struck the wall. There was something in her hand that struck the wall.

The gift! Abhi's gift!

"Your world. I'm giving you your world back."

What had he meant by those words? What was it that he had put in her hand?

The wrapper soon came undone. It was a phone. It was exactly like her previous phone - the one that she had burnt. It was exactly…

'No!…it…it's…oh!'

"Your world. I'm giving you your world back," the words swirled around her.

'I've had the world, Abhi,' Aashi cried out, 'I don't want it any more. I want you!'

Her fingers stilled at the little nick on the bottom right side of the phone. She knew how that had appeared there. She had banged the phone hard at the table in her fury and had had to call Abhi to find its back-cover and battery and put it together again. It was the same scratch. She could not be so mistaken. It was the same phone!

"Your world. I'm giving you your world back."

But she had burnt it. Why did Abhi save it? Why had he returned it to her now? What was the meaning of it?

"Your world. I'm giving you your world back."

She didn't want it! It was Raj's phone, she didn't want it now!

Her arm lifted up to throw it away again. She halted. It was a phone, just a phone, and she needed it to call Abhi.

Aashi carefully sought out the fourth key and pressed it hard. The phone rang, and kept on ringing for a long time. No one picked it up. Aashi pressed the key again. Still the ring went on, and remained unanswered. Again and again she dialled and waited to hear Abhi's voice.

'Why aren't you picking up the phone, Abhi!' she cried out, getting up from the floor and pacing around with furious nervousness. 'Why aren't you picking up the phone?'

A car zoomed by on the street, its horn blasting a loud wail.

Sudden dread overtook her heart. Strange, unbearable chill ran through her and she started shaking. Her hands trembled and could barely hold on to the phone. A loud pounding started echoing in her ears and sudden pain rose up from deep within her and rushed to prick her fingertips as if with a thousand needles. The mobile phone slipped down from her hand and she fell down again. 'Pick up the phone, Abhi…please pick up the phone…' she urged through her chattering teeth as she lay face down on the hard, cold floor.

Another horn rang through the air, sounding even louder than the previous one.

Voices rose up from thin air. Hawkers calling out, people jostling to rush past each other. The shops were decorated in their festive finery. That dress! She wanted it! It was the same dress. 'I don't want it! I don't want it, Papa! Don't go there! Come back! Oh, come back!' she cried out through her stupor.

She heard the blast. She saw the fire. She saw the smoke. She saw the blood raining down on the road. She saw the body parts pelting down in little red pools. There was her father lying dead. He had only one arm. He was dead. He was dead! He had only one arm. His leg…he…limp…he…

'Abhi! Abhi! Come back! I don't want that dress!' the scream filled the air for a moment. And then there was silence.

The door that Abhi had left ajar banged against the wall. Someone ran in.

'Aashi!' he shouted. 'Aashi!'

She was back in her home. She was back. Abhi…

'Aashi? Are you okay?' the person who had run in asked.

'Abhi!' she shouted out, though her voice came out in just a whisper. He had come back. It must be him. It must be him. She would tell him now. She did not want that dress.

Dress?

She…she wanted him. Yes, she wanted Abhi.

'Aashi? Listen to me, Aashi!' the visitor shouted again.

'Oh, Abhi! Thank God you are back. I…' she said, raising her hand to touch his face. Her fingers were instantly clutched in a warm grasp. 'I love you, Abhi! I love you!' she continued. 'I was mistaken! I thought I loved Raj. He's so perfect! But you are perfect too! And I love you. I was a fool. I never understood…I…but I know now. I never hated you. I love you, Abhi. And that's the truth!' she burst out.

'Say something, Abhi, I know you can't believe it. I know it sounds strange, but it's the truth,' she added when no reply came forth from the man kneeling beside her.

'Abhi?' she called again.

'Raj…I'm…Raj,' he finally answered.

'Raj!' she gasped, 'Raj?' she repeated his name, not quite comprehending what was happening.

Raj's eyes travelled to the mobile he had gifted her. It was lying on the floor, with its back cover open and battery a little way away. His lips twitched as he thought of the many times he had tried calling her and found her phone switched off. But now was not the time to make complaints.

He took a deep breath and turned his eyes back towards Aashi. 'Aashi,' he began, 'I…I received an SMS from Abhi, about…his…he…he wants you to see again,' he said. 'A little while ago, he was brought to our hospital…from… from …'

'A…Abhi?' she murmured, not understanding what he was saying.

Raj's voice kept on speaking further. He was trying to tell her something. What was it? She didn't want to listen. She didn't care. She wanted to talk to Abhi.

Railway line? Why was Raj telling her about the railway line? What did it matter to her if some stupid person had put his car in way of a speeding train? Last wish? What last wish? Whose? Operation? Eyes! EYES!

'Oh! Abhi would be so happy! He said I'll see again! He promised! And now he has found eyes for me. I'll see again. I'll see Abhi again and I'll tell him how much I love him. He would be so happy!'

'We must leave, Aashi. Abhi's eyes are waiting for you.'

'Abhi, Abhi is waiting for me,' she corrected Raj instantly. 'But now, his wait is over!' Aashi laughed, rocking herself with a furious energy as her teeth chattered and breath came out in rasping gasps. 'His wait is over. I'd tell him that I love him. He'd be so happy! He won't wait a moment in marrying me, now that I truly love him!'

'Aashi, did you hear what I just said?' Raj said, shaking her by the shoulders to make her listen.

'I'll talk to you later, Raj. I must talk to Abhi first. I want to tell Abhi how much I love him.'

'Aashi, listen to me!' Raj shouted.

'Don't be angry, Raj,' she pleaded, rocking herself even more furiously. 'I know I hurt you. But don't be angry with me, please. I never knew I loved Abhi. I never knew. But I'll tell him now. I'll tell him that his love has won. I'll tell him. There's no one else who loves me as much as he does. I know now. And I love him too. Abhi waited for me so long. But his wait is over. His wait is over, Raj…'

'You're right, Aashi,' Raj's voice interrupted her. 'His wait is over. That's what I've been trying to tell you!'

'But, Abhi…'

'Abhi…is dead.'

255